D0053615

COLUMBIA BRANCH
RECEIVED
MAY 21 2018

WONDERBLOOD

WONDE

BLOOD

JULIA WHICKER

ST. MARTIN'S PRESS
NEW YORK

This is a work of fiction. All of the characters, organizations, and events portrayed in this novel are either products of the author's imagination or are used fictitiously.

www.stmartins.com

Designed by Jonathan Bennett

Illustrations by Esbee Bernice

The Library of Congress Cataloging-in-Publication Data is available upon request.

ISBN 978-1-250-06606-0 (hardcover)
ISBN 978-1-4668-7337-7 (ebook)

First Edition: April 2018

10 9 8 7 6 5 4 3 2 1

FOR JOHNNY,
WHO GAVE ME FAITH

ACKNOWLEDGMENTS

I am indebted to many individuals: Peter Steinberg, my agent, who loved and encouraged this work from beginning; my coeditors, Michael Homler and Craig Pyette, who with extraordinary patience and kindness provided invaluable guidance; John Eicher, my husband, whose magic inspired every word, whose faith in my abilities still leaves me astonished, and who tirelessly provided me space and opportunity to write; Matt Williamson, lover of all things weird and wonderful, who published a version of this story in *Unstuck;* Sarah Whicker, my sister, for whom the act of creation is a necessity and without whose inspiration and support I would be lost; and my parents, Burton and Barbara Whicker, who earnestly believed I could do anything in the world.

I am also grateful for all the books—too numerous to name—that helped me make sense of a possible future by way of understanding the past. Likewise, I wish to enumerate the many places in which this manuscript was shaped, all of which gave me unexpected gifts: Richmond, Virginia; Iowa City; Austin; and Potomac, Maryland.

Lastly, I wish to thank Colette Eicher, my daughter, who arrived on the scene in the midst of everything, who changed it all, and brought the best gift—hope.

It detonated. Nature, God, mankind
Like sulphur, nitre, charcoal, once
Blended, in one annihilation blind
Were rent into a myriad of suns.
Yea! all the mighty fabric of a Mind

Stood in the abyss,
Belching a Law for "That" more awful than for "This."

—Aleister Crowley

WONDERBLOOD

CHAPTER 1

THE UNCRUSHER

When they rode, they took severed heads with them, in canvas sacks, in saddlebags, and set them out wherever they stopped, on rocks, or stuck them on pikes and tied the sticks with red streamers so the ribbon and the dead hair blew together with the wind. O, terrible Heads, gloomy-faced deaths—for the longest time, the girl remained afraid of them, even as she reached into her brother's canvas sack each night and withdrew one by its crackling hair, even as she gingerly poked it onto a pike and jabbed the pike in the earth outside her tent. She did not have her own magical head yet. But everyone said she should, so her brother made her one, cut it away from its body and powdered and magicked it so it would not go bad, so it would scowl always and forever in defense of her. He was twenty-nine, her brother. He could not read. He made Heads.

The Head had been a man named Cosmas, a doctor. Not a Walking Doctor, but a miracle healer, who'd once uncrushed an arm and made it work again by magic. He blew air into the arm like it needed breath and it plumped and warmed and worked again like new, but when the executioners saw that Cosmas was a miracle healer, they killed him and took his head. Her brother had fought three men for it—that was what he told her. "And now he's yours," he'd said, and presented to her a canvas sack, the kind he gave his customers, when he had customers. She was fourteen. Old enough to ride her own horse, to make her own camp—old enough for a Head. "Go on," he said. "Take it out." The skin, tornado-green, false-hard like a manta's eggsack; her fingers could punch through it if she pressed. She did not press. Eyeless, lashless Cosmas.

That night she put Cosmas in his sack and stuffed the sack into her saddlebag, but her brother banged into her tent with the Head, screaming, "Why isn't it out?" He was all flapping arms and dark hair, terrifying with his height and drunk eyes. She sat up in her blankets and he pulled her, shivering, outside, where he piked the Head and then made her do it as well, made her slide the sharp wooden pole into the hollowed-out neck, and it crunched and she cringed. "No crying," he said, when he saw her lip tremble.

"I'm not."

"Right, you're not." He stepped back and admired the Head. "Looks good. Did you know I make the best Heads in this sorry carnival? Always have. That's cause I have pride in what I do."

She nodded. They were camped on a plain, a field wild with weeds and prairie grass. Maybe food had been grown in a great field like this, before the Disease. She wondered who had figured out the field was safe to walk upon, how long ago that had been. It was early May, and the sky was mesh, stippled with stars. She was cold, in her nightclothes without a coat. Her hair, so fine at the ends it nearly winnowed away to nothing, was long and light brown. She was skinny, dirty, and had not seen her own eyes in a pool of water for months. She hated it outside here, and trembled in the chill. Argento saw her shiver but didn't give her his cloak. He was mean like that. Along the outskirts of camp, fires glowed, ten, fifteen of them, all guarded by sentries—do not cross the line, now, ever, you are not allowed. You are a little girl. The men are gates you cannot pass through.

"Can I go to sleep now?" she asked.

"Fuck no." He yanked her toward his tent.

"No," she said, tried digging her bare heels into the ground.

"Not that," he said. "It's your birthday, right?"

"I think not anymore. I think it was yesterday. That's why you gave me the Head."

He shrugged. There was a little upside-down moon, hanging like a backflip in the corner of the sky. "I got something else for you." He marched her past his own five Heads and their streamers, maroon-colored, hazard-orange, caution-yellow, and into the warm mustiness of his tent. She opened her mouth, but closed it when he didn't bother fastening the tent flaps. The blood in her heart slowed. From beneath a pile of blankets he pulled a square thing wrapped in paper, tied with a streamer and decorated with colored chalk. "I drew on it, lucky sigils," he said. In the coldish light, the chalk whorls were phosphorescent like plankton at the seashore. She became aware of a curious feeling—not exactly sorrow but something near it, like the lonely cousin of sorrow, and she knew it was homesickness and she missed her old life and her mother. A lump rose in her throat as she sat on her brother's bedroll and chewed her thumbnail. In her lap, the present felt heavy and she did not want it. The chalk rubbed off on her fingers and sparkled and her brother squatted next to her and punched her gently in the shoulder. "Open it," he said.

She paused. "You shouldn't have got anything."

He laughed. To her it sounded crazy. "I just stole it. Out of some other carnival fuck's wagon. He was riding around a month ago, five horses pulling this gigantic wagon, it made me mad. Who needs five horses? I would've shot his horses, but they were good horses. White and brown."

"What did you do?" she whispered.

He actually smiled. "I let them go." He made a motion of running.

"That was a stupid thing to do."

Then he wasn't smiling. "Open."

When she'd untied the streamer and piled it like entrails in a puddle of moonlight, when she'd ripped the paper away, she saw he'd given her a book. A heavy, huge book. And did he know what book it was? No, not at all. He gazed at her face, watching for her reaction—she felt hot and cold, feverish; she knew what he was going to do afterward. "Thank you," she said slowly.

"Do you not like it? What's it about?" he asked.

"I don't know."

"What's it say?"

She squinted. *Our True King,* which meant little enough to the girl.

The author was just as strange: An Executionatrix. She did not know what that word meant, but she saw within it another word she did know and fear. "It's about magic," she said.

"Well, every book is about magic, what's it *about*?"

She ran her hand over the fabric board-cover, curled her fingers around the fraying corners. A Head and a book. And outside an ocean of grass between her and the place she wanted to be, the place she remembered best, the cradle of the panhandle and its powderfine sand, its sky arcing overhead like green glass. Then tears came to her eyes but they were stupid—motion was life, even stupid men like her brother knew that. The word to name how she felt was nostalgia, a beautiful word that her mother had taught her was made of other words, foreign words, from the language of magicians: it meant return-pain. The girl felt sure her brother didn't know this, had never felt the feeling because he was too dumb, but she did, all the time, and suddenly her heart collapsed and she thought she couldn't bear it. It seemed her life flowed past her like a stream. All the time she fought this melancholic recognition of her female destiny, which was to be carried farther and farther away, forever.

She looked up at her brother. "It's about a king, I think."

"Is it about the Astronauts?"

"What?"

"Haven't I taught you anything? They were the Silver Stars, riding up into heavens, the kings of all magic once and for all. What have you been learning in this carnival if not that?" He stared at her goggled-eyed. She only looked at him. Her brother venerated the Astronauts like all the Head Makers in his carnival. Argento said these men had left the earth and now waited beyond the world until the land could be healed. *But how do you know?* she'd asked. *Well,* he'd answered. *Somewhere, someone has evidence.*

The girl knew nothing about other carnivals except that there were many, and they justified making Heads in various ways, because the Primary Law was bloodshed. Her mother had said the carnivals were a thousand factions of one idiocy. *There are innumerable ways to make a grave mistake,* she'd said, *and they are working on discovering all of them.*

Her mother was named Gimbal. Two years before, when Gimbal

delivered her to Argento in the deathscapes in the center of the continent, Argento had taken her straight into his tent and burned a unicursal hexagram into her thigh. The unicursal hexagram was a sigil with no beginning and no end: the symbol of their carnival, the Silver Star. It meant many things, Argento had said, especially the six great towers in Cape Canaveral where they returned every year to pay tribute to the king. She hadn't known then this mutilation wasn't allowed—only those condemned to become Heads were supposed to bear the hexagram. So now she hid the scar, because it shouldn't be there, and also she knew Argento had done it because he was stupid and crazy and didn't believe he had to follow rules.

She hated her mother for giving her to him.

Often, when she had nothing to do and she was alone in her tent, she traced her hand over the mark, down the lines that fell inward forever, and thought that if there was magic in this sigil, it was in the spaces bounded by lines, in the blankness between divisions, in the emptiness that held apart borders of the world. She understood this with some core intuition. Magic, like nostalgia, was like a lie; empty and full all at once.

When Gimbal abandoned her to Argento, the girl had cried. They had come to him from their peaceful southern settlement by the seaside, all the way across the continent, through the vast level plains that had once been Arkansas and Oklahoma. Those were the old names, her mother had murmured, though boundaries did not matter now because the land was useless. Sometimes the girl still thought her mother knew everything. Her mother could read the markings that other Walking Doctors left along the saferoads. A language of symbols that meant Sleep Here, Stay Away, Keep Ten Feet Back. Her mother taught her a few. She wished she had paid better attention. She often dreamt now of running away.

To get to Argento in his carnival of the Silver Star, she and her mother had walked across land gray as a storm-sky, through hail the size of fists. They stayed on the saferoads. They rode an old white mule decorated with a faceplate made from a piece of ancient plastic, they carried an old Head in a saddlebag—so they looked like believers on a pilgrimage. Her mother detested the ruse, but said they would be even stupider *not* to carry the Head. Anyone who stopped them would wonder what business two women had riding alone in the deathscapes. They could fabricate some relic, her mother said—even a shard of glass would do, for the magicians in the carnivals were notorious idiots who could be bespelled by a dung beetle. But having a Head with them would mark them as magicians themselves, and no one would question them much.

They'd traveled for months, from April to July, together on that mule, sometimes one of them walking, one riding, and they passed through fragrant mud and grasses heaving with summer and all the beauty and terror of the middle of the continent. They rode toward the heart of the Disease, where it had begun all those hundreds of years ago. That was what her mother had told her, with a sad laugh. *You best hope we don't encounter a Kansas Cow,* she muttered. *I for one wouldn't know how to kill it. If they can even be killed by anything other than the Disease, and believe me I have no idea. How do you kill what's already dead?*

Are the Kansas Cows real? the girl had asked, her eyes on the farthest horizon, a purple bank of clouds that flattened at its top into a deep blue dusk. She still remembered that day, the sky. She remembered so many skies. She had imagined a black Kansas Cow stumbling across the prairie on spider legs, eyes red and unseeing. She had heard of Kansas Cows, of course—everyone had. But she had never thought of them because she had never before left Florida.

Her mother, walking beside her then, shot her a look. *How should I know? People say they're real. People also join stupid carnivals and go around cutting off heads. You shouldn't believe everything you hear, because even if it's true, it could be wrong.* Gimbal's hair was long and dirty and she wore a plain dress with no buttons, for buttons were wasteful. She did not look like what she was, which was a dissident. She performed the illegal magic of surgery, during which she physically altered the human body in order to affect its form and function. A Walking Doctor, who went out on the saferoads to heal the sick and mend the wounded.

Gimbal's occupation had been cause for strife as long as the girl could remember. Once, her mother received a written command from the Hierophant himself in Cape Canaveral to cease and desist her "damnable surgeries and return to the proven methods of magic, astrologics, and bloodshed." He'd cited the carnivals as beacons of virtue. He'd invoked the doctrine of Wonderblood, the rinsing of the world in blood and pain for one Eon. "It is our collective debt," the letter said. "It is the Primary Law." If she did not follow it she would be executed. Her mother had torn up the letter, spat on it, and ground it into the dirt. *How's that for magic?* She had no time for the Cape's hysterics. There were people who could be healed, and she and her husband would heal them.

The reason she was abandoning the girl was: her newest husband was only twenty-five and a surgeon like herself, a true believer, and he had aspirations. They would leave the panhandle eventually, to go about as Walking Doctors on a wider circuit, just as her own parents and grandparents had done. It was true there was no cure for the Disease, but there were many people who would still pay for the old medicine. That is, if they believed it was tempered with a touch of modern theory. So she and her husband ground bird bones and collected thimblefuls of fresh morning dew. But those flourishes were for show; their *real* magic was that they'd memorized thousands of pages of anatomy diagrams, that they knew the names and formulas for ancient medicines that worked and tried to resynthesize them using molds and magnetic salt. On the saferoads, among the people, they used the incantation "primum non nocere," since it meant *do no harm* in the language of their books, and if people thought those were the magic words of a particular sect, so much the better. Though her mother hated to indulge idiots, she did it for what she called the *greater good.*

The girl had felt safe there in the settlement with Gimbal. Her two brothers, much older, had left years before, Argento off to the carnivals. The other one, William, had become a thief and was run out of the settlement. That was what Gimbal said, anyway. The girl didn't remember either of them. As she grew up, she even imagined she would become a Walking Doctor like her mother. But a time came when Gimbal explained that the larger world needed her more than any one child could. The girl was twelve then, almost a woman. Her mother had been a mother herself at fifteen, and that was that, her childhood was over. She'd said, *The time is coming for you to take care of others. That is the highest calling for any human being.*

But then the girl had seen her mother looking at her new husband, at his muscles like round machine parts under his skin and his smile like a fish hook, and then back to the girl, and the girl understood she was jealous. They began the long journey to find Argento's carnival in the deathscapes. Argento, her oldest brother, was also the most foolish and had turned religious for reasons unknown to any of them. He'd left for the carnivals before the girl was even born. She didn't remember him. Argento was his nom de guerre. She didn't know his real name, hadn't asked, didn't care. Her mother said the name she'd given him at birth was wasted on a lunatic.

But they went to him because he would be the only one stupid enough to take her. Just a pair of arms. The girl also saw that Gimbal hated Argento, or maybe she hated all religious men, and she meant the girl as a punishment for Argento's idiocy. The Astronauts, hexagrams, Heads as charms against the Disease—it was all nonsense; weakness and misplaced piety, her mother said. But he was her brother all the same, and if he wouldn't protect her, no one would. That, her mother told her in a sharpened voice, was life, that was living, get used to it.

When they'd finally arrived in the carnival country, in its cosmic wideness across which the girl sometimes thought she could see the curve of the world, and when her mother rode away home on her white mule, when she vanished across the grasses, when Argento used a hot iron to sizzle that six-pointed star on her upper thigh, where he licked her, when her mother was gone and the girl had nothing and no one to believe in, she traced the star and wished, hoped, wondered. The pain of it all—Wonderblood—made the unreal real and so sometimes magic didn't seem so much like a lie after all, and that confused her.

She glanced at her brother, now. He waited, his breath in her ear surprisingly soft, odorless. He reached past her and touched the book. She sighed.

"Come on. What's the book about?"

The pages were damp-heavy, words spidering across them, glaring up at her, but she loved them anyway because she knew she'd read this book again and again in the coming months, until she knew every word in it—she would read sitting under trees, hunched against the continental winds, she'd read it by the ponds where they'd stop to wash out their bedrolls. She'd read it in the timber cabin when they finally reached Manitoba, where the cold would freeze the eggs in her womb (her brother said), where she'd fall asleep thinking of crabs on the summer beach. O, lucidity, leave me, leave me. She turned the pages, full of words she didn't understand and names she had never heard: *Huldah, Lee,* and yes, *Kansas Cow.* "It's about the True King, I think." She paused. "It's written by an Executioner."

"The True King of what?"

"I don't know. It just says the True King. And then there are a lot of names and places." She flipped more pages over gingerly. "It doesn't look that old. Maybe someone made it."

Her brother made an expression, not a smile. "Someone makes everything. Read it to me. Why do you think I got it?"

She read to him, a long and incomprehensible genealogy, and he seemed satisfied but she knew he understood not a word of it, because she didn't. He was acting because he didn't want her to think he was stupid. Then he leaned back and said, "Do you think the True King is one of the Astronauts? That's got to be what it means."

She closed the book. A sadness had begun in her. She wanted to go outside the tent. She wanted to be away from him.

His face bent horribly and he hunched forward. "You do believe that they're coming back, don't you? The Astronauts. It's heresy if you don't believe that."

She began to panic. "Yes?"

He snatched the book from her and threw it into the corner, onto a pile of rags, where it sank like a fishing weight. With his other hand he pulled the cord on the tent flap, closed out the night and the glisten of dew on grass.

"No," she said, and braced her knee in front of her body. "Stop."

His almond eyes like unpolished metal. "No. Look." And he took a little box from his pocket. "This too. This is the best thing. Here."

A white paper box. Inside, sawdust. In the sawdust, a pin, black glass, jet maybe, or obsidian, liquid shiny and faceted. A black so black it was silver. He snatched it from her and rubbed it on his shirt, blew away the last shavings of wood, then needled it to her nightshirt. "Pin's loose. It's old," he frowned. "But I'll fix it."

"Where did you get this?"

"Ma. She gave it to me when she brung you here, told me to save it. Well. I saved it two years."

"I—" She felt numb. He called their mother Ma. The girl had never called her that. She wondered who Argento's father had been, how he had become *this*. Her hand on the heavy brooch, pulling the fabric of her nightshirt down toward her nipple. "I don't know what to do with it."

"Don't do nothing with it for all I care. Anyhow some loony crone would kill you for it if you ever wore it for real." He lowered his voice. "It's nightrock. Black amber they call it. Fuck if I know how Ma got it, maybe she stole it off the dead. Or out of some sick bastard's house." He touched her cheek.

"What's it for?"

He pinched her. "You wear it when somebody dies."

She began to cry, finally, big hot tears. "But somebody's always dying." In that moment, the girl felt the pain of the entire world and also her smallness in it, and it felt like: hopeless. There was another word. Endless. "I hate it here."

He seemed surprised she'd said it out loud. He looked at her the way adults look at children, with pity and sweetness and compassion, but then he hardened his face and nodded gravely. "Isn't anyone alive who wouldn't."

Banded blue and gold sky and no trees and stages everywhere, for the executions. There was an old sign someone had found deep in the ground, mostly rusted away, the rest so buried that it had needed to be physically dug out, which took a long while because the metal had turned to lace, it was so delicate—that was what her brother told her—a gigantic wheel with red letters. That was how they knew this place had been called Iowa. She had no idea when that had been—so long ago.

The carnival was made up of magicians and merchant Head Makers, and they set up booths and sold severed heads and polished bones and all sorts of intimidating talismans, and throughout the summer people came to the carnival country to buy their wares, to watch the executions, to trade horses, and to gamble. Always, this led to more executions. And more Heads, which was good for everyone, one and all. Her brother said so. Her mother had said they were all raving idiots.

Argento never killed people himself—at least, he never killed the people he made into Heads. He bought his Heads from the executioners, who sought out magical humans, captured them, and beheaded them onstage while uttering the standard incantations. In Argento's carnival, the incantations sounded like, Everymanandwomanisastar! and Silverstarfantasticspeardienow!

Or sometimes the executioners didn't behead their victims onstage, but hunted them like they'd hunted Cosmas the Uncrusher. Those Heads were harder to get and so more expensive to buy, so Argento charged triple for them. He threaded black quartz beads into burn marks on their foreheads to enhance their beauty. She'd watched him many times, outside at his workbench, squinting while he embedded the beads one by one. His tongue lolled to one side and occasionally he wiped sweat from his forehead. To embroider an entire unicursal hexagram took a day or more. The girl's own Head, Cosmas, had a glittering forehead star, an always-open eye, lumpy like the cancers her mother used to cut from people. The thought of touching it made the girl shudder. Everything about her brother's work revolted her, the way he made her sit by the tents while he sawed neckbones and yanked out the cervices of the spine, how he held each vertebra up to the light and inspected it, how he handed the good ones to her and made her polish them with a scratchy cloth until they were smooth, and then how he made her paint them bright black. How she had the feeling he would've kept her chained to the ground if he could've, if it had been acceptable, how he *had* chained her to the ground, actually—during her first weeks in the carnival—he'd chained her to the ground! *Just so everybody knows,* he'd said.

So everybody knows what? It was only a few days before some of the old women—there were never any young women in the camps—arrived to squawk at Argento until he used a huge pair of shears to cut the chain. *There?* he'd screamed back at them, brandishing the blades. *There, are you happy? If somebody grabs her it's gonna be your fault, you sickdry wrinkle fucks. Stupid women!*

One of them, the older one, although it was hard to tell, had taken the girl's hand and helped her up. She bent close and whispered, *You will never be more important than you are right now.* The girl had blinked.

Argento's carnival ran a northerly circuit, all the way up the center of the continent. It was dictated by Law that all carnivals had to winter over in the north, so that the countryland was free of them for some short time. She did not understand why things were this way, or who made the Law or what happened on the land when all the carnivals went north, but she knew she hated the cold. Her brother's carnival wintered with a small settlement of northern people. These people did not seem to care much about making Heads. They never judged the ways of others, no matter how peculiar. Many of the carnival men kept wives in little timber cabins: during her first winter there, the girl met Argento's wife, a tiny large-breasted woman who slept odd hours and cooked river-fish in three inches of grease. The girl dreaded that cabin—the fat bodies so close together, the nameless children underfoot, the putrid skins of caribou nailed to the walls. The wife had bright eyes but she never looked at anyone.

But if the cabin was bad, the journey to get there was worse. The merchants struck their booths in late summer and piled their furniture into wagons, repainted the giant skulls on the oilcloth tarps, re-shod their horses, and killed all the sheep and goats they couldn't bring with them on the journey. By the end of the three-month walk up the center of the continent, they were ragged and half-dead, and their northern wives sometimes could not recognize them. But the women still came joyously out of their timber cabins like they were greeting old friends, bearing gifts they'd stored up all summer—pelts and painted skis and beautiful bowls carved from gypsum, and they brought with them the men's children, too, now older and wilder. These children spoke a different language, so the girl couldn't play with them. She never knew what to do in the northcountry, so she prayed for the months to pass quickly and sometimes she prayed for her brother to freeze to death in a snowbank, and sometimes she prayed for the courage to run away. And sometimes she wondered if courage could well up like blood under bruised skin, and if what she needed was just a needle to poke herself with to start the flow. Like freedom might pour out of pain.

When the girl woke, Argento was already gone, his blankets twirled in a nest, not even warm. The tent flap was open. She saw clammy sunlight on the deserted fire-ring. A yellow streamer tumbled across the field. A dog barked, a lone sheep in a bridle stalked past on shorn and twiggy limbs. Then, high above, almost like a breeze, came the roars of men in the distance. She raised herself on her elbows and listened. Metal ringing against metal. Fighting. She pulled the blanket back over her head and underneath it was moist, coppery, the smell of testicles. She could not sleep and she shivered, and soon she heard thumping hooves outside, then the chain-clank of wagons being dragged past by teams of horses. The men were hiding everything magical: all the gypsum and the glass and the mirrors, the hanging charms. Still Argento didn't come for her and she felt like a fawn in the weeds—like her mother used to say—hide and wait for me, hide and wait. But when her brother finally stuck his head through the flaps, her heart popped, and she realized she'd been hoping he was dead.

"It's some other carnival." He had blood on his cheeks, his lips, a foolish grin. "They want this field, but we've had this field ten years now. I helped take it, and sure as shit I ain't about to let it go."

"The carnivals don't start for a month," she whispered. "Why do they want it now?"

He shrugged. The blood on his hands was gritty and black; he snatched her wrists and pulled her into the morning. He shook her. "This is dangerous. I got to put you in with the Heads—Storch is pulling all the wagons into a ring to make them defensible." He looked at her, her nightshirt, colorless fabric, and her knobby body beneath it. She felt him looking as though she were looking at herself. He wanted to protect her, not because he cared for her but because he wouldn't abide anyone taking anything from him. He rubbed the thin fabric between his fingers. "Don't let me catch you out once I put you away. Doesn't matter what happens. If I catch you out—"

A man staggered past, half his face hidden under red-purple pulp; clubbed. His destroyed head was a flower. She didn't want to look, didn't, but she did. Storch. He was bent double but glaring up at them as though they had hurt him, like he deserved more than this death, and she thought of Cosmas the Uncrusher, and wondered why anyone would execute a man who could heal. Storch's blood made her feel nothing. That seaweedy smell of gore, though, reminded her of when her mother practiced surgeries on dogs. She was thankful when Argento flung her aside to steady his friend. "Fuck!" Argento said. "Storch! What happened?"

A shattered skull. There was nothing to stop the bleeding. Storch wept, his eyes peculiar bright blue orbs. It would not be long before the blood was gone. He glowed the way dying people do. She dimly recalled that Storch was her brother's business partner, that they shared the same wagon and two bony yellow horses, but somehow, at that moment, the thought made no sense. She stared at the two of them tangled together, at Argento cradling Storch's head and cursing. He motioned her away and screamed, "Get to the wagon. Now!"

She couldn't move. Finally he kicked her.

As she stumbled across the camp, among the pikes and ribbons and dead hair blowing in the wind, she passed a pierced horse, men scrambling for more weapons, an old woman staring into her tent as though trying to decide what to save. She passed empty booths, devoid now of their wares. Above her, a flock of birds. Storch had already circled the wagons at the bottom of a slight hill, on the other side of the field, this field that lay upon the earth like an unfurled scroll. She could not have imagined this place before she saw it, the highness of the land, or maybe it was nearness of the sky; she felt she saw it now for the first time, even though she'd been here before. She heard the fighting better now, could even see bodies beyond a copse of trees, past the border-fires. People rushed by but no one looked at anyone.

Halfway to the wagons, she passed a tent, and beside the tent stood a man. He was not quite tall, perhaps her brother's age, with a slick knot of black hair and a long curved knife. Clean, the knife, and him. A vest buttoned halfway up and leather boots with brass buttons. He was strange looking, not like anyone she'd ever seen before, so her stomach lurched and she stopped involuntarily. But he was just standing, staring across the field, at the shapes shrieking and colliding beyond the trees. Like he'd stopped mid-stride to bask. He wasn't smiling but she got the terrifying impression he could smile at this fight. The girl turned to run but he'd already seen her and grabbed her and stuck the knife at her throat.

He didn't speak for the longest moment, but held her eyes, held them, and exhaled a word, nonsense, or maybe something in a magician's language. Then he laughed. Why was he laughing? His fingers around her arm hurt. She drew back as far as she could but he tilted his head and regarded her gently, with eyes like an illustration in a book—he was from far away, she realized, except when he spoke his accent was familiar. Her innards pitched at the sound—home, Florida. "What's your hurry?" he said. "I don't often see a little girl. Dangerous times, dangerous place, all that." At last he smiled, and she wanted to cry.

She couldn't reply. Terror twitched inside her and she was cold and hot again. Just do it.

"I'm Mr. Capulatio. You are?"

She shook her head.

"Name? Come on, you got a name. I won't tell."

She shook her head.

He took down the knife and slid his hand from her upper arm to her fingers, and clasped them. His skin was damp and callused. "Makes the heart glad to see a young girl. Makes me feel lucky." He pointed across the field at the killing. "That's my carnival. Better to be with me, don't you think? With us? We got this whole circuit locked up and then some. And for a grander purpose. What's your name?"

She felt tears and the powerful urge to tell him, but bit her lip until she tasted blood. He continued to smile. "That's all right," he said. He leaned toward her, blew sweet breath in her face. The air tasted like mint, like he'd been chewing herbs. She threw a desperate glance over her shoulder toward Argento, who was surely not watching, who was probably already dead, he was so stupid. Mr. Capulatio chuckled. "You look like a beginning, a sunrise. An aurora. A girl in white, on a battlefield? That's hope for a new day, if ever I saw it. So that's what I'll call you." Then he said frankly, "Nobody's going to save you, Aurora. Nobody will even try. Not from me, not now. You know why?"

She kept quiet. He began ushering her across the field. In the air floated a silence, eerie and loud and filled with the erasure of life. Soon enough they were stepping over bodies, and her feet were covered in blood and worse. She kept catching her legs in her nightshirt. He marched her to a great tent festooned with banners and garlanded with Heads, some old and some fresh, still dripping, uncured, spinal bones spiking obscenely from their necks. In her ear, he whispered, "I am the future. The True King. You can call me King if you want. It's what everybody is going to be calling me."

Mr. Capulatio sent someone for her belongings, because she kept crying. She couldn't stop, not once she understood what was happening. Her brother's carnival was mostly dead—she'd stepped in their viscera at the edge of the field—and the captives would shortly become Heads, and though she didn't care about that, she must've cared about something because she sobbed and sobbed in Mr. Capulatio's huge tent while he watched her merrily, drinking and occasionally consulting a mysterious book. He took notes. This lasted hours, him watching her and smiling. She watched him back when she couldn't cry any more: his eyes were mesmeric, suspended above the slashes of his cheekbones like leaping fish. He *was* some kind of king. People came to the tent and he told them what to do, many of them dressed in finer clothing than anyone in her brother's carnival. They wore yellows and purples and blues deeper than the middle of the night. And other men came and went too, these just as ragged as Argento, but their eyes burned bright with what seemed like a mad love for him.

That night he didn't touch her. She slept in a pile of blankets on the ground and he slept alone and once when he woke he yawned and said, "Aurora, you're killing me, come here." But she didn't and he didn't make her. He slept on his back all night and when dawn came, he bent down and kissed her eyelids.

That morning, the servant returned with her things. He brought the magic book and the black amber brooch and Cosmas's Head and laid them before her like a meal. Then two men dragged Argento, twisting and spitting, into the tent and pushed him to the ground also. Her heart sank. They held him there with long knives, smashed his face into the dirty rug. He was so frightened he could not stop panting, and a bead of spit slid over his lip and hung like ice. O, why didn't he have the sense to be dead? "That's my brother," she whispered. It was the first thing she'd said.

Mr. Capulatio, who was eating a shank of goat while sitting at an oversized desk, calmly gazed at her. She was still in her blankets, folded as small as she could get. "What a pretty voice," he said. "Truly. I'm so overcome." He sauntered across to Argento and turned him this way and that, inspecting him as though for parasites. He upturned Argento's head with the very tip of his index finger and scrutinized his neck, then said, "This is your brother? Astonishing. They told me so but I simply couldn't believe it."

The servant nodded. "We found him at the girl's tent."

Mr. Capulatio's face pulled into a smile, but not like his other smiles—it seemed mechanical, a curtain raised on an empty stage. He wheeled on his heels and knelt beside her. "Your brother, really? But you're so young, a fetus. And that"—he flicked a hand at Argento—"is ugly. And you're so darling." He snapped his fingers. "You there, Her Brother. What's her name?"

Argento always did the wrong thing—he was the kind of man who'd do anything, as long as it was wrong. If it was saner to die, he wouldn't. Though it would've been kinder to leave her with his foreign wife and his foreign son, he'd taken her on the carnival circuit instead, and made her ride her own horse and carry her own gear, and if the circuit was too arduous or cold or dangerous and she died . . . well, at least he'd gotten what he wanted, which was to have his way in all things, even when his way made no sense. She hated him, hated him. But when he opened his mouth and moaned, she understood that her hate had not kept her from loving him. Argento had been made cruel by the conditions of his existence. Just a string in a harp, plucked alongside the others. She was not too young to see that.

They had already broken his arms, and he was in pain. An odor filled the tent. Mr. Capulatio kicked him effortlessly. "Name?"

Argento did not reply. But nothing he did in that moment could be right, and for that she felt sorry.

Mr. Capulatio snatched him by the hair and hauled him upward a foot. "All right, then. Your name? We'll do you."

"Argento," he gasped.

Mr. Capulatio dropped him and shrugged. Argento couldn't catch himself on his arms and he fell facedown with a thud, and looked up with sick blood dripping from his nostrils. "O, a liar, beautiful,"

Mr. Capulatio said. "Argento, my good man, you are delightful. Since you're so shockingly delightful, I'll let you in on a secret. I don't want to kill her. Why would anyone kill her? So lovely. And do I want her for my bed?" He laughed; it reminded her of a dragonfly, something about that sound like hovering. "Well, maybe. But no, not really. Maybe a little. O, all right. You see, at this particular point in my life, I need something . . ." his voice wandered off—he wasn't talking to anyone. He gazed at her long and without any happiness. "Something to keep my mind off things. I am an ambitious man, you see, some might even say a regal one. I deeply hate the northcountry. It's unwholesome cold, terrible for my health. What a stupid Law it is that we should let the land rest for the winter. The stupid Law of a false king."

Argento coughed.

"O yes," said Mr. Capulatio. "A false king is King Michael! He is even now living in splendor meant for someone else. We have proof of this, in our texts. Exegesis, it's called. You're too stupid to know what I mean, of course." He gestured around him. "I have people trained to study the texts. They have worked years upon years and this is at last what they have concluded. So this year I proposed to these people, my distinguished consortium of magicians and merchants, that we simply not go. North, I mean." He blinked at Argento. "I know! An insane idea. What in the world are we thinking? That, my good man, is what you must be thinking, am I correct?" He waved a hand. "But I don't care what you think because you are about to die. You can clearly see, I do what I like. Your darling sister—if she is indeed your sister, which I doubt—is necessary for my comfort but more importantly, she figures into my destiny. Do you understand that?" He peered at Argento seriously. "She will be my queen. A miniature queen. The gemrock in my crown. A lucky sigil in the form of a beautiful girl."

Argento tried to snort, but he choked on blood. "You're not a king."

"Aren't I?" He grinned. "Well, who can say? Who's really anything?" He bent forward and brushed a smudge of blood from Argento's nose, rubbed it between his fingers. "It's not like it matters." He stopped smiling. "You're so charming. You charm me. You are the most charming man I've met in a long time. Charming enough to make into a Head, for certain." He straightened and cracked his neck. Boredom like a lightning bolt. "Is the stage up yet?" he demanded of the servant, who nodded. She noticed the servant had drawn back just a step, afraid maybe, of what might happen. Mr. Capulatio said, "Excellent. Tomorrow, dawn, you'll die, Argento or whatever your name is. It doesn't matter anyway, because we won't make you a Head, I changed my mind. But we will give your heart to little Aurora here—that's what I'm calling her, since no one has been kind enough to divulge her name. I'll cut your heart out myself and give it to her, an engagement present, and we'll keep you in a box and you'll be near us as we ascend the throne in Cape Canaveral! Yes? Beautiful. We are romantics, are we not?" He stepped over Argento and stood above the girl and her stomach heaved like when she fell from her horse, and she was floating, airborne, for the shortest moment as he pulled her to her feet and into his chest. He motioned to the book, her brooch, and the sack containing the Head of Cosmas. "Now show me these things that are dear to you. I want to know everything."

To the servant he said, "Escort this gentleman to the cages."

Mr. Capulatio talked to her all night but never once touched her. She did not sleep, but stared up at the striped fabric ceiling as he made outlandish claims she was sure did not make any sense, but in the night and in her fear they seemed true. He said that after the summer execution season, his carnival would head for Cape Canaveral, the holy city, the seat of government, and there they would unite with the other factions that supported his claim. They would mount an attack and take the throne. He knew he would succeed because he was divinely blessed, he said. Had been since the day he was born. Certain magical knowledge (like the exact date of the return of the five space shuttles) had been revealed to him secretly—the rockets *would* return, he assured her, even the incinerated ones. All five shuttles would be healed of their age and wounds, no longer patched trash cans, but miraculous elevators that would convey mankind beyond the sickened earth, the ionosphere, and into cosmic radiance. The names of the five rockets, he whispered, when said together, comprised the most magical word in existence. *Columbiachallengerdiscoveryatlantisend-eavour.* It was what he said when he cut off heads. It was what he said in the ears of women to whom he made love. It was what he'd murmured when he'd first seen her, a young girl on the carnival circuit—bizarre, surprising, and most of all magical. *Magical?* she whispered, almost too afraid to speak. Mr. Capulatio shook his head with a peculiar defiance. *O yes, you are mostly definitely magical. I found you, my Queen, the last augur of my destiny, exactly where I thought I would find you,* he said. *A battlefield. From pain and blood is born a new world order. Glorify. Columbiachallengerdiscoveryatlantisendeavour!*

Later that night, she imagined her brother dying to the sound of that strange word and in spite of everything, she couldn't batten down her eagerness to believe—what if even the smallest part of Mr. Capulatio's stories were true? What if he did take her to Cape Canaveral? What if the shuttles did come back, once the world had been washed in blood for one Eon? Maybe the Eon of Pain was ending? Maybe her mother was wrong and Wonderblood meant all the pain and horror in her life and all lives had been worth something, after all. She tried to make herself care about the magic—she pinched her eyes closed and tried to whisper Mr. Capulatio's word in thanks for her good fortune; she tried to believe it meant something. But really she only wanted to go home. With her eyes shut, she remembered the way the air and water fused on a warm day, exactly the same temperature, how she couldn't tell where one stopped and the other started and how much a part of the universe this made her feel. More than any word. If only he took her back to Florida, she would escape, vanish, go home. She knew the saferoads there, some of them. She'd walked them so many times as a girl, behind her mother, watching her dress sway as they went from settlement to settlement, healing when they could. She'd live in her own small house, she'd have a dog, she'd eat seagulls, grow her vegetables. She thought of Cosmas in his sack and wished he weren't a Head, so she could tell him about her plan. She'd ask him what it would feel like when her heart uncrushed. Like crying, he'd say, only the good kind of crying. She didn't know the word for that feeling.

Just before dawn, she'd pinned the black brooch to her shirt. Mr. Capulatio was already dressed. He'd fixed his hat upon his head at an angle and was flicking through the book Argento had given her. He glanced at her and nodded to the brooch. "O, perfect, I was just about to suggest that." He shrugged. "Can you read, darling?" he asked, his voice inflectionless.

She hesitated, shook her head.

"Why do you have this, then?"

"It's not mine."

"You surely don't expect me to believe it's *his,*" he said. She said nothing. He smiled again, bent until he was level with her, and batted at a piece of her hair. "All right. Impressive." She didn't know if he meant the book or her silence. His face close up was lineless, younger maybe than she'd first guessed and also cleaner than any face should be. "This," he began, handing her the book, "is powerful magic. Dates and names and history, on and on. Why do you have it? I must ask, you know I have to ask. You are my almost-wife."

"It's not mine."

"Not yours. I see. Well, that makes sense. Shall we go cut off some heads?" He shrugged again, and she sensed this gesture—this casual decisiveness—contained him more than any other.

"Please—"

"No please. Please is for later. Now is for thank you."

She stared. He stared back. Then he rose and said over his shoulder, "If you *could* read—and I'm not saying you can—you would know that the subject of this book is me. How felicitous, how scenic! That I would find you exactly where I expected to find you at the moment I knew you would be there, and you would have in your possession a book about *me*! How is that for harmony! Glorify, the universe is truly great. Now, darling." He looked deeply into her eyes and took his knife from where it lay on his bed. "Don't make me tell you again. Say thank you."

Colored streamers everywhere, ten thousand more than she'd ever seen, flapping as she walked with Mr. Capulatio across his carnival, which was huge, which had risen in two days like an enchanted crop.

Crawling with people who moved, built, sliced, hammered. A clockwork masterpiece, this camp, with massive tents and a stage flanked by booths where the customers would buy their Heads come summer. And a metal cage, encircled by lanterns still glowing in the bottle-blue dawn, and people inside with faces tightened by fear. People she knew. When they saw her with Mr. Capulatio, when they looked at her like that, their hands on the bars, she tried to hide behind him, she thought: *Don't look, I can't help you,* but he was walking ahead, wearing red pants and a tan shirt and carrying that knife. His hair was long and flashing black like a seabird, topped by a felt hat with an aigrette thrust through the hatband. He did not hold her hand. She followed him anyway.

The birds were singing as Mr. Capulatio mounted the stage. Loud as tin cans tied to a spit in a storm. The people gathering about the stage were louder still, and she felt so alone, ringed on all sides by this oceanic land—she wondered wildly if this place was the root of her nostalgia, this country of surging grasses and wind that looked somehow like tides and waves. Then the first ray of true light split the horizon. All she could see was the block at the center of the stage, hideous-smooth and black. A servant directed her into a booth where three crones in face paint offered to hold her, in case she fainted when the time came. They draped a shawl over her shoulders and one whispered, "Cover your eyes if you need to," while the other said, "I don't see why she'd need to," and the last marveled at Mr. Capulatio's new costume. At the first execution of the summer—which this was, had she known, wasn't she honored?—Mr. Capulatio was always resplendent, the old women said, with his unchopped hair and his knife made of pearlescent metal from the shuttle launch site.

She stared up at him. He was leaning on a podium and waiting.

Mr. Capulatio would execute six or seven, the women said, but Argento first, and this was an act of kindness. Mr. Capulatio must love her so, they chirped, and stroked her back. His new little queenlet, blessed with a grand destiny. Suddenly she saw Argento; he was bound, and two men conducted him to the stage, where he stepped up like a drunk. Silence swept the crowd. She heard her brother's footsteps, the whistle of breath through his broken nose, as he trudged over the boards and stiffly knelt before the polished block. He stared ahead with all the foreknowledge of a sheep, blue-blank membranous eyes, but then she saw his hands behind his back, shaking just a little, and a minute cry escaped her lips. She had seen executions before, knew to brace herself against those rolling waves of pity she couldn't enter, otherwise, that feeling she could not feel until a man began screaming and she imagined his family, watching him die like that, to be made into a lucky charm. She thought maybe Argento deserved his fate, but pity kept her from wishing it upon him. Mr. Capulatio certainly had no pity—he was half-smiling. And Argento had none, not even now. But they were men, and she was different. She hoped he couldn't see her. Better for him to die alone. But Mr. Capulatio straightened, pointed his knife, and announced, "She's right there." Argento wouldn't look. Mr. Capulatio took a powerful step forward and raised the knife and said, "Last chance."

He was not joking. Argento wouldn't look, and without ceremony, Mr. Capulatio brought the blade down, his face contorted by effort but not emotion. And in the end she couldn't look either, but hid her eyes in the shawl and wished she had never met Argento so she wouldn't have to remember him. The wet sawing lasted much longer than he'd earned. The crowd cheered. The birds.

Summer came and went, and though Mr. Capulatio tried to keep her from the unpleasantness of the executions, she always heard the beheadings and that gasping mob, their breath released together as laughter because laughter was all they could muster. He left her alone in the afternoons, when he left with bags of magic paraphernalia, and returned bloody in the evenings.

She walked around this new camp with an audacity she'd never had at her brother's carnival. She belonged to Mr. Capulatio and so everyone treated her well, and this knowledge shamed her because she felt so safe, and sometimes also it caused a twinge of excitement deep in her belly. There was a tent full of dancing girls, not much older than herself, and they caused fights between the men and even some of the crones, who considered them like daughters and fought over which one was prettiest or the best dancer. The girl liked to spy on them. She watched them draw on each other's faces before they performed, butterflies and stars, and once she heard them singing together in such a crystalline collective voice that it was like a knife in her chest. She imagined herself with them, laughing and shimmying onstage for the men, but stopped her spying when she realized she was jealous.

And sometimes, because she missed Argento, she went to watch the Head Makers at their task. Chanting and chalk and brands and blood. Heads were bought and sold at the booths, spines removed, ground, burned, eaten, sigils etched into dead flesh and live flesh. These Head Makers didn't venerate the Astronauts or the hexagram that symbolized the six towers at the Cape; their brand was a rocketship and there were booths devoted to each of the space rockets. The man in charge of the largest booth had a red beard and black hair and he was a ratty skinny thing but the way he said, *O, Queenie, you tell Mr. King I took extra special care with those Heads he brought in the other day* was genuine and kind, and his smile had a black front tooth but the way he smiled made her want to smile back. She was not afraid, even when he held a freshly beheaded body over a basin to collect its blood, he said. Collecting blood had been illegal in Argento's carnival, because according to Wonderblood the blood from the dead was supposed to saturate the earth. She had thought it was illegal everywhere because of the Primary Law, and wondered if the people in this carnival were happier because Mr. Capulatio was a blessed redeemer, or because he let them break the law.

Mr. Capulatio himself, though, confused her more day by day. He often took her outside to present the sky to her like a gift, something made special by his attention, and he bore it upward on his palms so familiarly, like it was his. Like a deep dark sapphire, he'd say, is the sky. Like the sea. They stood on a butte under the stars, at the center of five pikes and Heads, on these breezy summer nights. He could talk in such a beautiful way, it was hard not to listen. He kept his fingers clasped around her shoulders, so tight it hurt, and he said hypnotizing things like, *This field used to be underwater. Extraordinary, how the world reinvents itself. Inspiring. Promising.* Once, during a moment of mad terrible loneliness, she'd asked, *Do you believe that magic is real? My mother told me it's all just lunatic-ravings.* They were staring at the stars, like always. His mood darkened almost imperceptibly but then he laughed, rattled her hard. *My queenlet, are we not born in blood and pain? Is this not how we are squeezed grossly into the world? So then how should we atone for the sins of our past if what we desire is a new world order? Magic is about balance, sugarplum. If we once leeched, now we must gush.* He shrugged. *Your mother must have been a fool's bitch to believe otherwise, is all I'll say about her.*

She'd heard in his voice a trill of almost-laughter, which made her wonder if he was saying what he thought a king would say and not what he truly believed. She searched his face for lies and thought she saw many. Then he smiled cruelly and said, *You should believe in magic. You are magic, so if you don't believe in it, where will you be? Will you not exist?* He mockingly put a hand to his lips and made a surprised face. *Can a thing exist if we don't believe it?*

She had narrowed her eyes at this, unsure if he was making fun of her.

He hadn't touched her. At night, he sat cross-legged on his bed with a lantern, gazing at his many books—often with a puzzled expression but always with a singularity of purpose that troubled her. He'd be flayed alive by his constituents, he'd mutter, if he did not have all the answers by the time they arrived at the Cape, but she didn't know what he meant. He asked her direct questions that made no sense, like *Can you see me dying? How do you think I might die if I were to die in, say, two months?* Which was how long it was until they broke camp and headed south instead of north, until they broke the law and went forth to meet their destinies with brave hearts. He forced her to predict his death in as many ways as she could dream up, each more horrible than the last, until he sighed with a satisfaction that was nearly sexual and that frightened her because he'd never reached for her physically, never even tried. That troubled her. She began to believe he wanted something much more awful.

In October, they broke camp and marched over the plain. Fast, too fast, because they'd waited so late in the season, and soon they were riding in cold rain, against the wind, and she was miserable, wet, freezing, even in Mr. Capulatio's wagon, where his charms hung from the ceiling, tinkling and catching the lamplight and casting prismatic shadows along the walls. She sat wrapped in blankets all day, beside the sack containing the Head of Cosmas, whom she now kept close because she felt like they were in this together, and also because he reminded her of her brother. She watched Mr. Capulatio, who read, took notes, screamed at people, and laughed. Most of all he spent his time writing long tracts on page after page of parchment that he then scrutinized furiously. Often he threw them away and other times he locked them in a trunk.

Water seeped through cracks in the old wagon and she tried to sleep most of the day but the shuddering and bumping kept her awake, and sometimes when she opened her eyes she caught Mr. Capulatio gazing at her intently and perhaps sympathetically, but she could not really tell because she couldn't understand his face—it was written in a difficult language; the more she heard and saw of him, the less she understood. But forgiveness had been stirring within her a long while, perhaps since the moment he'd executed Argento, and when he looked at her she could not help but look back. He was a moon, pulling on the ocean of her pity. He was afraid, and she sensed that the first act of her womanhood would be to comfort him. Soon she would reach for him, not the other way around, and she knew then that was what he had been waiting for.

At a field of skeletal ruins, they camped for a day and a night. Still everywhere was flat, wide. Gaping holes in rusted cylindrical ruins. Metal scars in the fields. She overheard someone beyond the wagon saying "Arkansas," and for the first time she wondered what that word meant—our-kansas. She glanced at Mr. Capulatio, in bed with closed eyes. He nevertheless chuckled. "Wrong. Still Missouri. Miserable Missouri. Fools never know where we are. I have a state-sense that's never failed me." He rolled over. "Today's my birthday, did you know that?" He stretched his arms above his head and yawned. "Do you know how old I am? How old are you?"

"Fifteen."

"Are you sure?"

"My birthday was the day before . . ." She trailed off and looked around the wagon. *The day before you took me.*

"That doesn't mean you know how old you are."

She stared at him. "I'm fifteen."

He shrugged. "I was born on the anniversary of the launch of Cassini to Saturn. Today is a very important day, astronomically speaking. The book you have lists it out. It's all there, it comes together just so, like a fairytale." He noticed her eyeing him skeptically. "O, I've read that book you have, imagine that. It's about me. Sugarplum, I am one blessed son of a bitch, nothing else you can call me. I can do no wrong." He thoughtfully fiddled with his collarbone. "But you've never read the book, eh? Even though you *had* it." Outside people rattled cooking pots and laughed and someone was singing. "Well," he said at last. "What counts is what we do with our blessings, right?"

She remained quiet.

He took a deep breath. "What I'm *saying* is, I never get what I really want."

She drew her knees to her chest. "What do you really want?"

"Ah! Do you really want to know?"

No. No. A drop of sweat fell down the center of her ribcage, between her breasts, and she realized she was trembling, and Mr. Capulatio swung his legs around and sat upright and light seemed to pour from his mouth when smiled—that was his knifing smile. "No, I thought not. Do you have a gift for me?"

"No," she whispered.

He blinked. "Well, I have one for you. A secret."

"Why?"

"Why not?" He bent forward and pushed a few of the hanging charms away, holding them back while he seemed to consider. Then he let them plunge before him, a jingling curtain. He spoke and his accent had disappeared, she tried to hear it but couldn't—was she used to it or had it vanished? He said, "I know you think you're running away sometime, once you've ridden this train back to Florida. Do you think I'm a fool? Do you think I took you up just to lose you? Do you think I axed your brother for fun? Tell me what you think." He blithely inspected his knuckles.

All the blood drained from her face; she felt it slide into her heart, where it thumped about like a suffocating fish.

"Tell me: when I go off to do my magic, do you think I'm not spying on you?" He reached past her suddenly and grabbed the sack with Cosmas's Head, upended it, and dumped Cosmas onto the bed. The glittering forehead-hexagram caught the light and shot it all over the wagon. "It's called a Third Eye, Queen Stupid. It lets you see. Well, it lets me see. Even your idiot ugly brother could do a spell like the Third Eye. Thanks, by the way," he said, looking upward with phony gratefulness. "Saved me the trouble."

She could not stop blinking. How could he know? Was he just guessing, gauging her reaction? He couldn't read her thoughts, she knew he couldn't—it wasn't possible. Was it?

"I'm just telling you," he continued more softly. "Not to run away. Because I'll always know where you are. Unless you want to destroy good old Cosmas here." He extended the Head to her, dangled it by its straw-hair and swung it a little for effect. "Do you? Seems an awful shame to waste him. He gave his life for you. He's not the only one."

Her words were barely audible. "Are you lying?"

He shrugged. "Why would I lie? To you, I mean."

It sounded petulant even to her and she sat in stunned silence for a long moment. No crying, none, she told herself. The silence became an awkward void and when a tear rolled over her cheek, he rubbed it away with his thumb and he was sorry, she knew. He'd felt scared, that was all, and he wanted her to be scared too. "Why did you have to kill him?" she asked thickly.

He appeared to think, and then faced her. She wondered if such tension meant he loved her. He dropped Cosmas into his bag, dusted off his hands. "Well. It's not like you could have done it." He said it honestly, and gratitude jolted her like static, hot and surprising, and when he stalked away to sulk, she missed him.

Dark night. She crawled into his bed and into his arms and he held her and he smelled like rain. Hours passed. He stroked her hair. He ran his hands down her spine and around her neck, and he kissed her a little, not much—enough to make her feel protected. He was awake, she was awake, all night, and she said, "Thank you."

"For what?"

She buried her face in his hair. More time passed and she asked, "Will it be different with you than with him?"

"I don't know," he said. She felt his hand trace the star-shaped scar on the inside of her thigh. "Probably. The difference is that I'm only going to hurt you on the inside."

A new happiness had settled over him and he seemed relieved. She wondered if he'd been testing himself: how long until she trusted him, would she ever? A king must inspire trust. And for her, a miracle too: she'd chosen this, or felt like she had. He needed her. To keep him calm. To map out every one of a thousand horrible deaths that might befall him in the coming months or years. He was afraid of his destiny, chokingly, overwhelmingly afraid, and suddenly it didn't matter whether he believed in magic or she did or if it was real or if her mother was right and they were all just fools walking in a pointless, bloody parade toward the end of time. Her eyes were open. She could run or not, she could love him or not, she could miss her brother or hate him forever. It was all going to hurt.

"You know what I really wish?" Mr. Capulatio asked wistfully.

"What?"

"That I'd never been born. That would be really great."

She took a careful breath. "I think you're going to die by boiling oil. Our seventh son will have you fried and fed to crows."

Our.

She felt him smile. Sad, happy, deep, and dark. "O, sugarplum, I didn't know you cared."

CHAPTER 2

EARS

Marvel Whiteside Parsons walked across the palace courtyard in the morning rain, and paused for a moment to feel the drops on his cheeks. They wept sparsely from a marbled sky, and briefly he stopped to watch as they hurtled into the puddles gathering in the cart ruts. He'd once read that the oceans had formed drop by drop, from infinitesimally small amounts of water carried inside meteors until they struck the earth and released their contents. Each droplet a minor cataclysm. Men have held such strange notions of the world, Marvel thought, and wiped the water from his forehead.

Marvel had not spent much time thinking of nature. Rarely did he have occasion to experience it. He was a busy man, perhaps the busiest at the Cape. Certainly he was the most troubled. Although he had once crossed the continent on foot, he'd long ago counted himself lucky for that feat of survival and had never since tested his mettle against the elements. The elements could evaporate, for all they mattered in his life—the stars above were only lights to him now, no longer signifiers of the divine. Marvel passed his days signing letters, he appeared in public to grant blessings, he presided over beheadings, he advised King Michael, he concocted potions, and he managed all those matters that King Michael did not wish to manage. These were many. Marvel was tired.

And he had begun thinking of the weather again. He could not help himself.

He would be leaving soon.

Marvel Whiteside Parsons was the High Priest of Cape Canaveral, Hierophant and Head Magician. Born fifty and some years before in Dread Kansas, the Center of the World, he knew he was growing old, and yet still he felt like a younger man. Perhaps it was destiny that he should be robust. By design, his birth had taken place at the holiest spot in the holiest place in all the world: inside the Black Watchtower. His mother was a descendant of Huldah, the Mother Prophetess who had given the world the Primary Law. Wonderblood. His father had been a holy monk, one of the dark priests who prayed continually for the end of the world. Marvel was a man entirely *of* the deathscapes—he embodied their torment, so to speak, the way other men carried family names. His entire personage was to have been like those flat lands: alive with death, seething with righteous terror, unyielding and impartial.

But it had not happened that way.

Though Marvel was born to be a saving king from the great plain where the ruin of the world had begun—the True King, in fact—he was not. He was not even in Kansas.

He looked down the path at the busy courtyard. When people noticed him, they bowed perfunctorily. He often went about the palace grounds alone. He looked up again as another droplet splashed on his forehead. He was supposed interrogate a prisoner this morning, a job he preferred to delay.

The weather today, a spate of seasonal November drear. Rain had been falling from a sky the color of a kidney for how long? Maybe no more than a day, but if he were crossing the land, even a day of rain would be miserable. He must have the correct supplies for days and days of rain. And cold. The air today was uncomfortably windy and the gusts spat cold water blown in from the deathscapes. Marvel did hate the cold—he had grown to adolescence in the frigid stone rooms of Huldah's Black Tower. Here at the Cape, cold was never truly cold, but over time he had grown more sensitive to it.

He trudged through the courtyard, his black shoes dirtying in the wet paste of straw and sawdust. And there, look! A carpet thrown over a puddle. For who? His daughter Alyson perhaps. O, most certainly for her. *Michael* would never consider using a carpet to cross a puddle. What a waste, Marvel thought, of a perfectly nice carpet, and how like Alyson to demand something so frivolous. He shook his head and blamed her although he had no evidence.

He was unfair to his daughter. It was not her fault she was as vapid as the deathscapes were vast. Marvel had not been a good father. Where had he gone wrong? To look at her was a delight, but to listen to her . . . Marvel could hardly stand it. She thought only of sport and smoking. She may have resembled Marvel's pious mother Nasa Whiteside with her dark hair and round face, but she embodied everything he had wasted of himself during his years at the Cape: his virtue, his talent, his devotion. She embarrassed him.

But he was being petty. It was the weather, yes, his boots squelching in the mud; that sound made his skin crawl, the plump glug-glug of mud sucking at him. Something about it only just sickening. He was not by any means a precious man. He had some time ago discarded all the fine clothes his high office had afforded him and now wore only a plain brown cassock. He went barefoot to his prayers in warm weather. Marvel had shed nearly all the material trappings of his office over the years, yet couldn't contain his annoyance at this muddy courtyard. The *king's* courtyard. Did no one believe they were worthy of a clean and tidy courtyard any longer? Where was the man to lay down more straw? Marvel pulled his foot from the mud again and sighed.

When Marvel had first encountered the countryside outlying Cape Canaveral, he was struck by its utter inhospitality—and he had come from Kansas, Dread of the continent. He had been walking nearly a month. He was fourteen, perilously thin when he arrived, dirty. Like a scrambling vermin, his exhausted heart clawed at his insides, but still he lurched with wonder as he drew closer to the palace compound. He had crossed two stone bridges on pylons sunk into the shallow channel between the mainland and the Cape, their surfaces studded with fossilized shells and rocks—coral limestone, he learned later. When at last he sat in the sand at the Atlantic shore he sank to his knees. The sea here was so shallow and so lovely, like stained glass, with shallow panes of pale blue, its variegated green depths and its fleshpink sandbars gracefully lifting themselves like elbows above the water. The young Marvel had never seen anything so strange and darkly beautiful to his eyes, which had only ever beheld wide fields, dirt, skies. To his left and behind him was a sparse row of broken hexagrams, ancient cement markers in the scrub; these were the old shuttle launchpads, watched over now by palace guards with machetes. Still more patrolled in wagons drawn by mules. What they looked for, he hadn't known then, but they hadn't stopped him or paid him even a second glance as he'd passed them on his way to the water.

Now those guards did his bidding. Or rather, ignored it. This muddy courtyard.

He sighed.

The interrogation chambers were housed in Canaveral Tower. Its height was legend; the cylinder rose upward and upward, like a thin band of water siphoned into the sky, the most impressive construction yet built during the Eon of Pain. This was the spot where men had touched outer space. Marvel vividly recalled seeing the palace compound for the first time. He was a man tormented by a keen memory, embarrassingly old when at last he understood that many people simply forgot things, or—stranger still—didn't care enough to notice them in the first place. His first visions of the Cape were burned into his mind's eye. Perhaps more dynamic now than ever before.

After all, he was preparing to leave.

He would cross the continent again soon.

Marvel had first arrived at the Cape during the season when the carnivals returned to pay their tributes. Just beyond their lean-to camps, their cookpots filled with gruels, their casks of germed waters, was the great wall that surrounded the entire palace compound. Ten men high, encrusted with broken glass—greens and blues and browns cobbled together into a jagged mosaic that seemed at once to be depicting all the events in remembered history. Pieces of glass were thrust with their edges bared at the outer world, a spiked halo. Marvel knew that behind the wall lurked what he had come for: the seat of the magical world.

But nothing seemed magical here anymore. Not to Marvel. Not the wind from the sea or the glow of the stars. Certainly not this mud.

He had not progressed much further along the path before he noticed another of his staff's failures. A sleepy guard stood a fair distance away, one of the many posted to oversee the daily courtyard market. Merchants from beyond the walls came with their wares and sold them in booths. Magicked Heads, jewelry, leather. People pushed carts with wood for fires. Women carried water, men yanked horses through the mud, magicians shook their girdles of talismans. Still more carried fish and flesh and fabrics and pieces of found metal, balanced in gigantic baskets upon their heads. Courtiers, the families of the Cape who had lived here a thousand years, mingled in their finery and blew each other five kisses, the greeting their station demanded. Ochre robes, moonstone collars, blue glass rings on every finger in homage to the heavenly bodies. They were arrayed in splendor while their finely dressed children scrapped with each other and chased dogs.

But Marvel's eyes were drawn to the young-looking guard. He stood beneath the eve of a booth. His uniform was all wrong. It might not even have been palace issue. He seemed almost comatose, but as Marvel watched, he snatched an orange from a passing cart. Without offering payment, he peeled it and began to eat.

The whole fruit was gone in a few bites, the peel tossed underfoot. The guard ground it into the mud. Marvel stopped. Frowned.

The man would need to be reprimanded. There was no one to do it but Marvel. He realized abruptly that he hated to be in charge—when had that changed? At one time he had enjoyed it, craved it. Now he wished he could leave the guard to his stupid fruit. Should a man not have the dignity of sorting out those ethics on his own? But it was not possible. Others had seen Marvel crossing the courtyard: what if they had also seen the guard steal the fruit? What if someone had *seen* Marvel see the guard steal and do nothing? He clenched his jaw.

He took a weary step off the path, but at that moment a trumpet sounded the public prayer. It was led not by Marvel, but by the Royal Pardoness, Green Butterfly. Marvel turned from the guard, grateful but then at once reluctant for the distraction. The Pardoness emerged, shrouded. None of her skin was visible, only clouds of weightless fabric topped by a crown of polished green rocks. Like tombstones, or teeth. Her face entirely covered by pale diaphanous silk. Drops of water pitted the fabric here and there.

She revealed herself upon her balcony for a few moments every day in order to assure the people there still existed a link between themselves and the divine. Green Butterfly stretched her slender hands over them all each morning, in sunshine and rain. She was a direct descendant of a man who had walked on the moon. A feeling of peace *did* emanate from the act, if one had a mind to feel it: often, Marvel did not. There were people who said Green Butterfly lived in a room paneled entirely in opals. That she kept the finger-bones from every soul she pardoned. He was sure those things weren't true, but the people liked her nonetheless. Though she was now so frail her voice was nearly impossible to hear, though no one had seen her face in years, though she rarely granted pardons, still, she represented goodness. Kindness. Even love.

The spitting weather drowned her voice. The people in the courtyard stared at her anyway. Most of them. They knew what she would say, as did Marvel—she said the same thing every day. More important was to be *seen* looking at her. He supposed many of them admired her clothing, her headpiece, for he had authorized those, and knew how much they cost. Others were simply glad to stop working for a few moments. A few might even have wanted to feel her warmth, though from this distance it flickered like a candle across a bedroom. Marvel stopped along with them, splashes of rain on their faces together while they strained to listen.

She opened her arms, silks streaming off them.

A few murmurs, nothing discernible. Marvel knew the words because he'd written them. He found his mouth saying them, though he could not see her lips. One of his first acts as Hierophant had been to change all the traditional prayers. He had been young and passionate then.

He could remember many things, but could hardly remember himself. Who had he been in those days?

Then a trumpet blast barreled from another tower, signifying the end of the prayer. The Pardoness bowed to them all. She disappeared back into her chamber, and for a moment no one moved. The rain fell, and an indifferent silence filled by the sound of shoes shifting in mud, a mule shaking its mane. At last a woman sneezed, and the racket of the courtyard trading booths began once again.

Marvel's eyes fell at once on the offending guard again. He slumped against a pole. His chin nodded toward his chest. Marvel sighed again and went toward him, nearly knocked over in his haste by a handcart full of citrus greenery, likely meant for a courtier's bedroom. He weaved away from the cart and swore under his breath as the wheel splashed mud on his cassock. He was not angry, but it felt right to act as though he were.

He poked the guard in the stomach when he reached him. The man gasped and doubled over. On the ground lay the orange peel. The guard stood up angrily and glared at Marvel, not a shred of recognition in his eyes. "What the hell's wrong with you, eh?"

Marvel folded his arms. "Why have you stolen from your countryman?"

"Who the hell are you?"

"More importantly, why have you not addressed me honorably?"

The guard seemed confused. His face was unshaven; patches of wheat-colored hair growing out of tanned skin. Something about him off. That uniform, up close, looked years out of date. He shook his head slightly.

"Don't play stupid. I saw you," Marvel barked.

"Sir, I—"

"'Sir'? I'm no one's 'sir.'" Marvel paused. The man looked even more baffled. Marvel said, "*Do* you know who I am?" He had a deep voice, almost croaking, and knew he sounded intimidating. He was also tall, somewhat hulking, and only just a bit overweight. In his cassock he looked regal, though the garment was plain. Anyone should know who he was, Marvel thought, annoyed. His image was circulated.

"You're—" The guard's eyes darted left, then right. His head sat upon his neck like a goblet-bowl. "Obviously someone important." He tried to smile and mostly succeeded. He was a head shorter than Marvel, soft-skinned and loosely jointed. "I'm new to the job, please forgive me."

His accent was foreign—he might indeed be new. Marvel didn't concern himself with hiring guards, he had men for that. But this man could be a spy. Something about him bothered Marvel, apart from the stealing and the sleeping. Was it his clothing after all? With the thought came an unwelcome tremor. Who would send a spy wearing out-of-date clothing? Marvel could think of one place.

Kansas.

But how could the monks at the Black Watchtower have learned of his plans to return when he had told no one? Impossible. He leaned back on his heels and smirked, as he often did when he wasn't sure what to do. His presence was large; usually this was enough to cow his adversaries.

"Where is your firearm?" Marvel asked after a moment.

"My what?"

"Your gun. You're an elite guard. That's the uniform you're wearing, even if it's old. Or did you not know?"

"They didn't give me one. A gun, I mean," the man replied.

"Who is 'they'?"

The guard shrugged. "Whosoever's in charge of handing out weapons. Like I said, I'm new." The younger man looked at him buoyantly. Something striking about his eyes. It may have been cockiness; he didn't know who Marvel was, after all. How long since anyone had looked at Marvel that way? That sent another tremor through him. The man turned his head when he realized Marvel was still staring: the moment had stretched on inappropriately. "I just came here a few days ago." The guard shrugged. "I asked for a job and they gave me one. I didn't ask for a weapon. Should I have?"

"I see you have a knife right there." Marvel pointed to the guard's belt.

"That was mine. From before." The man's eyes were green. His hair was pale brown, cut poorly. Marvel rubbed his own chin. He hadn't shaved that day, or the day before. Suddenly he stepped back, aware of the gray in his beard, the other man's proximity. "Who hired you, again?"

"O, I don't remember his name. He was middle height?" the guard said. Then, more eagerly, "I used to go with the carnivals. If that's why you're staring at me like that." He gestured to his clothes. "I know I look bad."

"Carnival men can be . . . difficult to reason with. We don't often hire them as guards." Marvel raised his eyebrow. "You really don't know who I am, do you?"

Another cart jostled them as it passed. A palm frond fell from its overloaded basket and lay beside the orange peel. The guard's smile turned sheepish. He shook his head.

Surely a spy would know who he was, unless of course it was all an act. He crossed his arms. "Which carnival did you come from, I asked."

The younger man shrugged. Pale light filled the guard's eyes from the side, and with a jolt Marvel realized he had not *looked* at anyone for a long time, not really. He was thoroughly enjoying the experience.

His gaze fell on a tiny sack just peeking from the folds of the man's tunic. It hung from a cord tied to his belt, no bigger than a money-purse. The guard brushed it with his hand but that was all. A long moment passed. "I got work in the carnivals, that was all," the guard said finally. "It's better than nothing, eh? This was the only Head I ever made."

"The life of a guard will suit you better, then?"

"I think so."

A silence opened between them. It occurred to Marvel that this man might have spent all his life outside. His cheeks were roughened and red. Even if he was not from a carnival—which Marvel suspected—he had most likely walked long miles to get here. It was a hard way across the continent. Marvel had traveled it. When at last the other man began to fidget, Marvel said, "I'm Marvel Parsons."

"O."

The man knew the name. He cleared his throat. "O," he said again. "Many apologies. It wasn't . . . I didn't think you would be dressed so—"

He waved his hand. "You know, I think you're a spy. I'm almost sure. I might have you thrown in prison."

The man smiled again, while shaking his head. Perhaps he enjoyed being ridiculed. Marvel had met other men who did.

"But," Marvel went on. "I like you. If you've crossed the continent lately, I could see my way to a compromise." He shrugged. "Are you a spy?"

"Never."

"Did you cross the deathscapes to get here?"

Young and audacious and beautiful in the way that impudence can render a young man beautiful, the guard stood a bit taller and replied, "On my own. Without so much as a mule. No sickness, no death." He bowed at last. "Your Majesty."

Marvel found himself nodding. There would be time to discover who had sent him and why. But before then Marvel would hear about the deathscapes.

He had dealt with many smarter men than this. In these, his final days at the Cape, when his desperation to return to Kansas had all but transformed him from statesman back into a sort of cautious zealot, Marvel had begun once more to dream. He thrust out his hand, opened it, and waited until the guard placed his knife in his palm. Marvel clapped him on the back. The rain had stopped falling, but when? He hadn't noticed. He must become better about noticing the weather.

"Walk with me, young man. We have a few things in common," Marvel said, sticking the knife into his own belt and steering the guard toward Canaveral Tower, toward the jail. He would show him an interrogation, he would show him the jail in all its white horror, and then, perhaps, he would ask him again if he were a spy.

Or perhaps not. Marvel could simply kill him after he learned how the man had crossed the deathscapes. If, say, he was in possession of a map.

He had done worse things.

When Marvel was born in Kansas, his mother the nun laid him in a black stone cradle. She presented him with a swaddling blanket fit for a king, a sheer black cloth inscribed with gold thread that spelled out his name in stars. Later he was told the heavens themselves would have mirrored it, had he proven worthy.

Alas, Marvel had been an unkingly boy from his first breath, which emerged reluctantly from clogged airways—Marvel had been born dead. He came to life when at last a midwife held him up to declare him lifeless. As though he had considered her offer and rejected it. His mother cried with relief, but those tears turned quickly to despair. The Mystagogue at the Watchtower, highest priest of the Kansas sect, declared Marvel deficient the instant he saw him limply breathing in the cold birthing room. Barely squirming in that starry blanket. He turned the baby around so Marvel was no longer facing him and handed him back to the midwife, who handed him to his mother, who stared up at the Mystagogue in awe of his cruelty. By rights, said the Mystagogue, Marvel should be thrown from the tower, but his mother was a nun, after all, and more importantly a descendent of Huldah the Prophetess. Which made Marvel also a descendent of Huldah. Marvel would be educated as a monk, no more and no less, and Nasa Whiteside should be grateful for that small mercy.

He became ordinary in those first instants of his life, and his stricken mother became a failure. Nevertheless the account of his birth cheered him in a strange way. Even as an infant, he had been a complicated person, one capable of bearing tremendous weight as well as casting it off. Defying expectation was in his blood.

That was *his* destiny. He had faith in that.

He still had that swaddling blanket somewhere, shoved into a wooden crate and stored away. From time to time, Marvel enjoyed imagining himself from the vantage point of history, which stretches onward until the morality of events is winnowed until it appears to be fate—one action begetting the next and so on. Progress. This was the place where treachery and failure transformed themselves. What once seemed terrible could become courageous if given enough time. Marvel imagined that one day his sins might be tallied as virtues, that time could render him honorable, as he knew himself to be.

He would leave the Cape. He would leave them all, even his own daughter the queen, to their empty frivolities, their misguided readings of holy texts, to their gentle, ineffectual king who was not the True King.

He would go back to Kansas, he would start again, where he'd started in the first place. It was the only way he knew how to save himself.

Above the jail that housed all dissidents, Canaveral Tower spun sharply upward. The heartclot of the palace compound, of such terrific height and magnificence that even the macabre collection of corpses exposed on the eastern parapet could not detract from its excellence, the tower shone with a sunsharpened triumph both terrifying and cheerful. Together with its five flanking minarets, it represented the shuttles and their glorious passages off the world, and waited in bannered anticipation for their return.

Marvel and the young guard entered the jail through a plain door in the side of the tower. The jail was not wet or cold, which was itself an achievement of engineering given the high water table at the Cape. But all through it ran a smell of despair and death and rotting corpses from the bodies exposed on the compound's high parapets. The jail's walls and floor and even all the washstands in the cells were painted white—Marvel's idea. He had conceived of it as a maddening reminder of the light and air outside, but additionally it served to give the prisoners an endless amount of menial work, for the cells were required to remain spotless and the prisoners given only a few soft rags with which to clean them. Any visitor's feet left smudgy imprints on the floor.

He went with the young guard straight down a set of steps. Metal-white, perforated with many coin-sized elliptical holes, descending in wider spirals until the staircase ended at a metal doorway. There they stood in awkward silence, until Marvel used the knocker to rap five times. The door opened and that smell washed over them. Fecal and rotting. Each cell had a drain, and each drain was a horror. Marvel had grown used to it; the guard looked on the verge of fainting. Marvel smiled, shrugged. The jailer's face, when it appeared, was like a tree trunk, the bulbous nose and knotty lips eruptions on the rough skin. He was neither old nor young but struck Marvel as both bored and uncruel, qualities he supposed were desirable in a jailer.

"Here for a prisoner." Marvel withdrew a small bit of paper from his pocket and unrolled it. He and the guard stepped into the anteroom where the jailer had a three-legged stool set up in a corner, and next to it a bucket of oysters, some shells on the floor. "William Tygo II."

"Right," said the jailer. He held a brain-pink liquid in a thick, dirty glass mug. "I put him in the last cell. A real stick up his ass, that one." His eyes like wild malarial marbles. How could one bear this stench all day? The jailer seemed to have long ago lost some essential function of his brain—Marvel wondered how anyone could spend a lifetime sitting feet away from ranting lunatics. Yet apparently the jailer found his posting unobjectionable: he had performed his duties competently for many years.

Marvel and the guard followed him through the anteroom into the winding circular hallway that housed the cells. This was the most intense displeasure of visiting the jail. The incarcerated men and women called out to Marvel before the jailer shushed them with a poke from the back end of his pike. They screamed their innocence, threatened to have Marvel's daughter killed, insulted every feature upon his own body and hers. He didn't listen. The vulgarities had bothered him, until they had stopped bothering him, and he thought now that there was nothing the prisoners could say that could hurt him. Their words and spit misted him, but it was only a hygienic nuisance.

The young guard swayed uncertainly when the prisoners began their chorus. He had a boy's way about him, a boy's eagerness to please. It was not irritating, though in others this quality could seem calculated. He attempted to cover his alarm with a look of nonchalance until Marvel rapped him again on the shoulders encouragingly. "We're in this together now." He pushed the man in front of him. After hesitating a moment, the guard walked ahead.

Not too many months before, a woman had lunged at Marvel *through* her cell's bars. She'd starved herself until she fit between them and had thrown herself onto him like a cat of the jungle leaping from a tree, tearing the sleeve of his cassock from shoulder to wrist. Her face a firepit of insanity. Marvel was exhausted of ordering executions—instead of killing her, he'd had her forcibly fed and freed the next day. From his own apartments on top of Endeavour Tower, one of the other spires, he'd watched the jailer cast her into the sunlight wearing nothing but the rags she'd arrived in months before. He couldn't see her face, but she turned in a slow circle, blind to the commotion of the courtyard market. After a few moments, a servant woman brought her a brown dress, laced it up right over her rags, and held out a pair of shoes for her to take. The woman threw the shoes to the ground and kicked dirt over them. After the servant left, the woman returned to the shoes, dusted them off, and slid her feet into them.

Marvel did not often free traitors. He let that woman go because she was too insane even to question the circumstances that had set her free. Marvel had grown tired of exercising his power—even acts of mercy wearied him. He had watched the woman's expulsion from the jail from the safety of his balcony, uncertain of what he hoped to observe. Their eyes had not locked. She hadn't gulped the fresh air like a person thirsty to live. She simply went out through the nearest gate and drifted away.

"What's your name?" Marvel asked the young guard as they walked down the hallway, over the whoops and wails of traitors. The jailer clanged his pike on the bars, screaming at the prisoners for silence.

The young guard winced at the racket, as though sprayed with cold water. "Juniper, sir."

"That's a woman's name."

"Yes," he agreed. "No one's ever mentioned that to me before."

Marvel snorted. "I couldn't care less what you're called. But why would a spy choose a woman's name?"

"Because I'm not a spy."

"Ah." Marvel folded his arms behind his back. The man's knife was still in his belt. "Forgive me."

"If I *were* a spy, you'd lock me in here with the loonies, right? Or worse?"

Marvel shrugged. "You may have caught me in a season of tolerance." He pushed a thumbnail into the tough skin around his forefinger, watching the thick callus spring back after he'd pressed it. Suddenly he was imagining that wide land between Florida and Kansas again, those endless spoiled fields grown over now with grasses and trees but just as deadly as in centuries past. The precarious passage over the saferoads: he dreamt of walking the spindles through the wilderness, obscurely marked by scratches on tree trunks placed there by the Walking Doctors. Which reminded him to unfold the paper with the prisoner's name on it again. *William Tygo II, Walking Doctor.* He closed the paper and said to the guard. "You're not from a carnival, I can tell. You're too educated. So." He nodded to himself. "You've been lying."

"I went to the carnival once I was already grown. I wasn't raised there."

Marvel smiled and shrugged again and rubbed his own unshaven face thoughtfully. Still the jailer walked onward and they followed. The hall was long. Diffuse afternoon light poured through lozenge-shaped ventilation slits that lined the cells' upper walls; the dungeon was in fact only one level underground and received significant natural light. Finally the jailer stopped, gesturing to the very last cell with the sharp point of his pike. "Good luck with that one, yeah? He's the genuine article, an old-fashioned fanatic if ever I met one." He didn't even bother to glance in at the prisoner before he turned and left. No one shouted at him as he ambled back to his post.

The prisoner sat on the white floor of his cell, his back to them. He wore a suit of what must have once been a brilliant blue, a long jacket, quite expensive probably. Now the whole get-up was covered in filth, although it was *so* dirty Marvel could hardly believe all that grime could have come from the prison. He guessed the man had been picked up in fairly dire condition. Jail may even have been a mercy. So it was for many. Marvel leaned closer to the bars in order to see the side of the prisoner's face, since he had not yet turned around. The man's hair was tucked into his collar, obscuring the view. Marvel glanced over his shoulder at Juniper, who looked back blankly.

Marvel coughed. "So, I'm here at last. This is your hearing, prisoner, you'd better turn around for it."

The prisoner tugged his ratty hair down over his ears. It was long, after the fashion of the carnival executioners, and black, loose on the sides and wrapped tightly in back with string so it formed a pigtail of sorts. "I refuse to speak," he said sharply. "You're all idiots here, raving at the goddamn sky. This is the most humiliating thing that's ever happened to me. You have no right to hold me in this jail. None of you do." The prisoner's voice was unaccented. To Marvel's ear, he sounded local. Only a Walking Doctor. No terrible threat, just a routine dissident.

Marvel examined his nail beds once again. "Do you know who I am?"

"I can guess." The prisoner still did not turn. "You've come to torture me, I suppose. Nothing I say matters, but I'll still say it: I don't have anything to answer for. Not to you."

"I'm not here to torture you." Marvel inspected his knuckles. "But

I do enjoy a show." Beside him, Juniper remained quiet. Marvel tapped on the bars. "I'm here to establish your guilt."

"So this is my trial?"

He chuckled. "Trials don't exist except in books, my friend. You should have received a letter requesting you desist practicing contra-magical surgeries. You got the letter? Then if you still refuse—and I gather you've refused—a warrant for your execution is issued, you are captured, I establish your guilt. That's the part of the process we're completing today. You're lucky because I am a fair man." He paused. "At least today I will be."

A snort. "So after this I'll be executed?"

"It's the responsibility of my office to punish traitors."

"And what is your office? Who are *you*?"

"Marvel Parsons."

Marvel's words seemed to hang oddly in the air. It took a moment for them to float into the cell and land on the prisoner. The prisoner stood and turned around. He was much shorter than Marvel. He couldn't have been five and a half feet tall. "Marvel Parsons, the Hierophant?"

Marvel began a reflexive nod, but as the prisoner moved, his hair fell away from his ears—or the place where his ears had been. At once the warmth drained from Marvel as from a limb held above the head. "Your ears," he demanded. "What happened to them?"

The prisoner drifted nearer the bars of the cell, tugging loose strands back over the holes. Under that large, very blue coat, and dirty low-cut undergarment, his collarbones threatened to pierce the skin. And yet Marvel took in the wholeness of his appearance with just a glance, because he could hardly tear his eyes from those ear-holes. The prisoner twisted his lips to the side. "That? O. *That* was a punishment. I got on with my life." He seemed to speak from another dimension. Marvel could not stop staring.

The prisoner made a sad grimace. "I can still hear. It's not as bad as it looks, for the love of god. I'd like to think you've seen much worse."

Marvel realized he was not breathing. He had been sure he'd never see *that* particular punishment again.

The prisoner tilted his head, still fiddling with his hair. He stared intently at Marvel. "What's the problem? I thought you were going to execute me? A bit of disfigurement is that appalling to you? Or?" He lifted his eyebrows. "Or else you're from Kansas?"

"Of course I'm not." Marvel forced himself to speak at a normal volume. It was a fact that no one from the Cape actually knew where Marvel Whiteside Parsons had come from originally. The two kingdoms were rivals in both politics and piety, but centuries ago the Cape had become the capital. When, at fourteen, Marvel ran away, he had gone to the Cape because he believed that Leander, King Michael's father, was the True King. With all his heart he had believed that.

Only the mad monks at the Black Watchtower still thought the king would come to Kansas. But Kansas was the seat of the Disease. Where the Eon of bloodshed and pain had started in the cows and soil. Why should the king who would save them all be born in the place that had ruined the world? The endless reading and study the Mystagogue required had convinced Marvel that his entire denomination, all the monks and nuns and ascetics at Huldah's stronghold, the Black Watchtower, were pursuing a folly. The *True King* would not appear in Kansas, ever. Waiting for him there was pure vanity. The True King would reign at the Cape, where the shuttles had existed so many years ago.

What a fool Marvel had been in his youth.

He tried to wrench his gaze from the prisoner's missing ears. They were sure proof that this man had been a monk in Kansas. And yet, no one had used that punishment in Kansas in generations, except of course the Mystagogue himself, and only upon his personal retinue of zealous and dangerous monks.

But everyone knew the Mystagogue was dead. That he had been dead for a very long time.

Exactly as long as Marvel had been gone, in fact.

If the Mystagogue were not dead, Marvel could not go back to Kansas. Not after what he had done. Though the Mystagogue had deserved it.

He narrowed his eyes at the prisoner. "Who did that to you?"

Now the prisoner was as interested in Marvel as Marvel was in him. His eyes flashed. "Who do you think?"

Marvel would not say the Mystagogue's name or title aloud and give himself away. He tilted his face back and smirked again. Juniper looked at both of them and asked, "What's going on?"

"Yes, what *is* going on? Your paper says you are a Walking Doctor."

The prisoner drew himself up into his too-large jacket. "I am. My patients live. Almost always. That's why I'm here, isn't it? For doing surgeries." His black eyebrows knitted together and his irises shifted in such a way that Marvel felt he was being untruthful.

"There are no Walking Doctors in Kansas."

"There are, because I was there."

Marvel gestured for Juniper to come closer to the bars. "Does he? Come from Kansas? Do you know him?"

Juniper spread his hands. His eyes went to his knife, still in Marvel's belt. "*I'm* not from Kansas."

Marvel laughed suddenly. "O, of course." He gestured to the prisoner's earholes. "Your personal misfortune interests me—I would like to know more."

The prisoner smiled coldly. "I couldn't possibly."

"I think you should stay right here for now." Marvel checked his paper again and memorized the prisoner's name. He felt Juniper at his back in a way he had not, moments before. Were these two in collusion? How could either of them have known Marvel planned to return to Kansas? Or were they here for another reason?

"But—"

Marvel was overwhelmed by the desire to be away from them both. "There are larger fortunes at stake here than your own. You will be tortured if you are not forthcoming when I return," he said. "I would hate to do it." He paused. "For at least a moment I would hate to do it. But I must know the name of the man who took your ears. And why." He could not say anything more in front of Juniper.

The prisoner, Tygo, shook his head, and they left him there, gaping slightly like an askew window pane. Juniper tagged behind Marvel, taking longer steps than befitted a man of his height, but nevertheless keeping nearly apace with Marvel as he stalked down the hallway, through the gauntlet of wretches spitting and screaming. Marvel couldn't care less about them now. When they passed the jailer who was now nodding off in his chair tilted against the wall, Marvel kicked the leg and barked, "Up! Let us out! I haven't got time for this!"

In the courtyard again, Marvel tried to breathe calmly of the coming winter's salty air, but instead he felt a lurch of nausea. He saw his chance for escape diminishing. If the Mystagogue lived—and obviously he did—Marvel would die in this peacockish hellhole, he would live out his remaining years serving the wrong denomination, the wrong king. It would be the closing off of his soul from salvation forever.

He could not allow it. He had lived fifty and one years serving the wrong cause. No longer. He was a monk. In his heart, he was a priest. Not a king, a Hierophant, a soldier, or a malcontent.

What he wanted most was to go home.

Juniper had taken a deep breath of fresh air when they exited the jail, pulling a rag from his tunic to wipe his face. The fabric came away damp. An upswell of panic he tried and failed to hide. The young guard was most definitely a spy. Marvel considered having him thrown in the jail. But he had dealt with spies before. They were often more useful than otherwise, if one knew how to manipulate them. At least Juniper was nice to look at. Marvel, composed again, asked, "What did you think of the prisoner?"

"Probably not a Walking Doctor."

"Probably not."

"Or a carnival man."

"No," Marvel said.

Juniper said, "I'm not from Kansas. I want you to know that."

Marvel nodded. "You sound sure of yourself."

Juniper turned and stared up at Canaveral Tower behind him, squinting in the gray light of midmorning. "Look, all I can say is the truth."

"There are many truths, though."

Watching Juniper look up to where the Pardoness lived in her suite of luxury, Marvel had a strange idea. He was beginning to realize he was a desperate man. That earless prisoner had reminded him just how awful the Watchtower had been in those days, and probably so remained. And yet still Marvel longed to return, now more than ever. There was a way, though it would be violent.

Blood it must be, everywhere, and in everything. Wonderblood, the Primary Law. This time, at least, he would ask forgiveness.

If the Mystagogue lived, then he must be killed.

Marvel Parsons, a killer from the age of fourteen, would see to that unpleasant task once again.

CHAPTER 3

THE EXECUTIONATRIX

They had come finally through the drear of autumn and burst onto the whitish plain of Florida with its weedscrap and bloodsmell, and even as they crossed into the tropics, the girl knew she was home. Now she did not think anymore of running away, but sat quietly on Mr. Capulatio's bed in his red wagon as it bumped without rest along the saferoad on wooden wheels, and she listened to the jingle-jangle of his hanging charms. The sound soothed her. Nights, as they camped, she would watch him at his desk, writing and writing. In the warm red light from the lantern she could see he was troubled—his lips angled downward and formed a wrinkle just above the square of his chinbone. But when he turned to her and smiled all his worry seemed to dissolve. It was a smile that contained trust, and within his trust there was also safety, and inside that safety the girl felt growing the beginnings of her own power over him.

Sometimes she remembered to be afraid. If they were caught returning to the Cape out of season, it would mean more deaths in a world that was already overflowing with death. But she didn't desire anymore to escape Mr. Capulatio, who had rescued her from *certain* death—she saw that now. He had scooped her up before she'd been killed in battle or wandered lost into the country and contracted the

Disease and died a shivering chattering husk. Had she run off alone, she might have walked across one of a hundred thousand fields still harboring the blood-sickness. Her mother had said the Disease was a "predictable consequence" of the derelict society that produced it a thousand years before. Everyone called it the Bent Head Death, and no one wanted to die of it.

The girl had once gone with her mother to the bedside of a dying woman. The woman, dark-skinned and old, had wild eyes and thudded her head in an endless rhythm against her driftwood headboard, thump-thump-thump, the teeth in her mouth clacking almost angrily. The girl's mother could do nothing because there was no medicine on earth that could reverse the progressive spongifying of the brain due to the consumption of contaminated meat, which was what Bent Head was. Her mother believed that she and a few other Walking Doctors were the only people left alive who knew what *actually* caused Bent Head. As far as they were concerned, there never had been a cure, ever. They could find no mention or hint of one in their books. The best her mother could do was euthanize the woman and remove the brain for study. Bent Head was dreadful way to die—victims were transformed into angular, famished horrors. They could not be buried, as the fluid seepage contaminated the land for an Eon. The girl did not understand science or magic, or even if they were different from each other. But she knew it was Bent Head that had somehow brought Wonderblood into the world, and Wonderblood was the law on which all the other laws were based. It decreed that this purge was inevitable and sacred, and that until all lands were "rinsed at the cosmic basin in clean and virtuous blood," there would be no end to suffering.

Her mother scoffed: the religions had it all backward, she said—more blood on the land just kept contaminating it, and so they were now locked in an endless cycle of blood and sickness. But when the girl told that to Mr. Capulatio, he called her mother a faithless wretch who placed her trust in surgery instead of religion. Who could surgery save? A single person? In a lifetime, how many? A few thousand? Wonderblood, the executions, could save them *all,* eventually. Her mother's impatience was a great sin. Didn't she see that? Didn't the girl *see* that what they were doing was for everyone's good? And the girl could not at these times keep herself from marveling at the force of his belief. He spoke with such magnetism that she yearned to listen to him, even when she did not understand.

He answered questions she had not even known she was asking.

At last they made their camp outside the Cape compound's walls. Mr. Capulatio's carnival was already the mightiest in the land and functioned with a frightening efficiency. His men could raise it entirely in under nine hours. His own giant tent was so large it contained his wagon wholly; he and the girl used the wagon as their bedchamber. Outside, men laid planks for walkways, the merchants and charm-makers pitched their booths, and just as soon as they finished tying down the last tent pegs of Mr. Capulatio's new, great flag was hoisted over the encampment. This was a flag of conquering, he mused to her as he watched it unfurl. His chest rose and fell as they stood together in the tent's doorway. They looked out upon the carnival, and farther away they could see the metal spires of the castle beginning to whirl the morning light back to them and all around the land was low and flat, and the air heavy, and beyond that began the pink-blue crescent of the sea.

"Did you know," Mr. Capulatio began, and placed his hand upon her small shoulder and gripped the place where the bones knitted together. He pointed to the flag with his other hand. "I began sewing that flag myself when I was young?" It was made of five deep-colored oblong cloths, each representing a different one of Mr. Capulatio's constituents (whatever those were), all stitched together with golden thread. From afar it was uncommonly beautiful. Each of its oblong sections was made of some indeterminable color that wavered with the light like a beetleshell. He sighed. "Well, I'm still young. But in my childhood dreamings I *saw* that flag, and I knew that color was no color, but full of all the colors. That was my destiny. I couldn't sew, Aurora, Queenie, but I sewed it anyway with a needle, a whalebone from this place, from the beaches where I was born. I had the needle years before I had the fabric or the even the idea I should make a flag." He spoke with his eyes closed. "Sometimes it's a person's destiny to carry with him the sharp point of victory before he even knows what war he will fight. There is a preternatural sense of destiny among us chosen, I think." He rubbed the lump of her shoulder. "Did you have such a feeling?"

"A feeling for what?" she whispered. She was often still afraid to talk to him, especially when he spoke like this. His voice was soft. She found herself leaning into his touch. They stared out at the morning-wet landscape, and the girl felt hope stirring inside her. Hope for what? She said, "What kind of feeling do you mean?"

"That you yourself are important."

She thought, everyone feels that way. Because if you don't feel important, how could a person bear to go on? "I don't know what 'important' means."

He laughed sharply. "O my. I do."

Shortly afterward, Mr. Capulatio left to go tramping about his new encampment. *My final encampment ever, Queenie. Glorify! Soon we will live as we have been destined!* He locked her inside a cage in his tent and ordered two men outside to guard her. He told her as he shut her inside that this cage had been constructed to house his treasures, and she was his most treasured treasure, and now *Especially now!* he could not let anyone steal her away. She was the future. She was the rightful queen of Cape. He placed a lock the size and shape of an orange on the cage door and clasped her fingers through bars and twined them around his own, and leaned forward and looked into her face with his clear eyes the color of shallow creek water. "You are so beautiful," he said. "Truly. You are a gemrock."

He turned and dropped the key into a skin bag that hung from his belt, but spoke again before leaving the tent. "If I were a stronger man, if I were less mindful of the ways of other men . . ." he began, running his finger down the golden fringe that edged the tent flap. The length of his fingers always surprised the girl, and also they were thin and somewhat yellowish but from what she did not know, tobacco or an illness or some magic substance he touched in his workings. She liked those fingers that always touched her so very gently. They had, in their time together, become something she looked forward to.

He went on, "I would like to know you were safe no matter what, if I locked you up or not." He jerked his head back toward the guards outside. She imagined he might hand her the key through the bars of the cage. They both knew she wouldn't leave. But he stiffened when he heard the men outside laughing softly. She wondered as she looked at him whether he trusted anyone at all. This was wise in a way, and sad in another way, and probably unavoidable. He shrugged and blew her a kiss and then he went away.

The cage was not a terrible place to be. It was made of decorated metal with iron-lace flourishes. To pass the time, she slept and read from the book Argento had given her, which Mr. Capulatio had let her keep. The book was written like a fairytale, and it had been so long since she'd read anything at all. *The True King* was full of stories she had never heard. The people in the book followed a religion that was hardly anything like Argento's superstitious worship of the Astronauts: Mr. Capulatio's religion had real scriptures, they had relics from the old times. She braided and unbraided her hair as she devoured the handwritten pages, wishing she might never come to the end of it.

But before long, a woman strode in carrying a wooden basin of blood, which she set beside Mr. Capulatio's desk. The girl froze. The woman wore tall leather boots. She made straight for the crates of books and papers around the desk without even noticing the girl. She spent a long while bent over his desk, rifling through his stacks of papers, holding a few up for inspection and then setting them down again. Her back was to the girl, and her light brown hair disheveled but clean. Nearly the same color as the girl's, and just as long. As she leaned and stretched around the desk in search of more papers, her foot kept bumping the basin of blood. The girl thought she should say something, draw attention to herself, but for some reason she didn't. The woman had such a fierce expression.

She appeared to be searching for some particular piece of information, but other than the papers Mr. Capulatio had been recently working on, all his books remained in their crates. There had been little time yet to unpack. The woman took a pry-bar lying nearby and began jimmying the lid off a crate.

Suddenly she seemed to stiffen. She turned around like she'd heard a noise, though the girl had not moved. Maybe the woman had heard her breathing. Her age was impossible to decipher—twenty or thirty or even older—but her eyebrows were thick and darker than her hair, mussed slightly. Beneath them, her eyes burned with intelligence. She reminded the girl, for the slightest second, of her mother Gimbal.

A long moment passed before the woman smiled. A frightening smile, like a grotesque shadow on a wall. It contained many emotions, all of which the girl had seen before on different people at different times, but never all at once together. Anger, immediately. A shard of despair. She saw fear, too, in the woman's eyes.

The woman set down the pry-bar and approached the cage. "Hello," she said. The dimness obscured her eyes, but they were magnetic all the same. The girl stared at her.

"Hello."

"Well. You are not what I expected at all. At all." She blinked.

"Who are you?"

She came nearer. She wore a huge necklace of feathers. Each one long and brown and green and stained to look like blood. It was very well made. The woman fingered it absently as she stared. The girl wondered if people around here wore such things. No one from her settlement had.

"What *has* David done? What has he done this time? Who are *you,* is the question."

"Who's David?"

The woman squinted. She was slight but looked strong, with small, well-formed muscles like bits of rock crystal running along the insides of her bare arms. She wore a leather shirt, and her face was so small and her features so crowded together that the girl thought she appeared to be squinting even when she was not. Still, there was something lovely about her. Perhaps it was her very appearance of strength. Solidness seemed to gather around her like a wall. "O my. What has he told you? You don't even know his name?"

The girl felt her cheeks burn even though she was not afraid. "Mr. Capulatio?"

The woman laughed. Though not much taller than the girl, she seemed to crowd out everything else in the tent. She bent toward the cage, the necklace hanging off her chest, and examined the girl more closely. The girl could see her better too. This near, her cheeks were still supple, but the skin around her eyes had tiny fissures like drought-ground. The girl smelled a citrus perfume. She swallowed. "Mr. Capulatio took my brother's carnival. Everyone there is dead now."

"Except you? Unfortunately?"

"I was alone. My brother is dead." The words spilled out because she could sense this woman meant her evil. "He says I am going to be the queen."

The woman tilted her head. "How's that?"

"I don't know."

"*The* queen? Or just *a* queen? There is a difference." She ran her fingernail through the fronds of a feather on her necklace. "But how would you know that? You're just a child."

The girl felt her face tighten. "Why are you in our tent?"

The woman showed no expression. "*Our* tent? You are an *our* with him now? Says who?" She stepped very close and now the girl could see into her eyes, which were set deep in her face and appeared dark in a way that belied their actual color, which was the grayblue of a rock. But the eyes themselves in the riverbed of her face were awful to look at for some reason, so she looked away, until the woman called her back with a soft voice. "Little one, I'm talking to you. Explain to me this, if you can. Are you a prisoner? Perhaps a blessing and a charm to lend luck to our endeavors? Maybe through your honorable transformation from human to Head? Or are you some other part of our Great Work that is soon to transpire?"

"Great Work?"

"Hasn't he told you *that*?" The woman smiled strangely. "What *did* he tell you? Anything at all? How awful for you." She paused. "Where did you say he picked you up?"

"The field where my brother's carnival was—"

"Was it perhaps a *battlefield*?"

"Not until he came and starting killing them all."

The woman wrapped her fingers about the cage's bars, just as Mr. Capulatio had done earlier. Perched on one finger was a gigantic blue glass ring. "I see. And you were just an unprotected fawn, as it were, innocently standing there waiting to be found? In the center of the poisonous continental desert?" She looked over her shoulder at the desk and all the books in their boxes, frowning. "You were a girl on a battlefield."

"I guess I was."

The woman tossed her hair behind her shoulders. "That is—at least to my ear—highly unlikely. Is it not *more* likely that he bought you from someone or someones who were hastening to be rid of you? For their own reasons, of course." She clicked her fingernails on the bars.

"No."

The woman's hands were always moving. Now they were on her necklace, lifting and stroking the feathers, which were so glossy and long that they extended nearly to the center of her stomach. She wore a loose tunic, short-sleeved. Her knee-boots were constructed bloody-looking leather. Everything on her body was black but the feathers. "O," was all she said.

They stared at each other. The girl had a very bad feeling indeed. She longed for him to come back and make this woman go away. "Who are you?" the girl asked again.

But the woman ignored her. Her expression was quickly gathering a darkness. "Has he told you that you are part of a vision?" Her face dropped and she closed her eyes wearily. The girl thought she had seen them tear up for just a moment before she shut them. "One of his visions was of a small girl upon a battlefield who would become queen, but we—or should I say *I*—had not taken that to mean *his* queen."

"Why not?"

"Since he is lawfully married to me. He has been since he was sixteen years of age. That would mean that I am his queen already." She shrugged. "A man can have only one legitimate wife. That makes you something additional. A concubine. What was your name again?" she demanded.

It made sense now, her jewelry. She was his wife.

The girl found her voice. "Aurora is what he calls me."

"But what is your *name*?"

"I can't remember."

"How terrible for you," she murmured. She spoke very much like Mr. Capulatio himself: with half-threats and vague intimations. She shared his cruel manner of a manipulative child. Still, though the girl saw through this behavior, the intended effect of which was to produce in her a great shame, it worked. She felt suddenly stupid for even trying to talk to this woman.

"Well, I was abandoned by my mother when I was a girl and then my brother died a terrible death I had to watch, so I have no family. So I have no name." She glared at the woman. "Not that I would tell you, anyway."

But she did have a name. She would never speak it. It was her mother's name, and her mother had given her over to this life, whatever it was. How terrible or angelic of her, the girl did not know. Whatever risks were here, there would have been others if she'd stayed in the settlement with her mother and her mother's new husband, riding out on the saferoads with them to learn Doctoring. She was unsure if she had wanted that, or for her mother to become jealous of her youth. But she had not wanted to be abandoned, either. The girl stared now at this angry woman and felt that she had ended up just as bad off here as when her mother left her with Argento. Her punishment back then had been to be in the carnivals with her lunatic brother. What would it be now?

"You're right to keep it to yourself, at least in these times," said the woman. "I, for one, wouldn't ever trust anyone with my real name. Except my husband." She began to smile. "Who is apparently also *your* husband, or so you think. Have you told David your name?"

"He didn't tell me he was called David."

"Why would he? You're not his real wife."

"Not yet."

"If you were perhaps slightly more beautiful, I would believe he did love you, but his other concubines have generally been attractive or at least fertile. Do you have some other talent I am not seeing? Are you particularly good at cooking? Your mother, maybe, taught you that. I would teach my daughter to cook if I had one."

The girl scowled.

"You appear to have only recently, in cosmological time, mastered the ability to walk and talk. Tell me, can you menstruate? It's a fair question for a future queen."

"Go away." She had never bled. She felt ashamed of herself, her body. Her mother had told her how it would happen when it happened, and she wasn't afraid. She expected it soon, but there was the trauma of constant motion to contend with. And her thinness. The woman was nodding as though the girl had said all these things aloud. It was as if she could read minds. "Don't be sad. You can't help it." She stopped nodding. "Do you wish you were dead?"

The girl made a face. "Of course I don't. Who would wish for death?" In fact, the girl hadn't wished for death since Mr. Capulatio took her from Argento's carnival. Not since she'd hidden her eyes when Argento died. She straightened her shoulders.

"Many do. Many have." The woman studied her more closely. "It's a fact that I've killed more people than David. I am myself an executioner—an executionatrix. I took my carnival by violence from my own brother when I was not much older than you. In fact, it was a marvelous coup. Very bloody." She looked the girl up and down again. "I would even go so far as to say it helped David to love me. He likes a strong woman." Then she shrugged. "How does it feel to be in a cage?"

"I'm here to keep me safe. Not because I'm a prisoner. That's what he said."

"O, of course. And he always tells the truth, I'm sure you know that."

She looked to the ground, embarrassed. The blankets and carpets in the bottom of the cage made her feel like a captive animal. But there had been a needle-poke when the woman said she was Mr. Capulatio's wife. The girl felt it growing now, an envy so sharp and tiny she'd hardly noticed, but now it began to burn. This was his wife? This maniac? He had a *wife*? Other concubines? How many? She couldn't believe she'd never allowed herself to wonder about other women. The pricking oozed inside her like blood under the skin. She made a dark face at the woman, who tapped the orange-shaped lock with a clean long fingernail. "O dear, now don't be angry," she said. "You can't have thought you were the only one. What's he told you about me?"

She squared her shoulders and jutted out her lip, she couldn't help herself. "He never said anything about you. Or any wife. Except that *I* would be his wife."

The woman appeared to think. Finally she went back to the desk and pulled out the chair and sat down. She kicked the wooden bucket of blood for effect. "That's my offering. My thanks to the heavens for his successful return. Do you know how much blood that is? How many people? I've been very busy."

"It's grotesque."

"Is it grotesque when David executes people?"

She remembered Argento's dumb eyes as he was led to the block. Had he been drugged? She wanted to think Mr. Capulatio would have granted him—her—that mercy. She thought of her relief and sadness. She said nothing.

The woman began rifling through the papers again, this time with much more urgency. "My name is Orchid." She spoke with her head in one of the crates. "My carnival is called Loss, this is *my* tent and David is *my* husband." When she looked up, she was angry.

"What are you looking for?"

"A certain book."

The girl clenched her hands. She had the very sure, very irrational feeling this book was the one she herself had been reading in her cage only moments before the woman arrived. She had not yet admitted to him that she could read, but he knew. Of course he knew. He could see her eyes fly across the pages of his own writing that he brought into their bed, where he sometimes read it aloud, holding the papers at an arm's length as though this would give him greater clarity. When he hated it, which was all the time, he burned the papers with sulfur-sticks in a glass bowl set right between their legs on the blankets. They watched as the papers curled up like a dying centipede. He was destroying every evidence of his failures, no matter how small. He wanted to be very sure no one could ever accuse him of getting anything wrong.

The woman rummaged and searched. "Why do you need this certain book?" the girl asked, kicking it as slowly as she could under one of the carpets on the floor of her cage.

"I *had* wanted it so I could record the names and numbers of the carnivals that have met here today on the plain. To support him. To crown him. To defend him. But now I want it to prove to him that he was in error to have brought you here." She eyed her. "Grievous error." When she was met with the girl's uncomprehending grimace, she returned to the desk chair. She spun it around and threw her slender limbs over it, sitting like a man but much more beautifully. "I am his scribe."

"Did you write the book?"

"Do you know the book I'm talking about?"

The girl shook her head.

"Let me tell you a story, since you are just a child." She lowered her voice to a dramatic whisper. The girl could feel herself beginning to hate this woman. "Only I trusted him in the beginning. Because I loved him. He was just an orphan once upon a time, with strange visions that would possess him body and soul. And I was a girl, not much older than yourself. We had made our covenant already, passionately and many times, upon the green grass, in the streams and brooks of the countryside. Yes, we were careless. In our desire to be alone together, we strayed from the saferoads. So you must understand that at first we worried his visions might be a raving illness. Maybe Bent Head, who knew? We were on the land so often, and who could account for his frightening premonitions without at least considering a medical causation? We came from a settlement where they still ate cows. A backward place. Not far from here. Even I wondered if he was sick—I admit my faith was tested then."

"We ate cows in my settlement too," the girl whispered. "At least the other people did. My mother said it was bad."

"Florida, land of the cow-eaters. Only idiots and magicians are from Florida." Orchid kicked her heels on the carpeted ground and rolled her eyes. "How he does love strange women."

"I'm not strange."

Orchid ignored her. "The point is I *trusted* his divine knowledge. He told me he wasn't sick, and I believed him. Only me. Because I loved him. Do you know how he felt all those years? When it was only me who believed he was the True King?" She leaned back again, waving her hand. "Who are you, anyway, to comfort him? You're a child, you have no thoughts of eternity."

"I—"

She put her finger to her lips. "When he would go out with the carnivals preaching and cutting heads, before we ever had a carnival of our own, I would wait at the settlement, transforming his scribbles into legibility. His writing is unformed, it is . . ." She reached for the papers and shook one in the air to make her point. "I made sense of what he saw in the visions." She paused thoughtfully, her hand lingering on the paper. "I've been with him through all that."

The girl crossed her arms.

"Do you love him?" She came over to the cage again and picked up the orange-shaped lock and let it fall loudly against the bars, once, then twice. In her thin hand the gold lock bulged nearly obscenely and the girl tried to imagine this woman with a sword, hacking off heads before a windblown crowd, and found she could see it better than she would've liked. And then the girl felt a stirring in her chest that was difficult to bear: a renewed awareness of her captivity. The woman clanged the lock again and leaned her face in very close to the bars. "Love is impossible without history."

That was the very moment when Mr. Capulatio himself strode back into the tent and beheld them at odds—the girl standing on her guard at the center of the cage, and the strange woman with the necklace rattling the lock. He did not meet the girl's eyes or even look at her. He stared directly at Orchid, who sucked her cheeks in and pursed her lips. They formed a narrow "o. " "You're here," he said easily to her, after a long silence. "I was out looking for you."

"I was looking for *you*. But instead I found this." She fanned her hand at the cage but her face remained impassive.

"You won't even come kiss me? It's been a whole six months, Radiance. Come here." He opened his arms. That day he had worn his most spectacular cape, which was the color of goldenrod on the outside and lined with midnight blue, to greet his constituents at the meeting. The girl had watched him pluck the cloak from a trunk, shake it out, and admire himself in the small mirror above his writing desk. He swept this cape behind his shoulders, smiling handsomely. Evidently his meeting had been a success.

Orchid was not smiling. "O, but you had many other touches I'm sure in the meantime."

"That's the first thing you say to me after six months?"

Orchid's expression became a frown. "I shouldn't be saying a single thing to you. I've spent this last half-year at my desk working on the revelations you left in such a half-formed glob, making sense of them and circulating them here, at the risk of my own life and certainly at the expense of my own happiness. I've spent this last half-year readying all this that you see around you, this entire gathering, your constituents from all the corners of the land and who have met here to defend *your* cause because they believe in you and love you, despite dangers and troubles and unknowns! And I come to your tent to find this? This child?"

"Yes." He was nodding. "Another queen. Not any queen, but *the* queen. Of our revelation. My queen."

"*What?*" The girl saw her fingers knotting and unknotting behind her back.

"The fulfillment of my prophecy. This girl is a solid piece of our destiny."

"That is the stupidest thing I've ever heard."

He clasped her shoulder. "You should have been there! Her appearance! Upon the field! In a battle! Just as I saw in my head many years ago! In a white gown! Can I help it that she's beautiful?"

Orchid raised her eyebrows. "I was not there, *David,* because I was here. Doing what you needed me to do *here.*"

He wrapped his arms around her with a familiarity that made the girl's heart blacken like meat on a stake. She wished she could turn away, but instead she held on to a cage bar and interlaced her fingers through them as though they could pull her up out of her jealousy.

Mr. Capulatio whispered, "Perhaps, my love. But I found her just like my vision predicted. I can't take the Cape without my divinely appointed queen. It would be madness."

"The prophecy in the book is certainly not about anyone living now. I should know, I wrote it myself. It would be madness to enter the coming battle with a child by your side instead of me. What are you even thinking?"

"Hear me, Orchid—you haven't been infallible in the past, have you? Dearest? The girl queen we wrote about is not a future-queen of a distant age. She's here today, now, in front of you. This is her. That is my interpretation of the passage. Please consider it before giving in to this, ah, unflattering jealousy. How was I to know that you were wrong until I saw that you were wrong with my own eyes? When I saw the girl standing on the field?"

Orchid said nothing.

He said, "She was wearing white."

Nothing.

"I trust you. I have trusted you all along. I hope that you trust me too."

Orchid's silence went on too long and seemed like a challenge between them.

"It's *my* vision," he said at last. "I should be able to interpret it."

Orchid whirled on her heels and went back to the books. "O no," she repeated again and again, tossing books aside. "O no, O no, you are wrong wrong wrong. You haven't spent time with the words the way I have, you haven't studied them—"

He went after her and grasped her shoulder, pulling her back. "I am not wrong."

"I'll find it and prove it to you. It says, 'A young sigil dressed all in white shall appear when at last the rockets have returned to earth, and this sigil shall sit enthroned during all the days of heaven.' " She was muttering now. "I wrote it a hundred times in a hundred letters to a hundred of your constituents." She looked up and a plaintive note entered her voice. " 'Heaven' is not now, David."

"But how can you know?" he asked.

She threw some more books from the trunk onto the rugs and kept digging, all the while speaking more angrily. "I *know,* David, because this does not feel like Heaven to me. Seven in my own carnival died of Bent Head since you left, even though we created more Heads this season than we ever have. They did nothing. The Disease is still in the ground everywhere, even on the saferoads, no matter what you say. I *know,* David, because I am still here on his wretched planet with these wretched people and I am not gliding freely up through the sunshine glare of ozone in a celestial vehicle, like you promised, *David,*" she spat. "I *know* because my own humanity is not disintegrated, is not made perfect. I—" Her voice wavered slightly, but when she turned to make what the girl assumed would be a spiteful face, her eyes were dense and unreadable and showed no emotion at all. "The rockets have not returned for us."

Mr. Capulatio merely shrugged. "I love you dearly. You speak like a warrior-scholar, your gift for translating my words into beautiful writing has gained us thousands of followers. But Radiance, the rockets *have* returned. As I knew they would. Even at the precise time I suspected and not a minute sooner. I am here at the Cape, and so are they."

Orchid's brows knit together. "What?"

"Did you stargaze lately, my beautiful wife, wife of my boyhood, wife of my first heart?"

"Yesterday." She frowned. "No, two nights ago." Her face was losing color. The girl knew that Mr. Capulatio looked at the sky every night, without fail. Orchid wiped her forehead with the back of her hand. "The days run together. I can't remember. I have been so busy, I . . ."

Mr. Capulatio was nodding vigorously. "As sometimes happens. We are all busy people. But we shouldn't fall down in our worship, ever, especially in this Age of Times. Our hearts should always be afloat with the ecstasy of shame, which drives us ever toward vigilance. Constance, Radiance, is required of us all."

"Stop talking like that to me. I *was* constant." She spread her arms in a helpless flourish but her voice had weakened. "All this. This carnival, all this—" She paused and narrowed her eyes. "What is the Age of Times?"

"A new revelation. Soon we'll write it down together. But now is the time for rejoicing; we will go to the shore and build an altar of oyster-shells. Then, tonight when you go out to look at the heavens, you will see the new light of the first rocketship. You will know beyond a shadow of a doubt that I am divinely blessed. Tonight we shall make upon our altar a green phosphorescent flame and go on a raft into the circle of the sea and there you—you, Orchid, Priestess-Wife and scribe—will marry us. You will be her sister, her guidance, her own Radiance as you have been mine. Who better to teach her how to be the king's queen than the king's first wife?"

Orchid breathed quietly for a few moments. Then she turned to the girl and cried, "Did you hear? Do you understand?"

She did not understand. The rockets had returned? Did this mean the world was ending? Or just beginning? Their religion was strange to her, their faith baffling, but she understood that she was important to whatever they believed, just as she understood the look of eagerness in Mr. Capulatio's eyes when he gazed at her. Her mother had said all religions were madness, and here in her cage, the girl thought again she may have been right.

Mr. Capulatio unfastened his cape and stood before them both in his beautiful clothes. He opened his arms. After a time, Orchid slipped into them, all the while eying the girl with a look not of hate but of gigantic loss—fresh-cut, still squirting. She was not finished with her objections, far from it. The girl was more scared of her than before. With Mr. Capulatio's back to her, all she saw of him was the way his shoulders curved around Orchid's body, how they formed the top of an inverted triangle, and she saw how strong he was, and she again felt a thrust of agonic jealousy, so she turned her eyes away and did not watch them as they kissed in the low lamplight. She heard their mouths touching wetly together, and when she did finally look she saw Orchid's eyes blazing at her over his shoulder.

CHAPTER 4

THE COMET

It was a lonesome truth that John D. Sousa, Chief Orbital Doctor, astronomer, and scholar of holy texts, named as he was after ancient magicians both celestial and musical, had still not discovered how to make that which was *ún*visible visible. Though he used ancient mirrors and water tables and though he fasted and studied and sacrificed and calculated, he had not yet, in all his years, been able to call down any real revelation. Not a single one.

He was now nearly forty, and it was recognition of this monstrous failure that drove him at present to discount the manifold wonders he had created over the course of his life. During his tenure at court, John had adjusted and re-cast thousands of pages of his predecessors' charts, compiling them finally into what was considered the foremost work of scholarship of the age—a vast *New Cosmology of Orbits*. The book was expansive and contained information from hundreds of places, translated and reinterpreted and reimagined. It was a beautiful work. But now, when John looked at the book, he felt only revulsion. Huge and ungainly, it signified nothing but a torturous waste of his talents—as precise as it was uncreative. They were scientific but not revelatory. They declared, in short, nothing that was not already known.

He continued to pour over texts and pray as though he might yet make some discovery that could give meaning to his life. He still rose every day at the golden dawn and worked some nights straight through until morning again. But in those sweaty torch-lit hours John had begun to understand what was perhaps the most lonely truth of all: failure meant something far worse than he'd imagined as a younger man. For John had tried his entire life to predict the exact day and hour of the return of the rocketships, but recently, he found himself pursuing this vocation with not a little fear and trembling in the face of the what-if, for *what-if* he had indeed succeeded—not in predicting the exact day and hour—but *what-if* he had proved inadvertently that there were no shuttles to begin with? That *no such artifacts ever existed?*

Did John anymore believe it was even possible that the shuttles (which were supposed to convey the chosen heavenward into the forever of forevers) were really and truly coming back? If they had ever existed to begin with, why should they return? From where? They would come back to earth, *past* the dome of heaven? Preposterous. The only objects that ever descended were ragged pieces of burnt-up metal from the ancient past. And meteorites. And rain and wind. *What-if* all his scrying and magic and pursuit of the illusory had already revealed an answer? An unpalatable one, but an answer nonetheless? This was the bleak possibility that troubled him more each day.

It so happened that in the almanacs John drew up yearly for the court, he included all the changes an observer of the heavens might have occasion to witness, should he turn his eyes to the sky on any given night of the year—constellations, meteor showers, phases of the moon, star-risings and star-settings. Though valued by King Michael, who was particularly fond of divination, these predictions were an art to which John had not devoted considerable time in years; the formulas had been worked out centuries before his birth by men with more mathematical genius than himself, and John merely applied them diligently, like a fastidious clerk. They did not engage his imagination or advance his larger quest, which was of course the discovery of the Return Date.

So when, on the fourteenth day of November, after a tedious day of calculating horoscopes for friends and enemies of the crown, John crossed his own small courtyard and happened to glance into his newly filled reflecting pool, he was astonished to see shining in the center of the glassine water a bright, unfamiliar orb. He bent down and looked closer. Under the water were brocaded carp, just purchased for his new manor house. They were arm-thick tubes of variegated flesh, with fins wavering gently in the currentless pond. But atop them, on the water's surface, John saw the unmistakable curve of light that indicated a celestial body in motion.

For a long moment, he gazed at that radiant bend and felt nothing. Then a thin panic leapt into his throat and he realized he had been holding his breath. His heartbeat sped up. He had not forecast *this*—whatever it was. John flopped back on his behind in the sandy earth and looked upward finally, searching the sky.

He called in a hoarse voice for his servant Mizar. The man emerged shortly from the gardening shed and brandished a small box, talking as he approached. "You can see," Mizar barked, "how wonderfully the new pond comets are faring! The colors! The dealer said you cannot find carp this color anywhere, that he has made them himself in his own laboratories specifically for your lordship. And that we should only feed them these." He opened the wooden box and tilted it downward; John did not look inside because he was still looking up. "They are dried and pulverized tadpoles. I will of course do the drying and pulverizing myself for subsequent batches. But the catching of the tadpoles might better be assigned to a younger member of your household, although I suppose the exercise would be not so terrible for my"—and here he gestured to his paunch, John sensed it without even looking—"well, I could use it." Mizar paused and shook the box in John's face and then pointed to the carp. "Sir, do you like the pond comets?"

It was Mizar's habit to peck about fretfully. He was as boring as a woman, but John had long ago learned that Mizar had to be extraordinarily annoyed to raise his voice. "Do you like the new pond comets, sir! They only just arrived today. I acclimated them to the pool as instructed by the breeder, by submerging them in their own separate bowls over the course of five hours." Mizar knelt beside his master and pointed at the pond. "That is one of the new ones, I believe, with the darker head. Have you ever seen such a lovely fish? I say they were worth every cent."

"Look *up,* Mizar," John said gloomily. Mizar glanced at him. John said, "At the sky, look up!" He shrugged upward.

Mizar looked. The white underglobes of his eyes shimmered blue with the condensed light of the skies. He looked back at John. Between them lay some fundamental gulf that John had only ever been able to guess at in moments like this, when he knew himself to be filled with the horror of the possible, and Mizar to be merely amused by it. "A *real* comet?" he asked.

"I think so."

"Should that be there? I don't remember anything on the calendar about a comet . . . not this year or . . . in the next many?"

"I know." John thought suddenly of how he had spent the last several years intensively studying the old texts, revising charts and inventing new magics to determine the elusive Return Date. Over these years he had half-convinced the king and even himself that there *was* some way to divine it from nothing. Lately his search had grown more esoteric, and as he became desperate to prove to himself that the shuttles had in fact existed, he'd begun pursing the line of thought that the date might be revealed by some unearthly entity, through channeling. He also wondered if the date had already been disclosed—somewhere, somehow, to someone *else*—he only needed to learn where and how it had been communicated. It was a somewhat ludicrous hope, but anything was possible. Wasn't it? He had once believed so.

But many nights in his office he had looked through his window, out onto his private courtyards and slumbering astronomical apparatuses, and had pounded his fists because he could not understand everything all at once. No, not even a sliver of it; his mind was simply too small. And he fell into despair that he had spent his life in pursuit of folly.

Mizar coughed. "Could it be a fall of metal, sir? Perhaps just an old object coming down from the orbits?"

"It could be." John was himself an expert in Metal Falls, which occurred when fragments of the ancient satellites crashed back to earth. The recovery of these relics was deeply important to King Michael, who ordered each one studied and catalogued. John was less interested in the physical aspects of the heavens than in theoretical ones, and so had little energy for the king's insistence that these misshapen twists of metal meant anything at all, but he understood their importance as devotional objects and so kept a collection of interesting specimens in a cabinet in his offices.

"Should I bring your telescope?" asked Mizar.

"I doubt it will help."

"Do you want your books? This may be in the charts. Perhaps the printer of the calendar made the error, not yourself."

"It's not the printer's fault."

Mizar stood and his knees cracked. "Well, what should I do?" He looked unconcernedly again at the blazing arc.

John waved his arms as he was given to doing when he felt hopeless, standing up so quickly he felt dizzy. "What? You ask me 'what'? Here we have some phenomenon of a magnitude I cannot gauge and you want to know 'what' is to be done? You know, Mizar, 'what' is a word I am just now rethinking, and I—" He put his head in his hands. "I need to go to my study. '*What,*'" he sniffed. "I am surrounded by low hideous persons with visions only of 'what.'"

Mizar sneezed to cover a laugh. "What then should I ask, sir, if not 'what'?"

"Well, certainly not the obvious: 'why,'" John said, and squinted at the sky. "And any idiot might ask 'how.' You, Mizar, are not quite that much of an idiot, so I believe you will refrain from asking stupid questions, if only for my sake. But—" John felt his insides burning with confusion, for the reality of this streak of light was concrete: it existed, and he had not predicted it. "Perhaps even a half-wit such as yourself might stumble instinctively upon the correct question, or through a process of elimination might arrive at it. What, Mizar, do you think that question might be?"

Mizar's cheeks did not flush—he was a good servant, impervious to verbal cruelty. John had, in times of greater despair than this, cast his fury upon Mizar like a club, pummeling him with the hugeness of his own fear and pain, while Mizar cheerfully clucked on about selecting an entrée for a dinner party, or the soil in the garden beds. It was easy for John to believe Mizar had no concerns beyond the domestic. He truthfully considered him a kind of genius, though he would never have admitted it aloud. Mizar shrugged narrowly. "I believe the word you're after, sir, must be 'who'? Since you have kindly exhausted all the other alternatives for me."

John closed and opened his eyes. "Yes," he said. "You're right. '*Who*'?"

"Well, '*who*' what?"

"*Who* predicted this light, if anyone? I surely didn't. Better yet, *who* can explain it? *Who* is the person I should write to first and *who* is most qualified to interpret the meaning of this occurrence? *Who* is the fastest courier we have?" John's mind swam with the letters he knew he must begin writing immediately—to men and women he preferred to correspond with only in writing. He feared he might be forced to request the physical presence of one or more of them.

John greatly disliked sharing his laboratories. Actually, he greatly disliked sharing any portion of his private castle—several years before, the king had allotted him funds to construct a small manor just a mile from the walls of the compound, and John had named his new home Urania. He had installed every instrument of astronomical observation that he had so far collected. They were bolted tightly into his courtyard's ground and protected by metal domes that closed out the salt and the water. John was fiercely protective of them, as he had, after all, spent his life acquiring these marvels. He was not often moved to share them with magicians he considered lesser than himself; that is, with anyone else. The very notion of a swarm of interested parties converging upon his lovely, peaceful, near-complete castle caused his breath to race, so that he began to feel like his heart was flapping open and closed like a door in the wind. He found himself hating this bright streak in the sky.

He had secured from King Michael four armed men to guard his manor—one for each gate—and outfitted them with swords blessed by the Hierophant and forged from the metal of fallen satellites. His instruments were priceless, he would not leave anything to chance. And yet King Michael had insisted the manor be built with extra bedrooms to house other magicians he invited to the Cape from time to time. John could hardly object—it was not *his* money used to build Urania. But during the days and weeks these other Orbital Doctors used his equipment he lingered behind them as they worked. He knitted his fingers together, watching to be sure they did not smudge their face-greases on glass casings or jostle any of his precisely aligned water tables or scrying bowls. And yet now John must write to the other Orbital Doctors—*who*? All of them! In their own subpar astronomical spaces where they calculated with half, no!, a fourth of his natural alacrity—and he must ask them if anywhere in any of their own records and charts was this thing, this glowing streak, this cosmological rumination he himself had missed.

It was all too much for him to bear. John's already pounding heart sputtered. He could not catch his breath. He bent to his knees, staring up at the mysterious light in the late afternoon sky. Bright and beautiful. Mizar rushed to his side, patted his arm. "Sir? Are you all right?"

Then he fell backward. Mizar immediately clutched his wrist in a vain effort to find his pulse, for John had been somewhat prone to fainting in his youth. So Mizar was pressing up and down his arm as though testing fruit, and then a great wooly heat descended over the top of John's head. He could remember nothing, and then he passed from the realm of the physical and also from the constraints of his worry and into a gauzelike swoon.

CHAPTER 5

THE PARDONESS

Marvel Parsons had hardly emerged from the shadow of Canaveral Tower when a feeling of profound dread swept over him, and he turned and looked up. Beside him, Juniper did the same. In the white incandescence of the late fall sky, Marvel saw the light. Juniper said, "O. Well, shit." The young guard squinted and cupped his hands around his eyes for a moment, until he shook his head and murmured, "God, that hurts my eyes, the sky's so bright."

A very light wind swept over them. The rain had completely stopped. Other people in the courtyard, now hushed, had likewise turned their faces to the sky, their wares forgotten. They all stood like silent statues.

"O shit," Juniper said again. "What *is* that?"

Marvel found that he was comforted by the younger man's demeanor. "I have no idea. A comet is what it looks like." He turned to Juniper. "We'll go now to the Pardoness. You come with me."

"What? But the light—"

"Yes, it's probably a comet, as I said."

"What will the Pardoness do?"

"She'll do what she does," Marvel replied with straining patience. "Pardon us for crimes we will soon commit." When he saw the confusion on Juniper's face, he said, "You are a spy, aren't you? I'm taking you to an important place, perhaps the most important one we have here at the Cape. There you can spy all you please. Afterward I will need you to be of some assistance to me. Is that an acceptable deal?"

Juniper blinked.

"I will pay you. Whatever they're paying you, I'll pay you more. Double. Triple."

He shrugged at last. "If you say so." Then, his handsome face cracked open. "I'm not a spy, though."

He would act, and later he would consider his actions. It had been so for him during all the important moments in his life. This quality, he supposed, made him a good leader—it was politically expedient, at any rate. It gave him an air of authority.

Marvel had never actually been to Green Butterfly's chamber, though he had committed many sins. The zealousness of his youth and the trust he'd placed in his own judgment meant that he'd done little, over the course of his lifetime, for which he believed he needed forgiveness. Surely not the poisoning of the Mystagogue all those years ago. An unpleasant means to a holier end. In that matter, Marvel wanted to believe the balance of righteousness still tipped in his favor.

And yet that *light.* The light in the sky had rattled Marvel in a way that even the prisoner with no ears had not, or discovering a spy like Juniper, from outside the compound, slinking about in a poor costume. Both of those things were concerning, to be sure. But that light? The light was worse. It could be only one of two things: the space shuttles returning or some heavenly body hurtling perilously toward them.

Marvel had never truly realized how high Canaveral Tower was until he and Juniper had made it halfway up. The white metal stairs went on forever. After a few minutes, he felt the muscles in the tops of his thighs burning. Juniper, ahead of him and apparently still amiable, remained unwinded. To be young again, Marvel thought. But then he looked at Juniper's shoulders tilting right, then left as he climbed, and so forth inside their dust-colored fabric casings, and noticed the elbows of the jacket were patched with leather. The entire garment didn't fit him right; he was obviously not the first owner.

They climbed in tighter spirals until the staircase crested abruptly at a large solid metal door. There was no landing, just a massive door in the wall with a ring-knocker in the center. Juniper looked over his shoulder at Marvel. "What?" Marvel said. "Go *in*. I'm the Hierophant, I don't need permission."

Juniper nodded. "But shouldn't I knock?"

"O, probably." Marvel put his hand to his temple.

He knocked. Nothing happened. He knocked again. Then the door opened onto a circular room as wide as the tower itself, filled with uncomfortably warm, thin smoke that tumbled out onto the stairs and into their faces. Marvel and Juniper coughed as they entered. The only movement of air inside the room was provided by a single attendant—who presumably had also opened the door. She was nude, to Marvel's great interest, as he had always maintained a high degree of appreciation for naked bodies, male or female. Her peanut-shaped body swayed. Her nipples, flat and oval like galaxies, were the only thing Marvel could look at until he forced himself to look away. She walked quickly back over to the Pardoness and began fanning her with a sheet of paperlike metal.

What in the world were they burning? He glanced at Juniper. Juniper was staring at the attendant. Her skin looked wet enough to pull from her bones in strips, she was so sweaty. Why were they up here, sweltering? The Pardoness herself reclined on a couch, almost invisible under a web of diaphanous fabric. She peered at them serenely, and touched her attendant softly on the thigh. The woman stopped fanning. Marvel and Juniper stepped farther into the stuffy room and struggled not to cough. For furniture, the room contained only a few tables, the couch, and an amply sized bed at the back end of the chamber.

"Now, I know who *you* are," said the Pardoness. Her voice was melodious but strangely accented, as though she had never spoken to anybody and had learned to pronounce all her words from books. He'd assumed she would be older than himself, since she had been the Pardoness before he had even come to the Cape. But her age was hard to tell. Her gaunt face was all but hidden under the hood she wore pulled over her ears and hair. The skin around her eyes seemed sweaty and moist—hardly surprising, given how warm it was. Though the rest of her body was covered by beautiful fabrics, Marvel could make out the vague shape of her arms. Thin, spindly. But her lower half was difficult to see. Only the tips of her two swollen feet protruded.

Marvel took a slight bow and nodded. "Likewise, you need no introduction." Then he looked at the attendant as though she might yet introduce her mistress. But she did nothing.

"I must say I am surprised to see you here, High Priest. You must have committed a grievous act indeed."

"Why in the name of all that is holy do you have this *smoke* up here?" He waved his hand.

"For my health."

"That's insane."

"It's not for you to judge what is insane, Priest. Not in this chamber. This room is my own kingdom."

This was true. The title of Pardoness was a hereditary one, and had been passed down from mother to daughter for centuries, endowing its bearer with complete autonomy. It was said and most fervently believed throughout the land that she was a direct descendent of the ancient king Armstrong, who had once walked on the moon. Privately, Marvel thought that after so many generations it was impossible to know *where* the Pardoness's family had come from, just as his own family's origins were a mystery. But her title held meaning beyond that. Marvel did believe that men had once walked on the moon, and if she was their descendent then she must possess certain powers. Of that there was no question.

"Yes," he murmured. "I meant no disrespect."

"I think you did," she replied mildly. "But it doesn't matter to me. Why are you here? We are protective of our solitude, aren't we, Discovery?"

"Very." The attendant walked to a side table and lit a candle. A sweet smell filled the chamber, and Marvel wondered if the smoke was some kind of mild narcotic. The door clanged heavily as it finally shut, drawn closed by its own weight, leaving the chamber in near darkness. The smoking candle made useless light. A few clusters of tallow candles flickered in the corners of the room, as was the custom for royal chambers, set before mirrors to amplify their light. Marvel swept aside his cassock and went into the room as though it were his own. "Bring me a chair, girl."

"Can you not see there are no chairs?" asked the Pardoness.

"Ah." Marvel felt the ends of his mouth tug upward into a smirk.

"You're used to getting your way. I do empathize. But you will be disappointed here." She raised an eyebrow. "Shall we come to the point of your visit? Discovery and I are accustomed to spending our afternoons in relaxation and care of ourselves. Mornings are our work time, and this morning is quickly running out. In my older age, I am also somewhat protective of my health. Come to your meaning, please."

He wrinkled his nose. "Sitting in an overheated cloud of smoke is good for your health?"

"Come to your business."

Marvel tried to make out her body beneath the piles of shimmering fabric. He could see nothing beyond her emaciated arms, wrapped like tentpoles in carrying-bags. The Pardoness took a swallow of a dark liquid beside her bed, and placed the glass back on the table with a trembling hand, as though lifting it had been all she could manage. As he looked more closely at the protrusion of sweaty cheekbones beneath her large, dark eyes, it dawned on him that she might be starving to death, although he well knew from the account books the amount of food sent up to her chamber each week. Her fingernails were painted red. She might have been sixty. But she might have been forty, and just ill. He saw no malformations to speak of. There was something wrong, though, just out of sight—he could sense it, and was unsettled. She reminded him of an infant chick that could not quite hatch. That would shortly dry out in its enervated egg and die.

He took a breath. "I *am* here to ask your pardon. Your highest pardon. I ask you to forgive my future actions."

"What are they?"

"They will most likely be awful."

"I cannot forgive what hasn't happened yet."

"You must."

She shrugged. "I don't have to do anything."

He sighed. "They will be treasonous. The highest treason. I plan to disappear, to leave King Michael's service. Can you forgive me now?" He had not meant to reveal it, he was appalled that he had. But saying it relieved him. Beside him, Juniper tried hard not to react, though Marvel could feel the ripple of surprise pass through him. So Juniper had *not* known—at least, he hadn't known Marvel was planning to leave.

What had he come for, then?

Marvel stared at the Pardoness and she looked back without pity. "After you have committed these actions, come tell me again, and I will or will not forgive you. I believe now we are finished." Her eyes strayed to the door.

He shook his head. He had marched up this tower without a thought. That was his way when he decided on something. He wanted—needed—to leave the Cape. He would return to the darkness of Kansas with a clear conscience, and there he was certain he would find the Mystagogue alive. And he would kill him.

He wanted forgiveness for murder.

He had always been a zealous man, in whatever he did, even to the point of martyrdom; he *needed* to be sure he had the heavens' favor. The Pardoness was held by every denomination still extant, every carnival on the land, and every sect that worshipped the shuttles, to be an infallible oracle of forgiveness. She was the only connection anyone on earth had to the heavens.

"Have you seen the light in the sky?" Marvel asked. The room had no windows.

"I have not. But I have been told of it by my dear Discovery."

He wondered if they were lovers.

"What do you think it is?"

"It could be many things."

He sighed again. "When I was a boy, living far away, I had a vision. Maybe not unlike the visions you have as an oracle."

"Forgiveness requires no fortune-telling."

"Well." He grew restless. "I had a vision. Just one. I saw that the True King, the king who will sit on the throne when the shuttles return, the king whose ascendance would *create the conditions* for their return, if you will, would appear here. The Cape. So I did what I had to do to come here."

"We all have megalomaniacal fantasies. It's quite normal." The Pardoness lifted her chin so her eyes were even more deeply in shadow, and she tilted her face toward Juniper, who went reddish with embarrassment. "Less normal to act on them, but you seem to have fared well."

Marvel narrowed his eyes and began to dig at his thumb again. It was a habit that undercut his authority, and yet he had never been able to break it for more than a few months at a time.

"I killed a man so I could come here all those years ago. As you may know, I began my service here at the Cape as a lowly priest and rose on my own talents to the position I hold now."

"Impressive."

"You don't seem impressed." He cringed inside at his own petulance.

She laughed. "Not terribly. I'm sorry. Many men in many guises have lived this story, and none are more special than you. Or less special." She gestured to her handmaid, Discovery. "When you hear as many tales as we do, they begin to seem similar. Which is for the best. We must cultivate perfect indifference in order to forgive wholly."

"Do you understand what I'm telling you?" That smoke she inhaled constantly—surely that affected her judgment. "My vision of the True King reigning at the Cape was so strong that I *killed* a man. A very, very important man. I was young then—just a boy. And I put poison in his cup and he drank it, and he convulsed and he died, right before my eyes, and all I could think was, 'I am free now!' I felt no sorrow. No pain. I left that very evening and crossed the deathscapes to this selfsame palace compound, set myself up as a young apprentice priest, and I rose to power. The acme of power." He spat his words out like food that repulsed him.

"Ah," said the Pardoness, and shifted on her couch. Something bulbous under all that fabric, a part of her body? He saw it, just for an instant. "You feel moved to tell me your story. I am moved to listen." She glanced at Discovery, who smiled. "Are you moved?"

The handmaid nodded.

"I'm not trying to move you," Marvel growled. "The man I thought I killed. I have reason to believe he isn't dead."

"How unfortunate. But why haven't you asked for a pardon for *that* killing? Or, intended killing, as it seems?"

"Because it was justified."

"How so?"

Marvel grimaced. "I thought he deserved to die because he didn't recognize the truth of my vision. And other reasons. Back then I was certain my vision was from the heavens. And that he was stymying me wrongfully." Marvel held his breath for a time. "But not just for those reasons. He deserved to die for . . . other reasons. He himself has killed many."

The Pardoness was now nodding, the iridescent fabric sliding back and forth over her shoulders. "But now you think your vision was merely the fantasy of a fervently religious boy?"

Marvel swallowed. "In a sense."

"And?"

"Well," Marvel took a breath. "I have come to suspect that this same man, this very important man, is still alive. That I didn't kill him after all."

"Praise the shuttles," replied the Pardoness. "You must be grateful."

"You don't understand. Because I *must* kill him this time. He will never allow me to return to my homeland. He would never accept me back." Marvel did not say that he still harbored a cold fury toward the Mystagogue, that it had not dimmed after these many years.

"Why go back at all? Why not stay here, where you have ruled mostly wisely and mostly justly?" Her eyes sparkled. "Where you are mostly respected instead of reviled?"

Marvel's destiny, his only purpose, was to serve the True King, whoever he turned out to be: he had been sure of this since his earliest cognizance. This True King would appear in Kansas. It had been so all along. Kansas was where the Disease ruined the world, and Kansas was where salvation would spring forth. He tried to catch the Pardoness's eyes in a meaningful way, but they were shadowed by her veil and hard to see. Her lower face, cut deep with two smile lines, pulled into a frown or a smile, he couldn't tell.

The truth was that Marvel was not sure if it was right to kill the Mystagogue, but he knew it was necessary. In order for Marvel to end his days peacefully in Kansas, the tyrant must die. "Because. I know now the True King is not here at the Cape. My vision was wrong."

"You sound sure of yourself. But what of this new light in the sky? Could it not be the shuttles returning?"

"It could be many things." He said her own words back to her with a smile. This time she smiled back.

"And you are a man very convinced of the rightness of your faith. Even when your convictions shift with the wind. Perhaps especially then."

Marvel ground his molars together. He had the intrusive thought that he was merely acting out of self-interest, that he'd grown tired of responsibility and the decadence of the courtiers. He had grown tired of his own daughter. Perhaps so tired that he would *never* be satisfied until he left this place for the solitude of Huldah's Black Watchtower.

For the burnished memory of his pious youth.

Maybe he remembered the Black Watchtower as a place it had never been. It was a distasteful notion. That his deep righteousness could be nothing more than nostalgia.

"You are not easy to talk to," was all he said. "I thought I was supposed to confess my sins here."

The Pardoness continued to gaze at him. "You are having many thoughts. Let me share one of my own." She motioned to her hidden lower half without removing the coverlet. "I am a woman in pain. Over the years it has become unbearable. My misfortune was to be born to a very unmixed line, one which maximized the purity of my blood at the expense of my worldly body."

His eyes followed her gesture. Juniper leaned forward as though he could see through the blankets. "Well, what's wrong with you?" Marvel asked.

"I have tried many remedies. But due to the deformities I cannot bear children. There was never any hope for it, so I never missed it, and that time has passed at any rate. But this means my only heir will be Discovery, and she is not of the correct lineage. She will never be accepted as a new Pardoness."

"I'm sorry," he said.

"Don't be. All things must end. But I ask you this: if my line, for centuries unbroken, will now be snuffed out with no legitimate heir, couldn't it be that this is truly the Return? That the True King will or has already appeared?"

A buzzing anger rose in Marvel's throat. *Yes, of course that could be,* he thought. *And yet I still don't believe it.* "Anything is possible. But you have no idea where he might be."

The Pardoness folded her shockingly thin hands on her lap. "This is as good a place as any," she murmured.

"What is your ailment?"

"It has no name in the medical books. Surely it is the result of inbreeding." She moved aside one of the blankets momentarily. Discovery dropped her fan and rushed to the Pardoness's side. "Grace, don't." She clapped her hand over her mouth, as though the exposure of her Mistress would cause her physical pain.

But the Pardoness pulled off a portion of the coverlet to reveal the most hideous mass of tissue Marvel had ever beheld. Her legs, both as grotesquely swollen as skin bags filled with water, were six or seven times the size of a normal limb. The skin was dry, discolored in spots, pink toward the knee but blue and even purple by the toes. It looked dead or dying. The feet as large and bulbous as square stones. How could a person live this way? Surely she couldn't walk. The agony must have been unimaginable. His mouth fell agape until he was able to close it, which he did quickly, but not before she had seen the horror and confusion on his face. The Pardoness remained sanguine as she re-covered her legs, but in Marvel's mind's eye there were only those appendages, lumpy trees of burst capillaries and flaking skin. Every nutrient her body extracted from food must go to feed those bloated overgrowths—that was why her upper body appeared so fragile. "My god."

She nodded. "My given name, Hierophant, is Green Butterfly. I'm sure you knew this."

He nodded.

"Like my namesake, I long to be free. I long to fly away from this tower. Perhaps as you yourself do?"

He stopped nodding.

"These legs are rotten. They will be the death of me. And yet, I'm not ready to die."

He said nothing.

"I would like to be rid of this prison." She motioned to her lower half. "Just as you would."

"How?"

She rearranged her sumptuous fabrics around herself weakly. Discovery bent over her and fluffed them up, then went to the sideboard and lit another smoking candle, and yet more sweet-smelling medicine filled the air.

"That is a question I have long pondered. I have considered many different approaches, but now I have the ear of the second most powerful man in the land. How might I be free, Priest? I will not give the Cape another Pardoness. This light in the sky may portend death for us all, or eternal life. *These* are the times we are living in. Somehow I knew I would live to see them." Then she said: "I will forgive your past sin of attempting to kill this man. I will do this if you free me."

"I can't just take you out of the tower, everyone would see—"

"No. *Free* me." She pointed to her legs. Now that he knew what was beneath the fabric, he could not unsee it. They were like sausages bursting their casings. And Marvel had watched many a person be tortured. "I—"

"That little man. The Walking Doctor," came Juniper's voice in his ear. "The one with no ears. From Kansas."

"No," said Marvel, to no one. The word floating up as from the bottom of a well.

"He said his patients always lived, I thought."

"Are you suggesting he *take her legs off*?" He shook his head. "You're crazy. The blood alone—"

Juniper's clear eyes seemed strangely delighted.

"And anyway," Marvel said, disturbed. "With all respect due to your office, Pardoness, I'm not asking forgiveness for my past sins, I want forgiveness for my *future* sin. And if the sin was once justified, why shouldn't it be justified again?"

"I cannot give you that. But if, as you say, this sin is justified, you don't need my or anyone's forgiveness."

He tossed his hands up. "Why did I even come to you?"

"Because you are uncertain. You"—she spoke in a solemn voice—"are a man of uncertain faith. And yet you are also a man who deeply needs to believe you are right. Your longing for peace surprises you, am I correct?" She reached for her little glass again and took a drink. "My predicament, though less philosophical, is similar. I wish to be free of this bondage. The end will come, either now or later, but

I wish to use my remaining days as I desire. I wish to leave this place."

There had been a few, rare moments during his life when Marvel felt he truly understood other human beings. The isolation of his rank and temperament lifted, almost like a mist dissolving, and what remained was his hand in that of another human. Courageous, contented, unified. He glanced about, absorbing all he saw in this dreadful room, so unlike his own chamber: the medicinal smoke, the sallow nude sycophantic attendant, the grim deformities, and indeed he judged this woman's life to be a prison—and here he had thought she lived in luxury. Everyone did. What did this unsavory truth now require of him, as a man of religion? He could not *not* help her.

She gestured to the sky beyond the ceiling. "The world may change forever. This may be the Return. We may soon be transported upward to Heaven. Or we may live in a new way here on earth. No one knows. Not even me."

"I don't think anything is going to happen," Marvel said.

"That is your prerogative."

"And you say I definitely don't need a pardon?"

"Not if you believe what you are doing is right."

"But I don't know."

"Then no one does."

Marvel had spoken before he even realized it. "Bring the prisoner Tygo here. He will save her if he can." He paused when Juniper nodded eagerly. "It's the least we can do," Marvel muttered.

Juniper left and returned some minutes later with the news that Tygo was already out of his cell on the order of the Chief Orbital Doctor John Sousa, an ineffectual pipsqueak of a man Marvel had distrusted for years. And yet for the moment he felt untroubled by the hitch in his plans. The order had been issued. Tygo would see the Pardoness soon enough. He would look at her legs. He would do something to free this woman, if he could. Thus, Marvel would use this good deed to set in motion a string of treacheries he hoped were for the common good.

Just as when he'd left Kansas the first time.

This circle pleased him, although he could not quite put his finger on why. He bowed deeply to the Pardoness and turned to leave. "Grace, I have done what I can."

She nodded, and he strode toward the door, but she said something from behind him that he did not hear. He looked back. "What was that?"

"I said that faith is both reasonless and the reason for everything. Beware any certainty, High Priest. For not many things are certain, and the ones that are certainly have no reason to be."

CHAPTER 6

THE ANGELS

John Sousa, King Michael's Chief Orbital Doctor, knew at once when he awoke that the comet he had seen meant nothing and everything. Likewise, he knew he was not sick but also that he was very unwell, and outside the daylight was escaping and beside his window there chirruped a brushfire of birds, so loud he wondered at their purpose—what could they be saying to each other, over and over, in such screams? He knew by the organ-colored sky that it was late afternoon, for no one had seen fit to draw the curtains. He was naked. He had soaked his bed through with sweat, and he knew also that he had now wasted some un-wasteable amount of time with this wretched bedriddenness, and so he staggered to the window and threw it open, causing the birds outside to blow a fresh wave of sound at him before they ascended and reconvened on the east gate. He stared at the white comet. It was so plain in its thereness. He folded his elbows on the window ledge and squinted. John was so tired, so very tired of his life and everything he had ever done and every thought he had ever thought and now, even now, when faced with this bright and indisputably heavenly artifact, he could not muster a single interesting thought.

He could think, only, of how much he did not wish to think about it.

"No, he is awake, look!" came Mizar's voice from behind him, and also the clamorous unfamiliar footfalls of a group. John turned. In the doorway stood Mizar with one of the king's elite guards with his lion-shaped facemask pulled down, always a terrifying sight, for the masks the guards wore made them look like deranged partygoers. Beside the two men, or rather with them, was a slight, dark-haired man in the last gasp of his youth, chained around the ankles and staring at the entire scene with an expression of grateful hunger, the way John might have looked at his instruments after he'd been a long time away.

Mizar pushed aside the guard and rushed to John, taking him immediately to the bedside and sitting him down again and then easing him into a cotton robe. "Are you all right, sir? You are always so moved by everything, I tell you it's a curse as often as a blessing—" Mizar looked pointedly at the prisoner in chains, whose every piece of clothing was brilliant blue, or at least had once been so. The prisoner and his garments were presently covered in dirt and what might have been blood.

John, even in his wretched state, was sure he had never seen this person before. The prisoner met his eyes without smiling or nodding. John pushed Mizar back and pointed. "Who is this?"

Mizar motioned to the guard to unchain the man's arms and then to wait beyond the bedchamber, but he flicked his wrist to indicate the guard should remain vigilant to sounds of discord within. Then the prisoner came into center of the room, like an Orbital Doctor called to give a lecture.

Mizar cleared his throat and said, "This, sir, is a Walking Doctor. A champion of"—he cast his eyes this way and that and lowered his voice—"well, of Surgery."

John blankly stared. "And?"

"He is a prisoner, sir. Really more than a prisoner—he is set to be executed in not many days for his treasonous use of living bodies. But that is not relevant to your cause."

John could not make sense of any of this. *"And?"*

"Sir, you said to me 'who.' And, well, *this* is the 'who.'" Mizar beamed and the wrinkles around his eyes bunched. He was strutting about the room in his hennish way, clacking his shoes on the tile. John felt with a lurch the very familiarity of this man, with whom he had forcibly belonged for the majority of his natural life; he understood their unwieldy togetherness as a kind of punishment for his being born in this particular place at this particular time, at an astrological confluence of moments: here, at the Cape, at this time, the Eon of Pain, the ache of the world. Mizar was John's punishment for being the final preposterous product of his rich parents' miserable and ambitious begetting. John had been born a seventh son, a lumpy white potato with no heartbeat, but he'd lived despite his nursemaid's dire predictions, and when it became apparent that he would not expire naturally, they'd squashed him in celebration beneath heavy pearlized fabrics and earrings made from moonrocks. But still he lived on, despite these indignities. Small, delicate, and defiant. In this meek way John had discovered himself strangely invulnerable: sick but never dying throughout his whole endless childhood, until his parents died themselves—together, poisoned with fifteen of their own banquet guests in a stupendous and oft-spoken-of feat of intrigue.

At that time, John had been only eight. Since then, Mizar had been his sole caretaker. In John's worst moments, he felt himself incapable of any lasting devotion to another human being. If he could not love Mizar, who had fed and educated him, whom *could* he love? And now Mizar was an old man, one who soon would be in need of care himself. His face was a place where many things had happened and John suspected his mind was similarly beginning to deteriorate. He watched with some cloudy dissatisfaction as Mizar stood in the center of the room, still talking, gesturing up and down at the blue-clad prisoner. "This prisoner predicted the heavenly manifestation. He is the 'who,'" Mizar was saying. He nudged the small man forward. The prisoner recoiled at the touch.

John took a breath. "What did you say?"

Mizar nodded once. "Yes, it's true! This man, a self-taught surgeon and an accused traitor, was discovered by his jailer to have fainted dead away, just like yourself, sir, when he observed the comet in the sky this late afternoon. When he was revived he was heard to exclaim that his . . ." And here Mizar removed a slip of paper from his pocket and read from it an exact quote. "That his 'prediction had come to pass and that this omen should not be ignored by the faithful, or by any one of us alive in these times, as it signifies a shift in our cosmic destiny.'"

John touched his temple. Mizar's habit of writing every infernal thing down so he would not forget it was a great source of irritation, and yet daily it did prove to be useful. He narrowed his eyes at the prisoner, who was rather strikingly small, and who stood morosely with his black hair greased to his head in ugly whorls, and who had at some very absurd previous moment in his life decided to have a cluster of stars tattooed on the side of his face and who, even now, was making every attempt to hide this act of youthful abandon by affixing a swatch of hair over the area. He might have been thirty or thirty-two, and his blue overcoat and pants were fashioned from heavy, plush cloth, no doubt very expensive. But now, after days or months in the palace jail, they were torn and he looked quite like a penurious seizure of a person, the sort of man John might turn his eyes from if he were to spot him on the short ride from his own Urania castle to the king's palace compound, which was in fact the only time John went outside his own gates at all, ever.

Although chained at the feet, this small prisoner did command *something*—if not an air of authority, he had at least some magnifying presence, which made him seem, in his current state, cruelly afflicted by their skepticism. He gazed at John eagerly.

John coughed. "Well? Exactly how did you predict this happening? What's your name and where are you from?"

When the prisoner spoke it was as though he were continuing outward from the center of some already formed thought. His voice was nasal and all his words hit at the same pitch. "This whole world is filled with time, it seems like, but when time actually came to me I wasted it." He shrugged glumly. "I'm half-convinced at this point that it's because I was drinking too much back then, but you would have too if you were me. So anyhow, at my last . . . what do I call it? 'Appointment'? If you could even call such a shit-pile of a job an 'appointment'—and I think that's roundly debatable—I had extra time at that job. Lots. And I wasn't filling it the way I should have been." He paused. "So yes, I admit that I was drinking. I told you that up front, remember that. And so one night I passed out and had the most amazing dream. You know how hard it is to explain dreams, so I won't even try. But when I woke up I went to my mirror and looked at it, I was going to shave—" Here he reached up and felt his sparsely grizzled face rather thoughtfully. "Not that I probably needed to, so that adds a whole other layer to the mystery. I mean, it does if you know me."

John glared.

The prisoner hurried up. "And a trance came over me while I was shaving, and when I came back to myself, I had written all *kinds* of things. By which I mean the most beautiful, predictive things."

John continued to glare.

"And that is what really happened, I swear. I could show you, but these dickheads"—the prisoner gestured to the guards at the door but surely meant every person at the Cape, generally—"took everything from me when they threw me in prison and said they destroyed it. But I'm sure that's a lie, because why would they destroy evidence? They'll need it later if they want any semblance of justice, how else would they prove their charges at my execution? But what am I saying? You're all liars, I know you are. You don't need to prove anything." He cast his glance at John and Mizar angrily. "If any of the things they took from me still exist somewhere you'll *see* exactly what I'm talking about."

"You have something written down somewhere? Some proof? Is that what this rant is supposed to be communicating?" John rubbed at his forehead.

"I did. I do. Somewhere. They gave me charts and figures and et cetera."

"*Who* gave you charts?"

The prisoner stared dumbly. "The angels. I thought I told you. Weren't you listening?"

"Angels?"

The prisoner nodded, unfazed. "I dreamed about angels, I woke up in a trance, and wrote it all down. That's the whole story."

John's airway compressed, as happened when he became nervous. "Please. Slow down. A moment ago you mentioned a mirror. A scrying mirror? Are those not prohibitively expensive while also being tremendously illegal for anyone but the Hierophant and his Orbital Doctors?"

John's own favorite scrying mirror was a relic, a piece of black granite from the other end of Merritt Island, where nearly a thousand years before men had fashioned a stone mirror that faced the sky, bearing the names of all who had died in spaceflight. It was presumed to be a religious monument, but who really knew the motivations of the ancients? The sky mirror had broken over the centuries, but nevertheless it seemed concrete proof that men really had traveled outside the world, once.

When John was not even seventeen years old—a mere boy, still a student at the palace conservatory for astronomics—it dawned upon him that this relic might be where an attuned soul such as himself would be most likely to receive a revelation. So he'd stolen a shard from the ruins of this mirror; in fact it was Mizar who'd driven him in a horsecart to a dock on the far side of Merritt Island and bribed a skittish fisherman to row the young John Sousa through the festering rot that was the inner marsh, to wait while he chipped off a portion of the mirror large enough to be of use. The swamp was dangerous and malarial, alligator- and snake-ridden, and Mizar had given the fisherman a great deal of money to perform the feat and keep quiet about it.

Since then, John had been gazing every so often into his chip of stolen black mirror, looking for . . . what? And why? It was a mystery to him yet. He felt uneasy about it sometimes—there seemed a unique perversity in viewing vertical destiny on a chip of horizontalia, and this paradox had in recent years begun to seem irreconcilable. He could not reason his way around it, and John's scrying had lately, inevitably, come to nothing. When an irrefutable sign *did* come—a comet, no less—it showed itself to him in his *servant's fishpond*. Not upon an ancient monument. Not even a holy water table.

Such an irony was, in John's opinion, so predictable that it was hardly an irony at all.

The small blue-dressed prisoner was shrugging now, his shoulders swimming in the coat like two nubby goldfish blindly hitting the sides of a bowl. "Yes, illegal and stupid on top of it. I loathe divination, let me tell you. The idea is so boring to me. That we pick something, anything, at random and ascribe an equally random meaning to it is pure lunacy." He paused and seemed to wait for John to curse at him, but it did not happen, so he spoke again, this time with more warmth. "Listen, I am a Surgical Doctor, and I deal inside bodies. What can I say? If that makes me a traitor to you religious people then I'm a traitor, and you'll execute me for it, but my point is this: I deal in the physical. I don't abide your starworship. I don't do 'magic.' I wouldn't even know what it means to see an omen or predict a happening. To my mind, that's impossible." He paused again. "So I can't make you believe me because I can hardly believe myself."

John nodded shallowly.

"Listen," said the prisoner, apparently sensing the shift in John's mood. "I saw this comet in a dream, and even though I don't believe in your stupid rockets, I am here telling you that I predicted it, and it *happened.* And something changed, and inside me now there's an outpouring of . . . of something . . . of knowledge, maybe, but it's being choked to death by everyone's disbelief, including my own. So there it is, I don't even believe myself! Are you happy?" He was vibrating with what appeared to be rage, and thrust his mottled hands at his face to rearrange his hair again over the tattoos. John noticed, for the first time, to his amazement, that the prisoner had no ears.

"What happened to you there?" He pointed to the holes.

The man had surely known from the instant his ears had taken leave of his body that he would ever afterward be explaining their absence, thought John, and indeed he began nodding in earnest.

"Yes, that," he said rather sadly. "That was obviously a punishment."

"But why?"

He bridled. "Look it up. I'm sure somewhere in this disgusting place some record-keeping piece of goat shit has written down every single one of my offenses in hideous detail on my execution warrant. The ears, sir, happened many years ago, when I was in Dread Kansas, and I surely deserved it at the time, but these days I wonder if the punishment outweighed the crime, because now that I'm a visionary I'm thinking very different things about that period in my . . . ah, life. Let's call it a life. Yes." He smiled again, this time without pity. "Kansas is a place of hell."

John was fading. Endless talk, it seemed his life was nothing but endless listening and talking. The bed and the room beyond it formed vast empty spaces and he wanted to be alone in them to gather his wits. But something about the prisoner interested him—there was a yearning in him that went beyond this undignified attempt to save his own life. John was not blind or stupid, but he was an insatiably curious man. Which was, he supposed, its own exquisite kind of stupidity. He folded his hands in his lap as he sat still on the bed. The man was probably lying about the comet. It didn't matter. And he was dressed in clothes far too fine for a Walking Doctor, even a very successful one. Yet that didn't matter either. His transparent motive remained, absent of any discernable use to John. If he had come to deceive, he was not very good at it, and he did not seem the sort of man likely to subject himself to anything he was not good at, even to save his life, so it followed that he must have come for some other reason.

The prisoner took a hobbled step toward John. "You must forgive me," he said. "They will execute me here, certainly sooner rather than later. The Hierophant himself has already interviewed me once. I know I don't deserve to die."

"My job is not to pardon prisoners—"

"But I *did* foresee this calamity, and other things, and I know I could foresee more, with the right equipment and the right minds helping me interpret my visions. The fact of the matter is simple: I'm not educated in astrologics. Myself, I know the human corpus, I know medicines and surgeries and have been practicing them since I was a child at my mother's side. I don't know the skies and I understand even less about the voices I heard in my head."

John said nothing.

"It's been said . . . out in the country, I mean, not *here* . . . that you aren't like other Cape men. That the head cutting and the bloodletting and Wonderblood are just a means to an end, anyway, for everyone, but you're much more interested in the *end*. That's the rumor about you."

John raised his eyebrows and Mizar shrugged. Who knew what people said? It wasn't any of John's concern, though he did not put much effort into fitting into Cape society. It was quite possible the man wasn't just trying to flatter him.

The prisoner went on. "When this light struck by outside my window today, I knew I was still alive for this reason. To tell you—specifically you, Lord John Sousa—what I saw in my vision. I truly believe I'm alive right now to bear witness to my prediction coming true." He opened and closed his fists thoughtfully.

These words congealed around John and he quivered fruitishly inside them. Talking, talking! But outside, still, that comet, entirely there, entirely not going away. And here before him, a man who might (yes, terror—might!) be able or at least who might believe himself able to explain this marvel. It was that belief, which seemed itself marvelous and humble in spite of everything, that moved John so awfully. So that his heart skipped again, this time down into his feet where it remained, and he had to gasp for a new breath. O, his body, so frail a thing when pitted against the tireless lashings of his mind! He clutched the bedpost and leaned forward as if to vomit.

"Yes, yes," John replied. "Perhaps it does mean something. Nameless sir, we who love the truth are bound to be undone by it, as it seems always to be melting just as we grab for it. You are telling me you think you can see more and better things than *I* can in my own scrying mirror? Is that what I hear you saying?"

"It was just one time. I was in a trance. But . . . yes, I do."

"Where did you get your mirror?"

The prisoner glanced over his shoulder. "A simple—very legal—shaving mirror."

John waved his hand. "I know you're lying about predicting the comet. You're lying to save yourself from the executioner, but I don't care about that because I think you're not lying about being *able* to predict the comet." He spread his hands. "I would like nothing more than to give you unending moments of my time, but as it is I have so much work to do, and your views are so against my own philosophy that I cannot see what more there is to be gained from this . . . suggested partnership. That is what you're suggesting, correct? That we work together?"

The prisoner coughed. "Will you give me a chance to prove myself?"

This was what John had been casting for, some desperate act to match his own desperation. He felt himself begin to smile but instead he hacked phlegm into a ball of wadded-up bedsheet. "Go ahead, then."

The man glanced up and out the window at the coral sky and for a long time he seemed on the verge of weeping. Unfair, the weight of expectation, John thought, but then each one of us is given his own special dreadfulness to endure. Better perhaps to have been born as he himself had been, the seventh son of third-generation Chief Orbital Doctors, and better perhaps to have been raised inside the faith, rather than however this man had been raised—surely only inopportune circumstances could have led him to such a pitiful line of work.

But John felt no special sympathy for the downtrodden. He accepted things as they came to him, and sometimes they were good and other times they were unsatisfying. He supposed he had some persistent wish that others should do the same. After all, he'd worked all his life at something he could neither see nor touch, and there was dignity in that—he knew it existed somewhere—but he could not expect a man like this prisoner, who'd spent his life elbow-deep in human guts, to understand that.

After a long silence, the prisoner closed his eyes and began to twitch like worm cut in half, one side of him shrinking from the other as if in awful pain. John watched. The show revealed as much as the prophecy. The prisoner was a good performer at least. But presently he collapsed in a heap on the desk chair and said, "I can't, I can't, sir, I can't see anything right now."

"Ah well. Would that we could call down precognition when it suited us. Mizar—" he began. "Take this fellow back to the jail—"

"But what if I were to tell you something I already saw? It's real, I have it written in my notes that they confiscated, I can prove to you I wrote it a long time ago."

John leaned back on his elbows and into the fluffy boat of the mattress and didn't speak.

The prisoner's eyes widened, and a peculiar blush went over his face. He looked to his shackled feet. "I don't know if I should say it."

"Then don't say it, man. I haven't got time for dithering, I've wasted hours already in a damnable swoon."

The prisoner nodded. "What I saw, or part of what I saw, when I was in the trance months ago, was a feminine wildfire ripping through this very spot, in tandem with the comet, or rather *in relation to* the comet, and I know that if you were to check with the, ah, ladies of this court you would find that they are all, to a woman, ah, bleeding at present."

John raised an eyebrow, his habit since childhood, which he had learned from imitating Mizar. He detested this gesture now but could not stop doing it. "O yes?"

The prisoner winced. "It's true. Check. I have full confidence."

John frowned. But then shook his head. "You believe these angels—you called them angels, correct?—revealed *that* to you? That the ladies are bleeding? And you're certain you're not insane? Who cares about the menses of the palace women?"

The prisoner said, "I am only a mouthpiece. Which is why you must see this as proof of my visionary skill. Even when I didn't know what I was seeing, I was seeing something. Now it all makes sense. The angels told me."

"That we shall certainly see." John said with a dry snort. But the prisoner's claim was so extraordinarily bewildering that he found he could not rightly select a look appropriate to the situation—he felt his face begin to twist downward into an even deeper frown, but just as quickly he tightened back up the edges of his mouth. Could it be true? It was easy enough to verify and after all, what had his own prayers and magic revealed? Ever?

This. Perhaps. Perhaps *this* man, small and roguish though he may be, was the very thing John had felt approaching without being able to name. And the king, how thrilled he would be if John could finally make an accurate prediction of the Return. That was the entire reason for the favoritism King Michael showed John, for his continued monetary generosity, why John alone of all the nine Orbital Doctors had his own castle, and the blessing of exemption from the royal court.

The king wanted that date.

John peered at the small man in the peacock blue, who appeared now to be on the verge of tears. "I—" The man began to talk again.

John stood abruptly. "Enough, my god. Mizar, find out if what this man tells us is in any way true. And please discover these notes to which he keeps alluding, if they in fact exist. And you." He paused, turning back to the prisoner. "What's your name?"

The man stared. "We don't just *tell* our names. Not out on the land."

"Then make one up, I don't give a damn. You're not on the land, you're here, about to be de-headed apparently. What does it matter if you tell your name?" He watched as the prisoner's face fell. "Now, now, you won't die yet, good man. At least not if what you tell me is true. We may be able to help each other." He snapped around to order Mizar to unchain the man, and was surprised to remember that he'd already ordered him away. John sulkily stepped to the exit, motioning to the prisoner. "Yes, come on then, you will hobble along after me. We will see how you fare at my mirrors, yes? Maybe your angel voices will return. There's no time like the present."

At the door, the guard leaned over gingerly and whispered to him through his lion-shaped mask. John could hardly understand him through the thick resin, so he gestured for the man to pull it aside. "Go on, what?"

"We've just had word that a new carnival has set up outside the palace walls," said the guard. He had a black mustache with particles of food clinging to the corners. "They are flying a black flag. They appear to be . . ." He frowned. "Outlaws. They're here in the wrong season. And more than that, there are many more than a normal carnival. It may be dangerous to send a messenger on the road to the palace compound."

John felt not alarmed, but strangely disappointed by this news, and fought the desire to return to bed. A moment before, he'd had a strategy—now he felt the old shapeless anxiety gnawing at him once again, for this new trouble surely portended something as bad or worse than the comet or the vision-having prisoner. "Yes," he mumbled, as the guard replaced his faceplate. "I see. Well, at least take this man to a room and have Mizar dress him in something other than these filthy clothes. We will check on the ladies when the threat has passed."

John watched as the prisoner was led away down the narrow steps, then returned to his window. And it was there, in the distance, under the curious blaze of the new comet: settled in the scrubby awfulness of the coastal expanse was a dense thicket of tents and booths and stages. This new encampment extended all the way to the sea—a great yawn of humanity, all bustling like ants under a huge, iridescent black flag. John gripped the ledge with fingers he could not quite feel. The earthworks and the line of flimsy watchtowers that served the Cape were dilapidated and had further deteriorated after a minor hurricane. But that had been years ago, now. King Michael was not a man who valued his military. John peered over the plain, his heart in his throat, before he turned his eyes back to the sky and had the absurd thought that it would be far better to be struck dead by a heavenly body than by a living one.

CHAPTER 7

THE THIRD QUEEN OF CAPE CANAVERAL

That evening, the girl was released from her cage. Three old women attendants came to Mr. Capulatio's tent. They said he had sent them. The girl stood on a padded footstool as they fussed with her gown. She watched as though from afar, like her body in this new dress was an experiment that could go horribly wrong. The oldest woman remarked: "How can an aged person like me keep straight all the queens at Cape Canaveral now? Now we have *three*—three queens!" She bleated laughter, her eyes catching the girl's mischievously. A woman who had seen so many things she no longer took anything seriously. Her laugh trailed off into a gasping chuckle that caught in the back of her throat. Without thinking, the girl drew back, afraid as ever of any kind of sickness. The crone shook her head slightly after wiping her mouth, as if to say *It's nothing,* and went back to pinning the dress with sharpened sticks.

The crones were dressed in elaborate drapings of otter pelts sewn in random places to dresses of thick brown fabric, with their gray hair wrapped around forms to keep it high and stiff. The girl wished Mr. Capulatio had given her younger attendants—girls her own age, who would make her laugh and tell her gossip. Like the illegal dancers in his carnival. Where had they gone? Were they here? Why hadn't he given her *those* girls?

She looked across the tent at Orchid, who sat reading at Mr. Capulatio's writing desk, ignoring the preparations. The crones kept creeping toward her in an attempt to dress her, too, but each time she waved them away brusquely. She was scouring stacks of papers and books, copying words occasionally into a slim book of her own. Every now and again, she stretched her hands over her head, exasperated, pulling her fingers through her hair and shaking it back down over the front of her pinched face.

The crones rustled with the girl's dress for a long time. It was sewn from material that looked very much like Mr. Capulatio's flag. In fact the girl thought it must be exactly the same. It took her some time to realize they weren't simply pinning it so they could work on it later: they were sewing her *into* it. They stitched two panels tightly up the center of her back, pulling mercilessly until she could hardly breathe. To distract herself, finally she gasped, "What are you looking for, Orchid?"

Orchid spun around on her chair and glared. "*They* were brought in for you. I am not your nursemaid."

"I thought you were supposed to teach me things."

A sneer crept across her lips. "You want to learn from me how to be his wife? I'm sure you're quite good at it already. I can only imagine what has gone on in my absence." She turned back to the desk, muttering, "O yes, I'm imagining it, have no doubt. If I were not so indebted to the cause I would not stand for this chicanery."

"Who are the other two queens? She said there were three now."

Orchid sighed elaborately. "What does he see in you? Your talk. Your face. Your body. You might as well be a yapping dog. I haven't got time for this."

Orchid's every reply made the girl more determined to engage her, although not for any reason beyond bothering her. "What are you doing?" she asked.

Orchid rose unexpectedly. Her slender body was very beautiful, the girl could not help but notice. The strong thighs, her hips, which flared like a carved instrument. "Well, since you insist on being infantile, let us teach you, then. Let us count the queens. First, there's me: I've been his queen-to-be since we were sixteen. That was after my mother, our Prophetess Lois, had . . . passed from this realm. But I guess he hasn't told you that story, either, has he?" Orchid looked away, her face betraying nothing. A crone poked the girl and entreated her to remain very still while she finished stitching the back of the dress. "Then there's the queen *inside* the palace," said Orchid. "She's the second queen, King Michael's wife, Alyson. She is the daughter of Marvel Parsons, the Hierophant. Terribly spoiled, so they say. I wouldn't know, personally. We've never met." She said this as though the girl should know there was no chance they ever would have met. "Alyson is the one you will usurp once our uprising begins. You'll probably have to de-head her yourself. That's what I'd do. It would make a decent show of authority."

She came nearer to the girl on her footstool with widened eyes. "But then . . ." She trailed off and leaned forward, speaking more quietly. "There is another. She's not a queen, exactly. The Pardoness." The word hung in the air, changing the room. The crones stopping sewing. They seemed to hold their breath.

"Who is the Pardoness?" the girl asked finally.

"Who is that! She asks who is that!" The old women bubbled with nervous laughter.

At this, the girl felt a frenetic darkening begin inside her, little shadows flitting past at a preposterous speed, but she kept her voice light. "How should I know who she is? I've never been here before," she said carefully. "My mother is a Walking Doctor who abandoned me. She told me only mad people live at the Cape. I don't know anything about anyone here."

Orchid nodded. "Poor girl, abandoned by everyone who's had charge of you. It cannot be *your* fault they all left you, can it?"

The girl flinched.

"*We* are all just people, though we may be queens. Me, Alyson, you. The Pardoness is different. She is descended from a man who once visited space. Do you understand that? What that means? She is a living relic. She lives in the palace compound, as has every one of her forebears since before there even was a palace. Kept mercifully apart from the world's hideousness. Michael houses her high above us all in a tower." Orchid nodded. "From which she dispenses Cosmic Justice."

Orchid went to the door of the tent and drew back the flaps. She pointed across Mr. Capulatio's vast carnival to the tallest and brightest minaret in the palace compound. "In Canaveral Tower. She has lived there since she was a child. We do not dispute her authority as a beacon of justice. David does not intend to dethrone her." She turned back and spoke flatly. "What we were talking about? O, the queens. And then there's you, apparently. The third queen. You will be the third queen, after tonight."

"Why do you accept the Pardoness's judgments if you don't like anything else about the Cape?"

Orchid let the tent flap close. "*I* don't know why. 'Why' is a question most are not fit to ask." She flung her eyes to the crones like a person tossing a stick for a dog, hoping they might give chase. They all laughed. Orchid said, "Not even me. I don't even know why you are to be David's queen."

"You mean instead of you?"

Orchid met her eyes. "Yes."

"Can't we both be queens?"

"O, would you shut up? I'm trying to read, *Your Majesty*. Perhaps you should be reading about the religion you are so blindly entering as a leader," she muttered, casting her eyes at the girl's pile of books. At once her face changed, and the girl knew she'd seen the book Argento had given her, *The True King*. Orchid leapt to her feet and went into the cage, which stood open now, and snatched out the hardbound volume and held it up with one hand. "This!" she cried. "You've had it the whole time!"

"That's mine!"

"Why did *you* have this? This is my finest piece of scholarship. It's everything I have ever learned about our history collected and retold for the ages."

"That's mine," the girl said again, this time coldly. She folded her arms over her chest.

Orchid hefted the book up and flipped to a certain page as though she'd known all along where she would find what she'd been looking for. The pinch between her eyes deepened. "Here. It reads just as

I remembered, of course it does. '*She is thunder, the perfect mind who rings in a brilliant age. A young sigil dressed all in white shall appear when at last the rockets have returned to earth, and this sigil shall sit enthroned during all the Days of Heaven.*' This is the passage David is using to justify your existence. But he is wrong. Wrong wrong wrong."

As the minutes passed and Orchid read and took furious notes, as the girl stood quietly while the crones sewed her dress, she couldn't help but feel sad for Orchid. This empathy was her downfall, she was beginning to recognize it, for it had happened with Mr. Capulatio as well; she had begun to love him. Overnight Orchid's whole world had changed—the girl could imagine it all too well.

But Orchid also frightened her: the particular violence of being a violent woman in the violent world. What was it like to cut off heads? She looked at Orchid and shuddered.

Then the girl felt sorry for herself more than anyone. Orchid appeared to be the only companion she would have in Mr. Capulatio's world.

Orchid turned back to her suddenly, and after a visible struggle, attempted to smile. She came over to the girl and put a gentle hand on her hair. "I suppose I cannot be angry at you for not knowing our religion. For never having read anything I've written. That would be very poor character on my part. David has already explained the difference between you and me: *you* are mentioned in scripture, but I am not. To put it simply, David believes you are more important than I am. So you are supposed to be his queen."

"But—"

She nodded. "And I will be a minor queen. A glorified concubine. But since in this case David is wrong, it occurs to me that something I have recorded for him is likewise wrong. Over the years I have misled him, though I did not mean to. I shoulder the entire responsibility for this error." She blinked her water-clear eyes. "My task now is to edit the offending text. If you will excuse me."

She turned back to the desk, but the crone with the tallest hair, who seemed in charge, gingerly steered Orchid to another stool and began dressing her as well, in a slightly less beautiful dress but one that was lovely all the same. Orchid scrunched her nose as they flocked around her. "I suppose it doesn't matter if I formulate my reinterpretation of the passage now, or after this 'wedding' or whatever he wants to call this rude display of bigamy that we are about to embark upon. He has always listened to reason and this time will be no different."

The girl lifted her arm so a crone could stitch under it. She understood why Orchid hated her. How sad it must be to give up everything, your power, your influence, your husband, and then be forced to serve the person to whom you gave it.

Orchid's dress slipped off her shoulders while they began pinning. She looked beautiful, the girl thought without wanting to, so unsettlingly angry and lovely. "I will tolerate you," Orchid said, again nearly reading the girl's mind. "For now."

The girl scowled. Mr. Capulatio had made his choice. Orchid was the loser. In spite of her pity, the girl felt grateful to be the one in the more beautiful dress. Even if she was not more beautiful and accomplished herself. Orchid gazed back at her for a while as though she understood those thoughts too, until finally she looked away.

CHAPTER 8

THE RIDER

John, the Chief Orbital Doctor, reconsidered his options, and sought Mizar to dispatch a rider to the palace compound. The carnival was far enough away, and the rider would be fast enough, he reasoned, that they would have their answer about the women's bleeding in several short hours. John pondered, if the odd little prisoner proved correct in his prediction, what did it mean?

Mizar, always sensitive to the plights of servants, insisted that the rider would be dangerously exposed on the plain.

"We do not even know yet if the outlaw carnival is a threat," John growled.

Mizar stared at him as though his master were eight years old once again, all flapping arms and ill-advised schemes. "Of course they are a threat, sir. What reason could they have to break the Law and return here out of season? The question is, would they attack a rider on the way from an insignificant country house?"

At that, John bristled. "I would hardly call Urania 'insignificant.' I have more scrying instruments here than probably anyone in the world and I would assume, given the circumstances"—and here he gestured to the light above—"that they would find my manor house most interesting. But why am I arguing against my own position?" he demanded, to which his servant merely smiled. Mizar had a manipulative streak. At last John sent him to prepare a hot drink and went to his office to wait.

John begrudged Mizar his little insult. It dampened his excitement. He was sensitive about Urania Castle, even though he was the only Orbital Doctor to have his own separate quarters. Even the Hierophant himself, the king's High Priest and advisor, lived inside the compound. But then let us be honest, John thought, gripping the windowsill in his office and looking into the courtyard. Urania was hardly a castle at all, though he had taken pains to make it appear as such.

It was all vanity. He was the last scion of a family to whom appearances had mattered, and so they mattered to John, even though ostentation was not a feature inherent to his character. Primarily, Urania was a place to keep his instruments. He maintained them meticulously, tucked beneath weathertight mechanical domes of his own design. This was indeed a battle, a philosophical one for him and a physical one for Mizar, for the domes were not ever completely fast despite their combined efforts, and at last John had been forced to admit he was no engineer. Now he cursed the rust grinding in the dome gears each time he cranked one open; he cursed the broad speckling of salt-ruin on the deteriorating instruments. They'd become the easiest place upon which to fixate his self-loathing. His disappointment in himself, which like a desolate satellite circled the mass of his being, pulled up tides of shame regularly. When he looked at his courtyard of once splendid instruments, which he still loved for their mathematics and precision, he cursed himself for being as unlike them as seemed possible. So fickle he was, incapable of discerning truth.

The news about the women's bleeding arrived in a flurry of hoofbeats on the gravel at Urania's gate, more quickly than John had anticipated. It was borne not by his own rider but by a tall and thin young man wearing an ill-fitting guard's uniform. Spotting him through the streaked glass of his office window, John fairly fell over himself to get outside, all thoughts of past failures washed away now by the hope that the prisoner had indeed made a *real* prediction. As

John threw a coat over his bedclothes, he shouted to Mizar to fetch the prisoner from his room.

The young guard's mount was an exceptionally fine roan-colored horse. The guard was reaching forward to swing the gate open himself when John called, "Ho! Not so fast! It's locked!" But the gate opened anyway, leaving John to sputter impotent protest to no one in particular.

The guard stood in the open gateway holding his horse's reins, a smile on his lips. "Lord Astronomer?" He made a small bow.

John cleared his throat. "Who are you? Where is my rider?" He narrowed his eyes. "Is that one of the Hierophant's horses?"

"I was sent by His Majesty Marvel Parsons to collect the prisoner you're interviewing." The man's accent was thick and hard to place.

"I hardly think so," John huffed. "Where is my man? I sent him with a specific question and I require a specific answer. I cannot release the prisoner to you until I have it, it's impossible."

"Well, the Hierophant outranks you," he replied blithely. "Sir."

"That's preposterous." Like most courtiers of his status, John had discovered that the best way to communicate with the lower classes was with a certain blustering indignation—it relieved them all of the apprehension that friendliness might be possible. "What is your name?"

"Juniper."

"That's a woman's name."

Another sanguine smile. "I've never heard that before. Where is the prisoner Tygo?"

"He's here," came Mizar's chirp from behind John. He scuffed toward them across the scrubby courtyard, around the reflecting pond with John's expensive fish, leading the prisoner by a short chain. The prisoner—Tygo—by now had been shorn of his leg-cuffs, given new clothes, and chained again at the hands with a set of much more functional manacles. The clothes seemed to greatly displease him (they were Mizar's and therefore ugly, being brown and far too long and also too tight in the upper arms and legs). Mizar handed John the prisoner's short chain and hurried over to open the gate wider.

Tygo nodded his head upward at the young guard. The other man did the same.

"If the Hierophant outranks me, it's only because of tradition. Michael has privileged my work for twenty years and more." John sniffed. "You would be too young to know that." John did not add that, in his view, Marvel Parsons was the upstart poisoner with the delicate hand who, thirty-two years before, during the reign of Michael's father Leander, had murdered John's own parents along with their entire retinue of dinner guests. They had numbered fourteen that dreadful evening, all dead before dessert. John had been good that day, and so was permitted to eat with Mizar in the kitchen with the servants, which had been a treat until it wasn't, when he realized how undignified it was. There was never proof of the Hierophant's hand in the affair, of course. Only the most cursory of inquiries had followed the deaths. No one was ever formally accused. But ever since John had been of an age to reason, he had suspected Marvel Whiteside Parsons. There was an air of menace around that man, a kind of radical but rational willingness to play the game to its logical end. In fact John somewhat admired the derring-do such drastic action had required. He'd never been overfond of his family anyway. "You can't take him now," he repeated.

"But I must."

"Does the Hierophant not look up?" John was flabbergasted. He pointed to the sky. "What traitor's interrogation could be worth more than discovering what *that* is? I have removed Tygo for the very immediate reason that he claims to be a visionary who predicted this light. You go straight back and tell your master that I simply refuse. He can come here himself if he disagrees."

Despite scrying with his magic bowls and all the evenings spent in rapt meditation, willing his body to open like a night-flower to the celestial plan, despite locating himself at the navel of the world that connected the earth magically to the heavens, despite how endlessly he gave of himself, there had always been something broken about John's faith. Some enormous failure of will. Something faltering about his belief. He did not know if that was the cause of his failure but he suspected it. *How* could he release a man who might be the genuine article?

Juniper's horse stomped the ground. Tygo looked at him pleadingly. John felt a dizzy alarm, as though the two of them—Tygo and himself—were about to embark on a journey for which they were not prepared. Tygo straightened his coat. They looked up into the vast sky overhead and the diffuse late afternoon sunlight throbbing beneath the gauze of clouds, and yet the comet beyond was brighter yet and more mysterious still, and choked John with a presentiment of danger beyond the physical. He could not explain it.

Tygo's face, apart from the star tattoos, was very pale. "I'll go back with him, if that's what I have to do."

"It's not your decision." John closed his eyes and opened them again.

"It's not yours, either," said Juniper.

Tygo said in a pleading voice, "You don't understand."

"No, *you* don't," Juniper shook his head.

John looked between the two of them, bewildered. "Let's take my carriage, then," he said slowly. "I will talk to Marvel myself. My god, this is a gigantic waste of time when we may have precious little—"

Mizar clicked his tongue. "The outlaws on the plain, sir—"

He whirled around. "This miscreant got here all right, didn't he? I assume we will be fine."

Tygo laughed unhappily. "You should never assume anything."

John was already stalking back to the house to put on decent clothes. "I assume things only when blundering idiots force me to."

From John's vantage point in his open cart, in the darkening gray and green afternoon, he observed a crowd of carnival people gathering down by the shoreline. Peeking from between the dunes as the mule-drawn carriage bumped along was an impressive collection of booths and tents. There was a raft of some kind down there, some structure being erected a ways out in the water, past the breaking surf. The people milled about like they were waiting for something.

The outlaw carnival winked in and out of sight. Still, John could hardly believe his eyes; there were so many people by the shore, more than there were palace guards and infantry at the palace, that was certain. The landscape before their own carriage lay bare, exposed and open all the way to the Cape compound, and he suddenly felt they were very stupid to have set out upon this Uland. The guard riding his horse beside them gave him little comfort. If anything his uniform might attract attention.

Mizar, unflappable, did not slow or hasten the carriage, but muttered gently from the driver's bench, "They're building something down there, aren't they? If it's for a good purpose I'll be most surprised."

John's mouth was dry. His heart lurched but he kept his face expressionless. "Surely the palace guards are watching these outlaws."

Beside him in the back seat Tygo was kicking the wooden floorboards rhythmically with his heels. John saw in his face a firm determination to distract himself from their immediate task—it seemed he was tapping out some familiar tune, but John could not place it. The noise set his teeth on edge.

These ill omens will come to naught, he assured himself, they must, all of them. The comet, the prophetic prisoner, the outlaw carnival. All at once he couldn't imagine the idea that he and this ignominious man might be the only people in the world who could interpret the meaning of these strange occurrences. It seemed dreadful, and yet this was how the world worked, wasn't it? The world gave you nothing, until that nothing added up over the years in some obscure way to produce *something.*

"Speed up, you fool," he grumbled to Mizar, just so someone would be talking. "Do you think these criminals would not grab us for a ransom?"

"I have no idea, sir," said Mizar, and smiled. His knotty hands flicked the reins, and the two mules drawing the wagon roused themselves minimally, protesting with alternating percussive snorts. "You know," said John to Tygo after a time. "I confess I thought you were lying before. About predicting the comet." He considered. "I'm sure I don't need to tell you that you have a very dishonest face."

"Others have let me know."

"But do tell me truly, do you think we will be snatched from the road, here? Can you predict that?" John laughed uneasily. "Because I have a worry we will."

Tygo kept his eyes facing forward. "Prediction doesn't work like that."

"How then does it work? I'm curious."

He sighed. "I don't know. I told you, I'm a Surgeon. Ask me to pull out your bowel and have it function in a sack beside you for weeks on end and I can do that, I'd *like* to do it, it gives me joy to do it. But I don't know how to predict anything. It just happens. I went to sleep, I had a dream, I woke up in a trance and my shaving mirror showed me the comet. It showed me . . ." He paused, embarrassed. "Well, the angels showed me . . ."

John rolled his eyes.

Tygo said, "The proof is here before your face. The ladies are bleeding. You'll see. It will be just like I told you."

"You could have magicked those ladies at any point and this 'prediction' will be nothing more than a trick you devised to get yourself released. I wasn't born yesterday."

Tygo balled his fists and unballed them. "I told you, I don't believe in your stupid star-magic. I believe in science, sir, and that's the end of it. No spells, no magic, no bloodletting, no executions, no rocketships. None of that is for me. I don't think it *works*. Science is the first and the last, and whatever else there is in the world has got no business influencing anything important, least of all human lives. So call me a liar, by all means. I'm used to it. Or call me a con-man. But never say I've done magic. Nothing insults me more. I've spent my whole life hiding from the Law and groveling for my head when I'm caught. I'd slit my throat before I did magic, and maybe I will anyway in the end. Just to get away from you people." He spread his hands to encompass the Cape and all its environs, and he shook his head. "You're all morons."

A door in John's chest seemed to crack, and a peculiar light came in. He chuckled again. There was a darting quality to this man, a venomous puppy-snap that was appealing for all its sharpness. John supposed the prisoner was very clever indeed and yet disgusted by his own cleverness, an attribute John himself rather enjoyed, since he felt his own nature to be similar. "My friend, it's your mouth that's gotten you condemned, not your fool beliefs. But you do at least acknowledge there were once shuttles, correct? For godsakes, we have abundant proof. It's not as though we've based our Laws on nothing. You can see the launch sites yourself, man. We have people who can trace their ancestors to that time."

"Thousand-year-old structures you've rebuilt to suit your tastes don't mean a damn thing to me. Your asinine executions and dumping of poisoned blood have destroyed the better part of this land. And this land is *vast,* Mr. Astronomer. I can't begin to tell you the damage your priests have done. We'll all die of Bent Head thanks to them." The cart trundled over a bump and Tygo slid ungracefully into the side of the carriage, but righted himself and continued with a rueful smile. "It's a farce played out with an immensity that staggers the mind. If I hadn't given my life to opposing your idiotic Laws, I would've killed myself decades ago."

John nodded. "Is it true that you can heal people?"

Tygo's smile faltered. "My mother is a famous Walking Doctor. Or was. Maybe she's dead now. I wouldn't know."

John raised his eyebrows. "She taught you your Surgery?"

Tygo did not answer for a long time. Outside their carriage, the slender black scrim-lip of the marsh lapped at grass mere feet from the cart path, and the mules' hooves sucked up the grasses, and further beyond them a bedraggled pine tree stuck above lowland bushes. John peered at Tygo, who blinked slowly and tugged the hair down over his ear-holes. It was a habit, John noticed. "I came here to find my fortune," Tygo said with a straight face. "I'm a con-man. I thought I already told you." He grinned finally. "And. My mother hates me. She never taught me anything."

John nodded. "I have always enjoyed liars. I'm not sure why."

"They're much more fun."

"So you're *not* a Surgeon?"

"I go around as one. It makes good money. Finally they picked me up for it. Now I'm kicking myself, eh?"

John realized he was spellbound before this man, lost, almost in the way of a child whose father has journeyed to many unimaginable places. "Why do I disbelieve you?"

Tygo smiled wider. "Maybe you have trouble trusting people." He looked away. "I just like to travel. That's all. This was all a big mistake. Now I could lose my head."

John discovered that he was smiling too. "Except your prophecy. That is real."

"Well. Yes."

They rode the rest of the way to the palace in startled silence, the bloat of friendliness suddenly distending the air between them like a rude noise. This strange comfort struck the astronomer as ill-advised, for what good could friendship do him now, when it had never done him any good before? And as he thought this, his eyes were searching the countryside at the same moment, looking for outlaw riders or carnival men or legions of Law breakers. But no one came, and no one followed them.

CHAPTER 9

MARVEL AND THE ASTRONOMER

Following his interview with the Pardoness, Marvel Whiteside Parsons marched to his own chamber at the top of Endeavour Tower, where his window shades remained drawn, even though a wintry dusk was rapidly descending. He must have a moment to think. The cool gloom entered him like a trickle of water down his throat. He breathed a few times.

As soon as he'd stepped from beneath the shadow of Canaveral Tower, a servant brought him a note bearing the startling news that an outlaw carnival had set up on the plain, just between the palace compound and the shore. King Michael was unconcerned, the note promised. Marvel knew that meant nothing. Michael was always unconcerned—by worldly matters, at any rate. He was the sort of king who would fine the carnival rather than make an example of them for returning to the Cape out of season.

Marvel, for his part, could not help but suspect their arrival had everything to do with the light in the sky.

Why else would a carnival come back during the winter season? It was one of the oldest parts of their Law that the land should rest after summer carnivals, so the blood would have time to work its magic in the earth. It had been written by Huldah herself.

Was Juniper a spy for this outlaw carnival? Had he lied about coming from Kansas? And William Tygo, the earless prisoner from Kansas, why was he really here? No one just *came* from Kansas to be a Walking Doctor at the Cape. The deathscapes—even with a Walking Doctor's maps, one wouldn't risk such a journey without a reason.

At his desk, an enormous solid wood heirloom from the king's family, Marvel rifled unread papers absently. There was much to be done. Purpose had been his comfort, always. Even now his instinct was to *do* something more, to create some motion that would satisfy him.

But instead he attempted to wait. And think.

The smart choice would be to leave immediately. It was what he would tell himself to do, if he were his own advisor. There were too many coincidences, too many novel happenings. It must mean something. Leave, he said to himself, just pack your bag and leave now. He'd thought he could use Juniper as a guide in the deathscapes but there was no time now to ascertain the exact nature of his treachery.

Unless Marvel had him tortured.

Then, if Juniper truly had come from Kansas, Marvel would bring him along as a guide.

He sat down. He took a breath.

But that would be too dangerous. How could he be sure Juniper wouldn't murder him in the night? Marvel was fifty one, large and healthy, but no one could survive a head bashed to a bloody pulp by a tree limb. Or a throat slitting.

It was best he go alone. Now.

But the poisonous land. He didn't trust any Walking Doctor's maps, didn't trust himself to remember how he had crossed the deathscapes at fourteen—it had been luck, pure and simple, though back then he'd believed it was a divine blessing for killing the Mystagogue. He didn't trust a carnival man to take him because they often made mistakes in their navigation. Whole carnivals died all the time, it was well known.

And if Marvel did make it to Kansas, seat of Dread? What then? Where the gruesome cows still lurched on their cloven hooves, eating the dead and the living indiscriminately, where dark monks did dark magic and prayed for the end of the world? Marvel could hardly imagine it.

Only that morning, he'd assumed he'd soon make the journey alone, but finally doing so was not as easy as planning for it. He had known it would not be, and still he had not imagined he would feel such fear.

Marvel stared blankly at the desk. It had been Michael's father Leander's desk, and many other kings' before him, and was a thing of great beauty. Marvel had believed for years that he should give it up—he was an ascetic now. It was not his, of course, which lessened his guilt. Hewn from mahogany centuries before, deeply varnished and nearly as wide as it was long, it bore many of his tinctures and oils, and accounts, diagrams for magical rites, Michael's infernal horoscopes (how the king loved having that silly astronomer, John Sousa, draw up horoscopes for him, a habit Marvel found particularly repellent).

He picked up a bottle. The liquid could become poison if he wished, with only a few drops from another glass dropper. When, at the tender age of nineteen, he had achieved his first assassination for Leander, he had been very unskilled. He had accidentally killed an entire dinner party, and very nearly also murdered John Sousa, then just a boy. The intended victim had been Sousa's mother, pregnant by Leander and becoming very shrill about it. John Sousa had hated Marvel ever since, of course. As was his right.

He rang a bell for a servant, turned around in his chair, and opened his shades. There were the outlaws, camped down by the shore, not beside the compound wall where they usually set up camp when they brought their yearly tributes. In fact, the outlaws were very close to the first watchtower in the defense line, which was barely visible from Marvel's window. This was intentional, he supposed; the earthworks were long neglected. Why should the outlaws fear an unmanned defense line?

They had no intent to surprise, obviously.

The servant knocked. Marvel's knees cracked when he stood. He pulled open the slot on his chamber door. A middle-aged man with yellow hair whose name Marvel could never recall looked at him nervously. "You called, Majesty."

"I need a man to ride out to that carnival on the plain and discover their business. They shouldn't be here." He spoke as though no one should be worried.

"That has already been ordered by the king. The riders will be back shortly. But I have more news for you."

"Proceed, then."

"A guard has returned with the Chief Orbital Doctor. And a captive in chains. They wait for you in the Receiving Room."

"I didn't send for Sousa. I don't want to see him now."

"He would not *not* be seen, sir."

"Tell him to go away."

The servant bowed. "I would very much like to, but he's in a bad temper and he says he has something very important to tell you about the . . . comet, he's calling it."

It would not do to insult John Sousa. He was unfortunately one of King Michael's favorites. The Sousas had been at Cape Canaveral a thousand years. John had harbored an especial loathing for him since Marvel had registered distaste at the expense of Urania, John's gaudy manor castle. Had the astronomer *truly* needed his own observatory, a castle in miniature, with all the contraptions and instruments his heart desired? Marvel hadn't thought so. By that time, the extravagance of the Cape had worn him down, and he was rejecting plans for improvement everywhere. But Michael had been happy enough to override Marvel's judgment, with the caveat that the Astronomer should feed and house any and all of the numerous foreign Orbital Doctors who might come to cast yet more horoscopes and make yet more detailed predictions of the Return Date; it was, after all, His Majesty's passion to know the exact Day and Time.

"I will see them," Marvel mumbled, and slid shut the viewing slot.

He wanted to pray. He had, in past times of confusion, prayed before any decision. But today he felt empty of magic.

His rooms were paneled in stained wood, because the rooms in Huldah's Black Tower in Kansas had been made of volcanic rock and were very dark and close. Since he was a boy, work meant a dim room. Daylight was time off, a game, a ride on a horse. But Marvel's eye was drawn now to a gray trapezoid of light that had fallen on the floor when he pulled up the shades, and he went to it and knelt. His hands on the bare floor looked suddenly old to him, and he closed his eyes.

At the moment of his un-kingly birth in the Black Watchtower, his mother the nun had been nearing thirty-four years of age and had been attempting to have a child for seven years. Marvel had learned her age from a compendium of royal personages he found in the Tower library. She had been born of a family who claimed never to have lost a single person to Bent Head, and had become a nun of her own volition when she was only twelve years old. Later, the Mystagogue had her thrown from the Black Tower. The volume stressed her piety, her beauty—she was called the most beautiful woman in Kansas. A striking drawing of her accompanied her biography in the compendium, which showed her to have wide-set eyes and a square face. Straight dark hair plaited like a farm-girl's, with the half-moon fringe that all the nuns at the Black Watchtower wore in those days. Beneath the drawing was written her name: Nasa Whiteside.

He had since observed a very good likeness of that face upon the visage of his own daughter Alyson, King Michael's second wife. Alyson was a woman very much like the record described Nasa: libidinous, gorgeous, querulous, athletic. Above all else and in most situations easily bored. Marvel was as proud of her beauty as he was ashamed of her shallowness. She drank palm wine to excess with her handmaids and had bred a line of small dogs since she was nine years old, improving their appearance markedly in each generation. Other courtiers bought them from her now, so a parade of small black dogs with ribbons tied behind their ears was a feature at any court gathering.

Alyson had caught the king's eye (if such a thing can be said, for it was questionable that any woman or man anywhere had ever truly distracted Michael from his spiritual quest) after the unfortunate death of his first queen, Rachel Moonstorm. Rachel had been allowed to "fall from a tower" since she had not conceived a child in ten years of marriage and she came from a noble family too powerful to risk angering with a divorce. It had been Marvel's idea. Michael, reluctant because he actually loved her, had seemed unhappier since then, but it was not a matter that could be rectified by anything but time.

Marvel—gently—suggested that Alyson might make a lovely bride for him. Michael never asked why Marvel himself had sired only one child; perhaps he sensed Marvel's attentions ran in another direction. Children were a distraction to a religious man, anyway. And yet Marvel loved his daughter. He tried not allow himself to think of what might happen to her if she, too, failed to conceive for Michael. She had only been queen a few years. There would always be Michael's inattention to blame it on. He was forever at his meditative walking. Or having his horoscope made. Impractical and kind. The king's nature irked Marvel as much as it inspired him. He had controlled things for Michael for the better part of twenty-five years.

If Marvel left, however, Alyson would have to fend for herself.

He would write her something that explained why. He did not know what to say yet. But when he did, he would write. He might even invite her to join him, though he knew she would not.

Standing, Marvel dusted off his knees. So many hands holding back the pieces of his heart. So many people he would betray if he left. So many dangers he would face, alone or with Juniper as his guide. But truly, he had already made the choice. He felt an urgency now, a gift from the heavens to move him forward.

He went to his desk to mix poisons.

The Receiving Room was in Endeavour Tower, several levels below Marvel's private quarters. The chamber required formality to achieve its purpose, which was to intimidate and impress, so Marvel had kept all the fine chairs, the woven carpets, the embroidered hangings recording the Cape's history. Some of them were centuries old. The king's chair sat on a raised dais alongside another, smaller chair and Marvel sat there unself-consciously. Someone had to. Michael never used this room.

Finding his company waiting for him, he strode straight past the chair and only faced them once he had arranged himself. There stood three men of vastly different ranks: Juniper, still dressed in his shabby guard's uniform and now covered in dust from riding; Tygo, earless, wearing new clothes that didn't fit; and John Sousa, who looked as he always did—like a man who was so far from knowing he was good-looking as to persuade everyone that he wasn't. It rankled Marvel, that obliviousness. John's dress was, as ever, impeccable and fussy, though Marvel suspected this was entirely due to his overcapable manservant. Sousa was more than convinced of his own brilliance, however, and as soon as Marvel had seated himself in the grand chair, John said, "Do you have any idea what a nuisance you've caused me? What danger you've put us in to travel here? When there is an outlaw carnival camped just minutes away? Damn you. I have tolerated you forever, seemingly forever. I won't anymore. And that is all I have to say."

"You came a long way to say it, then," Marvel replied in a dry voice.

"Indeed I damn well did come. Because your man compelled me. The prisoner and I are at work on . . ." He sputtered, began to pace. "On a thing that could be everything. Do you understand? The light in the sky? Have you *seen* it?"

Marvel looked on with an icy stiffness.

"I want to talk to Michael," Sousa said at last.

"I don't think so. He is at his meditations. Tell me what this is about, because I have urgent need of this prisoner at the moment and will send you away."

Tygo paled, but mastered it so quickly that no one but Marvel noticed. Marvel leaned forward to get a better view of those ear-holes. Tygo shook his hair over them on purpose. Juniper was gaping at the wall-hangings, the floors, which were made of polished lime-stone and inlaid with mosaics of the shuttles, and the ornately carved chairs. A bench at one side of the room was covered in dark green silk that Marvel had always liked. Juniper looked at it. He might be from Kansas indeed if this ornamentation appalled him. Or he could be from anywhere else in the world. Marvel's head had begun to hurt.

"I have need of Tygo as well," Sousa was protesting. "More so, I say, than you. He's told me that he predicted this comet, he has writ-ings that prove it. I was skeptical. It seems a ploy to save himself. But as further proof, he's offered another prediction, one that I am at pains to discover the truth of. *That* is the most important matter at hand."

"I would say discovering the nature of the outlaw carnival is the most important matter at hand."

"And you would be mistaken, as you usually are." Sousa flashed his teeth in what Marvel supposed was meant as a smile, but which came off nothing like one. "These occurrences are connected. Have no doubt. If this convict has predicted the comet's arrival, then there is a chance we can ascertain the Return Date. Do you understand? We will know once and for all. We could *know*."

Marvel's certainty that the Return—if it happened at all—would happen in Kansas was firm, but he couldn't say it aloud. "The day that you could tell me anything I don't already know has not yet dawned, Astronomer. Michael may be in your thrall, but that's why I'm here, to make sense of the preposterous. You've calculated for twenty years, yet we've never had the Date from you. Why would you suddenly know it now?"

Sousa pointed to the heavens and then flung his hands to his sides. "I'd say there's your reason. Things are a bit different now."

Marvel snapped, "What is the prediction you're trying to prove?"

"There are two, I said. Weren't you listening? The prisoner claims he recorded this . . . comet, this *stella nova,* whatever it is, in his journals. They were confiscated when he entered the prison."

"Well, then, they are gone." Marvel shrugged. "Our common practice is to destroy the belongings of the condemned."

Tygo closed his eyes like he was in pain.

"Of all the idiotic excuses," Sousa exclaimed. "I simply disbelieve it. You expect me to believe that all prisoners' effects are burned with the trash?"

"I don't expect you to believe anything. This prisoner is only a Walking Doctor, why should we keep his filth around? He is to be executed forthwith."

Sousa, growing ever more annoyed, looked from Tygo to Juniper, who seemed somewhat bewildered, then came forward alone and spoke in a low voice. "Very well. I should have known you would have some bureaucratic reason for doing what you do. The prisoner's second prediction is more sensitive, and I've already sent someone to find out if it's true." Now he whispered. "The prisoner has informed me that all the ladies in the compound are bleeding in the feminine way."

Marvel knitted his brow. "What?"

"They are *bleeding.* In the feminine way."

Marvel stared at Tygo. Tygo met his gaze evenly. Those ears were the Mystagogue's work, or at the very least an apostle of his. Which meant Tygo's presence could not be accidental. The Mystagogue's priests did not simply run away. There was no escape from *that* place.

It was indeed strange that three monumental things had occurred at once—the comet, the outlaw carnival, and now this man who claimed he could heal people and predict things. Marvel's blood turned. He must secure his pardon. There was absolutely no going without it. He was too superstitious now, in his old age, to risk his salvation. He said, "Your name is William Tygo, do I have that right?"

"*A* name I have is William Tygo."

"You're a Surgeon?"

Tygo looked at Sousa before he looked at Marvel again, a fact that did not escape him. "The very best. My mother was Gimbal. The Witch, they called her. She crossed the continent in her youth. You won't have heard of her, you being religious lunatics. But others will have." He glanced at Juniper hopefully, but the young guard stared directly ahead.

"You can perform Surgery?"

"With my eyes closed."

He nodded. "I have a task for you, then. A very important person in this palace is in need of a complicated surgery. You will do it. Perhaps in the process you will save your own life."

"No, no," interrupted Sousa. "I doubt he is a Surgeon, but I'm beginning *not* to doubt that he's a visionary, and I must have my proof. Today. I want an answer about the bleeding."

Marvel chuckled. "You are very much in demand, William Tygo. It couldn't be that you say what you need to say in order to please whatever person you're trying to win over. Never that, eh?"

Tygo smiled. "Of course it's that."

"So you admit you are *not* a Surgeon?" Marvel raised his eyebrow.

"This is incredible," Sousa said. "The time we are wasting! I will go to Michael myself this instant if you do not release Tygo into my custody. You know I'll do it. And you know Michael will take my side."

He was right, of course. Michael was obsessed with the horoscopes Sousa drew for him on a near daily basis, no matter how Marvel had tried to dissuade him from the practice. In Marvel's experience, horoscopes relied nearly entirely on their interpreter: this was why the Mystagogue had hated them. When John Sousa interpreted them, they contained all the deleterious possibilities the heavens could dream up. Marvel frowned at the disagreeableness of the situation.

Then he frowned at Tygo, the hard nubs of his eyes boring into the smaller man like parasites. It was better not to involve Michael at all right now—Michael's gullibility would make things harder for Marvel. The king would ask, simply, why it was so important that Marvel send an illegal doctor to the Pardoness. And Marvel would have no answer.

In a black mood, he dismissed them, but not before Sousa's messenger burst in with the news that the ladies of the palace were bleeding, each one, profusely. At his words, Sousa turned somewhat dazedly to Tygo, who had gone motionless. Sousa winced. "Ah. It is true, then. I . . . actually, I don't know if I had expected it to be true. Well." He laughed softly.

The messenger informed the room that Queen Alyson was very keen to hear the reason for their bleeding. Incredibly, Sousa turned to Marvel, as if for guidance. Tygo appeared to have sprouted a glitter of wetness in his eyes.

"What are you waiting for?" Marvel growled. "My daughter has summoned you."

"I'm hardly ready to see the queen. My clothes—And I must take Tygo back to Urania so we can begin work. The Return—"

"You are an idiotic man, Sousa. If you've gotten what you wanted and yet still refuse to take it, I have absolutely no sympathy for you." He stood and smoothed his cassock down over his legs. "Leave me." They did not move. At last he stormed to the door, beckoning Juniper to follow him. "Tygo, you will answer to me after this interview. Mark that. My man will come for you. I will hear your story. I should have heard it in the jail when I first had the chance." He slammed the door.

Should have, indeed. Marvel Whiteside Parsons decided in that moment that he hated John Sousa. He hated Michael. All of them. He wanted only to be a good man. To pray in peace at the center of the universe. He wanted to be away from them all, but through some confluence of duty and curiosity and filial love, he had not brought himself to leave.

When he reached the bottom of the tower and burst onto the world again, it was nearly dark. The sky above was the color of a rotten lime, striated with thin wintry clouds, and there was the comet, the *stella nova,* Sousa had called it.

Juniper looked up too, his face unreadable. “Do you think it could be the shuttles?” he asked. “That’s what folk are saying. Even the outlaws.”

“How do you know what the outlaws are saying?”

“I heard some other guards say that. I don’t know if it’s true.”

Marvel did not reply. For the briefest moment, he entertained the thought that the incredible light was a harbinger of deepest darkness, a comet, a last burn of radiance before a final calamity befell the earth and humankind. It must happen sometime, perhaps now. The thought was black and he liked its blackness, reveled in it for a few precious moments before he shook it off.

“Take Tygo to the Pardoness whenever Sousa is finished. Send me a message when you are there with him, and I’ll come.”

Juniper nodded. Marvel went to find Michael. The king would hear what Marvel wanted him to hear before he heard anything from anyone else.

CHAPTER 10

THE CARNIVAL

Upon the advent of darkness, the landscape of the camp was studded with bright diadems, each lonesome fire leaping up and up into the gathering dusk, inviting booth dwellers to gather around them, murmuring and warming themselves as they waited for the ceremony. The girl stared out on them from the warmth of their tent, which was set higher than the others because Mr. Capulatio would be the king. She listened to crones behind her fixing dandelion tea and then sipping it ponderously. Their slurping gave her comfort as she contemplated just how many people were spread out before her in this dimly lit carnival of carnivals. Waiting for her to become queen. She felt the weight of her iridescent black wedding dress, which flowed down her legs and pooled about her feet on the beautiful carpets covering the ground. She had never dreamt of anything so luxurious in her life.

She had never known things like this fabric could exist. All she'd owned herself had come first from her mother (and that was little enough), then from Argento, who never gave her anything of value except Cosmas the Head, whose forehead was now embroidered with the unicursal hexagram and the Third Eye spell, so she couldn't even trust *him* not to tell her secrets. But Mr. Capulatio had given her so many things already: this dress, and jewels, and hats with feathers and even a pair of azure gloves he said were four hundred years old. *Do you know how old that is, can you imagine that?* he'd asked. And she had answered no, she could not imagine. He told her they were made from a kind of plastic fabric so delicate that she must never wear the gloves or even touch them, for fear they might flake away to nothing. He'd shown them to her one night while the carnival was still on the road; he opened a glass box inlaid with smooth bright blue rocks and displayed the gloves to her with great care. They lay upon a soft pillow. He lifted them ever so gently up, and turned them over and over in his hands, before finally placing them in a different box, this time the one where he kept her other belongings: the black amber brooch, the Head of Cosmas. He locked it and put it high on a shelf where she couldn't reach it. He said she would wear the gloves only one time, when they ascended into the heavens, so it wouldn't matter then if they disintegrated because they would disintegrate anyway because of the shining force of the light and beauty that would envelope them and raise them up. The girl thought the words insane, but beautiful when he spoke them.

She stood at the tent flap now, running her fingers over the watery texture of her dress almost obsessively as she gazed out at the land. Orchid had been forced by the crones to finish her preparations in her own tent, and had not taken the hardbound book because it did not belong to her. The girl felt the strange book at her back now, nearly pulsing with importance. She had been enjoying it, all the fantastical stories she had never heard before. But then she'd discovered it had been written by *that* woman.

She went over to Mr. Capulatio's desk and opened the book again, though she did not know why. The first page said:

THE TRUE KING

By An Executionatrix

New ages shall be rung in like thunder, by a perfect mind.

She flipped through the pages, the words spilling across them perfectly formed—the girl could read, but she could write nothing but the inane sigils her brother had forced her to learn, curses and charms.

What could that verse mean? Where had it come from? What did any of it mean? *Why* had he had a wife already and not told her? She was jealous again.

She closed the book.

Soon, all around her came the low singing of the men and the sounds of cooking and eating as the carnivalers enjoyed their evening meals. But there was more: among the tents and booths there were other wagons, heavier ones, pulled by big horses that now stood hobbled here and there between campsites, with bags of feces swaying heavily at their backsides, and these wagons were loaded with clubs and maces and guns, and the girl knew (but O, hadn't she known since the beginning?) that Mr. Capulatio's carnival was here to make war, and that other carnivals had come to join him in the war, and all at once she felt a certainty that the war would begin *tonight*. It would begin with the marriage, because he had been waiting for proof of his own divinity and he believed she was that proof.

Maybe if she did not marry him, there would be no war. Maybe he would give up and return to wherever he came from. A hut on a beach, maybe. He might slink off in the night and live out his life as an ordinary Executioner. Maybe she and Orchid wanted the same thing, for her not to be the queen. She tugged at her dress again. It was so tight and hot.

Then a restless breath seemed to pour across the carnival at once, like a birdflock rising in a single heaving motion. The people were drawn like puppets from their fire-rings to the center aisle, and the girl squinted into the darkness and saw that it was Mr. Capulatio himself at whom they were staring, striding across the camp toward his tent. He seemed to wave when he caught sight of her silhouette in the doorway. She glanced over her shoulder to be sure he was not addressing someone else. But of course he was waving at her, she was about to marry him. When he came closer, she could see he was smiling.

She thought she could number every tooth in his smile—they had touched their faces together so many times already in the early half-lit mornings, when he would rest his head under her chin and hold her very tightly. She felt she knew every place on him by heart. He was dressed for the wedding, in clothes she couldn't have imagined before this moment.

When he reached her, he took her hands in his. "Do you like my clothes, Queenie?" She couldn't stop staring at them. He did a little turn for her and then bowed. "These are real sharkskin from a real marsh shark," he said, pointing to the pants. They were smooth and dove-gray and so soft-looking. She nodded.

He laughed quietly. "Do you like your dress?"

She said nothing. He smiled wider. "That's why I love you, my almost wife! You don't need to talk to make your point. At first I was confused by it, but now I see this is precisely why we are a match made in heaven. It makes me gladder than you can know." He hugged her close and she wrapped her arms around his body, which was strong and warm. She could feel the smoothness of their fabrics rubbing together. He gathered up a handful of the dress and shook it at her. "Silk," he said, as though the word itself were magic, and who knew, perhaps it was? "Come, my bride. Let us be married."

They clasped hands again and he led her across the carnival, picking his way through tent poles and staked Heads and all the grotesqueries that accompanied the making of Heads, the basins of herbed water, the sand pits where they dried, and also they walked past ropes hung with curing meat, past herds of tiny goats, past a teenage boy with a bow and arrow who gazed at the girl with undisguised lust. She had just met eyes with him when Mr. Capulatio pulled her along more roughly.

They passed many faces—hopeful, skeptical, kind, hungry. The insistent attention began to make her even more nervous, so she kept her face down, watching the flamelight and the shadows twisting together on the ground while they walked, and she concentrated on lifting her skirt high enough to keep from tripping. Onlookers soon began to follow them as they proceeded out of the camp. Suddenly, bewilderingly, a sizable group had fallen in behind them, following them toward the ocean. The people in these carnivals were wilder than the ones in Argento's, with tangled hair and faces painted like stars. Some of them wore hardly any clothes, others were dressed in full robes and crystal crowns. They even seemed to walk with more purpose than the people in her brother's carnival. Like they had something to lose.

A crowd surrounded them now. Many of them kept looking from

her to the sky, and when she too looked up she saw, almost directly above her head, a bend of light arcing toward the earth. A returning rocket, just as Mr. Capulatio had said? It was brighter than she'd imagined. Or a comet? She had never seen one, but she had not imagined it would look like this, purple-white and motionless. Like a held breath. She kept her hand loose in Mr. Capulatio's as they walked. The soft mumbling of the crowd passed from her attention, as did all things except that light, and she watched it slowly burn for what felt like the longest moment, while inside her chest rose up a noise; in time, she realized it was the pounding of her heart. What terrible wonder could this be, what reckoning spilling over the heavens? And in spite of herself she felt of a piece with it, this light, for it had brought her with it to this place, on this night. As if it had been destined forever, as if it had existed always.

CHAPTER 11

QUEEN ALYSON

John had met Queen Alyson many times, and yet each meeting renewed his terror of her, not because she was herself terrifying but because she burned with a need to understand—not him, no, and not his work, and nor did she seek a definite prophecy about the Return or the endless remedial horoscope calendars her husband Michael so loved. But there was something fixed and slow and deep about her that caused him to trip up his words, to poorly explain even the most explicable events, to stumble about her chamber like a hyperactive child, sweeping his arms along with the peaks and valleys of his lecture. He lectured her, he could not help it, and her appearance of boredom never failed to horrify him.

She mostly called upon him to explain practical things: why, for instance, were all the ladies of the palace bleeding at once?

Tygo waited in the hallway in the care of another lion-masked guard, who had yanked him hard by the arm to stop him from entering the queen's grand chamber, as though Tygo posed some immediate threat, although it seemed plain to John that he did not. This evening, John faced Queen Alyson alone. She was gazing at him with her I-dare-you eyes, the way he assumed she must look at everyone, for what was he to her? A weak sneeze of a man. The king, although nearly middle-aged now, was broad and somewhat tall; Alyson was his second wife—the first queen, Rachel, had fallen from one of the palace minarets, or that's what everyone said, and frankly John had not cared for her, either; she'd been inbred as a lapdog and ugly as well. Alyson seemed somewhat young, but John was not certain she was. She had the sort of face that could exist mostly untouched for several decades, with faint lines and freckles across the forehead exacerbated by smoking, which she did in excess and was doing at the moment, holding her slender moonstone pipe a foot and a half from her lips. Her hair was the darkest brown and straighter than a normal person's hair—another artifact of inbreeding? He suspected. She was the daughter of Marvel Parsons but cared little for magic or ceremonies. She preferred to spend her time at golf.

"Your Beauteousness, forgive us. Your discomfort was not our intent."

She watched him. "Okay." Her pipe adularesced when she drew smoke through it, a throbbing opal, blue with gem-light. "I didn't say it was."

He squirmed. "O. Yes. Well . . ."

The queen waited. She had a girl's manner of waiting for him to speak first, a paroxysm of disinterest upon her even when she herself had asked the question. He wondered how she thought of him, if she thought of him at all—her life was in every way a mystery to him. What did she *do* all day? The vast room she occupied in the southeast tower, Columbia, was the same room her predecessor had lived in, but Alyson had removed every trace of the other woman (pinks, whites, sparkles on everything) in favor of a terrific and startling blue, an azure paint accented by cobalt rock crystal. Around the room, clear indigo geodes spilled light, from clusters of beeswax candles situated behind them. And there were more candles, candles everywhere. There must have been a hundred around her sitting area alone. Whenever John stood in her chamber he smelled something impossible to describe but that nevertheless described perfectly her entire existence, her experience since birth, a scent wholly hers and one he had never smelt in another place: a detached butterfly wing? The paint on the eyelid of a statue? Something powdery, something mineral. Alyson's life, her tenuous hold on the truth of the world, the terrible stinking gross world that John admittedly only glimpsed on his infrequent journeys to the palace compound, at times struck him as unbearably frivolous. And yet she did fascinate him. In the corner one of her small black dogs slept in an elevated bed shaped like a saucepan.

"Your Majesty, how shall I begin? We did not cause the bleeding." His voice splattered into the space between them like vomit into a bowl. "It happened in spite of us. Believe me, I would've done anything I could to spare you and every lady of the court such extreme extra unpleasantness, had I known such a thing was happening."

"'Us' ? 'We' ? Who is 'we' ?" Her face like a wide freckled ancient head. A feminine votive.

"My new . . . predictive assistant and myself. That's the title I've given him for the moment. I've only lately acquired him." He heaved his arm in front of himself in gesture of affirmation he recognized as overdrawn even as he performed it. Who was he in front of her, the palace fool? And still he could not stop grinning like a maniac. His dimples hurt. "This new assistant, he's a damn sight more intuitive than I am, that's for certain. You may not know, but I'm very, very poor at predictions myself. Or at least ones that aren't strictly astrological—now certainly I could tell you if the day of your birth is auspicious, or I could tell you when it might be fortuitous to conceive a son—" Was he talking about her womb? Was he imagining her beneath the girthy heft of their blond king, a hairy-backed board of a man (John had read the king's horoscopes to him in his bath many times), Alyson lying back under his spermy exuberance? He swallowed. "You might have asked Michael if I—"

"We never talk about you," she said, turning to her little black dog and scrunching her brow absently. She took a puff of her pipe. "Michael has his obsessions." A shrug. The dog caught her gaze and wagged hopefully, stepping out of its round bed. John's hands seemed unable to sweat properly. They felt numb to him, weirdly flaccid. The dog crossed the room diagonally from the back, and when it reached Alyson's couch in the center she kicked it playfully away, and when it would not retreat she waved at one of her servingwomen to hold it. "Michael talks about a lot of things. I just tell him to shut up." She turned her head back to John. "I asked him about this bleeding, though, and he said I should ask *you*. So. Lord Astronomer. What can you tell me?" She held up her own hand and studied each knuckle carefully. "Wait, did you just say you have an assistant now? Is that what you were talking about?"

When John had been a boy, he'd spent many an hour in what could only be called hypnotic fascination, the study of tiny things: a garden lizard fear-frozen on a coral statue, a swatch of fabric on his trouserleg, an engraved medallion his mother often wore—which became his after her death. Objects obvious and present to a boy, woefully unpresent to him as a grown man. He'd never concerned himself with time until it had already passed. When he was young, he'd nabbed that medallion from his mother for a few hours, studied the slender figures depicted upon it: two women seated on a chaise longue, a guinea hen, emblem of the family Sousa, scratching at the ground before them. John had dismissed easily the most obvious questions a child might ask about the scene—who the women were didn't interest him, but how they got onto the medallion did, what person or tool had machined them there so smoothly, and then there was the matter of the age of the metal. He'd sent his boy's fingers around and around it. So even and smooth it was. As though the medallion itself might answer him. The skill necessary to make such an object had astonished him, even then. John the adult was no different, only now he spent his time studying invisible magics. But had he not once studied his own knuckles as Alyson was just now doing, the marvelous utility of each bone-nub straining against the skin, and each mole, and each sparse shaft of hair? He stared at her.

She waited patiently, content, it seemed, to contemplate her hand and then him, watching him teeter from side to side, having got lost inside himself on his way to an answer. Her nails were painted, each one a different color, short and practical. At last she snapped her fingers to catch his attention.

John panicked. "Ah . . . yes, my assistant. He is . . . an unorthodox choice, I confess, and he has spent some time in prison. This prison in fact, only recently. Terribly recently. But I have cause to believe that his predictive abilities are remarkable. You see, it was Tygo who advised that I inquire about your . . . bleeding." The word was difficult for him to say. "I asked him to perform a feat of prediction as a test. His, ah, employment, shall we say, was contingent on the fulfillment of his prediction. And before you ask, let me inform you that I have not, as of yet, proven that Tygo did not do some magic of his own to *cause* his prediction to become true, but as we speak I'm working on it. I am as certain as I can be that Tygo is honest. Would you like to meet him?"

"What?" she asked. Still she looked at her nails.

"Would you like to meet Tygo? He's outside. Shackled, of course. Technically—you must be aware—he's still a prisoner. I ask permission from you to take him before the Pardoness. A royal pardon would unburden me greatly and legitimize our work." *And keep the Hierophant away from him,* he did not say. He stuffed his hands into the pockets of his coat, felt a rip in the lining of the left one. He knew he would forget to ask Mizar to mend it until he lost something precious through the hole.

Alyson put her hands to her temples. "You're so hard to follow. Are you telling me the man who caused the bleeding is here now, outside my chamber?"

"Not caused," John piped. "Predicted."

"Whatever. Yes, bring him in right now, I want to see him." She held up a hand. "Wait." She spoke to her handmaid. "Get the sheets."

The handmaid returned, her arms piled high with white sheets stained with russet blobs; John stared, uncomprehending. The young woman cast the sheets onto the tiled floor, spreading them out with a toe so they were all more or less visible, hills and valleys in a circle around her own rose-colored dress. There were at least seven or eight sheets, each ruined by brown-red smears. John knew Alyson, always inexpressive, was watching him. As he realized what the stains were, a blush mounted his face.

"This is gross," she said finally. "Just gross. You know it is." The handmaid had at last spread out each sheet and John could see the extent of the havoc: could normal women bleed so much and yet be unharmed? Alyson said, "They can be washed but the laundress says they'll never get completely white. I know *I* won't want to sleep on these, and Michael won't want to sleep or do anything on these, and other than the handmaids and servants I don't know a single girl who won't need new bedclothes, and who's paying for that? Are you? And"—she pulled on one of the two straight curtains of her hair, which divided and fell onto each shoulder—"as a side note, Lord Astronomer, when you're talking I immediately start thinking about something else. I used to think it was me but I actually think it's you. Don't they have some kind of class you can take to get better at it?"

He wondered what "they" she referred to and felt his blush ripen. "I—"

"Part of your job is to explain things to me when I wish them explained, right? But it's like you're speaking a different language. You do this thing where you start in the middle and then I'm lost."

"Your Majesty . . ."

"You're paying for these sheets. It's coming from your salary."

"I insist!"

"You were saying something about an assistant?

He was dazed. The handmaid still fussed with the sheets, using first her left foot and then her right to swab them into some unintelligible order. The heft and locomotion of them across the floor, all the blood—O! Might the women have died? *Had* Tygo magicked them after all? His mouth moved. "My assistant?"

She huffed. "This is what I mean! You were just saying!"

"Yes, my Lady Queen, of course. May I bring him in? I am sorry to say that only he can aptly explain it to you. Forgive me for everything. I'll pay, a hundred times over, I'll pay for all this."

"Yes, okay," she sighed, glancing at the door.

John called for the guard to produce Tygo, handcuffed again, but this time with his feet unbound. He came right into the room as though he had been waiting for just this chance to explain everything. His too-large pants gapped at the waist and dragged slightly on the floor. John noticed again then how uncommonly short Tygo was, and yet he did not *seem* short. Nor did he appear to have any misgivings about this or any situation John had yet observed him in. Tygo smiled at the queen, a quick and dazzling smile, and John could not understand the look that momentarily crossed her face: amusement?

"Hello," she said.

"Hello," he said, still smiling.

She waited for Tygo to speak. But he said nothing. John wished he were standing closer so he could nudge him—didn't he sense that Alyson did not like speaking first? But Tygo waited and waited. His smile slowly slid down his chin and left his body altogether. Alyson narrowed her eyes at him palely. John had often noticed she looked nothing like her rumpled, stocky father Marvel. He saw no hint of her father in her, except . . . except in her eyes, so very pale green, like diluted sulfurous nuggets, chalky and impermeable. They remained on her earless guest like veils, opaque partitions separating her soul from her face. Alyson gazed without blinking at Tygo, and at last, with no hint of retreat in her voice, she asked, "You are . . . ?"

"Tygo Brachio. Or people have called me the Peacock, or William Tygo, or one of a hundred other names. Didn't the Lord Astronomer tell you? I'm his new assistant."

She laughed. Laughed? Her cheeks crowded upward and forced her eyes into small crescents. Now it was she who blushed as her laughter left off, and still she looked at Tygo most intently, unconcerned, it seemed, with the livid pulsation in her face. "You're both dressed terribly," she said. "Didn't you have anything nicer to wear to visit the queen?"

Tygo pulled a handful of dull fabric free from his chest and let it fall back again. "Servant's clothes was all they gave me, I don't know his excuse. Also I didn't expect the queen to be a smoker. You must smoke all the time. It smells like it."

She ducked her head indignantly and waved her blue pipe with her other hand, dispersing the haze around her. "I can do what I want. I'm the queen."

"I'm only saying it's bad for you." He smiled again.

John's stomach dropped. "Your Beauteousness, I apologize again—"

Alyson ignored John and leaned forward. "You don't know that."

Tygo shrugged. "No, I do. I also knew you would all be bleeding, and here we are. You want to know why you're all bleeding. Right?"

"Do you know?"

"The question you're asking is really 'did *I* do it?' Am I right in assuming that? And the short answer is no, of course not, it's not possible for me or any other person, 'magician' or otherwise, to fix it so you and all your ladies . . ." He looked pointedly at John then, but John would not meet his eyes. Tygo straightened and enunciated, ". . . Are bleeding at once. That's the medical term. The discharge of blood from your bodies is not caused by magic. That's not my opinion, it's a simple truth. Now, I don't want to have a discussion about politics, so we should agree to disagree here. But let me promise you, Queen Alyson, I don't do 'magic.' The Astronomer and I have covered this at length."

"Well, did *he* do it?" she said, with a cursory nod in John's direction.

"From my admittedly short experience with him, I'll say that he doesn't do 'magic' either. He spends most of his time with his instruments—"

"His what?"

"Telescopes. Astrolabes. Charts," Tygo replied, with a wink at the queen, so quick John could hardly believe he saw it. "Math."

She smirked. "John Sousa, in my mind, is always doing spells or stabbing birds through the throat or something like that to make his predictions. But you're saying he doesn't?"

It was as though the little hideous man had put John over a burner, and steam rose up through the top of his head. "I perform calculations based on numbers our forefathers collected many years ago," he said through a tight mouth. "I would have been delighted to show you. I could easily make up a simple series of predictions while you look on—"

"O god. No." She was laughing again now. "No, please, it's okay." John's face went slack. Tygo smiled openly, and greater still was the joy in his eyes, precise dark pools with a black sheen, water at the bottom of a well.

Alyson said, "At least Michael makes it sound interesting when he talks about it. Which is *all* the time, god." She waved her hand, a swirl of multicolored nailtips. "You were saying, Tygo Brachio?"

He stepped forward. "I was saying this: although it's well known to most Walking Doctors that women, when boarding together, will often begin to cycle together, we don't know why. There doesn't seem to be any accepted explanation, but a guess recorded in the books has been that the lead woman—the most fertile woman, that is, in the group—somehow changes the bodies of the subordinate women to bring menstruation in line with her own cycle."

She smirked but said nothing.

Tygo said, "But obviously this is not what happened here, as you have all been living together for a long time. So whatever has caused the bleeding could only be something impressively out of order, a thing of the most extreme magnitude." He held up a finger. "I'm sure you and your ladies have noticed the *stella nova*?"

Keenly, she nodded. "We saw it earlier and now they are saying there is another."

John heard this but could make nothing of it. Another one? A deep distress began to crash within him, knocking his worries together like cylinders on a wind chime. Another comet? Tygo too appeared confused, but quickly blustered through it with a nod. They had just been outside, had they not? In the widening luminous evening they had just ridden through, cut as it was by gray-purple clouds stacked atop one another, they had seen no trace of another comet. Had they? Even as John uneasily recalled the landscape from their carriage ride, he knew he had been distracted and not at all in a state of mind to properly notice anything, least of all some new, miraculous manifestation that was most likely hidden by clouds. He hadn't *really* looked up, he who should always be looking.

He had read nothing in his books about a double comet, not during this century. O god, when had he last read up on comets? Would Mizar know? John looked about without realizing it, so used was he to Mizar clicking behind him in some spirit of helpfulness; Mizar had memorized almost as many of the charts as John. But his servant was nowhere to be seen, probably down taking a luxurious look at the exposed bodies on the east wall of the palace, holding his nose and cackling with some guard or another.

"Yes, another one," said Tygo. "And I'm sure you've already figured out what they must be."

Alyson answered, a slight pursing of her lip betraying her puzzlement. "Of course it must be the shuttles returning. Right? You're saying that's what's caused our bleeding."

Tygo began pacing in front of her. He hunched over just so, to indicate deep consideration, even a little confusion. John bristled in silence.

"Yes, it may be the Return." Tygo nodded slightly. "When I predicted the bleeding, I was hoping to prove myself of immediate usefulness to the Lord Astronomer—I confess that it wasn't so much a prediction as it was a guess. An educated one. I was hoping he'd take me in, let me help him sort all this out, since he doesn't seem able to make heads or tails of the physical aspects of what's happening to you all. And—" Tygo held up his hand. "I admit, I wanted to save my own skin. I don't want to die, your Majesty, just because I know a thing or two about the human body. Just because I've done some surgeries in my day. Anyway, I figured such an extreme celestial event was bound to be affecting you ladies bodily. I even feel it in myself," he said, lowering his voice and moving his chained wrists near his waist. "I'd tell you where, but . . ." He shrugged. "I wouldn't want to offend your dignities. I'm sure the Lord Astronomer concurs." He looked over at John, eyebrows high, and then Tygo flashed one lid up and then down; another wink, this time at John, and Alyson could not have seen it for Tygo was turned at that moment entirely toward John himself. "Would you agree, John?" he asked. "May I call you that, Lord Astronomer? John?" He leaned back toward the queen and said in a low conspiratorial tone, "We haven't even had time to discuss the formalities of our professional collaboration yet. But I think Lord Astronomer would agree that I've already made myself more than useful."

Agitated, John ran his dehydrated hands through his hair, which flopped back unworkably onto his forehead. Tygo was lying to her—he no more believed in the return of the shuttles than he believed in the efficacy of any magic, as he'd made plain on the carriage ride. He'd been cast into a jail cell precisely because of his heretical beliefs. Why would he tell her it was the shuttles? John felt he was losing track of some important thread, that he was watching it slip past him into the open world, and afterward that he would never see it again—the thread was his singular agency, that he would never draw back. Tygo even now was spinning out some story that made only the dimmest sense to John. To save his life. To impress the queen. And why not? It was a performance. It struck him that Tygo was an actor more than anything else.

He didn't understand anyone or anything around him. He found himself numbly agreeing with Tygo, even heard himself talking as if from a far-off prominence: "Yes. It must be the Return, I have every evidence of it. The charts indicate . . . well, there is much to suggest that we should . . . In fact, your Beauteousness, I was just about to insist that you bring the king thusly or else we should go to him; this is the moment. We should begin making a . . . a . . . a plan of some kind."

Her face, inexpressive still. "A plan for what?"

Tygo stepped between them. "We don't know, is what the Lord Astronomer is trying to say. What we're trying to say—both of us—is that please, please don't be distressed about the bleeding or any other vagaries of the body during this unique time. Something much more important is about to happen! Have you not wondered at the arrival of the enormous outlaw carnival?"

"They have their eye on it." She said slowly, knitting her brows. "We've had uprisings before, like during the Unrest. They never get inside the walls." Then she shrugged. "Nothing comes of it in the end."

"This may be different. Maybe they've come because they know it's the Return. Who knows? Maybe they've come because they want to be here when it happens," Tygo said.

She bent forward excitedly. "What do you think will happen?"

Tygo took his place by John—he was clearly closing the interview. An acrimonious bile rose in John's throat. Tygo had caught the queen's eye and now was looking somewhat impertinently at her, in way that John distrusted, leaning in to meet her with barely restrained interest. Her own eyes seemed to search every corner of Tygo's face, looking across the slope of his nose and up to those idiotic star tattoos, clustered like freckles on the left cheekbone. "Do we have your permission to keep at our magic?" Tygo asked. "Our work is important, John's right."

Her lips, full and small as two buttons, turned downward as she nodded. She said, "You know those tattoos look stupid on you. I just noticed you have no ears."

He bowed a little and swung his arms as if to stretch them above his head, if they had been unchained. "Youth!" he laughed. "I had a good time. And then a very bad time. It's a common tale."

"You'll come back in one day to tell me everything you've discovered?" Was she *asking* him? Her lips parted, resolved themselves again into a perfect bud.

"I'd tell you anything, my Queen." He smirked delicately. Tygo took John's sleeve and turned him physically toward the door. As they exited the chamber, they heard her giggling with her handmaiden, and then the dog was placed on the floor and they heard its jubilant scrabbling as it raced after them, but before it reached their heels the heavy white door slammed shut, and at John's side Tygo had also begun laughing. "I think she liked me, eh?" he demanded. "What a gorgeous creature she is. I can't stand it."

John glowered.

Then they were walking alone past one of the immense windows at the top of the tower, and John stopped in a stupor, squinting. Wait, it *was* there. Just there, in the gleaming dark. A second arc, faint to be sure, but soaring high in the sky not more than a few degrees from the first light. And beneath them, a growing mass of people had convened an outlaw carnival—for what? What reason could there be besides the obvious?

There came over him the undeniable impression that all reason was leaking from the world, that he was a faucet, that through his miscalculations all things would slowly but surely upend themselves. What could these lights be, if not the shuttles? It seemed fitting that after decades of failure, John, who had his whole life long desired truth and order, should now be reliant upon a con-man who may well have real visions. Why shouldn't the truth, when it finally came to John Sousa, be revealed by a liar?

CHAPTER 12

THE WEDDING

The way to the shoreline had been lit for them by a legion of the faithful. People lined the rocky path in a winding route that seemed meant to prolong their march to the sea. The surrounding crowd was innumerable in the half-light, face after face turned to the girl in a euphoria of shared belief: here a set of eyes that cried, there a pair of hands reaching to touch Mr. Capulatio or his betrothed. And somehow, she found she was on the cusp of sharing their hope. Excitement welled up inside her as she completed the final steps of the processional and arrived at the first dune, hand in hand with Mr. Capulatio. The ocean now was very loud, breaking only a hundred yards in front of them. They mounted a weatherworn set of steps that crossed the dunes and fell down again onto the soft pale beach. When their feet touched the sand, Mr. Capulatio whispered in her ear, "We've made it." And she didn't know if he meant to the sea or something else.

At the base of the steps, they removed their shoes. Piked Heads loomed all around, grinning deaths lit up by torches thrust in the sand between them, one after the other, all the way down to the foam of the ocean. The girl counted thirty, forty Heads at least, all lined up opposing one another to form a kind of aisle, and wafting around them a tangle of streamers in the colors of his carnival, purple, red, orange. Beyond this, the people were all waiting in the darkness, all watching her.

She was trembling—with excitement, confusion. Damp in her armpits. They were going to walk down the center of the aisle. That was how weddings went. Mr. Capulatio took her face in his hands while they still waited. Shadows, colored like the inside of an eyelid, bounced across the sand at her feet. Suddenly the crowd seemed quieter. There was whispering, the breathy sound of a wind instrument from someplace close by, and the murmur of the ocean. It was only then she fully realized she was back. He had taken her home, just as he said he would. He had kept his word—he had taken her to the sea. It lay black and silver in front of them like a wavering net. "Are you all right, Queenie?" he asked her softly.

How could she answer? Her mouth yielded up some formation of the word "yes," and then he had his arms all around her in a happy daze. They swung together like dancers. As he spun her, she looked at everything. The beach beyond the throng of people was dark, until a mile away the east wall of the palace compound rose up, with cords of hanging lanterns strung from the four towers to Canaveral Tower in the center, so it formed what looked like the frame of a large carnival tent. It was beautiful indeed. And then Mr. Capulatio's lips found hers—soft, unbelievably so, and she was looking at his face and nothing else. So many people were watching them. He kissed her fiercely and then they were cheering. He said in her ear, "Aurora. Will you marry me?"

Out of the sky came the warmest wind, and it stirred many emotions in her that threatened to bring her to tears. She did not know if she wanted to marry him but she had accepted—forever ago now, it seemed—that she would. As far as she could disentangle one feeling from the next, she found she was flattered by his public kisses, and she was full of pride because he was the leader, and she was pleased with her own beautiful wedding dress as well as the delicate opalescent crown he had set upon her head to signify that she was queen.

But mostly she was thrilled at her place in the center of this crowd, buffeted by the blaze of torches and smells, with him. The eyes made her shy, but she wanted them upon her. She nodded, "Yes." And at that he clapped his hands and thrust his hand high in the air together with hers and shouted: "The young sigil dressed in white! Here she is! Columbiachallengerdiscoveryatlantisendeavour!" Her loose sleeve sliding backward down the cylinder of her arm. The crowd cheered again, and the girl felt that this, this must be happiness, this, and if it was, then perhaps she had been happy all her life after all, so unsurprising was this feeling of inevitability and excitement.

Just as they began their walk down the aisle of Heads and streamers, a great globe of green light sprang up at the shore below, as though a lamplighter had been watching for a signal, as she and Mr. Capulatio passed some invisible marker. The path before them ran directly into the sea, and there at the seam where the ocean met the sand was a large raft, suddenly lit up brilliantly. A driftwood barge big enough to hold three people at least, and on the barge stood Orchid in her own fine dress, holding a burning torch in her hand that sent spirals of emerald light and shadow down her forearm, with her hair bound up on one of those stiff forms that the crones wore. She wore face paint like a crone. Her smile when she saw them was dreadful. The torch had been treated with some chemical that made it burn green.

At the water, the girl hesitated, but Mr. Capulatio tugged her into the sea, which swirled around her ankles and billowed her dress between them, and when they were knee deep he boosted her up onto the raft, which must have been anchored because it remained in place despite the jostling. The girl stood for a moment alone with Orchid, who glared without a shred of sympathy. She offered no encouraging word, not even a nod of acknowledgment. The girl looked at her, and Orchid, hard-eyed, looked back over the umber stripes on her cheekbones. Once Mr. Capulatio ascended the raft and they'd all regained their balance, he laughed and exclaimed, "My wives. My hearts." It was such a jubilant laugh. The torch in Orchid's hand winked in the breeze and she set it in a brace bolted to the back of the raft.

The crowd massed at the waterline. They stood shoulder to shoulder, and the low pitches of their voices were no longer audible. She felt the raft straining against its hidden tethers with the tide. Orchid moved closer to Mr. Capulatio. "Are we really going to do this, David? You can still stop this hideousness. I'll say anything you want me to say to them. But stop it." She paused. Though she was begging, she did not sound like it. Her voice, the girl noticed, was quite high. "I need time to read the texts again. There is a mistake in my interpretation."

"Read your lines," he replied, forcing her slightly away from him with his thigh.

"I will not," she hissed. "I cannot, this is too awful."

It seemed to the girl that Mr. Capulatio might strike Orchid. But the scowl passed nearly instantly and he grasped the girl by her hand again and stroked the inside of her wrist. "My Radiance," he said to Orchid. "Wife of my first heart—"

"Quiet with that!" she whispered. "I will *not* do this, David. Tell them that she is a sacrifice to the Great Work. Say that you will marry her here and now, and then we will make her a Head, together; she is our great sacrifice. Look, I've brought my knife." She lifted her dress and exposed her tall leather boots, the ones she had been wearing earlier. Poking from the left one, just visible up against her pale thigh, was a knife handle. "I've read the scriptures over and over today and I cannot agree with you. You are *not* supposed to take another queen. You are making an erroneous interpretation. Please forgive me for saying this, but perhaps it's brought on by your fear of what is to come. David, my dear husband, my spiritual master whom I have loved with all my heart since I was a girl. That was not so long ago, I am not that old! Please listen to me. We both know how afraid you have been of these days, of our Work coming to its apex. Let us at least admit that? Can you admit it?" She stared at him imploringly.

He said nothing.

"Fear has clouded your vision," she raised her voice. The folds of the silk around Orchid's thigh, the handle of the knife catching the light as she bent forward ever so slightly—the girl saw it. Mr. Capulatio was watching her leg too. He was barefoot, as was the girl. Orchid swayed as she spoke, then spun her hands in an odd circular motion; the girl wondered if she was trying to conjure something. "Husband, I cannot see as I once could. I grant you that. But my intellect hasn't changed, my talent hasn't lessened. I am still your Glassine Prism, refracting your dreams into words for the world."

He nodded. "Yes. You are. And this girl is my gemrock, my possession of highest worth. We are all the things we are. I am the king. She is the living sigil who ushers in our success, who appears at the perfect time, and whose appearance heralded the Return. Glorify." He spoke coldly.

Orchid turned to the sky with restless anguish. "There are two, now?"

"Yes," he said, going nearer to her. He pointed at the second star. "Yes. It appeared late in the afternoon. It's faint, but it will get brighter. You must know I consult minds other than yours. These wise minds tell me another and another and another rocket will come, until they are all here. Watch. Look." He held his hand before her eyes, extending each finger rigidly in sequence. "Five, all together."

"But—" she began.

"You are a translator," he said. "A scribe. Before your accident, when your visions were accurate, you'd earned your place with me. I trusted you, when we used to look at auguries of the future to discover how I died. *If* I would die. Do you remember? This girl is no visionary. I've asked her to predict my death many times. She makes up answers. They are wrong, only fantasies, but they charm me. She's charming. But you, wife, what do *you* do for me now? Find fault with what we've written? Tell me that I am not the best person to interpret my own visions? You hear how stupid you sound, don't you?" His eyes, flickering in the green torch, were blank. "We will perform the Star Sapphire ritual with Aurora, just as I've planned. First thing tomorrow. You will attend. Happily."

"No," Orchid clenched her jaw. "Never."

"Put down your dress. You are indecent."

Though they spoke almost inaudibly, the girl wondered if anyone on the shore could hear their argument. Orchid's hand hadn't moved, her fist a tight rose against her thigh, with fabric bulging from the crevasses between her fingers. The girl noticed with alarm that hand was creeping slowly toward the grip of the knife. Orchid's voice was throttled with jealousy. "David! My love. Say she is your wife if you have to, but say we will sacrifice her to the Great Work. Let me sacrifice her. I know what to do. I always know what to do!"

In Orchid's eyes an inchoate rage began to boil, and the girl sensed she would strike out with the knife at any moment. The girl began to creep toward the side of the barge. She would jump into the black water if Orchid reached for the blade. Mr. Capulatio, an executioner after all, must have felt the swelling tension, or else he knew his wife's nature well enough to predict what she would do.

In a single moment that passed almost too quickly to see, Mr. Capulatio darted at Orchid and pulled the knife straight out of her boot. He sliced her skin in the process. She howled a high and vivid scream but still managed to lunge after the knife with her fingertips. It slipped past. Mr. Capulatio had already swung it behind her, and in the same motion he grabbed her by the hair and turned her almost entirely around, until she was bent backward over his knee, where he held her, where at any moment he could break her back or slit her throat or stab her in the heart. Then, slowly, he pulled her long pale hair off of the hair-form and around his arm, and she was staring up at him with wide hate-filled eyes.

The three of them on the raft were at once alone in a world of their own making, roiling and rolling together like bubbles in a fountain. Mr. Capulatio raised the knife to Orchid's neck. The girl watched, her breath trapped. Orchid closed her eyes. A look of hunger on her face. And strange courage.

Hovering motionless on the edge of the raft, the girl became aware of a new emotion roaring in her heart like a beast: she wanted to protect her husband. She thought of him that way now. Her body tensed like a single muscle. Orchid's eyes remained closed in anticipation.

But when the blow came it was not to her neck, but to her hair. Mr. Capulatio sliced her hair off in four sawing thrusts, tossed it by handfuls over the side of barge. He was smiling now, a genuine smile, his head-cutting smile. But he was angry, too, she could see it. He pushed Orchid upright, steadied her, and then threw her knife into the sea as well with an angry grunt. It disappeared beneath the inky water.

"How is that for a sacrifice?" His voice frightened the girl.

A smear of blood stained the lower half of Orchid's dress. Her hair now floated in a jagged cloud about her ears, released of its former weight. Calm closed in on them like a cotton veil; some spell he had done in the cutting must have momentarily subdued her—the girl wondered, was it really magic?

"That knife was from the launchsites," Orchid whispered. "Where will I get another one?" It sounded as if she were trying to make a joke. Because of course she cared nothing for the knife, nothing for anything else she'd lost except her power.

Mr. Capulatio pulled the girl back into the center of the raft and wrapped his arms around her, tucking her in close. He laughed angrily. "O, but you won't need a knife in the cages, woman. Which is where you're going right after this."

She made no expression. "Who will do the Star Sapphire ritual with you if I'm in the cages? I had assumed such an honor would be my fate." Her words were bitter.

"You will do what I tell you to do. I think that's what annoys me so much about you these days." He wiped his bloody hand on the sleeve of the girl's dress.

Orchid closed and opened her eyes the way a person does when they are trying to wake up. The crowd had turned silent.

He pushed on her shoulder now, almost playfully. The girl could tell he was enraged, his chest was hot through his clothes. "Say your lines." He paused. "Loudly, please."

From some pocket in her dress she produced a folded square of paper and after the girl and Mr. Capulatio had taken their positions facing each other, and after the crowd had clapped for what felt like an age, Orchid began to read the words, haltingly at first and then with less apprehension, until she sounded not just normal but entirely convicted, and the magical words moved between the girl and Mr. Capulatio and snaked past them, out into the waiting host of people, each one of them a believer, each one filled with the wonder of ritual.

After a moment Orchid took from between her small breasts a vial of blood and continued. "This is the daughter of Fortitude, the fawn of the Battlefield," she called. "Behold, she is Understanding, and science dwells within her and the heavens covet her. She is ringed by the Circle of Stars and covered with the morning clouds. She is ravished every hour by Glory. She is deflowered, yet a virgin; she sanctifies but has yet to be sanctified herself. Happy is he who embraces her, for in the days she is sweet and in the nights full of pleasure. Her company forms a harmony of many symbols. So purge your streets, sons of men, and wash your lands clean with blood for this Eon. Make yourselves Holy and put on righteousness. She will in time bring forth children and these will be the Sons of Comfort in the coming age, the age of the True King, the Age of Times. Glorify."

And it went on this way, a chant, for many minutes until at last Orchid opened the vial of blood and poured it over their joined hands and kissed them both on the cheek, her mouth drawn closed over her teeth, and the girl felt the cool blood go over their skin. Whose blood was it? But it was Orchid's, of course, she knew without asking. Then Mr. Capulatio kissed her for a very long time and pressed his body against her. Startled, she felt his hardness and was confused. She had thought he was angry.

She let herself be led wordlessly onto the sand again. In the flickering light, her hand looked black with drying blood.

Orchid marched ahead of them on the beach and stood in front of everyone for a moment, appearing dizzy, like she had just awoken from a nap. Then she whirled around and knelt in the sand before Mr. Capulatio.

He looked at her, unmoved. Her body in her blue dress as she spread out on the ground was beautiful even to the girl. She chastised herself for her own jealousy.

Orchid thrust her face up. "I have misread the scriptures in relation to this wedding! When he returned with the lucky sigil, I admit my heart complained. I could not see his larger plan for our Great Work. I did not interpret the scriptures correctly. Our master has reprimanded me. We made our peace at once. He shows us daily what perfect love is. And witness: I am still his wife. Wife of his first heart. I am his first wife. He has not cast me out!"

But this was no apology: even the girl recognized Orchid was trying to force his hand. Mr. Capulatio watched with a placid expression. He bent next to Orchid and spoke a few words in her ear. Then he straightened and smiled brilliantly at his people. They stood all around, stunned. There would be no undoing this fiasco. Faces pressing inward upon them. He brushed sand from his knees. He offered a hand to Orchid, who did not take it. "Someone escort my Radiance to the cages—not my tent. This is my wedding night." He was still smiling. "And she has nearly ruined it. Do it now," he repeated, as two men picked up Orchid and pulled her bodily to her feet.

Though she rose calmly, there was something wracked and demeaned about the way she tensed her shoulders, with multiplicities of anger squeezing her like a vice, making her smaller and harder yet, her solid small arms and their muscles clenching and unclenching like breaths.

Mr. Capulatio turned his back on her. He called out for everyone to hear. "Now, we'll dance! And drink. And prepare. Come and greet your queen, the Third Queen of Cape Canaveral. She is the true queen for the Age of Times. Look to the sky, at the returning shuttles, and rejoice! From this day we enter a new Age!"

Everyone gazed at the shooting stars in the sky, now numbering two. There were definitely two, even if the second was faint. But the girl watched the two men pull Orchid away through the crowd. She watched the way the crowd closed up behind her like soft tissue after a puncture wound. The crowd swelled into the processional aisle and there was suddenly music again, and someone knocked over a torch and a man caught his cloak on fire and ran laughing and screaming into the sea.

CHAPTER 13

TELLOCHVOVIN

After his humiliating audience with Alyson, John Sousa, Chief Orbital Doctor, took Tygo back to Urania at a gallop, so Marvel Parsons would not have time to intervene. John had a set of gigantic stone spheres among his predictive devices that could be moments away from achieving their purpose, and he wished to see them with new eyes. The spheres were made of limestone rich in fossilized shells, and were numbered five, just like the shuttles. They'd been constructed for him over the course of twenty years, and they were, as far as he could measure, perfectly round. The magicians who made them claimed to have employed a potion that softened stone until it was workable as clay. John didn't doubt this, but he had never seen it. The spheres, when they were finally finished, were immensely heavy and had been moved out to Urania one by one by a team of seventeen horses, and each sphere was placed exactly on an astronomical alignment that should, according to every calculation John had ever made during the twenty years it took the magicians to prepare the stones, match perfectly with the position of the shuttles upon their Return.

He ran like an excited child into his observation yard, his circumferentor in hand and lifted high so he might begin to measure the horizontal angles before he even came to a complete stop. The two comets blazed now, one brighter than the other, in the night sky. In the distance he could see the outlaw carnival's bright green glow. He had never known a carnival to use green torches—what could it mean?

But after a few moments, he'd dropped his arms: he did not even need to use the circumferentor. His angles were plainly off. There was no alignment whatsoever between his spheres and these new objects, whatever they were. There was surely the chance that John's calculations were merely *wrong*—that he'd been wrong enough in his life, and it was his own vanity that clung to these erroneous positions.

But no. In the end the spheres seemed to signify nothing. He stood there, bereft of all direction, with Tygo at his side. Tygo, who knew nothing of the spheres or any of the other perfectly aligned water tables and dials and disks that John had used so inertly throughout his tenure as Chief Astronomer. Then, without knowing exactly why, a terrible anger overtook him—not at Tygo but at the *idea* of Tygo. At his luck. His faith in himself? The entire situation was preposterous. By no means could it be true that the "angels" had told Tygo about the Return.

There were no angels. There could not be. He would not believe it. And yet what could this be other than the Return?

John felt black with fury as Tygo was strolling around the courtyard with his hands still shackled, looking with passive interest at the circular metal domes hiding what was not in use. The torches along the front wall of the house had been lit, and in the shadows Tygo's ear-holes looked like pits. Here and there he touched the domes with his shackled hands, which sent John into a private agony until he felt like tossing up his hands in defeat. At last Tygo turned his eyes to John. He waved across the courtyard. John waved back.

He gloomily called out, "Why don't you call down your 'angels' now, since my own attempts have always come to nothing. I'd like to see you try, actually."

Light from one of the torches bounced off Tygo's manacles. "That would be a very good idea. Clarification. Assurance. But—" He shook the shackles and smiled hopefully.

"I'm sure you'll manage," replied John.

"You do know I've only ever spoken with the angels that one single time, using my own personal shaving mirror."

"Surely the angels wouldn't mind you using a less humble mirror," John replied acidly. "They are *angels,* after all. But I have many such mirrors. In fact I posses a *beautiful* mirror, a black granite chip of the Sky Mirror itself."

"Sky Mirror?"

"The monument here at the Cape? Built by the ancients for all the known martyrs who gave their lives in spaceflight? That also lists the names of the noble families for posterity?"

Tygo's expression didn't change.

"Surely the angels would prefer *that* mirror to a shaving mirror?" John pressed.

Tygo seemed confused for a split second. A shadow darted across his eyes but he covered it quickly. "Why didn't you tell me you had a mirror?"

John smirked. "Such objects are strictly for priests and magicians of the highest order. Did you not say you *hated* magic?"

Tygo nodded. "But I thought I made it clear that my conversation with the angels was an accident. I never called them. I wouldn't know how to begin scrying, or whatever you call it. I abhor the utensils of your profession, I told you."

John continued to smirk. "All the same, you are now in my employ, and it seems prudent to get to the bottom of this matter as quickly as possible. We did tell Alyson that we would report to her tomorrow with additional knowledge, did we not? Are you not looking *forward* to that?"

He shrugged. "It doesn't matter to me if we see her or not. She was the one who requested the meeting. But I guess we have to tell her something. Maybe I'll see something." He paused. "Stranger things have happened to me. Since I arrived here I've done so many things I never thought I would do. What's one more?"

It was a curious thing to say. What had he done that he never thought he would do? But John let it go, and led the other man to his office, where he peevishly lit a whole host of candles that spat their trembling shadows onto the walls. John kept his chip of the Sky

Mirror on an intricate holder he'd commissioned some years back. Draped over it, however, was a plain cloth—a dust rag, really. Old and stained from handling. He withdrew the cloth and presented the palm-sized mirror as though showing off a finely crafted art object. He couldn't help himself—he had gone to such lengths to steal it and hide it all these years.

Tygo snickered, but quickly tightened his mouth over his lips in an effort not to offend. John was offended. He used the underside of the cloth to briefly shine the black granite. Tygo came up to the mirror and hunched over it, peering over its flat surface and blinking. He glanced at John, scrutinizing his face for instruction. John frowned meanly. He had no intention of helping. At last Tygo placed his fingers on the rock's shining surface and John audibly laughed. "That's not how it's done, man."

Tygo tipped his chin up. "Well, you were probably doing it wrong, that's why you never saw anything."

"How do you know I never saw anything?"

"If you had, you wouldn't be so desperate for me to look." He paused. "What are we looking for, again?"

John roughly pushed him away from the chip. "My god, man! We're looking for *confirmation*."

"From . . . the angels?"

He tossed up his hands. "Look, in my career, I've written an entire reinterpretation of our cosmology. I've scoured records from a thousand years ago! I've spent twenty years and more at this task, I'm in midlife now and only just realizing that everything I've believed was likely based on faulty math and my own hubris and some gross condition of the world which had convinced me until now that magic . . . that it mattered. Bah!" He shook his head. "We're looking for the Sublime! What did you think we were looking for? Why do you think you've kept your head this long? You said you could see things. So see them!"

Tygo nodded and rolled his sleeves up. "Right. I'm sorry. I'll scry for you." He hesitated still, then placed a palm on John's shoulder. "I did have a vision. I promise you. I know your work may be have been misguided. But it hasn't been in vain."

"Bah." John said again. "Did you *see* the shuttles returning in your vision? Did the angels *tell* you they were returning?"

"What I saw can't be communicated in words."

John rolled his eyes. "How convenient. You know, I regret listening to you at all."

"Don't say that."

"No, I believe I've been taken in by some scheme. I'm sure I'll be punished soon enough for it. And when that happens, I won't forget you. You will pay for tricking me."

Tygo shook his head. "You have it all wrong. I'm not tricking you. I *need* you. You, specifically. To help me understand my vision. I've told you, I'm not skilled in astronomics. I have no idea what anything I saw might mean." He spoke more softly. "What I'm trying to tell you is that this may be the Return. It *may* really be."

"Why then did you advise Alyson that it definitely was?"

Tygo spread his hands. "I only said it may be."

"I don't think that's what she heard. It's not what I heard. You have confessed to me you are a liar."

"I'm not lying, Lord Astronomer."

John folded his arms calmly over his chest. "Then prove it. Scry for me."

Tygo nodded again. "Well. That was part of the bargain, after all."

"It was the whole point of the bargain!" John snapped.

Tygo gathered his wits and took his place again at the mirror, and, taking a bit of his own sleeve, wiped the rock absently a few times. "Can't you cut off my shackles?"

"Not even on my mind, my man. It hasn't crossed my mind."

Then John waited. Nothing happened. Finally Tygo said, "You may as well take a seat, I can't promise you'll see anything yourself. It was just me at the mirror, that first time. And . . . I think I mentioned that when it occurred, I'd been somewhat at the drink."

John raised his eyebrows.

"It was a habit I'd gotten into. Regrettable. But . . . when it happened before I'd had . . . O, several or three glasses of wine. Do you . . . have any?"

John stormed through the manor house, into the kitchens, and removed a bottle of citrus liqueur from the storeroom—used for flavoring, he assumed—and without checking the glasses for dust he poured two hasty cupfuls of the stuff and brought it all back balanced upon one of Mizar's many inlaid trays. The bottle, too. He thrust the assortment at Tygo, who lifted the bottle and inspected it, wrinkling his nose. But he said nothing, raised his glass, and took the entire drink in a single draught, and waited until John had done the same, although John had to take two swallows, as he was unaccustomed to swilling strong liquids.

After that first gulp, his chest and gut seemed to catch like a fire. He teetered on his feet. Tygo held up his glass as if for more, and John supplied it, and then he too took another cupful, and then he felt like sitting down, which he did on the chaise longue at the other end of the room. Tygo closed his eyes like a child concentrating, and then went back to the mirror, cracked his knuckles, gazed at his own reflection in the black opalescent stone, and steadied himself as though for a duel.

Then John waited. They both waited, for what seemed like an Age, in their respective positions—John on the sofa and Tygo across the room, standing unmoving over the mirror. John eventually slid into a slumber, for when he lurched awake the candles were much lower and Tygo was still standing, stock-still, at the mirror, his black pigtail hanging lank on his skull. John realized he was damp and chilled and saw the fireplace, empty. A bubble of irritation burst within him, and he creaked to his feet, intending to fetch Mizar and reprimand him for not making the fire. One evening duty! Was it so much to ask?

The bottle of yellow liqueur winked merrily at him from the side table, and John discovered himself pouring another drink before he managed to leave the room. He sipped it this time instead of gulping. He somewhat enjoyed the warm feeling of the fluid sliding down his innards. Tygo had yet to move, but his cup was empty. John went to refill it, but when he approached the other man, he saw Tygo was not asleep, not awake, but open-eyed and vacant with his mouth half-agape. The pupils of the eyes hugely dilated.

John tripped backward in a startle, dropping the liqueur glasses. They smashed on the granite floor.

Like some blind bird, Tygo turned slowly to John, his face dead-looking, mercury gray. Around them the air pulsed with motion, as though spinning through fan blades. A pleasant breeze. But John noted in a slight panic that the window was not open. Even if it had been, it was November and the wind could not possibly be so warm.

He gripped Tygo's shoulder and shook him. Tygo continued to face him with that horrible expression. John grew more and more alarmed. He lifted his hand and actually slapped Tygo across the face. No response. He yanked back his hand, shocked at himself. It was as though he had been driven to do it: he had not even known what he was doing.

Tygo loomed above the mirror, the black surface reflecting back nothingness. Where had his reflection gone? John choked. The small star tattoos on Tygo's temples stood out, almost raised, like the hair of a hissing cat.

Suddenly Tygo began to speak in a bizarre language. Words John had never heard and could not understand. Each word seemed to be longer than the last. Quite a few had escaped the other man's lips before John had the wherewithal to leap to his desk and pull out a pad and begin transcribing. They were strange to the ear and ungainly to write; he could not tell when one word ended and the next began. Frantic, he scribbled, setting down sound after sound, writing as phonetically as he could manage, and this continued for some amount of time, John was not sure how long, enraptured and terrified as he was to be receiving anything that even resembled a miracle.

It occurred to him momentarily that Tygo was playing him for the worst kind of fool, but he let this suspicion out of his mind as one might let a hound into the garden knowing full well it may dig up the flowers. This relinquishment oddly satisfying. Some time later, minutes or hours, John had no idea, Tygo's words ran dry and he was himself again, alight with excitement and confusion.

He still stood at the mirror, drenched now in sweat. The first thing he did was wipe his brow with his sleeve. Then he sank to the floor and began, improbably, to laugh. John thrust his papers up to the candlelight and poked at them. "What is this?"

Tygo continued to laugh. "Angel language. I don't know. You tell me."

"But what did you *see*? You looked ghastly, like a corpse someone dug up! You must tell me. I've never seen anything like that. Were you putting me on? How did you do it?"

Tygo sighed happily and put his hands to his face. "I—I don't know. It just . . . happened. Like before. For a long time nothing happened, I was just standing there feeling stupid. Then I was seeing these strange grids, one atop the other, with small portions of the grids laid out backwards. But after a while the squares on the grids flipped over and then I was seeing a whole idea, a whole world, and I could exist in angelic time. *Inside* an event maybe . . ." He trailed off, seeing John's expression. He shook his head. "See, I told you before. It's like explaining a dream."

"No, no, explain. You have to explain," John said, brandishing the paper maniacally. "I wrote down everything you said. I copied out the sounds of the language. We can figure it out. If you can recall any of the physical visions—perhaps we can match them to the words. I've spent my life studying arcane nonsense." He laughed bitterly. "Did you . . . is this the Return?"

They peered at the papers together. The pages were awash with impenetrable syllables, each more inexplicable than the last. Stunned by the sheer unreadableness, they sat side by side in silence for some moments. Beyond them shards of glass sparkled in the weak light—the broken cups. At last John remarked in a mild voice, "You can't know how it feels to watch a person truly experience the Sublime. I've waited all my life to . . . to see a miracle."

Tygo nodded.

"If you *are* a con-man, I damn you, and you should be hung off the walls of the palace as a bounty for the seagulls. But if you are a visionary . . ." He exhaled. "I have never witnessed anything like that."

Tygo nodded.

"Is this the Return?" he asked again.

Tygo pinched his temples with his fingers. "I don't know."

"What did you *see*?"

"I think we'll need to do a very thorough study of these angelic words and how they correspond to the data you've collected so far—"

"That will take weeks. What did you *see*?"

Tygo met John's eyes. "I saw what I saw before." He took the papers and held them once more to the light, pointing to a scribble near the end of the transcription. "That word there. You haven't written it right, but you got the general idea. I remember that word. I saw it in the first vision, too. That word is important. 'Tellochvovin.'"

"What does it mean?"

Tygo shrugged. "That's what you're supposed to figure out." He hesitated. "I do know what it means, technically. But not what it means, cosmically. If that makes sense."

John frowned at him.

"'Tellochvovin.'" The other man frowned back. "It means 'falling death.'"

Thereafter, elated but also peculiarly overcome, they each drank more of the citrus liqueur. They took turns at the bottle, enough to stuff their heads with pleasantness and wonder at what had just transpired, and it was altogether confusing but mostly agreeable, until Mizar inserted himself into the room and began fretfully to sweep up the glass, reminding John of how he never took drink and shouldn't he think of his health? John was then seized by an unreasonable aggravation and spent minutes lecturing the poor man on his negligence in regard to the matter of the unlit fire, until Mizar hung his head, which was as much of an apology as Mizar ever issued. By then John felt depressed by his own tantrum and unsteady on his feet. Tygo had passed out on the chaise longue.

It was with a heavy heart that John allowed Mizar to lug him off to his chamber and place him in bed. Beside him on the night table Mizar filled a blue crystal glass with water and instructed John to drink all of it before he slept, but John drank none.

CHAPTER 14

THE UNICURSAL HEXAGRAM

On her wedding night she thought of her brothers. Argento, of course, there was always Argento. But also she wondered about her other brother, William, who had been driven from her mother's settlement for thievery before she was born. Her mother said William had run off to be a con-man, a swindler who posed as a Walking Doctor. Could he have been in that crowd of onlookers? Was one of those faces his? If so, she wouldn't have known him.

She thought of them both as she walked hand in hand with her new husband back to the tent. Now she had a husband. He would protect her from men like them. Men who could hurt her. Mr. Capulatio had said *The difference is I'll only hurt you on the inside.* She remembered Argento's broken body, before Mr. Capulatio cut off his head. Argento had kept his courage in the end. The girl's hate for him had transformed, and her pity as well, and now she wondered how she had ever been afraid of him. He seemed so far away. He could not touch her.

When the wedding dance ended and they came back to the tent, Mr. Capulatio sat across from her on the carpets. There had been laughing and singing and dancing, and then cups had appeared and folk had begun a raucous revel. Mr. Capulatio had stolen her away, back here to the soft pillowed ground. The quiet. Then, slowly, as her head cleared, she found herself trying to transform her husband's face into her brother's. There were no wrinkles on Mr. Capulatio's forehead, but she remembered Argento's thick and somewhat scarred skin so fully in that instant that she couldn't believe he wasn't here, that she wasn't there, back in his musty tent beneath mildewed blankets. If she tried, she could see in Mr. Capulatio some likeness of Argento. If she looked hard enough. Their eyes, for instance, were nearly the same color. And their hair was not that different. Maybe they looked like brothers. Suddenly she couldn't tell. She wondered if she had drunk too much.

She searched for something on his face that *didn't* remind her of her brother, and it was a long while before she realized that they hardly looked similar at all—they looked nothing alike! Her brother had been tall, very tall. She remembered that well. But Mr. Capulatio was of an average height. Was she disappointed by that? How shallow. She wondered if she was also of an average height; Orchid was a woman, and taller than the girl, and there was no one else to compare herself to.

She felt her eyes closing. But he still wanted to sit there in silence. What was he doing? Now she felt sad that there had been no one she knew to witness her marriage and tell her if she'd looked happy. There had been no one to tell the girl if she looked beautiful. Had she looked beautiful? Had she been happy? She couldn't tell. She thought she should feel different, now that they were married. But she didn't know if she did.

And in that instant the dam of emptiness burst within her. She did miss Argento. He had burned the unicursal hexagram into her thigh and dragged her through blood-spattered fields on her knees and never spoken to her with any kindness at all, but she missed him. He was her brother. The only one she had ever known. She wanted to hold Cosmas, the Head he'd made her, Cosmas the Uncrusher, but Mr. Capulatio had hidden it high up in one of his boxes. She began to sob.

Mr. Capulatio studied her as though this were no great thing. They continued to sit across from one another while she cried, him with his legs crossed beneath him and she with her knees drawn up to her chest. At first she sobbed loudly, with heaving breaths, but finally they slowed and Mr. Capulatio extended a hand to her and caressed the bulb of her knee. His fingers were gentle. He pulled her forward by her leg and kissed her forehead. He whispered, "Did you not like the wedding?" He kissed her again. "I think other people liked it. I'm sorry about Orchid. She acted very badly." He shrugged. "But the wedding was still nice."

She said nothing.

"Do you know what today is?"

She shook her head.

"It's November fourteenth, your wedding day. We've been together now for seven months."

She began to cry again. She couldn't help it; all the moments of the life she'd lived with her oldest brother rushed back to her at once. It was a torture she could not will from her mind. She remembered the horse Argento had let her ride—a broken down palomino that he cursed and said was no good for pulling their wagon anymore. Where was that horse now? Surely dead, like everyone else. And also the way at night Argento had crept into her tent with his bottle of foul-smelling drink clutched like a baby to his breast, and how he would take long voracious gulps while barely sitting up, and sometimes he would choke, and she was forced to slap him on the back to clear the fluid from his windpipe and how he stared at her with watery eyes and smiled—something he never did when he wasn't drinking. And how he looked when he slept: so compressed and uncomfortable on his bedroll. How she had, at times, re-covered his feet when she thought he was cold. But when he woke up, all those moments were forgotten and his cruelty returned. Mr. Capulatio hugged her and whispered, "It's all right, Aurora."

She was happier now. She was sure of it. Mr. Capulatio smiled all the time, he slept with his cheek pressed to the pillow so handsomely, his breath easy, in and out, and inviting. She liked lying close beside him and had become accustomed to sidling up next to him, pressing into the curve of his body. She felt that they were two caterpillars, knitted together into a cocoon.

Mr. Capulatio was watching her tenderly. "You really don't have to cry."

But she could not stop. So he took her by the shoulders and held her face up to his own like a mirror. "Today is also the day I became the True King. Aren't you happy for me? For us? Aren't you excited that the shuttles are returning?"

"I was thinking of my brother."

He nodded grimly. "Yes. I've been thinking of him too." He extricated her from his arms. He grabbed her by the leg and thrust her dress up past her hips. She gasped, surprised. Had he gotten the idea from Orchid's display at the wedding? His hands were prodding the burn mark Argento had given her two years before, when her mother abandoned her to his carnival.

"This," said Mr. Capulatio. His fingers mushed at the skin, puckering it and smoothing it out again. The lines, inward-falling, boundless symmetry. As above, so below. "*This* is not fit for my wife. This is another denomination's sigil, the mark of a foreign cosmology and the personal brand of an indigent rapist. Highly, highly unfavorable for our magic. Very disturbing. I've been very kind. I overlooked it this long because I hate to cause you pain. But now is a time of change. For us all. That idiot cannot ride with us into the Cape when we take the palace. Not him, not his brand."

She covered the mark with her hand.

"I'm a kind man. I was just born with mercy, I can't help it. I've let you keep that marking longer than I should. But I'm sure you understand that no one can ever see it. So we will be removing it tonight. Right now." He said it like a taunt. He pulled a short knife from the waistband of his pants.

She backed away from him like a crab, terrified, until her shoulder hit a low-hanging lantern and sent a carousel of red and black shadows around the tent. She yanked the wedding dress down over her thigh.

"No!"

"We have no choice."

She stumbled to her feet and dashed to the far side of the tent, where she hid behind her cage. "You promised you would never hurt me."

"It won't hurt. Not much, anyway. Don't be a coward."

In the months since Mr. Capulatio had taken her, she'd become less and less accustomed to the awfulness that before had regularly consumed her life. She was rarely cold now, and never hungry, and when they collided together at night in the bed it had felt like love-making and never like whatever she'd had before, the pain of which she could stand but which slowly had chipped away at something inside her, leaving a formless emotion that she could not name. Her skin was softer now, her body was healthier, and her breasts had become larger. She realized she'd thought she was almost safe.

"Orchid was right, Queenie. We *should* make sacrifices for the Great Work. She should. You should. I should."

"What is the Great Work?" she shrieked. "Please tell me!"

He tossed his dark hair. "I'm not that easily distracted. Little manipulator. You're already learning from her, I see. But it will be a long time before you're smarter than me." He considered. "Longer still before you're smarter than her. What a fine play she made out there on the beach. The affront burns me up. But by heaven she's a woman of many intriguing talents. I don't think anyone could criticize my choice of brides, first or second." He paused. "Tell me, did you think our wedding was enough? Be honest. I think I heard people complaining of the food."

She blinked in bewilderment.

He flashed one hand at her dismissively. "O, what do you know, you're just a child." He turned the little knife over and around in his hands.

She wasn't sure where he was headed. He would never be so cold that he could cut out her brand while she thrashed and screamed beneath him. But she had seen him behead her own brother—had Argento deserved it? She didn't know. All the things she didn't know! Perhaps Mr. Capulatio really did know better than her. Slowly she peeked out from behind the cage. He was still talking. Often he talked to himself in the same voice he used when he was talking to her.

"People are so ungrateful," he was muttering. "I try to overlook it. I'm trying to overlook your ungratefulness right this second. What are you doing, hiding from me? I'm your husband. I queened you. You are the most important thing in all the land, maybe even more important than me. And you're hiding! Unbelievable! We came to the Cape to save people, Aurora. How can you save people if you're afraid to do this small thing? What if they see that brand and think you're a blasphemer? Your brother's carnival had an archaic view of the Return! Have you not read any of the books I gave you?" he demanded. "Of course you haven't." He smiled meanly.

"I was reading. I am reading. I haven't had any time!"

He laughed at that, a deep whirling laugh. "You do what I tell you to do. I told you to read the books."

"I will. I'll read them."

He smiled. "That's the first time you've admitted you can read."

"Well, I can."

He scooted on his hands and knees around the cage until he was sitting close to her again. She could smell a tinge of the spicy-sweet scent he'd worn for the wedding. This near, even with him holding the knife, she did not feel entirely afraid of him and she didn't know why. "You said I was important," she whispered. "You told everyone I was."

He took her by the shoulders. "You are. Very."

"Then you should ask me what *I* want."

"All right. What do you want?"

"I want to know what everything means."

He scowled. "How should I know?"

"Because you're the king."

"If I knew what everything meant, I wouldn't be in this drafty tent getting ready to cut a brand off a little girl, would I?" he snapped.

"What's the Great Work? Orchid told me about it. What is the Star Sapphire ritual?" She kept her eyes on one of the hanging mobiles of glass and chalk he'd hung from the eaves of his wagon. It did not turn; there was no wind inside the tent.

Mr. Capulatio lost his frown. "A good question. You're bright! So bright, a sigil of knowledge. I'm still so happy I took you away from that idiot carnival full of raving idiots. Did you know I grew up in a place like that? A carnival just like your brother's, with those backwards convoluted rites that went on for two weeks straight. And all of it was just sex magic, you know that? And it was lurid, it was repugnant. I left, that's all you need to know. When I was fifteen. I came to the Prophetess Lois and I met Orchid. And that is a story for another time."

"I wish you would tell me now."

"The Great Work is the work we've done since Lois became the Prophetess. To reform the texts, the cosmology, everything. I've spent my life at this work. Lois designed the Star Sapphire ritual. She was my spiritual mother, the first one who divined that I was the True King. It's a ceremony of power, where a woman may become one with Heaven. And only by performing this rite will you be truly fit to be the queen of Cape Canaveral."

"What do I have to do?"

"The Prophetess passed from this earth eleven years ago. She named me as her successor over her own natural-born son. She was an aged woman of seventy-nine when she died. She took me in when no one would—I was raised by degenerates in circumstances not unlike your own. But," he said. "The ritual is beautiful. Violently beautiful. *Her* ritual. She gave it to us because she knew I was the True King." His eyes were far away; the clear brown of that first inch of seawater. "You know, I didn't want to be the king at first." Then he shrugged. "We all must make sacrifices."

He moved toward her with the knife, and his voice was sad. "Queenie. Give me your leg. I must do it." He paused. "You know I don't want to."

She cried, "I can do it myself!" Her head now felt strangely hot and cold, a flush of fear rising through up the web of her veins and pulsing into her cheeks. A thought intruded: this is the world. This is the world. She took his wrist in her own hand with such strength it surprised even her.

"I will burn it off. It was burned on, we'll burn it off."

Mr. Capulatio eyed her intently. "Burn it? I suppose we could burn it. Blood is better, though. It is only by our collective blood-rinse that the world will renew itself. That is Wonderblood. You know it well."

But possessed by an inner vision, as if by dictating the terms of her pain she could control it, the girl recalled when her brother Argento had burnt the hexagram onto her thigh. How on her first day in his camp she was weeping angrily at Gimbal, her mother, heaving tears of pure, polished anger. Even after walking with her mother so many weeks overland through the wildness of the country, the rolling world a joyful sensual experience despite every ancient calamity that had befallen it, and even though her mother cursed it and called it contagious—even after anticipating her abandonment for the entirety of the journey, the girl had still failed to comprehend the scale of the betrayal. Only when she at last sat alone with her brother in his tent did she understand how alone she really was. Argento towered over her, this man she did not remember.

Her anguish had been enough to drown out even the sizzling of the hot iron on skin.

"But it's the Return," she said. "The shuttles are back. The Eon of Pain is over. I thought there should be no more blood spilled if the shuttles are back."

He set down the knife, wiped his hand on the ends of his shirt. "It could be. I hadn't thought of that." And he looked at her with new respect. "You are a thinker. I'll have to check the texts. But you may be right."

In the end they agreed to the burning—the brand would be obscured by a hot welt that would over time become a pulpy scar that would over time become a skin-colored raisin. A blemish, a nothing. By then, she felt unafraid. She felt full of magic.

When he cut off her wedding dress and she held the heated iron—this iron was her husband's own sigil, a rocketship, the brand that marked the bodies of his horses and goats, that was carved into the wagons and painted on all his canvas tents—he looked at her so lovingly, her pale naked body that was still not quite a woman's body. When she held the iron above her skin for a long moment, he was quick to show her a place on his body she had not seen before. On the back of his left thigh, under a whorl of dark hair, he bore the same mark. When she did it, she imagined Cosmas the Uncrusher, with his diamond-studded face, her protector. She imagined he was undoing her pain. It must have worked, because she was able to hold the brand steady. The heated iron on her thigh felt ice-cold. Afterward he splashed water on her face and made a poultice, bound the leg in a bandage. He kissed her.

It was more than Argento had done.

CHAPTER 15

FRIENDSHIP

Marvel Parsons spoke to King Michael late that night. He continued to have difficulty devising a believable reason for sending a convict Surgeon to attend the Royal Pardoness, so he decided not to mention it. Who else would tell Michael anything about the earless man, besides John Sousa, who was—as always—preoccupied to a fault with his divinations. The comets, whatever they were, had granted Marvel a fine enough distraction.

Yet he still keenly felt his duty to the king. Though he tried his best to ignore it, he could not help thinking of their friendship. Michael had been good to Marvel.

Perhaps this would be the last time they would meet. Marvel had mixed his poisons and made his bag ready. He could never have explained to Michael his decision to leave without notice. To disappear, to give up all agency. All responsibility. He probably could not have explained it to anyone.

The king lived in a simple three-room house far below the sweeping vistas and dizzying heights of his six beautiful spires. He had been eating a late dinner at his plain wooden table when Marvel arrived. "We have had an exciting day, haven't we?" Michael spooned soup into his mouth, his blond beard glistening. "The comets. An outlaw carnival."

"Very strange indeed."

"I think surely these comets must signal the Return." Michael laid his spoon on the rough wood and wiped his lips. "Sousa must draw up a horoscope. I wonder what planet is ascendant? If this is a favorable day?" He took a drink. His cup was wood, inside it only water, ever. "What a time to be alive, eh? You must admit it's exciting."

"Surely the outlaw carnival is more concerning." He sighed. "You know, I think one of my new guards may be a spy." He spoke offhandedly, but he'd already decided Juniper would go with him when he fled the Cape. The only way to ensure his loyalty was to remain friendly with him, to pay him as he'd promised, and to convince him, through the subtle art of manipulation, that it was Juniper's own idea to bring Marvel back to Kansas with him. Marvel didn't think it would be difficult; Juniper was an attractive man and Marvel liked him for more than his knowledge of the deathscapes. Trust would happen, if he gave it time. There was no need to torture him.

Michael waved a hand and spoke aloud what Marvel had already known he would say. "We have spies all the time. Have him executed if you think so. I don't like to hear of it. Take some soup, Priest."

So Marvel sat. "Michael, we are friends."

"Of course so."

"I have always thought you a fine king. Better than your father."

Michael nodded. "I've tried."

It was true that Michael was the best king the Cape had seen in generations. He was slow to judgment, kindly indifferent to women, he deeply trusted men more knowledgeable than himself, yet was not blind to poor character. He had executed many a false courtier upon the great execution stage, and ordered Marvel to take care of others more discreetly: unctions, potions, salves, tinctures, preparations. All that he had learned at the Black Watchtower, from the monks. And Michael had always trusted him to do what needed to be done.

Marvel ladled some soup from the pot that sat on the table. Michael ate the blandest gruel. It was part of his devotionals. "Sousa has a new assistant with him now—he freed him from the jail. He thinks this man is some kind of prophet. A visionary."

"Is that so?" He took a sip of water. "John Sousa is not one to delegate responsibility. That's always been my impression."

"The man is a convict, as I said. A con-man. I think he has befuddled Sousa in order to secure his release from the jail."

"Why is this a matter for my attention?" Michael said. Like a good king, he was rarely emotionally bound to the concerns of his advisors, even his most trusted confidant, Marvel Whiteside Parsons.

"Well. That your Chief Orbital Doctor may be under the sway of a convict. I thought you should know."

"What has this got to do with our friendship?" He set his spoon on the table top.

"Nothing, sire."

He chuckled again. "Then why did you bring it up?"

A swell of regret lifted Marvel, and as it crested he found he could not say any of the things he wanted—he would never have been able to say them anyway. That he was leaving as a traitor, soon to slink off like a dog in the night. That to set his own life back to rights, he must turn away from a good man, to leave him to his own fortune.

He regretted whatever might happen to Michael after he left. That was what he wanted to say but did not say.

He noticed Michael looking intently at him, his eyes overcast with worry. "I wonder," Michael said in a slow voice, "why you are more concerned with John Sousa than with the lights in the sky? I would think you would be enraptured even to *think* this could be the Return. I know I am."

Marvel smiled, a bit sad. "I have always detested Sousa. Much to your chagrin, I know. The thought of him wasting his time with that charlatan galls me. Especially"—he motioned upward, at the sky—"when we have real evidence right in front of us."

Michael slapped the table. "So you think the lights may be the Return after all? I must have a horoscope about it. You sly dog. You had me going."

"They may be comets. Or meteors. They may signify death for us all."

"Surely they would have hit the earth by now if they were meteors," Michael said, though momentarily he looked worried.

"Perhaps not. You should ask Sousa. He might know."

"He would have told me if they were dangerous." Michael leaned his chair back, catching his bare feet on the other side of the table, and folded his thick arms behind his head. He was a strong man from riding and walking everywhere; Marvel had always thought him beautiful in a certain coarse, active way. The son of thirty generations of Astronauts. The king gazed at the ceiling, wistful. "I must say a part of me doesn't *want* to know."

"I'm sure Sousa wouldn't be able to tell you anyway."

The king ignored Marvel. "Right now I'm not sure if I should be afraid or joyful. What a strange feeling," he chuckled again. He looked at the Hierophant, his face a disaster of hope. "What does your instinct tell you, Priest? Give me guidance."

But Marvel had hardened, already. "I don't know what they are," he said. "I don't think anyone does."

CHAPTER 16

A HEADACHE

John awoke late in the morning to a vile throbbing in his temples. Leaks of light poked from around the edges of his curtains and John scrunched down into his bed and groaned into his pillow, muffling the sound. His bed was splendidly comfortable, but all he could feel was a heavy pounding over his brows. The curtains were thick and blocked out most of the morning light, and the vast bed was overstuffed with feathers and covered in silken blankets. If Mizar heard him stirring, he would inevitably bustle inside, and then John would be duty-bound to rise. John rarely drank too much—there had been only one or two other times since he was a boy that he could recall such a revolting lapse in his judgment.

He was certain, when he awoke, that he felt a good deal worse than he had the previous day, and not just physically. But why? When they had succeeded in contacting *something* otherworldly? It was more than John had ever achieved on his own. He barely opened one eye, but still could see by the light seeping beneath the curtains that it was far later than he normally rose. Was there any point at all to waking up and taking yet another very dangerous carriage ride back to the palace compound?

Their meeting with Queen Alyson—he dreaded it even though

he had news to report. Tygo and Alyson's flirtation had angered him. He hated the ambiguity of emotion: this was why he had no friends, only servants. The idea of them thrilling one another with flutters of their eyelashes. As though he were a child who didn't understand.

John Sousa was many things, and he did know himself to be perplexingly unattractive to most people even though he had been blessed with a strangely handsome face and an equally adequate body and even a position he'd won through merit and heredity. And yet he remained unliked. There had been occasions when he did have some girl or another sent to him for pleasure, although the entire business was a distraction in the most base sense. What did he care what some low-born courtesan thought of his naked member? And yet always they seemed to judge him, rightly or wrongly, and enough of them had passed through his bedchamber that he'd decided there was no pleasing any of them. He had stopped trying. Now, it was only when his own physical urges reached a distracting pitch that he even remembered he could call for one of these girls. And it was always a different one. Did they wish never to return or was there some rule about courtesans visiting the same man over and over? John had never thought to ask, though it might have been nice to see the same one more than once.

He had given up the idea of a wife some ten years ago; no, longer. He found the prospect of living with a woman odd—he had shared his life with Mizar and no one else for as long as he'd been a fully formed and thinking human, and he saw no reason to upset that order. His health was weak enough. He needed significant rest and time to think. Truly, the arrival of Tygo was enough of an upheaval to cause a surge in John's chronic unease. So much that the previous evening, he'd drunk nearly three times the amount he had ever consumed in one sitting.

And now he was paying the price.

He turned over in his bed and finally pulled the cord on the curtain. In rushed cool gray light—odd to see clouds, he'd imagined it would be sunny. The air was a limpid glaze over his coverlet, his arms hairy pastel tubes atop the fabric. He could not get that word out of his mind. *Tellochvovin*. Falling death. Had he been more superstitious, he might've assumed out of hand that the word portended evil.

But John was not superstitious.

Chronically skeptical, perhaps. Demanding of proof, certainly.

Because of this quality of his character, he had begun to suspect that *no* shuttles were returning, ever, because none had ever existed. Or if they *had* existed, it was in such a way that man would never unlock their secrets to understand what they had meant to the ancients. They were as mysterious as the angel's language, artifacts of a past so distant now that it might as well have been a fiction.

In the morning light, John couldn't believe he'd swallowed Tygo's little show. Now that he was sober he saw it plainly.

Yet still there remained a niggling germ of belief. In the darkest part of John's heart, a hope. Tygo's word, tellochvovin, had remained with him, freezing his heart with fear even now, when he was no longer under the sway of Tygo's unseeing eyes. Even after his faculties had returned to normal.

What had happened in that room?

Suddenly, he felt sick. As soon as Mizar appeared with a bowl of steaming porridge, John threw himself across the room toward the washbasin but missed it entirely, and vomited on the floor, a scorched yellowish bile with a smell that caused him to wretch again. Mizar cheerfully withdrew a rag from his back pocket. "I had a feeling, sir."

John wiped his mouth, uninterested. "I feel terrible."

"Yes," Mizar agreed. "So does Tygo Brachio. What an odd fellow, that one. Inciting you to drink. That's not like you."

He spat out acrid saliva.

"You know he slept all night in your office, on the sofa? With his hands still chained. I offered him a bed. But he said he preferred to be near the mirror. What a funny man."

John panted. "You let him sleep all night in my office? All my records and books are in there!"

"I didn't see any harm in it. He was just as sick as you are now. It wasn't as though he was pawing at your belongings, sir." He paused. "His arms *are* chained."

"Have you given him free rein of my courtyard, as well?"

Mizar bent stiffly and began wiping up the vomit. "I thought he was to be your assistant. I didn't know he was to be watched like a prisoner."

"He was in jail for treason. You just said he was shackled. It should be evident that he's to be watched!"

"Not to me it wasn't."

"You left him all night with my mirror and all my books—"

"He was only checking the mirror for faults, he told me."

John goggled at his servant. "You let him touch it again? Mizar, that mirror is perhaps the only link between our world and the heavens and you . . ." he sputtered. "You just let a known con-man finger it as though it were his own?"

Mizar stopped wiping up the vomit and glared at John. "I don't know him to be any con-man. I thought he was a Walking Doctor."

John hurried to dress and went at once to his study, where he found Tygo standing in a corner with a large book balanced upon his chained forearms. Gray light fell from the window onto the floor just beyond where he stood, so he was partially in shadow. John noted with some relief that the mirror was still in its holder, unharmed, though still uncovered. He rushed across the stone floor and threw the dust-cloth over it again.

Despite what Mizar had said, Tygo Brachio looked just as well as he had the night before. No sign *he* had been sick. John ran his hands fretfully over the dust-cloth, feeling the shape of the mirror beneath it.

"Good morning to you, too," Tygo chirped, from behind the book. "Although maybe not so good, eh? How do you feel?"

John scowled. "I don't recall giving you permission to scavenge my rare books. What are you looking at? Those are some of my oldest volumes, not fit for daily use. Some of them are so old I've only held them a few times, for cataloguing. Don't touch them."

Tygo held the book up. "This one isn't too fragile, I don't know what you're so excited about." He eyed the mirror, John's hands on it. "Got it in your head that I'm a thief, did you?"

John flushed. "It's Lord Astronomer to you. You are to call me by my title. And you are not to read my books! You are not to . . . to do *anything*. Unless I say so. Give me that." He extended his hand and Tygo, snickering, gave him the book.

"O, I think you've read that particular one more than a few times."

John turned it over and looked at the spine. *Sexual Astrology: Effective Positions for Begetting Heaven's Children.*

"Were you intending to beget yourself some star children?" Tygo's eyes furrowed with laughter. "Tell me, have you used any of the techniques in here? It's so stupid. Look at this." He snatched it back and opened it. "'The position for a boy will be best achieved after a thorough massage to the feet and legs. You will find the leg massage tilts the cervix back, allowing for easier passage of the seed.'" Tygo flipped the pages. "There's more: 'Caress the underside of the breasts. Elementals delight in a winding motion applied to the nipples.' Did you know that a leg massage opens the cervix? I didn't."

John grabbed the book. "I've never read this book."

"But the drawings, you've looked at those." Tygo turned it sideways. "It has very good drawings."

John felt a glut of hate and jealousy for Tygo rising in his throat like more vomit. So at ease all the time; talking, poking fun, slinking along as though everything were a joke when almost nothing ever was.

"It may astonish you," John snapped. "But some people think about more important things than sex. That book is a relic. I inherited it from my father's library, and I imagine he inherited it from his own father's, ad infinitum. If you'd bothered to look"—now he was stammering—"you'd have noticed that this corner of the library is dusty. In fact I hardly ever come here. Not that I could expect you to possess such basic powers of observation. Being that you are a drunk. Now." He took a long, slow breath. "We're late already for our audience with Alyson. Although I don't know what we'll tell her. We haven't even begun studying the transcription."

Tygo's face lurched with pleasure. "There was a message from her earlier. She wishes for us to meet her at her golf course, since you were so late getting up. Did you know she plays golf?"

John could feel his still-hot face. "Everyone knows that."

"Fine. Sorry for asking," Tygo said.

"I'm sorry too," was all John could think to say.

"The Hierophant will play golf with us." Tygo's eyes became strange and bright.

John's head throbbed. "That's just wonderful. He will surely have plenty of wrong-headed suggestions about how we should do our jobs. He always does." He sighed. "You best not stare at the queen the way you did yesterday. Marvel is her father."

"I gathered that. I think the queen didn't mind being stared at, though."

John had to get away from the little man or else he would surely hit him again. He did not even check that Tygo followed him out.

CHAPTER 17

HULDAH

Mr. Capulatio woke her before dawn and went at once outside to urinate, leaving her in the knot of their blankets. She heard him outside talking to someone. It was some time before she smelled and felt the green fizz of rain in the air. She was surprised she wasn't cold. And then she felt it, all at once like slap. Pain in her thigh. In the dim light she examined the spot. A smear of yellow-copper had oozed through the bandage. It looked better than it felt. But from moment to moment it burned so hotly she wanted to tear off the bandage and pour cool water over it.

Mr. Capulatio came back inside the tent, yawning and stretching. Today they would do the ritual, but first he had to make things ready. He seemed tired, but she could tell he had something fixed in his mind. They'd slept with their foreheads touching but now he knelt before her while she lay on the bed, his face a limitless plain of calm. But she sensed his anxiety. "You really should read." He handed her *The True King.* "While you wait."

She stared at it. "Orchid wrote this."

"Ah, you've figured it out. A girl of many talents." He pulled his hair halfway back and secured it with a tie, then looked down at her sternly. "Let me tell you something before you get ideas. I do love her. She has been an asset. A great advantage to me in many, many ways."

The girl's heart contracted. "But she tried to humiliate you in front of everyone."

"Her magic is a special kind. She has bent the world to my own will with her words."

"She tried to kill me," the girl said in a flat voice.

"That will happen."

"But how can you let her try to kill me?"

"I'm not," he growled. "Leave it alone, Aurora. Read the book. When I come back you will have read it. As much as you can."

After he left, she was angry. But she had nothing to do. So she did what he said.

> "The carnivals began after the Blood Rain. They brought terror and relief by turns to the people of these lands, a people who are few enough these days and were even fewer in times past. The people were so enraptured by the carnivals that they kept proficient records, which I have long studied to collect this history. About the origins of the execution carnivals there can be no misunderstanding. I will tell you now how they came about.
>
> The history of the new religions and the carnivals begins some thousand years ago, when a rain of blood and viscera fell over a great swathe of land in the center of the continent. It fell upon the place that had been called Kansas, when it was but a wasteland ravaged by the Disease. The rain came from a clear sky, red drops and globs of tissue, and ever afterward people called it the Blood Rain. They did not know what it could be, if some gargantuan floating animal had exploded in the sky above them, or if the massacred dead from an unknown war had been lifted into the sky by a cyclone and then dumped upon them by chance, or even if the rain had been sent by evil forces or good ones. No one knew, and so the people were terrified.
>
> The Blood Rain occurred in April and lasted five days, soaking the ground in blood up to the ankles of the wild cattle that roamed freely in those days. Much to the astonishment of the Cape and

the king's court at Canaveral, the Blood Rain did not fall there. Even in those ancient times the Cape was already a holy and famous place, one filled with magicians and Orbital Doctors. They had already embarked upon the use and refinement of magic, the outlawry of medicine, and many more tenets of our faith that we still hold to be true. They had done all these things, and yet still nothing had been able to quell the spreading of a terrible Disease known as Bent Head, and people were still dying, and the world had continued to grow worse in every generation.

The Disease killed more people in Kansas than anywhere on the continent. Some even believe the Disease originated in the cattle there. Whatever the case, Kansas had become a wasteland, where nothing grew. The few people who still resided there lived like wretches in tiny settlements they were terrified to leave, in case they should stray from the roads they had come to believe safe. They were afraid to contract Bent Head.

But after the Blood Rain, the land, so long fallow, bloomed. Wildflowers, grasses, ferns, and rushes sprang up almost overnight, carpeting the countryside. The land brought forth greenery and living creatures, and for the first time anyone could remember, there were as many calves in the fields as grown cattle, and the cattle did not seem to die as they usually did when they crossed patches of Diseased ground. For several years the world was lush, even in winter. The fall of blood had nourished the earth itself, and its beauty was excruciating. There are records of men who went mad with the splendor of it, the rolling hills of soft summer grass, and the cattle which multiplied a hundredfold and then a thousandfold, until people could not look upon the land in Kansas without seeing cows walking dreamily from this place to that one, glossy and happy in their herds.

What were the people to make of this abundance, where before there had been only death? The folk had no inkling of the forces at work. So they reveled in the glory all around them, the warm wind blowing down the prairies, the birth of new calves. They spoke to each other in hushed tones, like the entire world was a holy space. And yet they were still afraid to walk among the cattle.

It was the case that the land looked beautiful, but they did not yet trust it. How many of them had watched loved ones die of Bent Head? It could not leave the soil—in hundreds of years it hadn't, why should it be different after the Blood Rain?

We still ask this question, but its answer is not one for our age.

Now, in that time and in that place lived a woman called Huldah, who would become the first Prophetess. All the Prophets and ultimately the True King descend from her line. Huldah was by then already an aged woman, and in the seasons following the Blood Rain she was first among those who wanted to understand why the land had changed. Each day she went onto the saferoads and made meticulous records of what she saw: how many cattle, how many calves, where they seemed to be walking, how many dead lay around. Soon enough there were so few dead as to be accounted for merely by natural causes. Huldah kept track of the plants as well, for it seemed to her that corn grew in places where it never had been, and higher than she had ever seen in any person's small garden, and there were soybeans again in the fields, and by and by she even saw wheat growing. But she dared not sample these blessings, for they grew some ways off the saferoads and she was still afraid. All the same, the people began to call the land the Garden, because it overflowed with abundance.

Huldah had two sons, Hector and Lee, but only one still lived with her in her small house in her settlement, which we still know by its ancient name: Lucas. At that time, Lucas was home to fewer than forty people, a fair-sized settlement for that time. Huldah's older son, Hector, was married and lived in his own home, but her younger son, Lee, was her constant companion and joy. The records speak very clearly about Huldah's love for Lee, for his energetic nature, for his curiosity and mischievous ways. He went with her everywhere while she was engaged in recording the effects of the Blood Rain.

Lee was by her side when at last she decided to sample some of the corn that had been growing, seasonless, for a year. Since the Disease first ravaged the world, fields where edible food could be grown had been reduced almost to nothing, as more and more land every year was found to be infected. But after the Blood Rain there had been no winter, only more and endless greenery, shooting toward the heavens, prairie grass growing even through the cracks in people's floors. Huldah went with Lee off the saferoad and out into a field, and they took in a basket of corn and boiled the ears, and then Huldah did eat one, with Lee watching and waiting to record what happened to her, and then they waited another year to see if Huldah would die of Bent Head.

Bent Head is known to strike in a very predictable way, so after a year of no illness, Huldah rejoiced that the fruit of the land was edible again. She called her son Lee to her and instructed him to inform the settlement at once, but Lee determined he must try the food as well, and he ate it and called it Holy, saying it was from Heaven, and Huldah declared it must have been sent by the Astronauts who had left the earth so long ago. The Blood Rain had restored the earth at last.

They went together to tell the people that the land was cured.

Also at this time Huldah, an aged woman, discovered she was pregnant, although her husband had been dead for many years. The land itself had given her a child, she said, for what else could it be? She had long ago reckoned her childbearing years were finished, and yet she was plainly with child. Moreover, during the pregnancy her health flourished. She blazed with vigour and walked about unencumbered through her ninth month, going from settlement to settlement and telling the people to eat the fruit of the land, for the Disease had been conquered by the Blood Rain. She was the proof. This was the occurrence that convinced many people in Kansas that Huldah was a Prophetess, as she had been inspired to observe the effects of the Blood Rain. Some celestial courage had made her unafraid. For her bravery, she was called High Priestess, and people came to her from then on to beg her wisdom.

After the birth of her daughter, who was very respectfully named Rain, Huldah began to receive visions. Lee recorded these visions with care, so Huldah would know every detail of what she uttered in her trances. She saw visions of a king—not the king at the Cape but a holier, innocent king, the True King, whose reign would begin when the shuttles at last returned to earth. The Astronauts who had sent the Blood Rain would return only when this True King sat on the throne—only this king could save the world from destruction by the Disease, and only those who followed him would ascend to Heaven within the perfected shuttles. Only they would be transformed into light and cosmic radiance and go on and on forever. Glorify! This vision gave people hope, and they were overjoyed to hear that this king would come from Kansas. Who would have thought such a cursed place might give the world salvation?

Huldah's most unhappy vision, however, concerned the Kansans' ingratitude for the Blood Rain, which had poured from the mouth of the cosmos—a gift, just when the world most required it. And how had they responded? With feasting and dancing and singing and lovemaking, but no great gesture of thanks to the Astronauts in Heaven for sending the rain, nor even a thought of how they *should* thank Heaven. When Huldah awoke from her trance and read what Lee had recorded of her vision, she was struck with grief and declared that men must at once build the most beautiful tower, a tower that would rival the Cape. Where the Astronauts had come from.

So the tower was built. It was made of an igneous stone, jet-colored, brought from the northeastern settlements, and when it was finished Huldah called it the Black Watchtower. There, the faithful would await the True King. During the years it took to build this magnificent structure, the land continued to produce staggering harvests. The Garden existed in such indescribable beauty that men believed they must surely have at last stumbled on the path of righteousness. The tower was a fitting tribute to honor the cosmos, and Huldah herself was the bravest woman in history, as well as a Prophetess whose words were wise and benevolent.

Now, at this time Huldah's older son, Hector, was jealous at the hand his younger brother Lee had in all their mother's affairs. Hector complained to his mother that he was the older son and by rights her heir and right hand. But Huldah only remarked that it was Lee who had followed her into the fields, and it was Lee who had accompanied her to tell men that the Blood Rain had healed the land, and it was Lee who witnessed her visions and interpreted them with her. Hector had been occupied with his own pursuits during these times.

Hector also protested her complacency with the perpetual growing season and the unending bounty of the land. It seemed quite an odd thing, as all Kansans were familiar with the harshness of the continental winter. Kansas had not seen a winter for many years. Four, he counted. Where was the cold? Did this aberration seem truly benevolent? Huldah chided him for his ungratefulness, and he went away unsatisfied.

Hector spoke of his disbelief with Lee, and the two opposed one another greatly, in both belief and temperament, for where Lee was bright and energetic, Hector was brooding and doubtful. They argued for many hours as they walked around the tower, their voices rising as they debated the unnatural weather and their mother's favor. At last their conflict came to blows.

Lee was the smaller of the two, but he struck Hector with a stone, his strength bolstered by his unwavering devotion. Hector limped away, bleeding and badly injured. Some time later, Hector crept into his mother's house and there, whether driven by jealousy or humiliation or greed, he poisoned Lee's drink with hemlock and within hours Lee had died a terrible death, paralyzed slowly until he could no longer draw air. Hector was incarcerated in the Black Watchtower for murder, and that was where he remained.

It happened that after five years of seasonless and overabundant growing, the land again became fallow. The marvelous numbers of cattle began not only to die but to *change,* for where they had once been lustrous and fat, they were now craggy and rageful, and they grew larger but uglier than before, and men could no longer approach them. They scraped their hides on the ground for days and weeks, until they wore away much of their skins and it hung in bloodied strips off their bodies. They teetered on skeletal legs, with eyes as dim and furious as demons. They became what we know as the Kansas Cow, that dreaded creature which still roams those dark places, whose saliva can kill a man on the spot. After several weeks of this terrible existence, they ran in wild circles before they finally, mercifully, died.

Men encountered other, even more monstrous creatures, the

manticore being the most fearsome, and all these still exist, although they have been seen by very few who are still alive. For with their appearance, men too began dying in droves—of Bent Head once again. So many died that it was impossible to bury them, and even Huldah feared for her life, for she wondered if their food was poisoned again with the Disease.

And yet she did not die. It came to her in a vision that her son Hector was to blame for the reversal of their fortunes. His jealousy had undone them all. This vision was recorded by a different scribe, as her son Lee was dead of poison, but we have copies of this scripture and thus can be certain of Huldah's intention. When she regained her senses after her vision, she understood that she must spill Hector's blood onto the land as a sacrifice. When Hector was taken from his jail, he was glad of heart because he believed he had been proven correct in his misgivings. The land was now in turmoil and they had all been wrong to trust the Blood Rain. But then Hector heard he was to be beheaded, so his blood would soak the earth in penitence for his ungratefulness, and he cursed his mother.

He did not meet his fate willingly, but grimaced and trembled. To immortalize his indignity and to remind all others of the consequences of ingratitude, Huldah asked her magicians to prepare his severed head in such a way as to preserve it for eternity. And ever afterward, Huldah kept the Head of Hector with her at every moment, sometimes gazing upon it sadly, for he was her lost son, sometimes cursing it angrily, as he had cursed her before his death. Soon his severed head became a charm she could not do without, a bitter memorial of Lost Hope.

Hector's blood did not stop the desolation of the land. The verdant hills regained their former character over time: dead, almost entirely poisoned and very dangerous: they became the selfsame land we know and live in fear of today. The great numbers of Kansas Cow and the other beasts died as well, since the land can support very few creatures of any kind, except those which still roam those wilds and terrify men who come upon them.

Huldah's visions revealed to her that her elder son's blood was not recompense enough for the slaughter of his brother, who would have been named Prophet upon her death, nor for Hector's denial of the beneficence of the Blood Rain. A larger sacrifice was in order. She meditated on this for several years, while she watched the world around her continue to die.

During this time of extreme darkness, Huldah was gifted. She saw in great detail the doctrine of Wonderblood, the rinsing of the world in blood for one Eon. She saw the legions of Heads, the stages for the executions, the blood running from the stone beheading blocks. She saw it and she commanded her followers do just as she had seen, and thus began the Eon of Pain. The first carnival was Huldah's own daughter's carnival, the Rain Carnival, and this miraculously conceived daughter became the next Prophetess, and it has been her line we have watched ever since for the emergence of the True King. Glorify!

The carnivals soon numbered many, each one believing a version of the story recorded above, although many are dangerously blasphemous and have veered from the truth. Still others are vectors only of violence and show no devotion at all, to Heaven or the shuttles or even the line of Prophets. These do none of the work for which they were originally intended: bathing the world in blood until the land lives again. They only are havens of sex magic and debauchery.

Cape Canaveral was the birthplace of a religion that found its perfection in another, sadder place: Kansas, the Center of the Universe. Only when the True King returns to the seat of Heaven, the throne at the Cape—where the men first took leave of this earth and journeyed into the cosmic openness—can the World begin anew. Until then, our carnivals merely staunch the flow of humanity's evil. When the True King emerges, the shuttles will return for the faithful.

This is the only truth that one must accept in order to begin the journey toward salvation: that we will be perfected and transformed and taken upward through the ionosphere. When the True King has taken his rightful place at the Cape, the Holy of Holies, when he sits upon the throne in his holy city, then surely will the shuttles arrive soon afterward. These days will be called the Days of Heaven, when the shuttles will deliver the faithful from the

Diseased earth and into the cosmos among our ancestors. Away from the earth. Away!"

She put down the book. The girl remembered her mother Gimbal suddenly, unbidden thoughts of her tumbling back—she had imagined Huldah in the story to be her mother. The long dirty white hair. Her doctor's bag slung across her body as she went up and down the saferoads. On a personal mission that even the danger of the Disease couldn't sway. It was the only image she could conjure of such a fearless person. Yet after all this, she had still not forgiven her mother. At all. She had forgiven Mr. Capulatio. Argento, even. But not her mother.

When she had ridden with Gimbal up to the carnival country two years before, her mother had said to her, *Fortune is a kind of uncontrollable ignorance, girl. You will know this soon enough.* Who says such a thing to a child, the girl wondered now, angry. Her mother had spoken in her ear, seated behind her on their white mule with the faceplate. The land was wide and calm—they were the only people for a hundred miles. That was what her mother had told her. Then Gimbal said, *This trial will better you, will move you closer to understanding the blind indifference of the World. There is no magic,* she'd said harshly. *Only fortune, good and bad, which you can meet with ingenuity or ignorance.*

The girl had argued. *Where does fortune come from, though?*

It's a gift.

So it's magic?

She'd clicked her tongue. *Maybe the only magic in the world.*

Her mother had taught her to rely on her own resourcefulness, which was a gift, to be sure. But from who? Mr. Capulatio said magic was all around.

Her fingers touched her oozing bandage, where she had branded herself with his sign of the rocketship. Curiously proud of the strength that had taken. She had changed his mind. She had done that herself. And the brand, a pain anyone would have dreaded.

She had done that herself, as well.

CHAPTER 18

THE GAME

John stood at the edge of Queen Alyson's golf course. He had never actually stood on the course before, and he didn't know anyone who had, besides Michael—but then, he did not talk to many other courtiers. He greatly disliked their chatting and rumor-mongering, and had been not in the least regretful to leave the compound for his own Urania.

Where at least he could work in peace.

Michael had razed a few courtiers' homes to make the course: he had known she would like it. The king himself never played, but would sometimes gaze out at her from a window in his modest house while John calculated the horoscopes, and he'd remark upon Alyson's beauty as she swung her club. Her long brown hair swaying with the strokes of the club. At these moments, John would pretend to look out the window as well, but really he fixed his eyes on some other point so he would not have to look at Alyson's lovely form, the pin-straight hair, the slender waist, all of which caused his heart to sputter.

John stepped tentatively upon the damp grass, blinking and disorganized in the cloudy noon light. It had rained in the morning, he guessed, but now the two comets—*stella novae,* rather, since no one was yet sure *what* they were—twinkled weakly overhead. They did not appear any larger or brighter, but there were most certainly two of them. He searched for a third but could not see one, so he turned his eyes to the course, which was roughly the size of several large tents and their surrounding booths, with each hole marked by a partition containing some particular challenge—knocking the ball through a small passageway formed by several wooden blocks, for instance. Or hitting the ball up a hillock but not *over* the hillock. He could not see what fascination it could possibly hold for a woman such as Alyson, who seemed uninterested in precision of any sort, but Michael once told him she'd read about it in an old book and had wanted to play it since she was a child. John could not grasp the point of the game. It seemed geometric, but Alyson was not mathematically inclined. Perhaps it was meant to be devotional? Did she meditate on the positions of the stars while she played through the obstacles? It did not seem likely.

John and Tygo were handed clubs and balls by a servant as soon as they stepped through the rickety gate and onto the course. From across the grass Alyson, dressed in loose white pants and an egg-colored tunic, lifted her own club and smiled at them. "I suppose we're actually doing this," John said dully, not even wanting to look at his companion in case Tygo was smiling effortlessly. He'd never walked on such perfect grass before and now regretted his choice of heavy boots.

"Just be yourself," Tygo said, stifling a chuckle. "I'm sure she likes you fine."

"I have no thoughts on that subject," John snapped. "I'm concerned that we actually have nothing of note to tell her, since all we did last night was become drunk."

Tygo swung his club in a shallow arc as they walked toward her. "That's not all *I* did." Then he said, "Tell her anything, man. You don't have to be nervous. She doesn't care *what* you say. She only wants someone to talk to her. For godsakes. It's incredibly obvious."

John snorted.

"Suit yourself."

He whacked his club on the ground, discontented, and said nothing.

They reached her at the seventh hole, concentrating on hitting the ball a short distance into the cup, having evidently forded the valleys and sand-spots within the enclosure in previous strokes. She didn't look at them until she'd hit the purple ball into the hole. When she did, her face seemed held together by strange smears of makeup. A cosmetic glaze one shade lighter than her actual skin hid her freckles, her eyebrows darkened with brown pencil. This mask moved barely at all when she greeted them, except her lips pursing into that bud. She leaned on her club and said, "I've been waiting all morning for you."

"We got drunk last night," blurted Tygo, before John could even open his mouth.

She appraised him with what John could clearly see was approval. "Very nice. I hope it won't affect your game. I hope one of you will beat me, no one ever does."

"So I've heard," said Tygo.

"I'm tired of going against my girls, I know all their moves. Most of them are up in bed with cramps, anyway. So when is the bleeding supposed to stop?" She swung her club and turned to Tygo. "Do you like my makeup? We were bored this morning waiting for you."

Tygo pretended to hit a ball. "I don't know. It looks a little . . . like you're trying. You know?"

Her eyes endless green phosphorescent nuggets. "We *were* trying! I was thinking I could surprise Michael with it." She turned her cheek to Tygo. John watched his assistant pull suddenly back to make it seem like he did not wish to be close to her, but then bend forward from the waist to study the spackle on her face. Alyson asked, "Well?"

"Eh," said Tygo. He removed a rag from an inner pocket and dangled it for her to take. His hands were still shackled. "You want to wipe some off?"

She swatted him away. "My best handmaid did it, the one who does my hair." She gestured to the length of brown silk falling down her back, but didn't ask what they thought of that. She gazed again at Tygo, not at all offended. "You're mean," she said, smiling. "Michael never criticizes me."

"Well, you asked," he said. "I just said what I think."

She continued to look at him, a half-smile trapped on her lips. "Why don't they unchain you?"

"Shall we play some golf?" he asked brusquely.

"If you're prepared to lose."

"You win because you're good, not because you're the queen and no one is allowed to beat you. Right?"

"I always tell everyone to do their best," she exclaimed, delighted. "If you can't compete, you probably shouldn't play."

And so John found himself, just as he'd feared, an observer to their coy match, a third when clearly no one needed one—O, he played with them, and quite glumly, but inside he alternated between seething embarrassment and dismal self-pity. Though neither he nor Tygo knew the rules to the stupid game, they kept whacking at the ball, which John surmised was meant to symbolize the moon or some other heavenly body. What other purpose could it possibly serve?

Alyson was correct, however; she was very good. None of Tygo's taunts, no matter when during the course of her stroke they were uttered, seemed able to upset her. Her concentration for this game flabbergasted John, but he reminded himself that people's talents could lend themselves to unexpected pursuits; one could never quite be sure who would be good at what.

At last Alyson, perhaps bored of showing off, placed herself directly in front of John, her square elegant head coming to his chin, and locking her eyes on his, said, "Well? When is the bleeding going to stop? I asked you once already."

"Ah. Well. We did an experiment last night that involved Tygo Brachio entering the trance state, but the information we received was hardly clear, and it shall need extensive study before we could possibly begin to—"

She pouted. "Then why did you even come here? If you don't know any more than yesterday?"

"Because you asked us to." Tygo said.

She smiled at him slowly. "So I'm just going to keep bleeding forever? How will I ever have Michael's child then?"

Tygo's eyes went up and down her body and John forced himself to look away, back toward the gate, where he noticed, to his surprise, Michael and Marvel Parsons standing together, deep in conversation. Michael, despite being an exceptionally tall man, the very physical ideal of a king, was dressed in unremarkable clothing: a plain white shirt with an open collar. He tended to wear his shirts until he'd sufficiently yellowed the armpits and neckband. He preferred the launderers to remove the stains with lemon juice rather than order a new shirt. The Hierophant wore his plain monk's cassock. Beside him stood the young pale-haired guard who had come for Tygo the day before.

Of course *Marvel* was already at Michael's ear. But saying what? What had he so needed Tygo for, when surely his time was better spent planning a defense against the outlaw carnival? Should that be needed. His presence annoyed John. Exhausted him.

He heard Tygo remark to Alyson, "Like I told you, pay no mind to the bleeding. It's bound to happen when something large upsets the gravity of earth. Trust me," he said, snickering. "I'm a doctor."

"But the shuttles can't be that big." Alyson said, doubtful. "Big enough to upset gravity? In ancient times did all the women bleed whenever the shuttles came around?"

"Who said it was the shuttles?" Tygo asked.

"You did! I remember it."

"I said it *may* be the shuttles."

King Michael was pointing to the *stella novae,* and gesticulating. The Hierophant, nearly as tall as the king, waited patiently until Michael was finished, then shook his head at the three golfers as though they were intruding on some previously arranged event.

Tygo was saying, "The shuttles may not be like they were when they were first on earth. We don't know what they'd be like, actually. They could be anything." He sounded so confident that even John found himself believing. Tygo tapped his ball lightly and it fell into the cup with a pleasant clacking noise. "O good," he murmured. "I'm getting better."

John still couldn't bring himself to look at them head on, but he sensed the queen had inched her body somehow closer to Tygo, who acted like he didn't notice. "What did you see in your trance?" she asked.

"A trance is like . . . it's like seeing different things out each eye at once."

"I can't imagine."

"Say you're sleeping. You're also dreaming. Inside the dream, you *know* you're dreaming. You wake up and you remember you've had a dream, but you also know you were asleep in bed the whole time. You can't remember the details, but you know you had a dream. You also know you stayed in bed for the duration of the dream. A trance is like that."

She hit her own ball. "So it's like having two present moments. One physical and one mental."

"Exactly."

Alyson giggled. "You're good at this. Can I hire you instead of John Sousa to be our Astronomer?"

John swung at his ball with a manic, too-hard swing, hitting it into a pit of sand lounging smugly in a far corner. It would be hopeless to get it out without several more swings. They were on the eleventh hole. There were fifteen. He could leave soon.

He ran sweaty hands through his hair, stared somewhat cruelly at Tygo. "Your Majesty, it might behoove you to note that this man was a prisoner for treason against your own husband but a few days ago, and just yesterday he did confess to me that he was a con-man in a previous existence. Just last night he was unsure if he could even enter a trance, and now he's speaking as though he's some expert. I would say that the evidence I have suggests that he's faking his visionary talent to save his own head."

Tygo smiled again.

"You aren't a man of religion, are you?" John sneered. "You've often reminded me that you abhor magic. Now you have the ability to enter trances? I think the evidence points squarely to these *stella novae* being ordinary comets whose paths have brought them nearer than usual to the earth." He shrugged angrily. "Perhaps they will veer away and we'll see them no more. Perhaps they will hit us."

Tygo's ball waited in the cup. He gestured for Alyson to go again before they moved to the next hole. "Well," he said. "There's an outlaw carnival camped at our gates. Maybe they know something. Has anyone asked *them*?"

John inhaled. "'Our'? So you are one of us now?"

Tygo smiled thinly. He pointed to John's ball in the sand pit. "Don't you need to get that in before we move on?"

John stamped over to it. "I say they're comets. Plain and simple.

That's what these things usually are, and we have no evidence as yet to the contrary. I say Tygo is an opportunist and that it was a grave mistake for us to have been taken in by his foolishness." He hit the ball. It did not come out of the sand. He hit it again. Alyson watched, her eyes folding upward like a dancer's arm. He hit the ball hard one last time. At last it flew out of the sand and back into the enclosure, where it nearly connected with Tygo's head. Tygo ducked so quickly that he lost his balance and fell onto the ground. Alyson dropped her club and rushed to him, kneeling by him and taking his shoulders in her arms. Incredibly, he was laughing.

He seemed electrified by her closeness, but pulled back as her hands came to rest on his face, near his ear-holes. Tygo dusted himself off.

"Are you all right?" she whispered, touching his hair.

John turned away just in time to see the Hierophant and the king making strides toward them. Michael, jolly and tranquil as ever, took large steps upon the springy grass, but the Hierophant scowled at them all, his daughter included. His frown visible even from across the golf course. "John Sousa!" Michael was calling him now, waving. "John Sousa, we have a most urgent need of you."

Michael arrived with muddied boots and a pinkish glow to his already pinkish face. He nodded affably at his wife, who had stepped away from Tygo. But Alyson's eyes were locked on her father's, whose frown had transmuted into a grimace of distaste at the sight of her hands upon Tygo. "Daughter," he said through a nearly closed mouth.

She threw her hair behind her shoulders and then gathered it into a bunch, which she fastened with a ribbon she'd withdrawn from her pocket. John watched with fascination. She was in her own way the most beautiful woman he had ever seen—this was a truth that now struck him with a wallop. Had it been Tygo's appreciation of her that had made him aware of his own? His cheeks, now burning, embarrassed him; surely they were red. Michael noticed them too, and clapped him on the back and said, "Yes, it is an oddly nice day, all things considered, warm too! We won't have many more of these before the rains come, and winter. You should be out and about more, Astronomer—you wouldn't get such a shock from warm weather if you took more time outside. I'll never understand how an Astronomer cannot like the outdoors."

"I take my outdoor time at night when the stars are visible," John sighed. "We are a fair race of people, the Sousas. And the data does take much sifting through, and that usually does entail . . . indoor time."

Michael laughed. "Yes, yes! Of course so. Speaking of the stars. Astronomer, I have quite the task for you today. We are greatly in need of a very accurate horoscope about these outlaws. Marvel here is telling me we haven't got time, but I say we can't even consider things properly without one. How quickly could you make one? Would an hour suffice? We'll go to my office to do it." He began to steer John in the direction of his residence, which abutted the course.

Marvel Parsons regarded John narrowly, his arms limp at his side. His eyes were concentrated green gushes of level-headedness, his only visible resemblance to his daughter, although on her they were as unrevealing as if they'd been drawn there in chalk. John did not bow to him. Tygo had sense enough to. The Hierophant spoke in a clipped voice. "I received a letter late last night from their leader, a young executioner named Capulatio. He wishes to meet with the king, inside the gates. Without weapons, as an act of good faith. He claims an undeniable proposition concerning the . . ." He waved his hand toward the sky. "*Stella novae*?"

"We should meet with him," broke in Michael. "Why not? He may know more than we do and they haven't threatened us in any way."

"There are many reasons not to," replied Marvel. "You're not swayed by his obvious breaking of the Law? By bringing several carnivals here at the wrong time of year? I'm very displeased by any act of open rebellion."

Michael glanced at John encouragingly, indicating he should join the debate, then said, "I've prayed over it. I feel no conflict, personally. Things do happen to change the Law. Miracles. If we don't pay attention at the right time we may miss them. What sign do you need beyond these two new lights in the sky? If a third appears we must have no doubt, I think. Something wondrous is happening, I feel it in every bone of my body. I've decided to be excited."

Alyson twisted her mouth to the side. "Lord Astronomer was just telling us the lights were only comets."

Michael peered at him, dismayed, youthful freckles standing out on his ruddy skin. "Really? How did you arrive at this very intriguing opinion?" he demanded.

Marvel smirked and John, pained, began, "Well, sire, I . . . you see I was merely attempting to make a point about basing conclusions on poor data. Which was only that we certainly haven't yet given the lights the study they deserve, so any conclusion we draw now would not be even remotely sound—"

"But when there's no time for study, what then? This could be the Return, whether you've studied it or not."

Tygo bowed deeply, inserting himself between John and Michael. "Your Majesty, I am Lord Astronomer's assistant, if I may explain? We have begun to study the lights in earnest, but the magic we're using is complicated and difficult to interpret, so we haven't drawn any conclusions—nor would we until we were completely sure that our observations are correct. This must take time. Until then I think a horoscope is a wonderful idea, if the Astronomer agrees?"

The king gripped the Hierophant's shoulder and erupted in a merry laugh, which sounded like air blown over the neck of a bottle. "John, I think you cannot refuse. What a catastrophe if we went in blind and it ended horribly?" He eyed Tygo's shackles. "Servant, have you done something wrong, to be chained up? Where are your ears?"

John watched as Marvel sank deeper into disapproval. The corners of his mouth formed a straight line—his face was a remarkable mask of restraint. "Excuse me," Marvel coughed in a brittle voice. "But this is the man I told you about. The convict. Sousa believes he is a visionary."

"Now see here. I don't know *what* he is. I just don't know."

Marvel nodded. "One minute he's a visionary and the next he's a con-man. Or a Surgeon. Maybe he's none of those things. Or maybe he is a spy as well. He comes from Kansas. That's all we really know," he said. He appeared on the verge of speaking again when Michael thrust his hand out and greeted Tygo as though he were a courtier—John knew this was Michael's way; he would have done it for Alyson's hairdresser or the court clown. "A visionary!"

"I would have him come with me to the Pardoness now," Marvel snapped. "I've waited long enough. *She's* waited long enough. The time has come for him to prove something to one of us. I'll wait no longer."

Tygo turned to John. Was it desperation in his eyes? John couldn't tell. But as quickly as John had seen it, Tygo nodded and bowed. "I'm at your service." What could it mean, Marvel's interest in Tygo? John had no time to wonder, however, before Alyson took her father's arm.

"Do you think the outlaw carnival means us harm?" she asked him quietly. "This meeting, will it be dangerous?"

He seemed to recoil slightly at her touch and acted as though she hadn't spoken. She said, "Father?"

"Alyson. I have no idea what they want."

She stepped back. If she was stung by his tone, she did not show it. She took up her club again and walked alone to another hole. Did she often feel alone, John thought, perplexed.

Then Michael rushed John into his office, and they had spread out their charts and water bowls. John was seated at the rough wooden table and locked for an hour within the heavenly math of so many overlapping orbits, and he drew triangles upon triangles upon semi-circles, and for the hundred-thousandth time he wondered if these shapes meant everything or nothing at all, and if people all did indeed live their lives as prescribed inside of them, or if the shapes were merely patterns thrust upon them arbitrarily. The king smoked as he waited, exhaling blue lungfuls of air that choked John until silently he opened a window.

Outside on the green lawn Alyson had begun her golf course over again, this time with another maiden for a partner, and they shrieked with laughter as a warm, gentle rain began, and John felt something inside him tighten and release, tighten and release, until he realized it was only his breath, entirely mundane and predictable. But suddenly he understood it had been the opposite all along: each breath he took meant *something,* in spite of his every effort to render it meaningless.

CHAPTER 19

THE THUNDER, PERFECT MIND

Mr. Capulatio came back to the tent. It was nearly afternoon, and the girl could hear sparse droplets beginning to strike the tent. He took the box of her belongings down again, and handed her her own brooch, the one Argento had given her that had come from their mother, and pressed it into her hand.

She said, "What is this for?" The brooch in her hand like a black spider.

"Black amber, sugarplum," he said, and picked up his hat from one of the sofas. "You wear it when somebody dies. Come on." He dusted off the hat and popped it back into a more perfect shape, then went into the damp light of the day, holding his arm above his head as though this could shield him from the droplets. She heard him laughing with another man just outside the tent. "Come on, I said," he called.

She put on the only clothes she could find, the white tunic she had been wearing before the wedding. She pinned the brooch to her chest and went outside. Whoever Mr. Capulatio had been speaking to had gone. Her new husband took her hand and opened a parasol above both their heads. For the first time since they'd camped, there was almost no one around. She was not cold. Her soft leather shoes wet through as they walked.

The black amber rock hung too heavily to the thin fabric of the dress-front; she feared it might rip. Her thigh hurt where she'd burned it. They walked out past the boundaries of the carnival. Past the sentinel fires and a field where some draft animals were pastured, then through a hedge of pricking bushes.

They saw a group of men when they mounted a tufted hill and came plodding around a thicket of low wet cactuses. The men stood in a slight natural basin. She'd never seen any of them before. They were huddled together around something she couldn't see. All of them were damp from the sprinkling rain. Mr. Capulatio led her closer.

The tallest was old, a dark-skinned barrel; he wore a brilliant yellow tunic and seemed like the sort of man she might have trusted if she hadn't met him here, now. So she did not trust him, but he smiled sympathetically at her anyway, as though he knew her from somewhere, and she had the same thought, but then she wondered if it just happened that way sometimes—if there are people in the world who are instantly familiar to you.

The other men parted to reveal what they had been crowded around. The girl froze. It was Mr. Capulatio's executioner's block, that black shining death-creation, and standing there beside it with her hair chopped to her chin and very dirty but calm as a lakeshore was Orchid. Her heavy blond brows smudged all out of order. She still wore the dress from the wedding, which had been a brilliant deep blue, though now it was dingy and stained all down the front with what the girl could only assume was blood. The girl felt hypnotized, rooted in place. It was a feeling similar to when she'd first seen Mr. Capulatio on the battlefield—a knowledge that she should run compounded by her absolute lack of ability to do it.

No one had held a parasol for Orchid; the rain had cut a rivulet down her face.

"Are you going to kill her?" she whispered.

"I don't like to talk about 'killing' or 'dying' in this special place," Mr. Capulatio said. He handed her the parasol, then swept his hand out over the whole of the landscape, which in this spot was ringed on all sides by scrub and palm-bushes. To the left she could hear the endless murmur of the sea. "My star," he said to her. "My sapphire. *This* place is the most holy in the world. This is where we left the earth, where we cut the binds of this sphere and blazed upward. Centuries ago. This, my wife, is where we first went to Heaven. It happened. It is here that you will ascend your queenship. It's only right. This is the spot that I first took on the mantel of king. Where I dispatched our Prophetess Lois, from the line of Huldah, using her own ritual, to set in motion all that has happened thus far." He pointed to the sky, although the lights were invisible through the rain.

He had killed Lois, Orchid's mother? Or had Lois allowed herself to become a sacrifice? The idea of Mr. Capulatio executing his own wife's mother was horrid to the girl, no matter his justification. She took a step away from him.

The four other men walked to four points surrounding the black block. Surrounding *her.* Mr. Capulatio went to the center, where there was also a shallow stone basin, presumably to collect blood.

"Are you going to kill Orchid?" she whispered.

His face was a wash of pacific resolve. At his feet, in the wet grass, his own blade, the pearlescent curved edge that he had used to behead her brother. She saw it now. His voice contained no doubt and no fear. "There is no death, Aurora. There is only Wonderblood."

The four men who stood with Mr. Capulatio all held their own swords like ceremonial staves in front of them. The rain had gathered and was now a cool mist, collecting as droplets of water on blades and clothing alike. She began to shiver. Two of the men were in middle age, and one was older and one was younger. The younger man was shorter and stouter than the rest and wore an otter-skin over his cloak. He had a close-trimmed yellow beard.

"But who are these men?" She tried to meet eyes with Orchid, who would not look at her.

"These are my Orbiters, the leaders of our four other carnivals. The same four carnivals which you've seen gathered here at the Cape in anticipation of my coronation as king. Five is the holiest number. As a group of five acting as one we cannot be vanquished. Each of these men has been convinced of the righteousness of our cause for many and many a year, and each has sworn an oath to die for me. They will be my cabinet when I ascend my kingship inside the palace compound. They have each forsworn their birth-names and taken up nom de guerres in honor of the shuttles. Columbia, Challenger, Endeavour, Discovery. And I am Atlantis."

"We have waited a long time for you, Sigil. You are the beacon that will bring forth the Age of Times. Glorify," one of them said.

Orchid was staring intently at Mr. Capulatio. Her arms were bound. The blond man held her by the elbow. Now Mr. Capulatio came to the girl and took the parasol from her and tried to push his sword into her hands. She kept her fists balled up.

He had executed her brother on this block. He must carry it around with him wherever he went. She looked at the stone as though she could burn it to death with her eyes. Did some small amount of Argento's blood remain in the rock? The day he died, she had been afraid. She hadn't watched; the guilt had closed her eyes. Now she was different. It seemed every hardship of her life had carried her here as if by design—her abandonment by her mother, her abuse in Argento's carnival, her kidnapping and enthronement, her marriage. All these past moments aligned perfectly, one atop the next, and she saw through them like a telescope: the thing she saw at the other end was her power. The girl had survived each and every trial and they had led her here.

The blond man brought Orchid forward. He pushed her to the block, where he bent her neck down and to the side.

The girl did not know if her mother was right and all magic was lunacy, or if magic was surely everywhere, waiting to be known at the precise moment one was able to know it and never an instant before. But she knew she felt power coursing through her and it made her brave. She had power to do this, or refuse. She thought maybe she *was* magical.

Mr. Capulatio said, "I'll hold your arm. It takes more force that you'd expect." He raised his eyebrows to the other men, who all chuckled darkly.

The girl pulled at her white dress, which was sticking to her body in the light rain, and gathered herself to her full height. "I don't need any help."

He peered at her closely and spoke after a long moment. "Do you know what we're asking you to do?"

"Yes."

The girl could not stop looking at Orchid, the bloody dress, the eyelashes wet from the drizzle. Now that she stood so close to her, Orchid seemed very pale, and smaller than the girl had imagined. Her body rigid and defiant still. The muscles in Orchid's arms flexed with tension. What would it take, she thought, for them to live together in harmony?

She took the sword from Mr. Capulatio. Orchid's face remained still. The girl spoke to them all, meeting in turn the eyes of the four Orbiters and trying very hard not to sound afraid. She was not. It was as though she had never been afraid in her life. "I am the sigil. You were waiting for me. I'm here now. The Great Work is finished and the world is different now," she began slowly. "I'll show you."

She raised the sword. But it was not Orchid's head she cut off. Instead she pushed Orchid back to her knees, grabbed her bound hands and cut the rope with a fluid *swish*. For a moment, Orchid's face went entirely blank; she could not have imagined this. But as soon as the girl had cut the rope, she brought the sword back down, the force of the metal driving through the bone grotesque and crunching. She did not pull back when the blade connected, even as Orchid let out a scream of fear, pain, confusion. Like any ordinary woman who was afraid.

The girl had severed one of her hands.

All the men yelled together in a panic. Orchid continued screaming, blood pouring forth into the basin, and she flopped to the ground where more blood soaked the earth as she rolled around clutching the stump. Her hand lay dead on the block.

Mr. Capulatio was by Orchid's side at once. He picked her up, pulling half her body from the wet earth and roared at the girl, "My god, what have you done? You've ruined the spell! Everything we've worked for!"

She spoke coldly. "I've given you a new spell."

"*What?*" he yelled. Orchid's blood soaked the front of his clothes. She still wailed. He looked as though he wanted to throw Orchid down and strangle the girl, and also like he wished he could pull his first wife to his chest to stop her pain.

"I told you last night," the girl said. "But you didn't listen. The

Eon of Pain has ended. The shuttles are back. Hers is the last blood to be spilled, but not for magic's sake. This a punishment. She tried to kill me."

They fell silent. Orchid opened her eyes. A weak laugh came from her. "A Law of Mercy," she gasped.

"What?" he demanded.

"She gives you a new Law of Mercy."

Mr. Capulatio stroked Orchid's face. He pulled off his cloak and wrapped it tightly around her bleeding arm. "What are you talking about, my Radiance?"

"The texts say new Ages shall be rung in like thunder, by a perfect mind. Remember? Here is your Thunder, your Perfect Mind. Listen as she gives you a new Law, David."

He paled. "What creature better than a woman to stay our hands at the executioner's block?" he whispered. "To stop our swords at the very moment when bloodshed becomes a sin again?"

But Orchid had stopped listening. She was gazing out over the soggy field in the direction of the compound. Then she fainted. Mr. Capulatio gathered her into his arms and held her body to his with such familiarity that all at once the girl felt like a stranger watching them make love. She stepped back, her heart thudding.

Just then he looked up at her with blazing eyes. "It is always a woman whom the heavens come to. It was a woman who gave us the doctrine of Wonderblood."

"Killing is wrong," the girl said.

He stared at her from the ground, then stood up, holding Orchid as though she weighed nothing. "Let me tell you, there is no right or wrong in magic. Magic is. Magic exists apart from your belief."

"I believe in magic," she said coldly. "But killing is still wrong."

Mr. Capulatio conferred with his Orbiters. The seconds stretched on, and the girl felt them draw out like the long blade of his knife. Might Orchid die from her wound? She was strong, the girl doubted she would die. With their backs to her, the girl could see only the chin-length jagged remains of Orchid's light hair. One of her arms—the one with a hand—hung slack along Mr. Capulatio's leg. After a time the Orbiters were nodding together, agreeing with each other.

They had accepted her Law of Mercy: Mr. Capulatio had saved face and won them back.

They all returned to the carnival then. The men went away—where, she had no idea. Mr. Capulatio carried Orchid. He gave the girl the severed hand to carry. A pale heavy lump. It was like a living being still, she could almost feel Orchid's fingers moving among her own. In the tent he took it away from her and placed it in a canvas sack. He summoned the crones to care for Orchid. He bent to his first wife's face, smoothed her mussed eyebrows, and kissed her as deeply as if she were awake.

Then he strode past the girl without looking at her. She had the feeling that by doing what she had known to be right, she had done her husband a gruesome wrong. The subjectivity of truth, for the first time, kindling within her a confusion she could not ignore. *O, lucidity,* she thought. *Leave me.*

CHAPTER 20

THE WATCHTOWER OF THE UNIVERSE

Marvel Parsons watched the king and John Sousa leave the golf course to make their silly horoscope. He stood there a long moment beside Tygo, watching his daughter begin another round with one of her handmaids. She looked happy, but he could tell she wasn't. He hadn't missed her flirtatiously gazing at the earless convict—how baffling, women's hearts. Who would want such a man?

A woman who had everything, he supposed. Who was very bored.

His mood blackened as he considered his failings as a father. He had not raised Alyson—he'd left that to nurses and servants. Her mother, a courtesan, had died a few days after Alyson's birth. Marvel had not cared for the woman, really, beyond her pedigree as a daughter of a fine family of the Cape. A few pangs of guilt when she died. He'd prayed over it. Women died in childbirth. It was sad. He had needed a child. He had gotten a child. Glorify.

At times, Marvel felt as though he didn't care what happened to anyone. And just as often, he felt the weight of his guilt like armor, impeding his every attempt to free himself. Why had he not left last night, after speaking with Michael?

Alyson looked at him from across the golf course. A few drops of rain fell from the bright gray sky. The sunlight had been swallowed by the clouds and now the comets, the *stella novae,* whatever they were, were hidden. Alyson's round face broke into a tentative smile as she motioned for them to join them again, waving her club in the air. Marvel shook his head darkly. He sighed. This was what he truly needed a pardon for.

Abandoning his daughter.

Tygo coughed at his side. "Are we . . . going somewhere? Or should we begin another game with them?"

Marvel chuckled. "I'm sure you'd like that."

"She is a beautiful woman."

"Lonely," said Marvel suddenly.

"Aren't we all?"

He glanced down at Tygo. This close, he could see the ear-holes, the scarring around them like puckered, waterlogged skin. "Very profound. In Kansas you were a priest, I take it?"

"Who said anything about Kansas?"

"Do you know who I am?" Marvel asked suddenly.

"Marvel Parsons."

Was Tygo sent to bring word to the Mystagogue that Marvel was High Priest of the opposing sect? To learn whatever secrets the Cape knew of the cosmos that Kansas did not? Was this why he'd ingratiated himself to John Sousa? Or had he come simply to kill Marvel and be done with it? "No. Do you know who I am, *really*?" *Born to be the True King.* A failure.

Tygo's hands, still shackled, did not shake. He took a long breath. As though he were tired of talking about it. "That's not why I'm here."

"Ah," Marvel leaned back. So he did know. Or was pretending to, for some reason. "Tell me, then. You know I can have you tortured. Why *are* you here?" He paused. "Why *are* you here?"

Tygo tugged his hair down over his ear-holes. When at last he spoke, his voice was soft, almost helpless. A droplet of rain landed on his eyebrows and he brushed it away. "Because I'm a visionary."

"What did you see?"

"The truth," Tygo said.

"We all receive portions of truth, I think."

He faced Marvel head on and said, "I saw the end of this world."

Marvel began to laugh. "O. Only that?"

They went to Canaveral Tower, where Juniper was waiting for them. He had run ahead to warn the Pardoness of their arrival. He was a good servant, Marvel decided, after all. He would like to keep him.

The pardon was all he needed. Or rather, *wanted.* Then he would leave.

The Pardoness received Marvel this time in a loose golden robe. She sat in her bed again, her gigantic legs lost somewhere in the folds of blankets. Her hair and face were uncovered now. Her cheekbones pressed against her skin. All that she consumed feeding those enormous legs and nothing else. The ledges of her clavicles made Marvel want to touch his own to make sure they had not broken through his skin.

There were no servants attending her at this hour. To her right was a very tall bookshelf containing old books, so many that some were stuck into the shelves two or three layers deep, overflowing even to her bedside, where there was yet another stack. A small collapsible wooden table sat at her elbow. She was bent over it, writing. She glanced up as Marvel entered, placing the pen in its inkpot. She said, "Puzzles. There is a man in the palace who makes them for me. That is his entire purpose." She pointed to Tygo and Juniper, who had been waiting by the doorway. "Well, here we all are. At last." She nodded skeptically at Tygo. "He is quite small, now that I see him. How will he manage to remove my legs?"

"What?" Tygo paled.

"My legs. How will you remove them?"

His mouth seemed to have gone dry. "I'm sorry. I don't understand."

Marvel took Tygo by his chained arms and dragged him into the center of the chamber. "Surgeon. Whose patients live, almost always. Take off her diseased legs."

Tygo cursed under his breath. He swept back his black hair and it stayed just where he left it, in a swirl above his right ear-hole.

"You can do it, can't you?" asked the Pardoness. "I can see by your face that you think you can't."

Tygo flushed. There was none of the medicinal smoke filling the chamber this time, but the smell was still peculiar, like no one had aired out the room in the longest time. Marvel noticed there was only one large airway, a closed door that led to the balcony. "What's wrong with your legs?" Tygo croaked at last. She pushed the folds of fabric away and heaved the appendages toward the front of the bed, each leg a hundred pounds—more. When Tygo saw them he gave no reaction. Juniper crept forward to get a better view. Marvel yanked him back again.

"My name is Green Butterfly," she said to Tygo. "If you did not know already." Marvel took pleasure in her voice, which was unusual and beautiful, even though he realized now that she had some speech impediment, or had never learnt to speak correctly in the first place. The thought made him sad. "I wish to be like my namesake and fly away. Please remove my legs if you can, so I can leave this place."

"I—" Tygo began to shake his head. "No. These are . . . what disease is this?"

"You're the Doctor, you tell us," Marvel barked. But darkness had begun forming again inside him at Tygo's obvious confusion. Of course he was no Surgeon. What a fool Marvel had been to even think it. That a Walking Doctor had come from Kansas to the Cape? Who had even ever heard of such a thing?

"Walking Doctors take an oath to do no harm," Tygo muttered. "*Primum non nocere.* If I took it upon myself to operate, I couldn't be sure you wouldn't die—"

"Escape is my aim," she said, leaning forward and meeting his eyes. Her own were dark brown, almost black. "Whatever the means, at this point."

Marvel rested his eyes on Tygo. "If you are not a Surgeon, what are you?"

The Pardoness joined him in staring at Tygo, her eyes disappearing into her face, dark circles acute with comprehension. "Then have you come to confess? If you are not a Doctor?"

"I did some healing in Kansas, some simple things I learned from my mother, and the rest I . . ." He seemed to slump. "I was just getting by. I never thought I'd get picked up for it. Much less asked to use it on someone so"—he swallowed—"important."

In a flash of impotent rage, Marvel shoved Tygo to the ground. He spilled onto the floor and slid for a few feet, unable to stop himself with his chained arms. "Who took your ears? Was it the Mystagogue?" Marvel shouted. "How did you get here from Kansas? Why did you come? Who sent you?"

Juniper instantly was at Tygo's side, pulling him to his feet. Marvel turned on him as well, his suspicions erupting from him. Suddenly awestruck by his own complacency. "And you!" he yelled to the guard. "You are a spy, I've known it since the beginning. You're not from a carnival, you're from Kansas, too! You were sent to flatter and trick me." He shoved Juniper away. Marvel wished he carried a dagger instead of poison. "I'll have you thrown in the jail if you don't confess."

Juniper stumbled backward, the small sack on his belt containing his Head bouncing against his thigh.

The Pardoness only sat in her nest of golden silk, unsmiling, unruffled. "Yes. Confess. Perhaps everyone should confess."

Marvel whirled toward her, about to scream at her, too, until he felt the Pardoness's eyes. Gentle. Calm. In the round stuffy room he became at once aware of his own petulance, his own pointless personal agony. Green Butterfly watched them all. Then, at last, she smiled.

She cleared her throat. "My, my. What excitement." She kneaded her knobby fingers together like she was knitting a garment in her lap. "All because of my poor legs."

"Pardoness—forgive me," Marvel said, smoothing his graying hair and arranging his cassock's belt. He bowed shallowly. "I lost my head."

"You are forgiven." She pointed at Tygo and Juniper and spoke in a quiet voice. "I see I am not to be freed by anyone here. But perhaps you men might be. Shall you two receive pardons as well?"

They both stood motionless.

She beckoned to Marvel. Against his better judgment, he went to her. She reached for his hand and cradled it in her own. "What do you want, Marvel Parsons?"

"Forgiveness."

"For what?"

"For—for leaving when there is a threat at our gates. For wanting to go home. For my nostalgia. For . . ." *For everything.* "My daughter will never be able to follow me, if I leave. The king will never know why I've gone. The outlaw carnival . . . For using those two"—he gestured at Juniper and Tygo—"for my own aims." Then he took a heavy breath. "For all the murders."

She considered. "You were going to kill the Mystagogue, yes?"

"Do you know of him? Is he alive?"

"He lives, yes."

"He would never let me live if I return to Kansas."

"No, he wouldn't."

He paused, defenseless. "Is it right to kill him? It's the only way I can be free."

"All *I* want is to be free." She lifted her bony shoulders into a shrug. "We all want the same thing." She laughed—it was a light laugh, a girl running among flowers. "I cannot make you free if you are bound to do evil."

"But I'm not," he whispered. "What I'm doing is right. I'm almost sure of it."

"How do you know they are not right, also?"

"I—" He slumped a bit. *I don't know what to do.*

She held his hand ever so softly. "Marvel. The truth comes unbidden to us—completely without warning. Go to Kansas. Don't go to Kansas. The truth will find you eventually." She nodded. "You are forgiven for your past sins. You may forgive yourself for your future ones."

Marvel remembered suddenly a bright day from his boyhood. The summer sky like a wild flashing fish, his hands in his itchy cloak-pockets as he climbed to the top of a butte and looked with pleasure at all he could see. This land, so beautiful, poisoned ground and all. He stood with his bare feet on the dirt, gazing over the grasses and the fields, and in the distance reaching skyward was the Black Watchtower, its crenelated spire, its monkish austerity, where his own mother Nasa Whiteside had been thrown to her death for finally failing to conceive the True King. He'd struggled, even then, to understand the beauty and horribleness of their condition. How, amid all splendor, they had come to be wretched. Warm breezes had swept the plain, turning the rose-colored grasses this way and that, and Marvel was so moved that he could hardly stand the feeling, and climbed down again.

Wandering away from their settlement alone had been a stupid thing to do, and when he'd returned, his nursemaid demanded to know which saferoad he had taken to climb the hill. When he told her he didn't know, she fell to crying, certain that he'd contracted Bent Head. But somehow, Marvel had known that he had not. Just as, a few years later, he had known he would not die when he crossed the continent on his journey to the Cape.

He had *known* then, just as he knew now. But this time he had needed to be told.

He would meet the leaders of the outlaw carnival. He would advise Michael. Then he would leave.

The Pardoness smiled.

Tygo's face was still red from his fall, but suddenly he came toward the Pardoness with an eager look on his face.

"*Tellochvovin,*" Tygo said.

"What?" she asked.

"The angels told me that."

Marvel pushed him away. For a moment all he could think of was holding the Pardoness's hand as long as possible, the papery skin so soft it could have been silk. He longed for her to smile at him again. But she said, "Let him speak."

"*Tellochvovin.* It means falling death." Tygo stared pointedly at the door to the balcony, then at the Pardoness once again. "I'm sorry. I did lie about my abilities. It's what I've always done. To get by. I had no idea it would lead me to Kansas, and certainly not back here. Or to you now. I meant only . . ." He glared at Marvel. The ear-holes gaped. Then his face showed only fatigue. "I only wanted to do the right thing. I came here for a man named David. I don't know where he is. I've been trying to keep myself alive until I find him." He chuckled. "It hasn't been easy."

"But who sent you?" Marvel asked.

Tygo blinked. "You've known since you first saw me."

Marvel sighed.

Juniper was looking at the balcony door. The Pardoness sighed too.

"Well, who sent *you*?" Marvel asked Juniper.

He shrugged. "The Mystagogue. I came to make sure Tygo didn't get put in jail. Which he did. But I don't know why the Mystagogue sent me. That's the honest truth." He frowned at Marvel. "There had been rumors about you, that you were alive here. But the Mystagogue didn't believe them."

"Rumors," Marvel muttered. He felt a stinging, a sensation confusing and inexorable. The Pardoness smiled at all of them. Her golden robe shimmered. She settled herself back in her bed, as if to indicate the meeting had ended. Drained of all his energy, Marvel stabbed his fingernail into his callus again. "They call the Mystagogue's tower in Kansas the Watchtower of the Universe. But maybe you see farther even than that, Pardoness." He bowed.

She shrugged. "I see what you show me."

Tygo came toward the Pardoness again, passing Marvel without a glance. He took her hand, which was as skeletal as a bird picked clean on a doorstep. Her expression was one Marvel could only guess at—the look was the kind one could see once and never forget, though in the past he'd often considered such sentiments to be maudlin. Within that exchange was contained the arc of lifetimes: love, hope, disappointment, acceptance. The Pardoness had looked at him with that expression moments before, and he had known the experience would never leave him. Now she looked at Tygo the same way, and Marvel understood forgiveness existed beyond a person's capacity to accept it.

Tygo stared into her eyes. "The word from the angels, *tellochvovin,*" he said. "Maybe they meant it for you."

She smiled again. She was gazing now at the balcony door.

"What a strange turn of fortune, to learn this word. You are all marvelous indeed."

CHAPTER 21

THE PARDON

Mr. Capulatio blew back through the curtains in late afternoon, a murky look on his face. His hat was gone. His hair was undone, sad-looking. Blood on his forearms. She had been trying to sleep, but none had come for her. The crones had taken Orchid away. The girl could not decide if she wished the other woman would die of her injuries.

"Don't stare at me like that!" he barked. "It's a nice early winter day, let's be happy!"

But he did not look happy.

She wanted to go closer to him but found she couldn't budge from where she sat on the bed, among his blankets and furs.

"You should be in your cage," he growled. "Where it's safe."

She said nothing.

"We'll have our day, today. We are going to the palace to talk to the fools in charge. They have agreed to see us. It is truly hopeless for them to resist. And they won't. Not after the magic I'm doing." He began to take off his clothes, stripping out of his still-wet shirt and dark red pants. He stood naked, his member slightly swollen despite the chill in the air, and she couldn't keep from looking. It was not as large as Argento's, but more nicely formed. It bobbed when he walked. "There isn't much time now," he was saying. He began rummaging in one of his boxes. The shadows formed by the indented sides of his buttocks as dark as eyes.

His mobiles of sacred glass tinkled as he knocked against them while he gathered more things. She found him beautiful. When had it changed that she couldn't stop looking at him? She wanted desperately for him to come over to her. For him to wrap his arms around her. He had a way of kissing her that drove a burning spike into her heart. But he wouldn't look at her. "You have humiliated me. And maimed my wife," he said after a long time.

"I thought you wanted me to kill her."

"The Star Sapphire ritual is not about death. It's about life!"

"You told me to cut off her head!"

He shook his head. "You are an idiot. 'A new Law of Mercy'? You are weak. A coward. Orchid would never have hesitated to cut *your* head off." He turned on his heel and bent close to her face. "But it's no matter. We've put into motion our petrifying destiny. We've begun the spell which will grant us our kingship. We are ready, even if we are not ready, to take the Cape."

Then he was at his washbasin, wiping down his arms and hands, removing the visible bloodstains, then his underarms, which he perfumed with a citrus-smelling talc he kept in a lidded dish on his desk.

"But I do think Wonderblood has ended," she said, standing. "It must have."

"What do you know? Have you even read the book?"

"A little."

"Then tell me, girl, since you're an expert now. Since you're qualified to interpret the texts you didn't even know existed until lately. *Why* did you cut off my wife's hand? My Radiance, my Glassine Prism? My scribe. Why did you take from her that which she needs for writing?"

"I don't understand." Her voice was cold. "Why it matters. If you wanted me to kill her. Why don't *you* just kill her, if you want her dead?"

"Because that's not how the spell works!" he yelled. She shrank back and sat again on the bed. He followed her and spoke in her face, his breath hot. "When I killed our Prophetess Lois, Orchid's own mother, I was little more than a child myself, though she called me a man. She gave her life to me so I might have this chance. She gave me her *daughter,* the heir of Huldah, so that our children might be legitimate heirs. My child with the aged Lois died in his sleep, not seven weeks old." His voice softened, becoming almost sad. "But Orchid cannot have children."

"So I was supposed to kill her?"

"To legitimate our line! Her death would have been a sacrifice, an unparalleled gift to the heavens. Who knows where *you* are from, you came from a field! Who will your children be? We have no way of knowing. You've said yourself that one of our sons may kill me."

"I—I was just saying what I thought you wanted to hear."

He weakly closed his eyes. "Please don't tell me that. I cannot bear it." Then, still naked, he strode past her, toweling moisture away with a cloth. He opened another box and pulled out a new set of clothing. Mr. Capulatio stepped into the pants, these ones made of pale leather and stitched with gold thread, and pulled them halfway up. His thighs were covered in sparse black hair, the muscles standing out like cords. He tucked his member into them and adjusted it to his liking. "I made these. Do you like them? When I was a boy myself I sewed for our Prophetess. She liberated me from that soulless carnival I was born into. I sewed there, too. Bags for the Heads. Wretched Heads they made in that carnival, even worse than your brother's—ugly and terribly magicked. Barely worth the effort." He glanced up. "My other wife recorded all the events of my life for posterity. You should read it some time." He went to the corner where the dripping sack containing Orchid's severed hand was still oozing, picked it up, and placed it into another bag, this one made of a tough horse-hide that wouldn't leak.

She hardened her voice. "It's better not to think about the past."

Mr. Capulatio, when agitated, had a cold mania that seeped into his voice, that same bland restlessness that had so terrified the girl in the first moment she saw him on the battlefield. Standing beside the striped tent. Like he owned the world. She tried to remember how he'd seemed in those first moments before she knew him, before she had begun to love him. Composed and unhinged all the same. How that combination had stopped the blood in her heart.

Mr. Capulatio was now donning an eye-blue vest. He slipped his arms through the holes and dusted himself down, although he was impeccably clean. In the mirror, he frowned. "You can make it up to me. How do you think I might die, sugarplum? My Queen? Try again. Isn't it likely I might die inside that massive castle, outnumbered a thousand to one?"

"Maybe. I don't know."

He sat beside her in the tumble of blankets, stroking her hair. "Tell me about the Law of Mercy. There will always be dissent, and dissidents are exempt from the Law of Mercy, I'm sure. For instance, what if a queen disobeys her king?"

"I—"

"There must be a codification of this new Law. Some way to understand its nuances, since surely it will be revealed to have many. Tell me, who will do that?"

"I will."

"You? You are a fetus! A child."

"You said I was the queen."

"You're beginning to act like a queen, I'll say that." He unbuckled his pants.

"No," she said, her breath speeding up. She did not think he would. He had never struck her. He had never even touched her when she did not touch back. The thin leather bunched as he pushed his pants down, and out sprang his member, already hard. He pushed her back onto her elbows, her skull striking the headboard. It didn't hurt, but the surprise brought tears to her eyes. He pulled her dress up with the other hand, his fingers lingering for a moment on the bandaged spot. "It's good we got rid of it," he hissed. "It would have been a bad omen indeed, it would have cast all this into doubt. But there is no remnant of your past unfaithfulness now." He swept aside the thin white skirt.

Something in his face—it was like she wasn't there. He had gone from familiar to ghastly in half a moment. It must be the magic he had done, she told herself. He couldn't be like this. She tried to scramble away. "Don't," she said. "Please."

"There is another bit of magic we can do. Don't you want me to succeed?"

"Stop."

He held her neck to the bed, his other arm supporting his weight, the veins standing out from exertion.

"You said sex magic was bad, that it was for degenerates!"

"'*I was just saying what I thought you wanted to hear,*'" he replied in a singsong voice. He rubbed himself against her leg.

"You said you wouldn't hurt me."

He was nodding. "Yes, and then I said 'except on the inside.'"

"You'll be breaking the Law of Mercy!" she whispered, as she felt him begin press into her. But then he stopped. She was not crying. He hovered over her, the slick knot of his hair undone now, and they both panted as they stared at each other through the revolving shadows cast by the hanging charms.

"What would happen to someone who breaks the Law?" He sat back suddenly. "Do you think they would die?"

She moved as far away from him as she could, pulling all the blankets over her lap. "I think anyone who hurts another person will regret it."

"Well, I must kill their king after we take the compound. There can be no other way."

"You'll know the right thing to do when the time comes to do it."

His face softened. "Aurora. You are kind. You are the sigil of peace. A girl in white upon the battlefield. You are better than she is—" He gestured at the bag with Orchid's hand. "She who is always grabbing for power, willing to do anything. But you stood your ground. You stand your ground. Against me. For me." He gently kissed her. "If cutting off her hand was what the magic told you to do, it must be right." He pulled up his pants, then cupped his own face in his hands. "What am I becoming? Who am I? Only degenerates work in sex magic, I did say that." He shook her, a bit roughly. "You must forgive me. It's this place. It's . . . I'm losing my mind, Aurora. I don't know up from down."

Cautiously, she caressed his knee.

"Lead me to the truth."

She kissed him. He kissed her back. Again he took up the bag with the hand in it. He said, "Right seems wrong and wrong seems right."

She nodded. He left and she felt her heart, a feather, floating down from a precipice.

She had thought he would save her, but now she understood she would have to save herself.

CHAPTER 22

FAITH

Tellochvovin. It was the language of angels, so said Tygo. Falling death. Of course he might have made the whole thing up. It was very possible. With the two *stella novae* hanging above their heads, an ominous quality could well be ascribed to the word. But John was not so sure Tygo have ever "seen" anything more remarkable than the weaknesses of others. John's own, for instance. John Sousa did admit that he was in search of a miracle, and had been for a long time. A vision of the Sublime that might, once and for all, convince him of its truth. Tygo need not have been a genius to see that John was a man who had always wanted to believe.

If the *stella novae* were *tellochvovin,* they would all soon be dead and none of it would matter. John cast his eyes out the window of this great lower hall of the southeast tower, Columbia. There the lights burned, through the gray haze. He was seated at a long table with Tygo and King Michael and the Hierophant, flanked by four armed guards. They awaited the outlaw carnival's faction—somewhat too jovially, John felt.

The horoscope he'd drawn up had been predictably vague. He and Michael had taken their usual roles. John urged caution while Michael laughed and replied that John was far, far too cautious. *There are so many ways to read that, John! Why do you always choose the worst?* But there had been a worrisome aspect to the reading: two opposing planets, one ascendant, one on the wane. In his view the ascendant body did not represent Michael himself—but of course Michael had not taken it that way.

He had pointed to the offending planet and its aspect, his narrow finger jabbing the chart. Michael had nodded eagerly. The horoscope showed at least one thing clearly: that the True King would be present at the meeting today. John's thoughts had taken an odd turn: does Michael even believe he *should* be king? Would he be happy to be overthrown?

The whole affair had unsettled him. Now John and Tygo were seated a bit to the right of Michael and the Hierophant, lower than the dais that elevated the more important men behind the table. Michael had changed out of his plain clothing into a robe of cosmic black, sewn with moonstones. John had also affixed a dress-collar onto his own astronomer's caftan—moonstones, again, patterned like the constellation of Orion, repeating around the length of it: the collar was a very old Sousa family heirloom, with the hereditary peacock insignia engraved in miniature upon the surface of each gem. Lately the collar had become too loose and John felt it drooped unflatteringly. Mizar had been wise enough to pack the collar in the carriage in the first place (how did he always know what to bring? And yet he did; some servant's wizardry), as well as an extra set of clothing for Tygo, who had finally been unchained. He wore a plain dark velvet robe—probably the finest garment he'd ever worn.

The Hierophant still wore his plain caftan. He energetically glared at the large metal door, as if willing the other party to appear, his fingers absently tugging one of the hems on his sleeve. John wished the other group would never arrive—his own palms were dampening. He wiped them on his chair cushion.

Michael spoke in a low tone to Marvel. "They stated only that they had a proposition concerning the *stella novae*. I'm more than certain they're here to request revisions in the Law now that the shuttles are returning. As rightly they should! I'm willing to make changes to the Law when the world itself changes. I am not my father. I will show them that."

The Hierophant narrowed his eyes. "That this is the Return is quite an assumption. And how did these outlaws know when they would appear? How did they arrive at the perfect time? We had no idea ourselves. No warning." He shot a pointed look at John. "By the looks of their crowd, they intend to assemble here for quite some time. Our scouts say they are armed."

"Of course they're armed, they're carnivals."

And they continued this way. John, stinging from Marvel's passive denigration, could tell Tygo was listening as well, but felt himself pulled out of the conversation again and again by some formless anxiety, a threat of especial doom that had fallen just now upon him like a band of shadow. He was, he supposed, given to hysterics but this was different, not just a minor churning of the gut. John stared at the great ceremonial door at the bottom of Columbia Tower. He felt guided quite firmly toward the inescapable conclusion that *something* was about to go very wrong.

The group of five carnival men were escorted in by the lion-masked guards. Two guards took their places by the door, crossing their pikes to bar any exit. To John's surprise, the retinue included a woman. She was nearing thirty years of age. Her dress had sleeves that covered her hands. Her face was incredibly difficult to look at, but whether this was because she was very beautiful or very ugly he could not tell. The eyebrows were pale and heavy. The mouth, childlike. The eyes, ravaging, painful to behold, like wounds in her head. Her hair had been fixed into a high hair-form, which was the style in the carnivals, though women at the Cape had long since given it up.

The entire cadre was an unpleasantly rough-looking sort, even though they were no doubt combed and powdered to present their best faces. There was no hiding the dirt of their world—John saw it in the corners of their eyes, under their fingernails, even from this far away. What lives they must lead, out there on the continent. He realized he'd never *thought* about people beyond the Cape, except when the carnivals returned once a year to make their offerings to the crown. Even then he was hard pressed to leave the comforts of his own offices unless it was absolutely necessary. Carnival people seemed simple. Cut off some heads, spill some blood, hope for a miracle that never occurred. Where was the exactitude? The tedious devotion? John had not the boisterousness for their kind of faith, nor the bloodlust.

Each of the ruffians exhibited different colors on their persons. Surely they represented different carnivals. Try as he might, John could not recall the names of even the more famous carnivals in history, even though he'd learnt a rhyme as a school-boy that listed them all.

They all sat down opposite them at the long table. This close, they seemed no less foreign—faces uniformly hardened, sun-speckled from the past summer's adventures. Two of them were darker, obviously brothers. One was a stocky pale-beard, the other tall and dark-skinned. The last was the youngest, who wore his oiled hair in a center part and plaited down his back in some ghastly outlaw style. He sat upon the cushioned chair with a dreamy aplomb, taking in the great hall and all the beautiful wall hangings and carpets and seemed singularly delighted by all of it. His face was the face of an innocent dreaming.

The Hierophant had several folders ready, large vellum envelopes he shuffled pointedly as the five men arranged themselves at the table. The innocent-looking man laughed softly. "Well, gentlemen, I won't beat around the bush," he said. "That would be undignified, wouldn't it?"

The Hierophant cleared his throat pointedly. "It is customary that introductions are made before any business is discussed. And then it will be the king who speaks first."

The man grinned. "Is that so? I have so much to learn about decorum. By all means, let us introduct, then!" He swept his arms out. "I am Mr. Capulatio, chief executioner of the Atlantis carnival, *my* carnival, which if you will recall was once the carnival of the Prophetess Lois, whose son I did wrest control of it from some years ago. This radiant star is my first wife, my scribe. As you can see, she is a breathtaking personage. A power beyond powers. These men are my Adepts, my Orbiters, my constituent brothers—"

The Hierophant held up a small bottle. "Before introductions even—if you had given me a moment to speak—I must insist that we bless this meeting with an unction I have prepared."

The four other men exchanged concerned glances, finally turning to Mr. Capulatio. He continued to smile. "Ah, but we don't share your religion, Priest. That is the very crux of our problem." He spread his hands. "We don't wish to offend, never that. But we won't be blessed by any unction concocted by the priest of a man whom we know to be a false king."

Michael barely raised an eyebrow. "Am I a false king?" He looked to Marvel, John, Tygo, the guards, his expression one of pure enchantment. "I had no idea."

Mr. Capulatio continued to grin, the corners of the mouth drawn up unflappably. He met each of their eyes in turn, including John's. "Yes. A false king. I am the True King, you see. I can't blame you for not knowing. There's probably no way you could've known."

Michael's own smile did not falter. "I had thought I was king. I live here. I've lived here all my life. That's because my father was king and his father before that and so on. I had supposed that made me the king also." He began to laugh, then looked to John and Tygo as if to say, *Is this truly happening?* "So you and your band of men have traveled all this way in an illegal season to tell me—quite politely, might I add—that I am not the king after all?" He pushed up his sleeves and revealed his blond arms, where he wore a bracelet of metal forged from the launchsite. He said, "If this is true, I believe I've heard enough." He paused, glancing at John specifically. "Though I *would* be interested to know what divination you used to reach this conclusion, I doubt I'll be encouraged to stay and listen."

Marvel chuckled. "This man is obviously mad. It seems the zealots can still organize themselves from time to time." He raised a hand and two of the guards advanced on the table with their pikes drawn.

The woman shook her head. Her face was so pale that John wondered if she would be sick. Her hair, colorless and wispy as a girl's, was parted low on her forehead so she appeared to have a very small face—upon which all her features were tight and refined. The hair was shining markedly for having no particular color. He decided he found her beautiful although he did not know if she actually was. "He's not mad," she said in a slow voice. "He is the True King."

The Hierophant continued to shake his head.

The woman went on stiffly, "Astrologically speaking, there can be no fault to his claim. We have evidence. Years of scholarly study done by myself and my predecessors led us to *this* man, at this time, and now that we have arrived at the correct location, the last piece of the puzzle has fallen into place. There are records we could present you here if you want to read them."

"O, but what evidence do you need beside the lights in the sky?" Mr. Capulatio pointed to the tall windows. "I'm here. They're here. I'm sure you don't know, because how could you know, but we've entered a new Age of Mercy. I want so much to do this without violence. I've been violent all my life. And I can't regret it. But I'm tired of it. My men are tired of it. We've come to you with open arms to ask that you hear reason. The lights in the sky signify that this is the Return. *Right now.* If the wrong king is on the throne—that is, if we have done wrong for all these centuries—we will pay for it when they arrive. Now is your chance to put things right. I am giving you that chance." He smiled again, emptily. "Because I'm the king."

The Hierophant opened one of his folders. "Do you suppose we will just give you the Cape? The whole compound? The king's clothes and books? His precious metals?" Marvel's face betrayed nothing. "Should we give you the king's wife, as well?" He threw a long piece of paper onto the table—a map of the Cape and its surrounding marshes, with areas darkened and crossed out. "Our scouts have been all over your camp. We know where your men are, even the ones you believe we don't know about. We have twice as many men as you, but we will kill you right now if that's the easiest way to put this nonsense down."

"You won't defeat us," Mr. Capulatio said.

"We will. We've done it before, with others. I shouldn't have to remind you of the Unrest." Marvel dusted his map off somewhat primly. "Michael is a descendant of the Astronauts. A direct descendant. If the Return is now, he will greet them gladly and tell them himself." He met Mr. Capulatio's eyes. "*If* this is the Return."

All this time, Tygo had been scrutinizing Mr. Capulatio, looking at him in the most peculiar way. "I know what the lights are," he said softly.

Everyone turned. John gaped at him. He seemed to John so foreign in that moment, a witless combination of assurance and naïveté—a man willing to climb on a box to speak before a disparaging crowd even after having done it before. "What?" Tygo stared at them. "I do. I know what they are."

Mr. Capulatio nodded. "And who are you?"

"My servant," John said sadly. "My assistant."

Michael was thrilled. He looked back and forth at John and Marvel. "Tell us, then. Johnny, this man is a treasure. I have no idea who he is or why he's here, but he is an utter treasure."

Tygo patted his hair down over his ear-holes. "The lights in the sky are angels. They're guiding the shuttles back to the earth. I know because I was in Kansas, and in Kansas I had a vision, and that vision revealed this to me." He stared again at all of them. "It sounds insane, I know. But the truth is stranger than anything anyone can make up. Ask Lord Astronomer. He's the one who freed me so I could help him ascertain the Return Date."

John remained silent for a long moment. "I don't know why I freed him. He is a madman."

"The Return Date is now," said Mr. Capulatio. He looked annoyed. "Angels? That's some fairytale. It's not got anything to do with our religion."

"It does. That's what they called themselves when they spoke to me—angels. And why not? They bring messages from above. And they speak their own language . . ." Here he trailed off helplessly, unable to explain. He blinked at John, nodding slightly. "I can't understand much of it. But some words come through, maybe by the very force of their will that I *should* understand. They told me the word *tellochvovin*. Which I understood." He turned about in his seat. "Which means 'falling death.' "

The Hierophant fingered the unction in the bottle. He kept his eyes on the bulb of the small glass stopper. For the first time John wondered what he had intended to do with it. The liquid in the glass was very dark, almost black, but when the light hit it just so, it shone gold, but with weight, like mercury.

Mr. Capulatio, impatient, watched Marvel's hands on the bottle as well. "I could be wrong, but my ears aren't hearing an overwhelming agreement to our righteous proposition. Which is a shame. You have every opportunity to do the right thing. You haven't even reviewed our scholarship. I would have thought you would at least do that, or have your man here"—he gestured to the Marvel—"do it. Where's your curiosity? In your minds is there not a chance, even a slender chance, that Michael may just be a man, like any other, and that I might be the True King who will reign over the Age of Times?"

Michael's smile had faltered slightly. He turned to the Hierophant, who gripped the unction tightly. "There is no chance." Marvel spoke calmly.

"I am the True King. It has been me for all time. But it was only recently, in cosmological time, that I became aware of it." He laughed again. His laughter was full of fearful anger. "I act out my Destiny. I can do nothing else in my life."

His men were nodding. The two brothers and the blond stout one were fidgeting; John supposed glumly that they'd concealed weapons somewhere on their persons, and that now he would probably die. They would be mad to come unarmed like they'd promised. For the first time he wished he had a dagger of his own—not that he would have known how to use it, but having one seemed suddenly so obvious. He was such a fool. The guards stood with their pikes behind them all, but they would protect Michael first, then the Hierophant.

Tygo beside him had straightened. His voice was unafraid. "The angels told me something else."

"Really, Sousa. Quiet your servant. He's making this worse," Marvel snapped.

John looked away.

"The True King was part of my vision. The whole reason I came here to begin with, before they picked me up for treason and threw me into the jails. The angels told me the name of the king. They—"

Before he could finish, one of the dark-haired brothers signaled to the other one, and with a floating motion, like the descent of a hummingbird, the one on the left reached into his cloak and threw a wet and heavy thing onto the table. The guards jolted forward, but stopped when they saw the object was only a sack, and that it lay on the table inert.

Mr. Capulatio's face was impassive. "In there," he said.

Michael eyed the Hierophant. Marvel turned to John. Horrified, he nudged it toward Tygo, who rubbed his hands together as though they were cold, but upended the bag on the table.

How he felt when the contents of the bag were spilt: drawn forward, pulled as if by a spell to look and look, eyes all over the bloodied and hacked disfigurement resting there, after rolling lazily for one half-turn and spattering blood on the table, before them all. And then, while his mind worked out what this object could be, revulsion exploded like a grease fire in his gut. He had seen his fair share of severed limbs—they all had, since childhood. The parapets around the east wall of the palace were always strung with dead bodies, headless trophies atrophying and putrefying in the moldy Cape air. But out had tumbled a delicate and beautiful forearm and hand; feminine, almost childlike. Gray as a winter day, except for the blue tips of the fingers and where the ovular bone had been cut through. This itself gave way to red along the ragged edges of the skin, and in the gory cross-section, the thin bone, white, impossibly fragile, surrounded by as many colors of dark red as he could imagine existed under the sun. Mr. Capulatio was not smiling now. He looked very near tears. "How many fingers do you count there?" he asked them.

Marvel, the Hierophant, had puffed up to his full roundness. "Get this abomination away from us. Guards."

The guards stepped forward, but Mr. Capulatio raised his voice. "How many fingers?"

"Five," said Tygo.

"O! You are the brightest star in the room, that is clear! What a servant! They are lucky to have you. I would make you my advisor, angel-talker. Yes," he said at length. "There are five. This, gentlemen of the court, is my wife's hand. A powerful magic took it from her: the Law of Mercy." He held up the woman's arm and her sleeve fell down to reveal a bandaged stump. Her eyes were closed. "Orchid, my scribe, has given her writing hand for my cause." He closed his eyes, seemed to whisper a nonsense word, a prayer. He spoke it five times under his breath, then faced them once again. He was, it seemed, in an ecstasy. "So our two factions will clash here at the mouth of the sea. How fitting! For so like the sea is the sky, from which those metal luminaries will descend to take us into the ionosphere, the Age of Times, the Days of Heaven. Glorify!"

Michael gazed at the hand as though it were a dying baby. "He is entirely mad," he whispered.

"The hand signifies the five carnivals we have outside the gate, five armies waiting for my indication that they should once more do what they have done for this last terrifying and holy Eon of Pain—to fight. To battle for their last field. It may be the Age of Mercy but we cannot grant mercy to everyone. We cannot grant it to you if you will not receive it." He frowned. "I have a great fear that you don't know what we're capable of. I'm sorry for it. But there's nothing to be done. You had a choice and you chose wrong."

Marvel picked up the hand and flung it across the great room. It smacked the far wall with an animate thud. "This is beyond abhorrent. You, my unfortunate zealots, must die now, every one of you. And your people at the gates will be executed upon our black stage for months and years to come. We will kill every one of them we catch; their blood will run into the earth and cleanse it of your sin."

He reached for the unction, but before he could grasp it, Tygo leaned over the table and clasped Mr. Capulatio's hands between his own. Like a lover. John had already pushed his chair slightly away from the table in case things became violent, but he stopped now, fascinated with horror. Tygo said, "The angels told me the name of the True King. I heard it in Kansas and followed that word all the way across the land, to this moment. Is your name David?"

Mr. Capulatio seemed confused. His attention had flown with the hand as it sailed across the room. He seemed to want to fetch it, to go comfort it. "What?" he asked in a soft voice. Mr. Capulatio's eyes went from each of their faces to the next, and finally at last to Tygo's, to whom he nodded with grim pride. "My name is David. Though how you could know it must be a deep magic indeed. Who are you?"

"No magic," whispered Tygo. "I saw it. I heard it."

One of Mr. Capulatio's men had drawn a dagger and John saw it in an instant. He leapt up and back from the table, just as the man with the dagger, the blond stocky one, pulled Mr. Capulatio back and behind him, brandishing the weapon in front. The other three men surrounded him as they began backing from the room. The woman did not move.

The guards surged forward with pikes pointed viciously, but they'd waited too long. Afterward, John would think often about this mystery—why had they waited? Perhaps they were afraid of the four men conjuring more magical weapons from the folds of their robes. Or perhaps they'd hesitated because of some feral strength in Mr. Capulatio's voice when he said, simply, "Be still." For John had become still then too, without realizing it, freezing in place just steps from the table.

Then Marvel Parsons cast his glass bottle and whatever enigmatic liquid it contained at the group of outlaws, and the bottle shattered and exploded upward some concoction of gases and fumes that began immediately to choke them. They fell to their knees. The cloud enveloped them and John could see nothing of them for long seconds—he only heard their choking and gagging as he backed away into a far corner of the great hall, distancing himself as much as possible from whatever had been inside the bottle. The Hierophant and Michael immediately slipped out through a small service doorway located just behind the great table.

The cloud spread to the main entrance, where even the two guards posted by the door succumbed to it. John realized Tygo had followed him. He was there too, pressed into the corner, listening to the death of the men inside the miasma.

There was nothing to do but wait. He looked down at the smaller man, pained. "Do you really speak to angels?"

"Only that one time. With my shaving mirror."

"What about *tellochvovin*?"

Tygo had a manner of looking entirely calm, even disinterested, when he said surprising things. "I made that up so you would believe me."

John only nodded. *O. Of course.* "Is this the Return?"

Tygo raised his eyebrows. "No. But we'll all die if we stay here. That's the truth. Those lights are meteors. Bound for the Cape. Nothing here will survive when they hit."

"There will not be three more appearing soon, to make five, to carry us heavenward?"

"No."

A muted thud: it was his heart sinking. He hadn't realized how he had hoped. "O."

Almost off-handedly, Tygo said after a time, "That man Mr. Capulatio is the True King, though. We should save him."

"What?"

"I saw it in my vision. He is David. He's needed in Kansas. That's where I came from." Now Tygo was shrugging. "I told you *some* of the truth."

John wrinkled his brow, putting his fingertips to his temples. "Why didn't you just tell me all of this?"

"You wouldn't have believed me." Tygo's face, unmoving, until his mouth twitched downward into a small smile.

Then they saw the one-handed woman. She was walking toward them around the cloud, just skirting the edge of it. Completely fearless. Her expression made no sense—she was smiling. "You *believe* in him," she said to them.

But before Tygo could move, the four guards advanced on the thinning cloud and began stabbing the four men, until they were covered in blood and motionless, just piles of bloodstained clothing, limbs splayed this way and that. John hoped they were dead before the blows, but he suspected they were probably not. John's eyes fell on the pile of men, and he saw—at the same time Tygo saw—that David, Mr. Capulatio, the True King—was nowhere.

The guards turned their pikes toward the woman, but she raised her arms again, so her sleeves again fell and revealed her stump. "I am helpless," she said. "Just a mutilated captive!"

They looked to John. "Don't just stand there, seize her!" he said, although he did not know why. The woman looked dangerous, but not like she would do them immediate harm.

One took hold of her. She held John's eyes with her own horrible ones; they were like holes gored out by an animal. "A long time ago, I had an accident," she said. "It cost me my ability to bear children. Before my accident, I could see things. Not the future. No one can see the future. But I could see other things. People's hearts. What drove them. But seeing made me unhappy." Her cheeks had flushed with the exertion of speaking. "You had a vision," she said to Tygo. "Of my husband?"

"I suppose."

"Tell me."

"There's a man in Kansas, a kind of high priest. The Mystagogue. I was taken up on charges of Surgery. To work off my debt they made me his servant. That was when I had my vision. He believed me." Tygo's face seemed to dissolve and re-form. "The Mystagogue knew my vision to be genuine. So he sent me here. To get David." He pointed to the dissipating cloud. "To bring him back."

"You believe," she said again, to both of them this time. "Without a text to guide you."

In the weird light choked by the fumes of the phlegmatic gases, John wanted to answer yes. But it was not that he believed in that man, her husband. He believed in Tygo. He believed in Tygo's vision. John pulled at his ill-fitting jeweled collar, finally yanking it off. Without thinking, he dropped it onto the floor.

Tygo replied, surprise in his voice. "Yes, I guess I do. I didn't, until I did. And then I had no choice."

"What about you?" the woman asked John.

But Tygo answered for him. "John requires proof."

She nodded like the answer satisfied her.

John muttered, "Shouldn't you two save your king? He must be unconscious by now, or dead."

"What should I do with the woman?" asked the guard.

"Let her go. What can she do? She's a cripple."

When she was free, the woman remarked, "It is the way of faith that it often feels like despair."

John and Tygo walked out of the tower and into the courtyard, across a plank bridge that led over the ornamental stream that trickled through the compound. The evening stillness breathtaking. No siege had yet begun. Just a few courtiers strolling the closing market stalls. No murmurs leaking from beyond the walls, none they could hear, anyway. It was unclear, in that moment, what would happen. The strange woman had simply walked away from them.

They stood in the hushed glare of the sunset—at the very end of the day the sun had broken through again. John watched the sky, feeling the weight of his accumulated failures begin to dissolve. All his life he had suffered to make his work matter, and of course, he had been wrong the entire time. Altogether wrong.

About all of it.

But then he thought of the horoscope he'd drawn up a few hours ago, the ascending planet—there was hope there. For his methods. The methods might yet be sound. Perhaps if he directed himself more properly. If he gave up this place, the Cape, its overindulgences. For twenty years he had been laboring under a set of false parameters; his work, yes, all flawed. But perhaps recoverable. It would be difficult, it may take another twenty years. He looked at the *stella novae,* brighter now in the fading light. Still numbering two. "When is the Return?" he asked no one, but Tygo answered.

"I don't know. No one does."

John nodded. He motioned to the *stella novae.* "Tellochvovin. You may have made it up, but it's true anyway."

"There's not much time," Tygo said gravely.

"I see him, I think," John said, his voice light. "David. Over there. He's behind that cistern."

"Ah. We should get him, then."

John felt calm, even as he stared up into the sky at his own certain death. What was there to do but move forward?

When Mr. Capulatio saw them, he didn't run. He coughed, wiped his hands on his pants, and nodded to them both with a restrained elegance. His Adepts, it seemed, had managed to cover him while he ran from the room. John was unamazed. They had seemed wily enough, the group of them. After all, they'd gotten this far. Mr. Capulatio's slick black hair had fallen from its arrangement. He looked despondent. When greeted with the news that his four henchmen had been brutally struck down, he did curse the Cape and all who dwelled within. As though he had cared for his men in some regard. "What of my wife?"

"She escaped."

He smiled. "Of course she did. She is a miracle." He then gripped Tygo's shoulder tightly and thanked him. Tygo said nothing. Very quickly they were able to arrange Tygo's dress cloak over Mr. Capulatio so that he was mostly hidden.

So they went out of the compound in broad daylight. They took

John's carriage, Mizar driving them to the outskirts of the outlaw carnival, the village of booths and tents and streamers and Heads. Mr. Capulatio rode the entire way with a look on his face that could have extinguished the sun.

John watched it all with the bland tolerance of one who trusted. This irony struck him only faintly. It was as though he had been wound up all his life, a toy, an automaton, and at last he was slowing down. His true nature had lain just beneath his anxiety all along. It was quietude. It was acceptance. He sat in the carriage, silent, suddenly grateful for every single thing—even for the years of struggle he had endured. As they entered the outlaw carnival, he looked at the unfamiliar world around him, the colorful tents, the basins of blood. His leg itched. He was, for a moment, happy in spite of all of it.

"My wives," Mr. Capulatio was saying. "I must find my wives. Before they find each other."

CHAPTER 23

ESCAPE

Marvel Whiteside Parsons watched Michael pace and complain that he was not born a monk. This was irritating to Marvel. They had escaped down the service corridor and emerged into another grand empty room where the floor was a magnificent mirrored tile. From here they could hear nothing except their own footsteps as they echoed around the space. No fighting. No ringing of metal. This room, a somewhat smaller banqueting hall, was never used. Or it had not been since Leander was king. Marvel went to one of the tall windows and pulled up the hammered metal shade: the golf course. Peaceful evening light, slanting over the ground like a stencil. A golden dog running across the seventh hole. And a man on the grass now with a rolling blade, cutting it shorter.

Michael could not be still, his steps ricocheting on the cool floor. He was speaking, but Marvel was hardly paying attention. The most important thing in the world seemed to be these few creatures just outside the window, going about their business, unaware of the encroaching danger. He thought of where his daughter might be at this hour. He didn't know what she did in the afternoons. Probably she smoked and gossiped with her handmaids. Or she might be walking one of her dogs.

He knew he would never see her again.

"The Law does sanction war when heresies are manifested bodily. That is this. Clearly. I never saw such a clear case. There is no question," Michael was saying. "I remember my Law classes. Somewhat. I'm definitely sure we're justified to send our soldiers against these madmen."

"Of course we are."

"Have you really scouted their camp?"

"Certainly."

"And do we have twice as many men?"

Marvel pulled his gaze from the window. Michael stood in the center of the room, like a motherless fawn in a clearing. "Of course we don't."

"How many do we have?" He was nodding as though he'd known this all along.

"Many less. Half as many. Don't think about it. We have the advantage of superior weaponry and, of course, our wall."

"Yes," Michael continued to nod. "The wall. It was magicked recently?"

"Better. It's been reinforced many times from the inside. The outer layer of glass is less majestic than it once was. But from the inside . . ." Marvel tried to smile encouragingly. He was trying to figure out how he could escape, alone. He had to leave now, or he would get caught up in the fighting. "It's impenetrable."

Michael went back to pacing. "What did you think of their nonsense about me not being king?"

"It's heresy. You said so yourself." Marvel turned back, impatient.

Michael had thrown off his bejeweled robe and stood anxiously in his undershirt and the plain pants he'd kept on beneath the robe. He twisted his bracelet on his arm, up past his wrist, apparently seeing how far he could push it up before it cut off his circulation. "Heresy. Yes. And yet . . . Sousa's horoscope." His voice ran off somewhat dejectedly. "It does make me more uneasy now, after this confrontation. What do *you* think?"

"Sousa is an abject failure. All these years he has had one job—one job, Michael—and that was to predict the Return. He's never done it. Why you put any stock in his astrology is baffling to me and always has been."

Michael sputtered a laugh. "It's only . . . John's horoscope did show an ascendant planet—and not my own planet. What am I to make of that? When confronted by this new man who claims to be king?" Then, because he couldn't restrain himself, "It could be that this other man *is* the king, Marvel. Anything could be."

Marvel Whiteside Parsons knew that Michael was not the True King. Apparently Sousa knew it too. Tygo knew it and even that outlaw Pretender knew it. Marvel felt a sudden anger form a molten ball in his stomach. If only he had left earlier! His dithering, his endless coming and going, such weakness he had shown. Now was the worst time to leave. Michael would be lost without him and yet if Marvel himself wanted to live—if he wanted to spend his last days in Kansas, serving the religion of Huldah, his ancestor—he must go. He shook Michael slightly, only slightly, and looked into his greenish eyes. "John's horoscope is nothing. You are the king."

"But how will I know if I am?"

Marvel tried not show his frustration but couldn't help it. "Knowing!" he choked. "How does one *know* anything? You *are,* Michael. King. Because you are here, right now, and your people within these walls look to you, and on top of that a large majority of this great land honors your authority. *That* gives you kingship." But even as he spoke he could see Michael's doubt giving way to crisis—and Marvel Whiteside Parsons knew that feeling well: he had left his own kingdom, his own chance to be king, in search of this thing that so moved Michael now. Where was the truth, and how does one find it?

The Pardoness had said truth finds everyone eventually.

He peered at Michael. His outburst had been unkind, and yet Michael did not look upset. "I know I am a good king," Michael muttered. "The True King, what is that? Some sort of Kansas nonsense?"

"Yes," said Marvel. "Just something someone made up. It's meaningless."

At the window again, Marvel could not help but watch each oblivious person tottering about their work, going from tower to tower, through the small streets and around corners. Each one following a course he set for himself, as well as one set for him by others. He heard Michael breathing at his back, more calmly now.

In due time Michael was standing at his side, coherent. Marvel had called for writing implements and they drafted a Summons requiring all men within the compound to present themselves at once for war. Boys, too, older than fourteen, though no one would ask their ages before sending them into battle. Marvel could not quite guess how the battle would unfold, though he was unsurprised to learn from a messenger that Mr. Capulatio had escaped the melee. How remained a mystery. But the guards were certain he was still in the compound. No one had seen him leave. How could he escape, after all? There was no escape.

Marvel kept his doubts to himself.

As the Summons was being read from every balcony, in every lane and every path within the compound, Marvel and Michael still stood in the abandoned great room, alone again. It had been very speedy, all of it. The others had come and gone, a parade of guards in masks trotting before them, ready to be ordered here and there. The master of the stables. The master of the canons. There was some talk of preparing oil to disperse through the outlaw camp, which could then be set on fire if it came to that. Michael had thought of that—but he wanted to use it as a last resort. There was a goodness in the man that no amount of pragmatism could put down. Marvel did admire that, in a way; it made things difficult, but he could not deny the grace of it.

He once again turned his gaze outside, through the window glass, which was very old and had sunk somewhat, pooling at the bottoms of the panes in graduated ripples. His attention was drawn by a general clamor and uproar as word of the Summons spread.

But Marvel felt compelled to look also because he was looking *for* something.

He knew the grounds so well. They had changed little since Leander was king, except for the golf course. A silly notion compelled him to keep looking down again and then he saw, with his own eyes, John Sousa the Chief Orbital Doctor mounting his carriage in the courtyard. Climbing in behind John was Tygo and another figure, this one taller and draped in a ceremonial robe. John's manservant was already in the front seat of the wagon.

It was the leader of the outlaws, David. A wire seemed to pull taut within Marvel, a blaze of recognition. Tygo had been sent to find that man; well, he had found him, and now he was rescuing him.

Whoever David was, he was wanted badly enough by the Mystagogue that he had sent two men over the deathscapes to fetch him. Marvel did not know if that portended good or evil, but his heart leapt in his chest as he gripped the window ledge.

Nudging Michael, he motioned to John's wagon, which was just now pulling around out of sight, toward the door they used for larger cargo. Michael shrugged. "He's not expected to fight, he's imperative to the crown."

But Marvel pointed at the extra figure in the open carriage, and Michael rounded on him with wide brown eyes. "The outlaw is escaping with them?"

"It would appear that way."

"But why in heaven's name are they helping him?" As though the idea of such insubordination exasperated his capacity for understanding.

Marvel walked quickly over the tiled floor, ordering guards in pursuit, but he knew it was too late. He left the room, determined to keep walking until he had walked away from the Cape forever.

This was the moment of his decision, he must seize it.

It was like walking away from a pan of boiling water. Eventually it would dry up, bubble and warp. There would be damage. It would not get better before it got worse. But then, it would be over.

CHAPTER 24

THE LAW OF MERCY

The wives Mr. Capulatio sought were not easy to find in the commotion of the outlaw carnival. John identified at once that it was several different groups, with correspondingly different tents and different booths and different-looking people, milling together now as though assembled for a bazaar or a trading fair. But their faces were odious to behold. Each man, each woman (and there were some women, he was surprised by that—he'd always heard they were not allowed on the carnival circuit) strode about fixed by some purpose of violence, and the wind was drawing up now as the first fires of evening were lit, the torches that lined the long rows and seemed to form the basic organization of the paths. Heads on pikes, everywhere; at every turn John felt he might walk straight into one. He stepped gingerly, his arms held out before him, like he was afraid of walking through a cobweb. How awful that would be, to touch noses with one of those things, his own face pressed up to one of those sunken green snouts.

They had left Mizar with the wagon, in a circle with other wagons. The livery of the Sousa family stood in contrast to the black carnival wagons, painted with skulls and rocketships and other magical things. Mizar looked helpless as he stood there beside it, still in his servant's jacket. John told him to stay put and stay hidden. *You're an old man now. Do what old men do and take a nap,* he'd said, cruelly perhaps. It was difficult for him to ever know how he sounded to Mizar, who only nodded congenially as he always did and at everything, every sight he had ever seen and every command he had ever been given. Then Mizar had crawled up into the wagon and tossed back a swig of water from a canteen hung on his belt. John envied that, the water—Mizar, eternally prepared.

Then John and Tygo were walking with David all over the wretched dirty camp. Past frying whole goats, women in black masks, past buckets and basins and vats of soapy-looking blood. His head swam. John found it was abuzz with motion, small movements and large ones, torch-shadows flickering, men stacking things, men draining things, people pouring from this place to that one in anticipation of some grand signal. Or so it seemed. *But how?* he'd asked Mr. Capulatio—David—trotting along behind him as they looked for his two wives. He did for an instant wonder if that was a code word—*wives.* So lost was he here, and Tygo beside him, taking it all in with a face like a docile sheep, but as tense beside John as if he were about to have a tooth extracted. *But how?* John had asked again. *How is it they are so well prepared?*

He imagined the scramble inside the palace compound. And he *was* glad to be out here, though he did wish someone would give him a weapon. A knife. Anything. David had laughed at John's question. *These are carnival men. They've been waiting for war since we got here. They barely need to put on their shoes.*

Finally they stopped walking, when David was approached by a crone. She was horrifically old, with a hair-form that sagged—perhaps she'd been caught in the rain. She was fat, her face painted as crones often do before executions, with two long ocher smears beneath the eyes and above them. John drew back slightly. The woman whispered to David for a long time, and his expression fell with every passing second, though he was nodding in agreement with whatever unhappy news she bore. Nothing on her face registered emotion. "Ah," said David. "What I feared."

"What is it?" asked Tygo. His face was wet with sweat—John had not realized how hot it was in the carnival, with all the fires raging around them. The crone had caught them just as they passed a thicket of Heads on pikes, perhaps fifty of them, propped up almost like a memorial. To what John couldn't even imagine. The Head closest to him appeared to be a child. But no, he looked closer: it was a man, just shrunken with age and rot, the eyes sewn closed with red string.

David sent the crone away. "She brings me news of my First Wife." Then he glared. "Appalling news."

"Well?" said Tygo.

"You're not my advisor, what does it matter to you?"

"You can't waste your men on storming the castle. It will do you no good, and it will cost hundreds of lives. Let's go away, now. Back to Kansas. It's unsafe here. The lights in the sky—"

"Yes," said David. "The Return."

"No," Tygo hurried. "That word I said, *tellochvovin*. It means 'falling death.'"

David vacantly nodded, and John shook his head.

"The lights are meteors! We'll all die if we stay here," Tygo shouted.

"The lights are the shuttles." David glanced toward the grove of Heads on pikes. For a moment he seemed to be considering dashing among them, hiding there perhaps. "I haven't got time for this. The crone has delivered very disappointing news. Orchid has taken my second wife, my Sigil." He paused, wrapped his hand around one of the pikes. "This is very worrying to me, actually. She is in my estimation the finest executioner ever to live in this world. She has a way with the blade . . . O! I see your faces, gentlemen! Damn her injury. It's not about strength. It is about . . . well, it is about magic." He cradled his own head in his hand. "My Orchid, my Prism of Accurate Divination. She was the daughter of our Prophetess Lois, who did bed me as a youth, and who in her great age conceived a child by me! Just like Huldah!" His eyelashes sent lacy shadows over his cheeks in the firelight. "You know, a part of me always believed Huldah's child was conceived with her own son, Lee." He laughed, surprised at himself. "I never said that to anyone before. But it's really the only explanation. O, and Huldah's age . . . well, what does 'old' really mean? She could have been forty. Or thirty! We will never know her age for sure." He blinked. "The Prophetess Lois was not really seventy-nine when she died. It was just what we told everyone."

John eyed Tygo. "What is he talking about?" he whispered.

The streamers on the pikes whipped around in a sudden gust of breeze. Yellows and reds, maroons, illuminated by the fires spluttering. The dark was complete now. It was fully night. Tygo shook his head. "Come with us, David."

David pulled up one of the pikes, then drove it down again in another place. He seemed not to like this placement either, and repeated the gesture, hissing an incantation beneath his breath, some string of words that John couldn't catch. Then he spoke louder: "Orchid still believes she is meant to be queen of the Cape."

"*No one* is meant to rule here. Damn you, listen to me," Tygo said. "We should leave. We must." A plaintive note entered his voice. John had heard it only once before, when Tygo was begging for his life, making his prediction about the ladies' bleeding.

"We'll take the Cape. It's what we came here to do," David said.

"The Mystagogue needs you alive."

"I'm a lucky son of a bitch, I was born for this." He straightened his shoulders. "I won't die. It's not possible."

Tygo opened his mouth again, but suddenly the ground shook with a force that knocked the three of them to their knees. Many of the piked Heads fell over and one landed next to John. He batted it away, even though up close the Head was somewhat less upsetting than he had imagined, just the hardened leather of skin, the smell of sand and sun and a wisp of rot thrown in. No more redolent than a mildewed bedsheet. There were only X's for eyes to look back at him. "Are they trying to blow up the wall?" John choked, clamoring to his feet. "It's ten feet thick, it's stood for a thousand years."

David pushed a stack of pikes and Heads off his back. "They will get through." He reached into his pocket and pulled out a small thing, a black amber brooch, just a plain piece of polished stone with a pin stuck to the back. It caught the torchlight. John knew these things. They were for executions, though the ones people wore at the Cape were much more finely crafted, often made in the shape of a family's patron animal. He owned himself one that looked like a guinea hen, passed down from his mother. He'd never worn it.

David pinned it to his shirtfront. "Ah," he said. "They will be needing me at the front for inspiration."

He strode away from them then, his hand wandering to his belt in search of a knife. Finding none, he picked one up off the ground, checked it over, wiped the blade between the folds of his shirt, and kept walking.

At once terrified of their surroundings, John and Tygo scurried after him. In this place everything blinked in and out of shadow and every eye seemed alight with madness. David was hard to catch—he so quickly blended into the crowd. A mile away in the distance and to John's right, he could just see the metallic castle within the compound walls. The high outer wall, encrusted with broken glass, reflected the torches of the approaching carnival men. Shanties and booths and huts and people appeared in increasing numbers, clotting as they went closer to the wall. He passed sheep and goats, spindle-legged and black with curved vicious horns and daemonic eyes and hooves that could kill a man with one kick. Farther down the path they met men on horses, magicians with their girdles of chalky severed heads and intoxicated eyes. Carts with wood for fires, a man with a musket, a barking dog.

The fighting had begun. David was lost in the crowd.

The battle raged on unchecked around them, people circulating like blood. Standing, falling, crying out at the moment of their own deaths. For the longest time, John just watched, until a huge man came at him with a club studded with spikes. He was confused momentarily, because it was a palace guard and John was obviously *himself,* a court official, an important courtier. Whyever would this guard run at him, with such a look of bloodlust in his eyes? But that was exactly why: it *was* a lust, John thought, the idea coming to him wildly as he dodged the blow. Some instinct kicked in, a kind of levity raised him out of his body. He saw himself narrowly avoid the clubbing. He saw himself turn, and take up a pike from a man who had fallen dead beside him. Then, he saw himself thrust it deep between the guard's shoulders.

The passion ran past the moment of doing it, and after the man had fallen, John stood there, panting. Tygo shrugged a little, as if to say, *It was that or die yourself,* and then John pulled the pike from the still-breathing man. He did not look back because he did not want to see a thing he could never unsee.

After that, he found himself a part of the battle, not as a believer fighting for the truth, because in the moment of the fight all ideology, old and new, vanished. He fought as a person who wanted simply to keep on being alive.

He received a bash to the head. A slash across the back of his thigh. All that mattered was that he would live. It was within his power to keep himself living. He vacillated between hiding behind wagons and ungracefully striking out when he gathered the courage. Beside him, Tygo kept slashing forward: the momentum of activity was enough. He had learned to fight somewhere—at least much better than John ever had. He watched the other man drop his pike for a knife as the opportunity presented itself, and then the knife for a sword, so John did the same, fumbling with the heavier and heavier weapons. Every so often he caught a glimpse of David far up ahead, smiling as he cut people down. Once he stood tall and met John's eyes, a head dangling by its hair from his fist. He looked different on this battlefield, and certainly different from how John had imagined a True King might look—and yet, David seemed to have been born for this, exactly.

John stopped to rest. Many hours into the battle, there were fewer people. The outlaws had breached the compound wall. They streamed inside. The fighting continued there. The screams grew farther away. John sat down in a pile of canvas—it had once been a tent. Tygo had gone for water.

Then he saw her through a maze of toppled stones. She wore a plumed helmet now, with the short ends of her hair sticking out. She'd cut her dress off at the knee so she could run. Overhead those two amazing lights shone their alarm down on them all, like an awful being waiting for them to die. Behind them their arcs of light. John felt he was looking into a dream. She did not seem afraid of any living being. Handless, covered in blood. Yes, smiling. Just like David. She was smiling at him now, she *saw* him. John's heart leapt into his throat.

A young girl in white stood behind her, her wrists chained together, fastened to a metal collar around her neck.

Orchid nodded to him. She had noticed him walking toward her before he'd noticed her.

When he reached her he could not speak. He'd gone to her like she'd summoned him. She touched his shirt. Behind them something

caught fire. A sound like wings beating as it went up in flames. Neither of them looked. The heat coming off it made John's left side redden. She didn't seem to notice. "The man who needs proof," she hissed. "You must have found something undeniable, to have left your friendly palace for *this* filth pit."

The girl lurched from behind her, screaming. "Help me! She's going to kill me!"

"For my bastard of a husband, you came here?" She looked beyond him over the field of dead and dying people. All her features were crowded on her face, the upturned snub of her nose bathed in the light of the fires. "O, but so did I, I suppose. What a fool I've been. This will not end well for any of us. I have a feeling."

"The end," John gasped at last. "Is coming."

"O, I know it well."

"No. The end of the world. Of *this* world. The Cape." He felt that he was a carving of a man about to fall from a great height. What would remain when he smashed open? "The lights in the sky. They're meteors."

Now she did not speak. Her bandaged stub was dark with watery blood. The girl's chain was fastened to a thick girdle around Orchid's stomach.

"She's going to kill me," sobbed the young girl. "Please save me."

"Don't kill her," John implored. "Leave. We all must leave."

"I'm the rightful queen of the Cape. This is *my* kingdom."

Then John pulled her close to him, their chests touching. They were each covered in blood and sweat. She let him hold her, even sinking into him. The fire flickered over her helmet. "I cannot kill the stupid girl," Orchid whispered in his ear. "Wonderblood is over. There is a Law of Mercy now. I cannot . . . I cannot de-head her as I once would have."

He did not know what she meant.

She pushed back from him, her face turned up toward him like a heliotrope. "Will you kill her for me?"

The girl met his eyes across the dark. "Her men chained me! She has the key around her neck! Save me!"

"I—I . . . I can't execute anyone."

Orchid pushed him away. "Then what good are you to me?"

"Leave, I said." He grasped her hand with both of his. "You have to."

"Not without the sigil. David cannot do a thing without her."

John looked to the girl, then back to Orchid. "Take her with you, then."

"No!" the girl screamed again. "Don't let her take me!"

"Where would I go?" Orchid spat. "Back on the circuit? There are my people. Helping *him*." She motioned with her stump toward the fighting, which was now raging inside the compound walls. "All I've made of my life is his now." She pulled on the girl's chain again, and the girl cried out as her head was jerked down with her arms. "Where is my sword? I cannot even use it, she has cut off my good hand." There were no tears in the woman's eyes.

John did not know why he was talking to her, what compulsion drove him, except that now, having been shown the truth, he wanted—needed—to tell someone. "Go to Kansas," he whispered. "We are. It's where we should have been this whole time, where the True King will rule. We've been wrong this whole time."

"But the texts—"

"Everyone was wrong."

"How do you know?"

He gazed at her helplessly. "I just do."

"David will never leave this place. He has dreamt of the Cape since killing our Prophetess Lois. He was born for this moment." The woman was backing away from him now. She was singularly the most magnetic person he had ever seen—even handless she throbbed with a power that could not be contained. She pulled off her helmet with her one hand. The feather plume fluttered to the ground, where it soaked through and disappeared in a puddle of mud. The girl sobbed as she was yanked behind Orchid. "You can tell David you killed me," Orchid sneered. "He'll probably name a tower after you."

She walked away, dragging the girl dressed in white. As the women were swallowed up by dark, the girl's pitiful cries grew quieter, and that most terrible and terminating of words came into John's mind, over and over and over again. *Tellochvovin.*

CHAPTER 25

ORCHID'S LOSS

It was not far from the flickering fires and the crash of fighting into a dense dark hell of wilderness, where the dark and the shadows and the smell of winter-wet foliage caused the girl's panic to rise, even as her eyes struggled to adjust to the deep colors of night. She was cold now, in her thin dress, but she had stopped crying. She could feel the tight trails on her cheeks where the tears had dried.

She followed Orchid through the sticking fronds of low-lying palms. Her feet sucked at the sandy mud. The metal collar around her neck never seemed to warm against her skin. In the distance she could still hear screaming, and every now and then a cheer. She had not noticed the coordinated whoops before—had they been doing that all along? Were the sounds rallying cries from the palace soldiers, or the carnival people? She wondered if Mr. Capulatio was dead.

She tried to shut everything out, the screams, the yells, the cold, the scratching underbrush. But she was more afraid here than she had been at the camp. Even on the battlefield. And she was more afraid of Orchid than she ever had been of Mr. Capulatio.

Or Argento.

Mr. Capulatio had killed her brother. Would his wife now kill her?

When they had walked a mile or so, Orchid turned slowly around.

The moon overhead cast scant light onto her face, but enough that the shining glint of her eyes looked unearthly to the girl, like a rabid animal in a trashpile. She shrank back, but Orchid pulled the chain, forcing the girl's head and neck forward. "We are in this together now," she muttered, and reeled in the chain with her one hand. The girl could not believe how strong she was, even injured.

"No," she said, her voice hoarse.

"Yes. I hate you nearly as much as I hate him, but we are in this together, little Sigil, and as long as you are mine, he will never have his kingdom."

"You don't even believe I *am* the sigil!"

Orchid pulled the girl to the ground, where they sat on a carpet of rotting leaves. The girl felt them sticking wetly to her thighs through her dress.

"He may have misinterpreted the passage. Or I may have. I . . . I don't know. I need more time to read," Orchid said. "To study the texts. My books—" She looked back in the direction of the carnival. For a moment it seemed like she might return for them. But then she let out her breath so slowly the girl wondered if she were trying to calm herself. "I would never get through the fray like this." The chain. The one hand. "I am a cripple thanks to you. You will pay."

"Would you rather I'd killed you?" the girl shrieked. She couldn't help herself—they had walked a long way but they had not spoken. "I could have. If you kill me you'll break the new Law of Mercy."

"Shut up. Did you hear what I said? As long as you are mine, he will never be ascendant. It doesn't matter what the passage says, or even what it means. He *believes* it. And so he is bereft without you." She smiled. "His little fantasy of the girl on the battlefield will cost him his kingship." Orchid spat on the ground and cradled the stump of her wrist. "O, not to worry, little Sigil," she muttered. "I shall not kill you, not now. Who would be my servant if I did? I'm a queen, I cannot be without an attendant."

The girl looked about for a rock. If only she could get the key from around Orchid's neck. The woman had to sleep sometime. Then she would hit her and escape.

The moonlight made deep, ugly shadows under Orchid's eyes. Orchid was watching the girl closely. A new expression rolled onto her face like a stormcloud, one of recognition. Her short hair dripped with moisture and blood. "Tut tut, little one. What of your Law of Mercy? How can you kill me in my sleep? Surely you are not so evil. Where would you even go? Back to him? Into the forest alone? A young girl will not be alone for long." She laughed meanly.

She gasped. "Do you read minds?"

"Never once in all my life. But I know your heart, because all people are the same. Selfish, grasping, lustful, prideful." Her voice was sly. "You cannot break your own Law, though, right? There is to be no killing."

The girl could not confess she'd made up the Law of Mercy in order to spare herself the horror of de-heading Orchid, because then Orchid would kill her. But suddenly she couldn't be sure if she'd made up the Law, or if it had been divinely sent; it seemed real now that other people had begun believing it. What would it feel like to be given a revelation?

Like this desperation?

Wonderblood had ended. She had ended it. There would be no more making Heads, no more carnivals, maybe. No more executions. She stared at Orchid. All around them were the wet smells of ferns and mosses, water flowing under the ground, the cries of night animals, shrill and sweet. The fear in the girl's heart began to slow. The woman sitting across from her was without a hand. In the weak moonlight she could see darkness on the bandage; the wound was weeping. It was likely Orchid would die on her own. In the distance the girl heard not just the fighting, but the ocean, too, where she had been married only a day before on the barge, before the altar of shells and the phosphorescent fire.

Orchid turned her face toward the fires and the far-off glint of the towers. She shook her head. "*I* should have been king. I was Lois's heir. Why not me?"

The girl nodded, hesitant. "My mother was a Walking Doctor. Maybe I can make something for your—hand. So you don't become fevered."

"You'd poison me just as soon as to look at me," Orchid snorted.

"I didn't kill you before, did I?"

"That's because you're weak."

"You haven't killed me yet. Are you weak?"

To her astonishment, Orchid wiped her face with her good hand. Was she crying? The girl was much too frightened to touch her.

"My books. My texts. My carnival, which I took from my wretch of a brother by my own force. Gone. Every good thing I ever did in my life. Ruined. Or else it belongs to him now." Her eyes roared at the girl. "I would have burnt it myself to keep him from getting it if I'd known it would turn out like this." Her face closed all at once, as though on a drawstring. She cradled her stump.

"I'm sorry." The girl did not know why she said it, but it was true.

They sat a long time in the wet forest, listening to the distant clamor of battle. The sounds grew dimmer and dimmer and the coolness swelled around them until they were both shivering in the fall air.

Then after a while the girl woke up. How could she have fallen asleep right next to that woman? But when she rubbed her eyes, she saw Orchid was sleeping too, her neck bent unnaturally and her face pinched as though she were having a nightmare.

Frantically, the girl searched for the key to the metal collar. It had been around Orchid's neck, but now it was nowhere. She didn't dare move more than a few inches, for fear that the chain connecting them would rattle. It was difficult to see in the dark. The only thing to do would be to hit her with a rock. Several small pebbles were within her grasp—big enough to stun her, if the girl hit her very hard.

She grew more agitated as the seconds passed. This might be her only chance. But still the girl could not pick up a rock.

At last she sat very still and let the breath go in and out of her body. She imagined she was a wind chime, air passing through her, transforming into beautiful sounds. She knew she would not kill Orchid. She'd had the chance before, and she had not taken it. She would not take it now. The Eon of Pain was over. The girl did not know why it was true but she had felt the truth of those words as soon as she had spoken them aloud, and so had everyone else. They had power. It was the Law of Mercy.

She knew something else, too. Orchid would not kill her.

She closed her eyes and slept.

When she awoke again it was still dark. Orchid's face was inches from her own. The woman's clear eyes, in the shine of the two comets as bright green as glass, for the moon had sunk below the tree line and the girl's body was covered in chills, still blazed at her, but this time Orchid appraised her with more nuance, for finally she said, "You did not kill me."

"I could have killed *him* every one of a hundred nights too," she retorted. "But I didn't do that, either."

Orchid nodded. "Though one of us should have."

"Is he the True King?"

"Yes." Orchid sat back. Her thighs were muddy. Her hand. She wiped it on her dress but it did no good. "Of that I am most sure."

"Will we die if we stay here?" The girl thought of the strange man from inside the palace who had told them the lights were meteors. She recalled her mother saying that word, *meteor*, but she did not know what a meteor was.

"I care not what happens to us," Orchid sighed. "My texts are lost. My life's work. Lois's work. It's all gone. How could I even begin to interpret what's happened here? How will anyone know what to believe?"

"Are there more texts?"

"In there." Orchid pointed toward the compound with her good hand, the finger dirty. "And in Kansas. But those are guarded by insane sorcerers who are ruled by a despot. The Black Watchtower. No one goes to Kansas."

"We could."

Orchid's laugh was hard. "O yes, the two of us, a handless executionatrix who cannot kill and the concubine who maimed her. We shall save the world."

"I only want to save myself."

Then, oddly, Orchid smiled, as though some private thought had cheered her. "The Walking Doctors have their maps, don't they. For the saferoads. You know these?"

She shook her head. The maps she remembered from her childhood were as long gone as her mother's comfort, swallowed up by the immensity of her circumstances. She hesitated, though. Finally, she murmured, "But there are markings on the trees."

"I learnt a few once, from an old book." Orchid nodded. "But—most foolishly—I entrusted navigation to others in my carnival, as did David. One can only perform so many duties." She shook her head. "Do you know them? The markings?"

The girl shrugged. The chain clanked. "Probably some." Then she stared. "Could we really get all the way to Kansas?"

"Others have. Why not us?"

"You just said no one goes there."

"No one with anything to lose." Orchid's eyes glittered darkly. "I have always wanted to see a Kansas Cow. Perhaps those priests on the deathscape could do with such a learned scribe as myself. Perhaps they might see value where others have so callously discarded it." She flung a rock toward the compound.

"What about me?"

"What about *you*? You are my hostage. You are my ransom. You are," she breathed, "an apprentice of a kind. A sigil, yes. But not what he thought. Not an ornament. A law-giver." She bent forward. "You will be a woman soon." As though that explained everything. She looked toward the burning compound. "Do you really want to stay here?"

"What about Mr. Capulatio?"

"Tragic." She pushed back the wet strands of her hair. "He chose worldly delight over Heaven. It's a story for the ages. Not our problem."

"I thought you loved him."

Orchid yanked the chain, but gently. "More than you could ever know."

They began walking before the sun rose. Orchid had not unchained her. The girl did not expect her to for a long time. A burst of doves from the brush on one side startled them and the girl shrieked, but Orchid laughed. The way they were going was unknown to both of them, until at last one of the Walking Doctors' symbols appeared in the shady murk of the forest morning, on a tree trunk, when the sun had risen to just above the tree line but all the moisture was still trapped below it as under a dome. The mark was small, shaped like a weasel inside a wheel. The girl said, "I can't read this one."

"Try."

"I was only a child when I would go around to the sick with my mother."

"You are only a child now. Try."

But it was useless. The weasel could mean anything. They might as well have been stepping onto a field soaked with the Disease. "I don't know."

They went helplessly forward, for what could they do, until many hours later they discovered another mark, this time on a narrow-trunked pine. Behind them was a flat field with white winter flowers. A mule walked unbridled in the grass, grazing, flaring his lips and chewing. The girl put her fingers on the mark. A square, plain, and a woman's body floating above its left side. Something about the image weightless. She remembered it. "We go left. Right is the Disease."

And so in this way they began to make their way toward Kansas, from tree to tree, pole to pole, leaving behind the countryside outlying Cape Canaveral. A myriad of changes to the landscape as they crossed it—even the ground became more solid, the low tree branches no longer twisted by ceaseless coastal winds, the piles of storm-shredded debris thinning out as they walked—they left the Cape behind, the girl and the woman, as they walked toward the Center of the World, what Orchid said was called the Watchtower of the Universe. "We will discover the truth in the texts there," said Orchid as they walked, through tight lips. "The truth is knowable to those who would seek it."

Maybe, thought the girl. She wished all of a sudden that she had managed to take Cosmas, the Head Argento had made for her. So they would look like magicians. It was stupid to travel without one. The girl still did not know if magic was real, or if her mother had been right and faith was a delusion. She did not know if Orchid would kill her. Or if she herself was a law-giver, a sigil, a concubine, or a queen. She felt like none of those things, and all of them.

She was a girl with feet walking toward Kansas.

She was a girl who had delivered the world from Wonderblood.

She was mercy, and mercy was a woman.

CHAPTER 26

THE BREACH

Marvel had thought he would have until dawn. In his wildest imagination, he hadn't believed the outlaw carnival could mount so quick an attack. He'd barely left Michael to prepare his own flight when he heard, from his own tower chamber, an explosion as the outlaws blew up the water-gate. The only point where the wall was not ten feet thick.

When he heard the blast, Marvel had taken a deep breath. Yes. He would probably die now. Certainly. Not even as a deserter, or a martyr, but simply a casualty of an ordinary coup. The irony almost amused him.

He stood in the black night air on his own balcony. He'd been in the middle of throwing a few things in a sack when the blast rocked the ground. He had been, in fact, holding the drawing of his mother, Nasa Whiteside. At the explosion, he teetered unsteadily but caught his balance against his desk. The framed picture fell to the ground. His mother, the failure. Pushed to her death by the Mystagogue.

Her death would most likely go unavenged after all.

He went to his balcony and looked through a spyglass, trying to see a route of escape. The wind was blowing. Water had rushed in over the limestone streets. An icing of water, thin as a cake topping. Below him the world was awash with noise and flickering torches—screams, grunts, cries of pain. Fighting seemed to have sprung up without warning. The sound of it was both immediate and distant, like a noise one hears in one's sleep and is reshaped by a dream. For a moment he didn't care what happened to anyone, even himself.

The outlaws had gained the compound but were not near the towers yet. They were vastly underarmed, slashing forward only with their clubs and pikes. They kept exploding some substance—he suspected they had barrels of oil, scavenged probably from the same spots where the Cape got theirs, the hidden troves abandoned by the ancients all those years ago. When a head guard had come to him for guidance after the explosion, Marvel slammed shut the slot on his door and locked it. They would break it down to get at him, soon. Someone would.

At his desk he swept more of his bottles and droppers into a hard-sided case. Whether to take them with him, or to have something to do for the moment, he wasn't sure. He had already packed his most important unctions. The bottles made a sound like water as they fell together. He could sort them out later, if he was alive. He knew each bottle by color and quality.

He looked down on the floor at the portrait of his mother. She peered back at him from behind cracked glass. Such a beauteous and terrible frown—the convention of the artist, perhaps. How she did look like his Alyson.

His mother had probably never been happy, either.

It was Juniper who got to him before the others. He called out to Marvel from behind the locked slot. Marvel fairly hugged him with delight once he'd opened the door. "My god, why didn't you run away?" he almost cried.

Juniper paid him no attention. He held a finger to his lips and whispered, "Michael is ranting and raving for you. More guards will be here soon, they can't understand why you don't open the door. They think you might have poisoned yourself."

Marvel peered around the younger man into the hallway. A single body—a lion-faced guard's—was sprawled at the head of the stairs like a carpet, run through with a pike. Blood had not even stopped pumping from the wound. Juniper's cheek was smeared with red.

Marvel nodded, grabbing his bag and stepping into the hall. Only a few torches remained lit, the others had burned out. They cast wobbling shadows on the rounded walls. One of the decorative tapestries had fallen from its hanger and lay in a pile on the floor. Marvel toed the dead man's arm. "You found a weapon, I see."

Juniper joined him, glancing around them apprehensively. His shoulder brushed Marvel's. "You said you'd pay me three times what the Mystagogue would."

Marvel actually laughed. "I believe I said two times."

"That's not what I heard. I've got an exceptionally keen memory. That's how I crossed the continent."

"Really?"

"Everyone's got a talent," Juniper said as they crept down the stairs.

"How lucky for me." Marvel attempted to sound restrained, but could not contain his pleasure. "You know, I was going to have you tortured for whatever information I could get about the deathscapes. But then I thought better of it."

"A true statesman, you." Juniper regarded him closely in the dim light. "Tygo will be going back, with or without David. A catastrophe is about to unfold here."

"I'd say it already has," replied Marvel. They took the steps two at a time.

"A different kind of catastrophe."

When they reached a side door on the bottom floor, Marvel threw his hood over his head, though he knew it would make little difference—his figure was too well known to remain hidden. "I have my horses," he offered.

"They're not in the stable, I checked," Juniper said. Even now he looked a bit as though he had just woken up. He'd found a helmet somewhere, probably on a dead man. He pulled the faceplate down. "You got any armor?"

Marvel blinked. "Not here."

"We'll have to make a run for it, then," he replied. "There's no other way." He pushed his shoulder against the door. But he stopped and turned, his brow furrowing. His ill-fitting uniform was pasted to his body by sweat on his chest. "I'll take you back to Kansas. But when we get there, you have to do a certain thing for me."

"What?"

"Something that requires powerful magic."

Marvel almost asked, *What?* again, but a crash echoed from the other side of the tower, and he nodded, wiping nervous sweat from his forehead. "If you get us to Kansas alive, I'll do anything for you."

Then they were in the fray. The clanging pandemonium. They had only to cover a short distance before they could escape through a cart-gate behind Endeavour Tower. Marvel prayed under his breath.

They drew closer, closer, sliding along the compound wall, their feet wet from seawater that had flowed in when the water-gate exploded. Carnival men surrounded the small service gate—they must wait for a distraction. They hid for a long time behind the same cistern that had shielded the outlaw king only hours before. Marvel was astounded at the disarray of the courtyard. How had the outlaws destroyed things so quickly? They had even set up a wooden plank bridge where the water-gate had been and were wheeling in more exploding barrels.

No one noticed Marvel and Juniper.

While they waited for a distraction, Marvel became aware of a wagon, at first far from them, then nearer, until he craned his neck and realized that it too was making for the cart-gate. Barreling over men as it surged forward. He saw one of Alyson's handmaidens in the front, and his heart sank. Michael and Alyson were surely inside. Marvel watched in slow horror as a carnival man threw a burning stick at the horses. They reared up and the wagon toppled.

Marvel nearly stepped out from behind the cistern. His mouth opened. He took a breath as though he meant to speak, and improbably Juniper heard it, for he turned to Marvel with wide eyes. Marvel opened his bag, fingered one of his vials. It would be easy to throw another potion, to cause a momentary distraction. But then the outlaws would surely come toward them.

There was no stopping what would happen. Whatever would be, would be. And yet Marvel did love them—both. He loved them as he ever had—flawed and lost, his only child and her husband, his friend. A painful spasm overcame him as he thought, *In my way I created this. All of it.* The thought did not ease his guilt.

He watched the outlaws yank them from the upended wagon, along with their servants. He watched them throw his daughter and Michael to the ground, their faces now in several inches of water. The scene grew harder to see as men crowded around them.

His daughter screamed. There was a scuffle, a wallowing of people, a splashing of bodies atop one another, slipping past one another. Then there was another awful scream, much more terrible than the scream of fright moments before, and Marvel sealed shut his eyes but of course that did nothing—still he heard his daughter screaming. When he opened one eye, he saw one of the outlaws stepping away from her body, her neck half severed by an axe, certainly a death blow. Then another uncontrolled howl, this time Michael, who crouched over her body like a demon and held her to his great wide chest, her head lolling to the side grossly, and Marvel gagged, he couldn't help himself, her hair down her back wetted on the ends now with her own blood.

Marvel and Juniper were invisible now that the greatest prize had been captured. Juniper dragged him forward, toward the gate. Did he know Alyson was Marvel's daughter? Marvel felt demented. He ran with Juniper not thirty feet from where Michael was lying in the cold, shallow water, half his body above it and half his body below. He held Alyson still.

Marvel slid with Juniper through the cart-gate, onto the plain, into the night, away from the torchlights and the smoke and the guards in their masks and the carnival men with bloody smeared faces and their piked Heads. Juniper led them through it all as though he had done it a hundred times before. Marvel took one measured breath. It was over. He could have done nothing, in the end—what would his poison have done, besides prolong the inevitable? They would still have been killed. He told himself that. He must believe it.

Juniper walked just in front of him now, his own Head swinging from the canvas sacks on his belt with every step he took. *That's the only one I ever made.* He had stolen a torch and lit it once they were far enough into the forest.

Suddenly, watching the guard's dim form, Marvel felt a cold dread seep into him.

The Head. He had forgotten about that. Only magicians made Heads.

But he followed because he did not know what else to do.

The world beyond was dark, and they had a long way to go.

CHAPTER 27

FORTUNE

The dawn birds cheered when David mounted the giant stage inside the palace compound, crying out their morning songs, though the sun had yet to break the horizon. A song of wild anticipation, the new day, the new day.

John stood below the stage, far enough away to be out of reach of the blood, though he was still soaked head to toe with blood from the battle. His hands as he studied them; the blood had dried in the lines, forming broken trails, like a map someone had drawn and erased. Tygo had had the sense to wash. John looked over at his earholes, the wet hair slick on the sides of his head, and then back to the stage.

Michael was dragged up on the shell-shaped stage by two of David's men. John had never seen him look so confused. David bent and whispered something to him, and Michael seemed to agree, his body arranged tightly now in anticipation of his death. He wore wet and dirty clothes: no time to spare, John thought, when there is a new king to be made.

Michael was so unsteady on his feet that John wondered if he'd somehow gotten hold of one of the Hierophant's unctions; that would have been a mercy. John did believe he deserved mercy. He moved as if sleepwalking, over to the block, and there placed his head on the smooth blackness. A wide silence opened over the crowd.

David called out, in a startlingly hoarse voice. "I am the True King. I have taken my seat at the most holy place in the world, where man did once take flight and where he did leave the world and enter Heaven. Today we depose a false king, from an unrighteous line of false kings. Today we are set right, cosmically. With this act, we enter an age of mercy. Wonderblood, the rinsing of the world in blood for one Eon, is over." He paused. "After this, there will be no more beheadings. After this, the world is healed and we await the imminent Return."

Michael looked up from the block. He had no one to look at. John hoped that he could see him there, watching.

Then he realized Michael would think him a traitor, and felt sad.

"How does it feel to be last?" David asked Michael loudly. "That is a fate any king would wish for. That his death might stay the hand of bloodletting and set free the earth from pain. Rejoice, King Michael."

Michael whispered, but David called out the words for everyone to hear. "He says: *I have been first and I have been last. I have lived the sort of life that any man would want to live.*" David clutched his sword approvingly. "Those are good last words. I will give you the easiest death. Mercy," he said again, this time speaking it over everyone in the crowd. An attendant gave him an ax. He had put down the sword.

John didn't watch the beheading. He heard the thud of the head as it rolled onto the stage. The crowd yelled. When he looked back, Michael's body emptied its blood out onto the ground, for some time, gushing and gushing, and David leaned on the ax handle and gazed into the distance.

John turned to Tygo. He had decided he would travel with Tygo to Kansas. They would meet the Mystagogue together. They would tell him what they had seen. "We should go," he said.

"We have to get David to come back with us."

"He's a lunatic. The True King is a lunatic. We must leave him."

Then he saw David pike Michael's head. He thought he would have been sick, but instead he watched it all. The head. The people. The stage. The sky.

John D. Sousa stood with Mizar and Tygo before his carriage, full again of all the uncertainty that had plagued him for his entire life. He was, after all, descended from a line of Chief Orbital Doctors and Astronomers and courtiers and fools. He had lived his life inside the geometry of his astrological charts. Now he had no guide except Tygo, who was only a man, fickle and lying, and yet John was prepared to follow him onto a dangerous plain where they would surely die.

What if, what if, what if? It occurred to John as he watched Mizar packing the carriage with bundles of food, a few weapons—gifts from the carnival men—that he was finished with horoscopes. But as he checked the wagon over with Tygo and Mizar, he could not help but wish he had some map for what was about to happen. But John knew that believing in Tygo's vision of the world to come was also him taking ownership of his own. There would be no shuttles. At least not now. The True King would not be returning to Kansas with them.

If only he had a few of his instruments. It would have been nice to bring them along. But going back to Urania would be madness in the commotion, especially driving a cart with a Cape insignia. Outlaws marauded everywhere, looting. His precious instruments had probably already been dismantled for their metal. He sighed.

"What's wrong?" asked Tygo. He chewed on a piece of tough meat while he strapped down a few pikes. John noticed he avoided the pile of Heads the carnival men had given them, stepping gingerly around them every time he walked past.

"O. My instruments. Nothing."

"That's a shame, Lord Astronomer. A real shame. Which brings me to a confession."

"O?"

"I hadn't thought we'd be together this long, to be honest. It just . . . it wasn't in my mind. I'm sorry."

John shrugged. "Mine either."

"So I stole your mirror. The black one."

"What? My chip of the Sky Mirror? Whatever for?"

Tygo blinked. "So I could have another vision."

"You said your vision that night was false. You said you made up *tellochvovin* and the rest of that gibberish."

"I did. But maybe . . ." He trailed off. "Maybe we could try again." He kicked at the dirt, embarrassed.

John was amazed. "I told you, I never saw a damn thing in all my life." But a smile broke over his face as he clutched the chip of mirror, its surface cracked only a bit. He held it up and dusted it off. "How did you keep it safe during the battle?"

"Luck, I guess." He rolled his eyes. "Magic."

John laughed, a gush of relief sweeping him from his toes to the top of his head. At least he had this, a small piece of his collection. "How fortunate for you." He took a breath as Tygo looked away. "And for me."

At last, they disembarked, Mizar at the reins. John looked up at the sky he had pondered all his life. He could see the palace and the spires for some time. In the sky, those two arcs bending over the Cape, drawing nearer like fish swimming toward a succulent waterplant, their paths exactly like lines one of his compasses might draw, *just* like that. Except they had been predicted by no one—not him, and not anyone who had come before him as far as he could tell. They were here of their own accord. Even holy perhaps, even if they were not the Return. The cart turned away then, and they went into the wilderness. Beside him, Tygo sat with his eyes closed. Tygo was the failure, now, returning to the Mystagogue without the True King.

John felt calm. Perhaps all moments of peace were like this: just perilous calms between one catastrophe and the next, for eternity. That these quiet periods could last a hundred years, or a thousand, or a hundred thousand—this seemed less interesting to John than those bookends of calamity. The Disease on one side, and on the other, these two lights, whatever they were.

Moments of unaccountable terror and irrevocable change. *That* was what changed the ordinary into the Sublime. Was that, John wondered, the only real miracle the world could offer men? A reformation of the ordinary, bent as if by magic, by an infinitely mysterious force, indecipherable as fortune?